Rave reviews for Marta Acosta's
delightful romantic comedy debut

Happy Hour at Casa Dracula

AN AUGUST 2006 BOOK SENSE PICK

Catalina magazine's Top Humor Book of 2006

"A winner . . . quirky, surprising and cinematic."

—*Star Democrat* (Baltimore)

"Clever and amusing."

—*San Francisco Chronicle*

"Laugh-out-loud funny. . . . Acosta's narrative zips along, keeping the pages turning faster than a salsa dancer."

—*Fresh Fiction*

"Darkly hilarious. . . . Acosta flings every vampire cliché out the window. You'd have to be undead not to enjoy this book!"

—Julia Spencer-Fleming, author of *To Darkness and to Death*

"A fun, snappy read."

—*Booklist*

"I couldn't put this one down . . . now I'm a fan."

—*Contra Costa Times*

Also by Marta Acosta

Happy Hour at Casa Dracula

Midnight Brunch

Marta Acosta

POCKET BOOKS

New York London Toronto Sydney

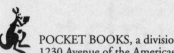 POCKET BOOKS, a division of Simon & Schuster, Inc.
1230 Avenue of the Americas, New York, NY 10020

Library of Congress Cataloging-in-Publication Data

Acosta, Marta.
  Midnight brunch / Marta Acosta.—Pocket Books trade pbk. ed.
    p. cm.
  1. Hispanic American women—Fiction. 2. Vampires—Fiction. I. Title.

  PS3601.C67M53 2007
  813'.6—dc22

                                                                2006038393

ISBN-13: 978-1-4165-2039-9
ISBN-10:   1-4165-2039-2

This Pocket Books trade paperback edition May 2007

10 9 8 7 6 5 4 3 2 1

POCKET and colophon are registered trademarks of
Simon & Schuster, Inc.

Manufactured in the United States of America

For information regarding special discounts for bulk purchases,
please contact Simon & Schuster Special Sales at 1-800-456-6798
or business@simonandschuster.com.

With love, to my parents Esperanza and Fidel,
who gave me hope and faith.

one

snappily ever after

I was sitting on the edge of the claw-foot bathtub, blow-drying the insides of my sodden work boots and conducting a state-of-the-*chica* analysis. My dwindling bank account had a disturbing inverse relationship to my increased efforts to sell my stories.

Oswald poked his head into the bathroom and asked, "What's that funny smell?" Looking at him made me feel as ebullient as champagne fizzing over the top of a glass.

Floating over the smell of my cooked leather boots was the faintly herbal scent of multispectrum sunblock. Oswald had to wear sunblock every day because he had a genetic autosomal recessive disorder that made him highly sensitive to sunlight and subject to unusual food cravings. On the plus side, he never got sick and healed rapidly from injuries.

Otherwise, he was perfectly normal. It was ridiculous that

1

people harbored primitive superstitions against anyone with a medical anomaly.

I flicked off the blow-dryer. "That's the smell of my *botas* cooking. Your grandmother told me I can't put them in the dryer anymore because the thump-thump-thump sounds like a body. Which begs the question: how does she know what a body in a dryer sounds like?"

"Why are your boots wet?"

"I fell into the pond when I was checking on my planting of native wetland grasses. They're doing great, by the way."

"You should buy an extra pair of boots."

"Of more critical importance is something to wear to Nancy's wedding. Like Thoreau, I'm wary of all enterprises that require new clothes."

"I thought you liked clothes," he said, and leaned against the door frame. He was dressed for work in a slate-gray suit of light-weight wool, a shirt the color of forget-me-nots, and a tie in a diamond-pattern silk.

I surreptitiously brushed dirt off the knee of my worn jeans. "I do like clothes. It's the enterprises that worry me. On the flip side, are you sure my old skirt and blouse are fine for the baby's christening tomorrow?"

"It's not a christening," he said. "It's a naming ceremony, very dull, and you still can't go to it because it's only for family."

"That seems rather churlish," I said. "If my niece was getting baptized, I'd invite your whole family to both the ceremony and the party afterward, and it wouldn't even be BYOB."

"You don't have a niece."

"She's a theoretical niece. Her name is Elena and she adores me."

He sighed. "A skirt and blouse are fine for our get-together *after* the ceremony. You can use the card I gave you to buy something for Nancy's wedding."

The shiny new credit card lay hidden beneath my favorite lace *chones* at the bottom of my underwear drawer. I had no intention of ever using it. "I dread going to the wedding alone."

"You'll be fine. You'll like seeing your old college pals."

Nancy and I had met at a Fancy University, but we'd run in different circles. Her snobby F.U. friends had a way of looking past me and talking around me that made me yearn to stick gum in their shiny rich-girl hair.

I decided that my boots were dry enough and shoved my feet into the damp, smelly things. "I find this whole family situation very perturbing. I'm beyond perturbed."

"Let it go, babe. Besides, once you meet them you might be glad you don't have to spend much time with them."

"But your parents are nice, right? I mean, they raised you."

Oswald shrugged. "They take a little time to warm up, but once they get to know you, they'll love you."

I hoped so, even though I was not one of them. I was just an underemployed girl who'd grappled romantically with their son after a party and been accidentally contaminated by their condition. His people were stunned that I had survived. I had a freakishly efficient immune system. Perhaps I was born with this immune system; perhaps it had developed as a result of my mother Regina's malignant neglect.

I stood and went to the mirror. Using my fingers, I parted my hair into three sections and plaited it into a braid. When I'd lived in the City, I'd been used to a hectic social schedule. But after months of calm routine in the countryside, the prospect of three events within a week—Oswald's family visiting, Oswald's departure, and Nancy's wedding—seemed overwhelming.

Oswald stood behind me. He was just above medium height, but he was tall enough to rest his chin atop my head.

His lovely pale, creamy skin contrasted nicely against my black hair. I admired his gray eyes, high brow, rich brown hair, and the smooth line of his cheekbones.

"You're beautiful," he said as he pulled me close.

I always appreciated him saying this, even though I had a look common to Latinas: black hair, brown eyes, olive skin, and a curvy figure. Whenever I saw a girl who resembled me, I secretly fantasized that she was a long-lost relative and that when the connection was discovered, we'd become loving *primas*.

"Why are you making that face at me?" Oswald asked.

"I'm raising one eyebrow cynically at your ploy to divert me from the issue at hand."

"Keep trying. Focus on isolating the occipitofrontalis muscle on the right side of your face."

That's why I so treasured him: he thought any problem could be solved by exercising the old gray matter. I said, "Dr. Grant, I'm going to miss you while you're gone."

"I can cancel my trip, stick around for Nancy's wedding if you need me."

"Yes, I'm so pathetically insecure that I would take you away from children who need surgery."

"That's not what I meant. But you don't always have to put yourself at the bottom of every list."

"You spend your time around too many spoiled, self-involved women."

"Yes, I do." He kissed my neck and I tingled all the way down to my popsicle toes.

"*Hasta*, babe," I said. "See you tonight."

I went to the hall of our love shack. It was a charming one-bedroom cottage tastefully decorated in classic blues and whites. My friend Nancy had once told me, "Taste is not style." I'd been using this aphorism to justify cluttering up the cottage with rural treasures, like old signs and vintage kitchenware and smooth stream rocks.

I picked up my stack of envelopes to be mailed. I had written a duo of novellas, titled *Uno, Dos, Terror!,* about brave young women who encounter diabolical creatures: genetic crop engineers, fascists, and a poltergeist. These novellas were a homage to the political writings of Mary Wollstonecraft and her daughter's classic political horror story, *Frankenstein.*

My shaggy dog, Daisy, gamboled with excitement when she saw me preparing to go outside. I had never had pets before, and I still marveled at how happy they could make me feel. Four other dogs lived at the ranch, but Daisy had latched onto me from the moment I'd arrived. She looked like a cross between a herding dog and a caterpillar, with luxuriant fur in many colors and golden eyes.

I opened the door and lifted my face to the cloudless sky. The air smelled damp and clean. Petunia, my chicken, was scratching in the dirt path by the garden fence.

In our little shack, I could pretend that Oswald and I were equals, but in the bigger world, Oswald Kevin Grant, board certified plastic surgeon, was a Big Enchilada. He earned a fortune nipping and tucking, slicing and dicing, plumping and sucking, sewing and gluing people into new, improved versions.

He owned the large house across the field. He owned the animals, the tractor, the trucks, the small vineyard of cabernet grapes, and the fields that spread out past the creek and the pond to the rise of the hills. He had other properties and investments that kept the money rolling in.

Oswald resided in the shack on a whim, and sometimes I worried that I was also a whim. He brushed aside our class differences, but I was always keenly aware of them.

I raced with Daisy across the green field to the car park by the main house. We hopped into my little green truck. After I went to the post office, I would visit shops in town and try to get a few more gardening clients.

I hadn't planned on gardening professionally, but my F.U. degree had not trained me to do anything other than write unmarketable fiction and say gins and tonic, not gin and tonics, a distinction that impressed no one.

My mother Regina would be disgusted that I was laboring "like an immigrant in the dirt." After I'd gone off to F.U., my father's landscaping business had thrived. He'd started with a humble residential service and had expanded Jerry D-Lightful Landscaping to corporate campuses and shopping malls. My mother Regina equated my proximity with her miserable days as a member of the lower classes.

As I drove round the impressive pale sandstone house, I honked my horn. Edna, Oswald's grandmother, appeared at a window. I couldn't tell if she was waving me good-bye or flipping her wrist in dismissal, but I decided to stop and check.

I went to the Big House through the back entrance. I pried off my damp boots and left them in the mudroom by the cupboard with the hats and sunblock lotions.

Everything in the capacious kitchen was coordinated in clear yellows and blues, very Monet-meets-restaurant-quality-appliances. Something deliciously cinnamon was baking, and I remembered those weeks when I'd lived in the cozy maid's room adjacent to the kitchen. The family had grudgingly taken me in after Sebastian, my Lunatic Incensed Megalomaniac Ex-boyfriend (SLIME) tried to kidnap me. According to SLIME's delusional rantings, I'd been infected with vampirism. SLIME's group, Corporate Americans for the Conservation of America (CACA), had planned to extradite my friends offshore and experiment with their DNA for fun and profit.

Yes, I had been dreadfully ill and perhaps I'd had a yen for uncooked meat, and I won't argue that I'd reacted negatively to sunlight, but I was fully recovered now. I did have a few felicitous side effects from the infection. My eyesight had improved, especially my night vision, and I healed immediately from minor cuts and scratches, a handy trait for someone who liked to grow roses.

Besides, as the family frequently reminded me, there was no such thing as vampires.

Edna came into the kitchen, her espresso-brown boots clicking on the terra-cotta tiles. She was sleek and petite, wearing a deep chocolate sweater and a moss-green skirt. I despaired that I would never be as elegant.

"Young Lady," she said curtly, "we need you to give Winnie a hand with the baby this morning and help me get the guest rooms ready."

"I have a full agenda, which includes stopping by the post office, doing some garden stuff, and writing."

"You don't have time for that nonsense today."

"So I'm expected to help with the chores even though I'm still not invited to the christening?"

"Yes," she said. "It's ridiculous that you don't have your own phone and I have to wave you down like a fishwife."

Because the cottage was a retreat, not a real residence, a phone line had never been put in. "I am loath to get a phone because psychopaths will harass me." Although SLIME was far away, I still got the uneasy feeling that he would come after me again someday.

"It's possible that the non-insane would occasionally like to contact you, Young Lady. Perhaps your mother Regina might even want to talk to you."

The family called me "Young Lady." Edna said that she was still hoping that I'd become one. I called my mother Regina "my mother Regina" because it kept me at a safe emotional distance from the woman who had unwillingly borne me and even more unwillingly lived with me.

"Possible, but unlikely, Edna. If you need me *tout de suite* you can call Oswald and he can tell me."

"My grandson has more important things to do than to relay messages to you." She had stunning, exotic green eyes, and now she lifted her left eyebrow almost to her hairline.

She was my role model for all facial gymnastics, and I sighed with envy. "Okay, once I get paid for my last gardening gig, I'll get a phone. *¿Donde está la niña?*"

"Winnie was in the study with her," she said. "That infant is not a toy for your amusement."

"Let us agree to disagree on this point."

The Big House was a solid two-story structure with beamed ceilings, white plaster walls, random plank floors, and Mission-style furniture. I went through the dining room to the entry hall, which led to the living room, study, family room, and reading parlor. A staircase with a graceful wrought-iron railing led to the bedrooms upstairs.

The study was very macho, all wood, leather, and hefty non-fiction volumes. So many books, yet nothing to read. When I'd suggested a few vintage chintz pillows and a collection of novels to Oswald, he'd looked at me as if I'd thrown holy water in his face.

The bassinet sat atop the large desk, and Winnie dangled one hand to the baby's fingers while talking on the phone. By her affectionate tone, I could tell she was talking to Sam, her husband and Oswald's cousin.

Sam and Oswald were as close as brothers. Things had been a little messy when Sam and Winnie fell in love while she was still engaged to Oswald. But we were all so fantastically mature and sophisticated that we were able to live happily at the ranch together.

Prebaby, Winnie had always been flawlessly groomed. She was a doc at a community clinic and had a wall full of diplomas from hoity-toity European universities. Now her polished cotton blouse had a wet splotch at the shoulder, and wisps of her cornsilk hair fell from a ponytail.

She put down the phone and said, "Hi, Young Lady."

"Hey, Winsome." I peered into the bassinet and said, "Hey, baby girl." The baby looked at me with her father's serious brown eyes and made some delightful infant sound. "Winnie, I can't believe you haven't named her yet."

"It's tradition to wait for the ceremony. It gives me more time to think about names, too. I'm thinking of Tabitha, but Sam says that sounds like a cat's name. He likes Elizabeth."

"I like Elizabeth, too." I picked the baby up and cradled her across my generous bazooms, which probably gave her the false impression of an impending feast. "I can take care of Baby now if you have anything else you want to do."

"Would you?" she asked. Before I could answer, she had rattled off a list of instructions and was out the door so fast she left a draft.

"When you learn to talk, we will have witty and insightful conversations," I told the baby. I brushed my lips against the soft fuzz of flaxen hair on her head.

We did all the baby activities, some exciting like dressing her in a cute gingham jumper, and some not so exciting like changing her diaper. Then I set the infant in a custom baby pack with a UV filtering fabric screen, and we left the house for a walk.

After checking to see that no one was around, I stopped at my truck and got out a sheet of sandpaper that was hidden under the seat.

The horses were a pretty sight as they grazed in the green fields. I took a path that skirted the barn, to establish the location of Ernie, the ranch hand and family confidant. The dark, compact man was hammering away at some wood and wire fencing, being all manly. I waved to him, and he waved to me, but he was engrossed in his project. This was my window of opportunity.

I la-di-da'd along my usual route beside the narrow creek that bisected the property. I talked to the baby, describing the oak-covered hills that ringed the valley, the beauty of the gray-blue rocks in the creek, the red, black, and white markings of a woodpecker.

Then I casually swerved forty-five degrees to a path that led behind the barnlike structure that housed the swimming pool. Because of the family's skin disorder, the pool was enclosed, but the sliding roof was usually opened at night.

The family had told me the pool was off-limits due to an accidental spill of cleaning chemicals. Although I hadn't studied chemistry at F.U., I was highly skeptical of the toxic pool story, especially since I'd spied Ernesto hauling lumber into the enclosure.

Once out of view of the Big House and the barn, I looked for the knothole in the redwood fence that I'd noticed before. Using a nail file, I worked at the knot until I could pry the chunk of wood out. I peeked inside.

To one side of the pool was a square platform with a canopy of dark red velvet. In the center of the platform was a rectangular table that held a large marble basin. Two rows of wooden chairs, ornately carved and black, faced the platform.

Whatever they were planning, it was more than a simple naming ceremony.

While the baby slept, I rubbed the sandpaper around the perimeter of the knot until it was smooth, and I did the same with the hole in the fence. Then I placed the knot halfway in the hole. When I pulled, it slid out easily.

I wasn't going to miss the show just because no one would give me a ticket.

two

what's blood got to do with it?

When I returned to the house, I put the baby down for a nap, and Edna commandeered my assistance to prepare rooms for our visitors. Winnie's parents, Sam's parents, and Oswald's parents would stay in the guest rooms upstairs. Oswald's cousin, Gabriel, would take the maid's room beside the kitchen. Other relatives and guests would stay at the old Victorian hotel in town.

As I changed linens, arranged flowers, and vacuumed, I fixated on the plethora of fashion crimes I might commit at Nancy's wedding. Sadly, women's magazines didn't offer advice on social armor for soirees filled with people who esteemed lineage above boobiage.

Between a bout of pillow fluffing and furniture polishing, I went to the study and phoned Nancy. "Nancy-pants, 'tis I, Milagro."

"Milagro!" she yodeled. "I am thrilling to see you. Everything is going *très* fantastically, and in a few short days I will be living in wedded blish."

"It's *bliss*. Have you been drinking?"

"Not yet. I like blish. It's like blush, the color of my gown, which is to die for, and lisps, which are the sexiest."

"I totally agree—about lisps, not blush. I thought everything was going to be puce."

"How could I when you told me puce means flea-colored? Yeuw. It's *pêche* and blush and blish."

"On the topic of clothes, what should I wear?"

"Whatever—all eyes will be on the lovely bride. Am I going to finally meet this mysterious Osborne of yours?"

"His name is Oswald and he still can't make it."

"Oh, Mil, *quelle pathétique*! Don't I sound just like Leslie Caron?" she asked. "We're going to a French place for our honeymoon, so I rented *Gigi*. Do you know the most shocking thing in that film, besides the fact that Louis Jourdan so obviously dresses to the right?"

"What?"

"When he's about to take innocent virginal Gigi as his mistress, and Maurice Chevalier says, 'She will amuse you for months.'"

"I had no idea that movie was so cynical. How awful to think that a young lady is only temporarily entertaining."

"That's why a prenup is essential."

"Now you are being cynical."

"*Au contraire, mon petite chouchou.* I trust in Todd's undying romantic love for my father's money," she said matter-of-factly. "I'm putting you down for the wedding as 'and guest.' But don't bring one of your 'arty' beaus."

By "arty" she meant unemployed.

"Where in France are you going?" I asked. "Somewhere on the Riviera?"

"No, the hot French island with the tropical beaches. Tibet."

"Don't make me laugh," I said, but I already had. "Tahiti?"

"You're no fun when you guess right so quickly." Nancy then launched into a detailed description of her beach wardrobe and said, "Mil, is it okay that you're not one of the bridesmaids? Todd's still upset that Sebastian isn't coming."

"Nancita, I'm just happy to be there on your day of blish," I said. We had had a falling-out because of her fiancé's association with SLIME and CACA. We were trying to mend our friendship. For her sake, I hoped that Todd wasn't as much of a repressed, corn-fed, entitled jackass as he appeared to be.

When I was done with my chores, I reported to Edna, who was in the kitchen. This was the time we usually had drinks on the terrace and shared a tranquil *espíritu de los cocteles,* but our drinks and dinner would wait until the guests arrived.

Edna looked me up and down and said, "Young Lady, you will make yourself presentable before everyone gets here."

"Edna, I will try, considering the circumstances."

"What circumstances?"

"The circumstance of *still* not being invited to the baby's christening and having only work clothes."

"Work clothes? Remind me of your profession again."

"I bitterly resent your implication that my clothes are trashy. The few clothes that I do own are trashed from honest labor in the garden."

Edna was making a supercilious snarking sound, something between a laugh and an "ack!," when Oswald came in the door. He kissed Edna on the cheek and gave me a more substantial smooch.

I said, "Your grandmother has been working me to the bone."

Oswald reached over and pinched my fanny. "Grandmama, you've still got a long ways to go," he said. They thought this was hilarious.

The phone rang, and Edna said, "Oswald, I have a feeling that's your mother again." She went to take the call in the study.

Winnie and the baby appeared just as Sam got home. Sam strongly resembled Oswald, but his nose was a bit narrower, his jaw a little rounder, and his cheekbones not as angular. He had big, brown somber eyes and wavy brown hair that he tried to control.

We were chatting away when Edna came back into the kitchen.

"Was my mother sidetracked by a sale?" Oswald asked.

Edna said calmly, "It wasn't your mother. It was Ian. He's coming here."

I couldn't have been more surprised if she had slapped me upside the head with a ten-pound coho salmon.

Ian Ducharme was Winnie's distant cousin. He had visited last year, and we had spent a few debauched days in each other's company. I'd found Ian dashing, compelling, and quite depraved, and he'd been inexplicably fond of me.

In the tradition of blaming the messenger, Oswald stared stonily at his grandmother.

Sam said with his characteristic solemnity, "No matter what our personal experiences with Ian, I am glad that he is interested in seeing the baby and establishing a relationship with her."

"Sam's right," Winnie said. "It's an honor for him to come . . ."

"Why is it an honor?" I asked. What was so special about having a jet-setting bon vivant at a baby party?

"I meant that it's very nice of him to come," Winnie said quickly. "Isn't it nice, Sam?"

Sam agreed that it was nice and quickly added, "It's nice to have relatives who care."

I couldn't comment, since I had no experience with relatives who cared, except my long-dead grandmother.

Winnie gave Oswald a steely glance that made us all remember that she routinely controlled a waiting room full of meth addicts, rowdy drunks, and screaming teenagers. She said, "I am happy that my cousin is coming for the baby's sake. Anyone who isn't happy can take it up with me directly."

Oswald gave a brief nod of concession.

Winnie smiled and changed the topic to the baby's name. Most of the family members had taken presidential last names when they immigrated to this country, so the kid would be stuck with Harding-Grant or Grant-Harding.

"What about a presidential first name, too?" I asked. "Warrenette or Millardina."

Winnie looked so affronted that I shut up.

When we walked back to the shack, Oswald was quiet. Finally, he said, "Goddamn Ian Ducharme."

"I know you have your Issues with Ian; however, I was free at the time, and you were engaged to Winnie. I've reconciled myself to your past, and I think you should do the same."

"That is a false comparison. My engagement was practically an arranged affair and I never had a physical relationship with Winnie."

"Really, Oswald, you're arguing the technicalities."

He glared at me, and I quickly added, "Think of the baby. Be tolerant for the sake of the wee infant, *pobrecita* Calvina."

After a moment, he said, "Little baby Woodrowette. Sweet Lyndonissa."

"Darling Rutherfordyne," I said.

When he said "Adorable Ronald-Ann," I laughed so hard my sides hurt.

Once inside the shack, I said, "I don't know why you get jealous of Ian, anyway. I'm the one who should be jealous. You feel up nekkid women every day and I understand that it's just your job."

"Liar. It drives you crazy."

"Of course it does. I want you all to myself." I slipped my hands under his shirt and along the smooth skin of his back.

He looked down at me. "Ian's coming back for you."

Ian still sent notes and gifts that I hid in the closet, but I said, "I'm sure he's forgotten all about some silly Mexican girl he once met."

"I couldn't." He kissed my mouth, running his thumb against the artery in my neck. "We have time before they come," he said. He took my hand and gently bit the skin on the inside of my wrist, signaling what he wanted from me.

I pulled off his jacket, slipped his tie over his head, and unbuttoned his shirt. I undressed quickly and he pulled me to him, running his hands down my back and over my hips, nipping my neck playfully.

I kissed his chest and tasted the subtle saltiness of his skin from a long day at work. I thought everything about him was perfectly right. I unbuckled his belt and tugged his slacks down. He whispered my name as his hands explored further, stroking me until I felt drugged with pleasure.

"May I?" he asked politely. He always asked. His voice was low, melodious.

"Yes." I would have said yes to anything then.

He reached behind a painting on a shelf, finding the scalpel where we always hid it.

He removed the protective plastic sheath over the blade.

I shivered despite the warmth of the evening. I wasn't a girl who sought pain, but some activities, like planting a garden, were worth the petty injuries suffered.

Oswald caressed me until I arched back and closed my eyes, aware of nothing but his hands. I felt the cut across the top of my breast, so fast and light that it was virtually painless. I opened my eyes and watched as he bent his head to the welling of crimson blood. He shuddered in pleasure. Seconds later, when he drew his lips away, the cut had mended and the skin was as it had been.

We slipped down to the wool rug and made love. He pricked my forefinger with the tip of the scalpel, sucking at the droplets of blood. I rolled him onto his back and had my way with him.

I was drowsing contentedly when I heard the dogs barking as the first guests arrived. I glanced at the clock and squirmed out of Oswald's embrace. "Do you realize how late it is?" I asked.

"How late?"

"Really, really late."

He remained on the rug, watching me as I went to the closet.

The burgundy cotton blouse and skirt I planned to wear looked shabbier than they had last night. There was nothing I could do now, so I laid them on the bed.

"Let me shower with you."

"We don't have time. I need to shower like Speedy Gonzales." I rushed to the bathroom and worried through my three-minute shower about meeting Oswald's relatives in general and his parents in particular. Mr. and Mrs. Grant had just spent a year in Prague, and I'd seen numerous photographs of them doing all things Praguish: reading at cafés, visiting museums, attending cultural events, and discussing existentialism.

They had raised a marvelous yet down-to-earth son, so how could they not be wonderful? I secretly hoped that they would embrace me fondly and that we would grow to care deeply for one another. Perhaps Oswald's mother and I would have long phone conversations and she would offer kind and wonderful advice. We would all join in holiday celebrations, and they would keep a photo of Oswald and me on their mantel.

I dried off with one of Oswald's thick Egyptian cotton towels and towel-dried my hair. After slathering myself with lotion that was supposed to impart a subtle glow, I dashed to the bedroom.

Oswald, wearing only boxers, sat on the bed, one leg slung over the other, humming to himself.

"Honey, you're sitting on my—" I began, but he wasn't. I glanced around the room. "Where are my clothes?"

"I think you look better without them," he said with a crooked smile.

"And I love your delusions. Now, where did you put my clothes?"

"The living room? Try there."

I was saying "Ha, ha, and ha" as I walked in a crouch to the other room, so that anyone strolling by the shack wouldn't get a full-frontal of my *chichis*. Oswald trailed after me.

On the sofa there were several garment bags and packages

from an expensive department store. "What's this?" I asked, standing straight.

"Open them and find out."

It was like Christmas. Not Christmas at my parents' house, where my mother Regina opened the innumerable presents she had bought for herself, but Christmas in television shows, where the kid is surprised as her loving parents look on.

There were pretty summer frocks, sandals, a chic black suit, silk blouses, sleek trousers, soft shawls and sweaters, and matching accessories. There were elegant flats, saucy high heels, and cool sporty shoes. One box was filled with lingerie wrapped in crisp tissue paper. And there was a dress, the perfect dress for Nancy's wedding: a deep rose silk dress edged in velvet, simple and beautiful.

"Why did you . . . how did you have time?"

"I can't take credit for anything. Grandmama suggested that I have my personal shopper pick everything."

It would have been so easy, too easy to take things from Oswald. I wanted to love him for being Oswald, not for the things he could give me. "I can't accept all this from you."

He looked exasperated. Then he grabbed a pair of filmy black panties from the pile of lingerie. Reaching down, he lifted my right foot and then my left, pulling the panties up on my hips. "Now you can't return them," he said. "Get dressed and let's go face the firing squad."

While he showered and shaved, I examined the clothes again and wondered what instructions he had given the personal shopper. While some of the clothes had classic lines, many had a distinct prelude-to-a-boink aesthetic. I picked out a pale blue blouse and darker blue skirt that would be suitable for an introduction of parents to their son's lovely girlfriend.

Oswald held my hand as we walked to the Big House. The windows were open to the mild evening and lively voices carried across the field.

"I'm nervous," I said.

"Don't be," he said. "Oh, one last thing, Milagro. Some of the guests are here because of their position, and their views may seem eccentric."

"Eccentric? In what way?"

"Uh, they're a little paranoid about outsiders, that's all. So don't get riled if they say anything weird."

Expensive cars with a new layer of country dust filled the car park.

"Do not worry your very pretty noggin," I said. "I shall be the very picture of tolerance and solicitude." The more anxious I was, the more ridiculously I nattered.

I took even breaths as we walked into the living room. It looked like happy hour at a country club, which was enough to make me want to run away screaming. The men wore polo shirts, khakis, and large gold watches. The women had neat suburban hairdos and wore light blouses and slacks or skirts. A few of the group had suspiciously orange tans. A woman who was an older version of Winnie held the baby in her arms while other women hovered nearby, admiring the munchkin.

I did a quick scan for Ian, who wasn't there, and saw two men who looked out of place. One was an elderly fellow with a head as bald and fragile as an egg. Despite the pleasant temperature, he wore a three-piece wool herringbone suit and perched in a wing chair by the fireplace. The country-clubbers stood around him, heads tilted down to listen as he spoke.

At his right was a narrow young guy in black slacks and a

black shirt, with ferret-sharp features, hair bleached to white-ness, and watery light-blue eyes. There was nothing extraordi-nary about his appearance, but he drew my attention like a monkey to a shiny coin.

"Mom, Dad," Oswald said, and let go of my hand.

He hugged a small, attractive woman, who stroked his hair and said, "Ozzie, how's my handsome boy?" Her face was youthful, but not scarily taut and frozen.

Oswald then hugged the compact, good-looking man at her side. "Hi, Dad."

"Oswald," his father said warmly, as if the name were enough.

Oswald brought me forward. "Mom, Dad, this is Milagro. Milagro, these are my parents, Conrad and Evelyn Grant."

I'd been wondering what Edna's son would be like. Conrad Grant looked like the fathers who showed up on move-in day at F.U. He had upper-middle-class ease and good grooming. His gray eyes had a slightly almond shape, a more masculine and re-strained version of his mother's.

"Hello," I said, giving a firm—but not too firm—grip, try-ing my best to look like an upstanding and worthwhile human being. I hoped this would be the start of a long and marvelous friendship. "I'm so pleased to meet you."

"Yes, we've heard about you," said Oswald's mother.

I was so fretful that I could have sworn she said it in the same tone that she would have said "Yes, we've heard about flesh-eating bacteria."

"Nice to meet you," said Mr. Grant flatly. His gray eyes lacked the genial mischief that brightened Oswald's. I took him for a solid, salt-of-the-earth type of man. A man of few words and deep thoughts.

"How long will you be staying here?" asked Mrs. Grant.

"I live here," I answered, glancing at Oswald. He'd said she knew our situation.

"I know you live here *now*, but what are your plans?"

"Milagro is a writer, Mom," Oswald said.

"My plan is to keep working on my fiction and other writing. Did Oswald mention that I contributed a few chapters to Edna's book on country living?"

"Edna and her books," Mrs. Grant said disdainfully. "Her roman à clef risked exposure of the whole family."

Edna had written the risqué *Chalice of Blood* when she was young and frisky. She'd spoofed vampires and the people who hated them. I'd loved it.

"Evelyn," said Mr. Grant, "it was a good book and everyone knew it was fantasy, right? No such thing as vampires."

"That's not the point," Mrs. Grant said. "Milagro, you never told me how long will you be staying as my son's guest?"

Edna came up at that moment and said, "Evelyn, behave yourself."

Oswald's mother opened her mouth, closed it, and then said, "I don't know what you mean, Mother Edna."

"I'm sure you do, and please don't call me that ridiculous name." Turning to her son, she said, "You're looking very well, Conrad. How did Prague suit you?"

"I could have done with less classical music," he said with a wink at his son. "I never want to set foot in Smetana Hall again."

Evelyn pursed her lips. "You were the one who wanted tickets for the whole series."

"No," said Mr. Grant. "I only wondered if it was more cost-efficient than buying individual tickets."

"I'm sure Conrad remembers correctly," Edna said innocently. "He has always been very precise."

23

Mr. Grant and Oswald both turned away, but I caught them grinning.

Edna tapped my shoulder with an elegant shell-pink nail and said, "Young Lady, I expect you to help me with dinner."

Before I could respond that I'd already been laboring all day for her, Edna went to talk to the egg-noggin, the elderly man who was still surrounded by other guests.

Oswald's father began quizzing Oswald about property taxes.

How had the meeting with Evelyn Grant gone awry so quickly? I smiled to show my good will and my earnest intentions and asked about her year in Prague. She told me about the city's cultural life, but the subtext of her dialogue was, "You're not fit to clean my brilliant boy's handmade Swiss shoes!" Mine was, "I really, really like you and you'll have to pry Oswald away from my cold, dead fingers!"

Oswald stood beside us, pleased that we were talking.

Evelyn smiled warmly at her son and said to me, "What is it that you do exactly? Besides this writing and living with my son."

"I also do garden design and maintenance," I said. "I made the courtyard garden here for Edna, and I've designed a few gardens in town. I'd be happy to show them to you."

"Oh," she sniffed, "Oswald's other girlfriends were successful career women, like Winnie." She looked over at my friend and said, "Such a brilliant and beautiful young woman."

"Yes, she is," I agreed. "What I like best about her is that she is so kind. Kindness is so underrated, I think."

Evelyn paused to consider attacking me on the kindness front. Then Oswald's cousin appeared in the doorway, so I said, "I could sing Winnie's praises all night, but I see Gabriel. Please excuse me."

"Of course. I must pay my respects to our honored guest, anyway." She turned and walked over to Mr. Egghead, and I went to Gabriel.

He had grown his red hair long and it curled romantically at the collar of the ivory shirt that hung loosely over his snug jeans. "Gabriel, you look practically pre-Raphaelite," I said.

Gabriel was a small man, but he gave huge hugs. "Young Lady, if I swung your way, I'd swing your way," he said.

I liked that he'd used one of my phrases, and I laughed.

He dropped his voice and said, "How are you?"

"Surviving," I answered quietly. "Oswald's mother didn't tell me flat out that she wished I'd crawl back under the rock from whence I came, but that is the general drift." I looked into the living room and asked, "Are your parents here?"

"They couldn't make it," he said.

"That's too bad. How's the security biz going?"

Gabriel was responsible for handling threats to the family, which was a full-time job. He had helped bring down CACA and negotiated a deal where SLIME could not approach me or the family. "No one's been gathering the villagers and shouting, 'To the castle!' but there are some developments I'm watching."

"Another crazy group coming after the family?"

"Not exactly," he said. He was studying the fellow with the white-blond hair, which surprised me because he didn't seem Gabriel's type.

I would have tried to find out more, but Sam's parents descended upon us. They believed I was responsible for Sam and Winnie's union, so they were very friendly. I began to feel so welcome that I told them all about my dog and my chicken. I don't know why Oswald said they were boring.

Now and again, I caught the fellow with the white-blond hair glancing at me. No one had bothered to introduce us, so I made my way to him. I had to wait until the circle around the older man opened up. "Hello, I'm—"

"Milagro De Los Santoss, the Miracle of the Saintss," the white-blond man said with a smile. He spoke with a slightly sibilant *s* in so leisurely a tone that I knew it was an affectation.

"Yess," I said.

"Your reputation precedess you," he said. "The only person known to have ssurvived infection."

Although his eyes were pale, his stare was intense; but his study of me was not sexual. I felt both complimented by the attention and uneasy. "Is that a bad thing?"

"On the contrary! I am impressed and intrigued."

I smiled and stared back at him. "Now that we're old friends, who are you?"

"Ssilas Madison," he said. "A distant relation, but the birth of a baby is such a rare and sspecial occasion . . ." He dropped his voice and said confidentially, "I welcomed the opportunity to meet you."

"Now you're making me feel like an exhibit at the zoo."

Suddenly Gabriel was by my side, saying, "Young Lady, Grandmama kindly requests our assistance with dinner."

As Gabriel and I went through the dining room, I stopped in my tracks and asked, "Who is Silas and who's the old guy?"

Gabriel fiddled with my arrangement of white roses on the table.

"The old guy is Willem Dunlop, who lives in Europe most of the time. You probably guessed by Silas's last name that he's an American. He's Willem's assistant."

"An *aide de corpse*," I said, and laughed.

Instead of laughing with me, Gabriel said, "Don't let anyone hear you say that. They're eccentric, but important to the family."

I shrugged. "So where is Willem on the family food chain?"

"What food chain? There's no food chain."

"Gabe, there's always a food chain. You'd know if you were ever stuck being the catfish, eating garbage off the river bottom."

Edna glowered at us from the kitchen doorway, so Gabriel took my arm in his and led me to the kitchen. "Willem is like Cher, respected as a dignitary, but without much chance of rocking the top twenty at this point."

"Cher would have worn a fabulous wig," I said as we walked into the fragrant kitchen.

I'd arrived at the ranch a year ago knowing only how to make quesadillas and one meal that I reserved for fourth dates. Edna had taught me everything from appetizers to desserts, and I was still learning. I loved it when Gabriel came over and we all cooked together, crossing paths, calling out for assistance and advice, and sharing tastes.

When we sat down to dinner, I was shocked to see Silas help seat Willem at the head of the table, in Edna's spot. I looked at Oswald and we both looked at Edna. Her eyes narrowed so very slightly that I would have missed it if I hadn't been watching closely. She was about to sit at Willem's right when Silas took that chair.

Edna froze for a second before moving down the table. She picked up a platter and held it toward Willem. "Tomatoes dressed with balsamic vinegar, basil, and garlic," she said dryly.

The egghead winced. He opened his lipless mouth and rasped, "We do not partake of the foods of the lower lands."

"The lower lands?" I asked.

"Italy, Greece, Africa, Central and South America, the southern lands with their sun idolatry," he explained.

"Tahiti?" I asked. "Cabo? San Diego?"

"Most definitely," said Willem with a bob of his noggin.

"But why do you have this dislike for foods of the 'lower lands'?" I asked. "How can someone not like a potato?"

"Whether it is the food or the sun, the peoples of these lands lack intellectual acuity," Willem said tersely, breaking into my wistful memory of eating my *abuelita*'s tender potatoes with a warm corn tortilla. "Their literature, science, and art are inferior."

The rest of the table was silent, and I felt Oswald's hand under the table, squeezing my thigh in a babe-please-don't-start-this gesture.

"I am boggled by your grand and sweeping dismissal of all the accomplishments of these so-called lower lands," I said. "How did you arrive at this opinion?"

"Opinion!" Willem spat out. "This is no mere opinion. It is fact. An outsider, a low-lander such as you cannot comprehend."

"Try me." I smiled coolly. I didn't break eye contact with him, letting him know that if he wanted a fight, I was ready.

Silas looked positively distressed. "Willem," he said in a placating tone, "Milagro iss new to our thinking."

"Yes, but I'm a fast study, and I've got mad comprehension skills," I said. "Toss a few of your analytical processes for establishing the inferiority of the lower lands in my general direction."

"You are a freak of nature. You will never understand our ways and our philosophies," Willem said.

I briefly considered the advisability of slapping an old

codger at the dinner table. Then I kicked Oswald's foot. This was his house, and I was his girlfriend.

Oswald opened his mouth, but before he could speak, Silas said, "Philosophy iss sso somber a subject on ssuch a joyouss occassion. Let uss sspeak instead of this new happy family." He raised his glass toward Winnie and Sam. "My most ssincere wishes for your happiness."

I admired the grace with which Silas deflected the conversation to a safer topic. I was happy to toast my friends.

Then Sam's father stood and said, "I would like to toast our honored guest, Willem, and thank him for joining in this blessing of our beautiful granddaughter." He raised his glass and said, "To Willem."

I didn't feel like toasting the eggman, so I tilted my glass and pretended to sip.

The relatives told stories about their children and their own childhoods. They were overly animated as they spoke, as if they were hoping that anecdotes about kindergarten would make us all forget Willem's earlier comments.

Their stories were not much different from the stories of other people of their generation, but I listened carefully. I was always interested to learn how people lived, people in normal families. Even so, I found my eyelids growing heavy. It had been a long day and I was exhausted.

When dinner was over, I excused myself and said good night to those nearby, one of whom was Willem.

He leaned toward me. "Why aren't you dead?" he asked as if genuinely confused.

"Just stubborn, I guess," I said.

"I would have said 'contrary,'" Edna said with a smirk.

The idea of enduring Willem's idiocy for even five more

minutes was more than I could stand. I said, "Do excuse me. Very nice meeting you all, but I'm a little tired. Not *dead* tired. Just tired." I gave Edna a kiss on the cheek. As I drew away, I saw Evelyn glaring at me from across the room.

I was heading out of the kitchen when I heard footsteps behind me. Oswald swung an arm over my shoulder. "Willem is very highly respected," he said as we walked outside.

"So I gathered, but he is a horse's ass," I said. We moseyed across the field. "How come you didn't speak up for me?"

"I was kind of hoping it would blow over. Everything had been going so well until then."

"He called me a freak of nature," I huffed.

Oswald laughed. "You are a freak of nature, but in the very best way. It bugs the hell out of him that you are resistant to our condition."

"Mmm." I was a little less annoyed that Oswald hadn't fought for my honor. "Don't you want to go back and talk with your family?"

"I'll talk to them later. It was great to see how well you were getting along with my mom."

His comment threw me off. Maybe I had been misinterpreting perfectly polite remarks. "Are you sure she likes me?"

"Absolutely." He pulled me close and said, "Let's open a bottle of champagne and have a lingerie fashion show."

"Oswald," I said, and stopped there in the darkness.

"Yes, Milagro?"

"Thanks for coming with me."

"To the ends of the earth, babe."

three

once bitten, twice dry

If I dressed a little nicer the next morning it was because I had new clothes, not because I was trying to impress the vampires. I caught myself thinking that word, "vampires," and I pushed it to a dank recess of my brain while I slipped on pink capris, a white eyelet blouse, and dangly earrings. I couldn't figure out what to do with my hair, so I just let it fall over my shoulders and hoped that the day would not be windy.

Oswald had taken the day off so we could spend it with his parents. Although I kidded Oswald about his spoiled clientele, he also did a lot of pro bono work for those with more critical problems. He'd fixed cleft palates for the poor, repaired features for those in accidents, and made a special effort to help returning soldiers.

This morning I found him at the turnout checking on the horses. I saw him before he saw me. He was wearing a faded black *Dawn of the Dead* T-shirt that had shrunk in a charming way. As he reached to scratch his bay horse, the shirt rode up and exposed a delicious slice of his smooth back.

"I hope you put sunscreen on your back," I called.

He looked at me and gave his lopsided grin. "I put sunscreen everywhere."

"Do you think your parents are going to appreciate your T-shirt?"

"My parents think I can do no wrong."

"That must be nice."

"It is. But sometimes I want to step off the pedestal."

"I'd be happy to give you a hand down," I said. "Or a hand anywhere you might need a hand." I swiped some hay off his jeans-clad bottom. "Even two hands. I'm feeling very helpful toward you at the moment."

One side of his mouth rose higher than the other. I loved his asymmetrical smile. "Don't tempt me. Stanley's been limping and I have to take a look at him before we go out." Oswald had studied veterinary care in order to look after the animals.

I scratched the bay between his eyes. "Okay, I guess that is more important. I'm going to have breakfast at the Big House."

"I was just there. I told my parents to meet us at ten thirty, and I made lunch reservations for one."

"Sounds good. Later, baby."

In the kitchen, the relatives, with the exception of Willem and Silas, were drinking coffee and noshing on pastries and fresh fruit. They chatted about the beauty of the countryside, and Sam's father waved a camera and said he'd already taken over one hundred photos of the baby.

Oswald's mother poured a glass of dark red juice and

handed it to me. The family preferred juice from blood oranges and ate lots of red food because that color staved off their cravings for blood.

"Thank you, Mrs. Grant," I said. "Oswald said he'll be ready to go at ten thirty. He made reservations at a winery restaurant."

"That's very thoughtful of him. Of course, Oswald is a very thoughtful person," she said. "He hates to disappoint others."

I couldn't really argue here, since he had had a problem breaking up with Winnie when he'd had a bad case of Milagro fever. "Oswald tells me you've only been here once before."

"Yes, when he was living here in the house, not off in the guest cottage."

"I know that seems strange, but it's really very cozy there."

She frowned. I was trying to think of something pleasant to say when Gabriel came over and slipped an arm around my waist.

"Auntie, I'm taking my honey out for a walk."

"See you later, Mrs. Grant." It seemed odd to call her Mrs. Grant when I called her mother-in-law Edna.

Gabriel wore a wide-brimmed hat, sunglasses, and a long-sleeved shirt because he was especially fair and sensitive to the sun.

"Milagro, may I ask a favor?"

"Spit it out."

"I can tell you're aching to antagonize Willem, but please don't. Believe it or not, he's making a huge concession allowing you to be here now."

"Allowing me here? This is where I live," I fumed. "He's a bigot."

"I'm not making any apologies for him, but the family in

the old country has a long memory for the atrocities we suffered. If he sees you as a security risk, my job will get more complicated." He sighed. "Believe me, it's already complicated enough."

Gabriel was being serious, so I said, "Okay, I won't cause you any grief. I wasn't looking for trouble."

"I know, but it seems to find you anyway."

"Not always. Only with SLIME. Have you heard anything about him lately?"

"Still slimy," he said. "CACA has completely disbanded, and Sebastian seems to have settled into his exile for now."

"I never would have believed that he would accept living in Nebraska."

"You'd change your mind if you saw Omaha's downtown," Gabriel said. "Sebastian bought a historic warehouse and completely renovated it. It's an amazing space, with views to die for."

"You got all this from your research team?"

"That was from a spread in *Architectural Digest*, but we keep an eye on his movements. I think he's happy there for now."

We stood by the creek and watched the water sparkling in the clear morning sun.

Business concluded, my redheaded pal was happy to gossip. "I hear Ian is coming." Gabriel grinned. "What a man."

Laughing, I said, "Does he know about your crush?"

"I don't think so, but what I don't know about Ian Ducharme could fill a book."

"The Dark Lord!" I said ominously, repeating the name Gabriel had once called him.

Gabriel's smile froze. "Please forget I ever said that—it was just a stupid joke."

"Sure," I said, "I know it was a joke. Anyway, I thought you were dating someone."

Gabriel looked away. "Not anymore. He kept wondering when he was going to meet my family and wanting to know details about my business. I'd take off on so many mysterious trips, he started to think I was cheating."

"I'm sorry, Gabriel."

"It's okay. It's not like I didn't know it would happen eventually. It always does."

I offered a sexual favor, "but only to help you relax," and he laughed easily, so I assumed he wasn't too crushed by the breakup.

I ran into town to pick up and drop off mail, and when I came back Oswald had washed up and changed into a sea foam–green button-down shirt and olive-green slacks. His parents were waiting for us by his car. Mrs. Grant got in the passenger seat, and Mr. Grant and I sat in back. I hadn't been able to get a sense of him yet. As we drove past a field of yellow flowers, I said, "That's wild mustard, generally considered a noxious weed, but I have a hard time hating it."

"Oswald says you like plants," he replied, as if liking plants was indicative of serious brain injury.

"Yes, I garden for pleasure and profit," I said idiotically. "How nice for you to be retired. You have so much time to travel and, um, pursue hobbies. Do you have any hobbies?"

He turned his head and gave me a long look that reminded me of his mother just before she delivered an insult. "I travel and golf."

My own father loved golf—not the game, but the courses, those vast expanses of emerald lawn rigorously maintained by excessive labor, water, and chemicals. I could have expressed my own opinion of golf courses in a drought climate, but I thought it wiser to keep quiet.

In the front seat, Mrs. Grant chattered happily with Oswald. Her side of the conversation consisted primarily of "How interesting!" and "You're so smart!" She was as cheerful as someone getting paid by the smile.

Oswald drove along the gently winding roads through nearby vineyards and orchards. We stopped and took a walk through a wood of oaks. Oswald walked ahead with a stick, checking out the ground.

"Ozzie, what are you doing?" his mother asked.

"Looking out for rattlers," Oswald said. "We had one at the barn already this year."

"Don't bother, son," said Mr. Grant. "Your mother hates reptiles, but a snakebite isn't going to kill her."

"Milagro's not immune, Dad," Oswald said. "So far as we know."

"You could let a rattlesnake bite her and find out," Mrs. Grant said with a fake-innocent laugh.

I wanted to reply with a scornful "Ha, ha, and ha," but Oswald had already joined in his mother's little joke. Was I overreacting, or did Conrad and Evelyn simply lack the social skills of my friends at the ranch?

The path narrowed and somehow I got left behind, trailing Oswald and his parents. The day was warming and the air carried the scent of leaves crushed underfoot, earth, and stream. We rested against a boulder shaded by a tall pine. Mr. Grant pulled a silver flask out of his jacket. He took a sip and said, "Evelyn?"

"Thanks," she said, taking the flask. She reached past me to hand it to Oswald.

He saw my expression and said, "It's calf's blood, Milagro."

"Oh, I'm sorry," said his mother. "I didn't know if you drank."

"Not blood," I answered, trying to sound pleasant. "I did once, but I don't have the urge anymore."

"Oh, that's too bad," she said.

When we finished our walk, Oswald drove us to one of the bigger wineries, a favorite for tourists. "It has a funicular," I said with some excitement. I could say the word "funicular" all day long. I loved the view from up high and the swaying of the compartment as it traveled along the cable.

"We're not taking the tram," Oswald said as he drove by the parking lot for the ride.

"I don't do heights," Mrs. Grant said.

Well, what was the fun of a mountaintop winery without taking a funicular? As we drove along a road lined with olive trees, I stared longingly out the window at the funicular suspended above us. We went past a pond with a fountain and to the paved lot beside the stark white modern structure with narrow windows.

The temperature in the winery was chilly, and we joined a group that was just beginning the guided tour. I'd taken the tour before. This winery was impressive, all stainless steel drums, metal walkways, and scientific technique; but I preferred the funky little tasting rooms that operated out of converted barns and garages, where the vintner himself would open a bottle for you.

The Grants were at the front of the group, listening intently to a lecture that made winemaking sound about as much fun as a pop quiz in thermodynamics. Actually, the tour guide used the word "thermodynamics" twice. "The condensed tannins used in winemaking are polymers of procyandin monomers," said the guide, which made me lag behind the group, fearful of what other atrocities she would inflict upon my ears.

So when the brawny, ruddy blond guy strutted up to me with a big toothy smile, I smiled back. "Hello, love. Where can a bloke get some grog?"

"Does laying on the Aussie accent work for picking up chicks?"

"You tell me, gorgeous," he said, with an exaggerated leer that made me laugh. A few of his friends materialized, and I got the distinct impression that this was not the first of their winery visits. Wearing T-shirts and shorts, they were in their late twenties, tall, muscled, and tanned, with rough good looks.

"The tasting room is downstairs. There are signs."

Another man shook his head dramatically. "He can't read, sweetheart. Can you show us?" The men circled me and gave pleading looks.

I could either catch up with the tour or help these hunky men. The tour group had turned a corner, and Oswald hadn't even noticed that I wasn't with them. "Sure," I said. "Follow me."

As I led them downstairs, they jostled and slugged each other amiably.

"What's your name?" asked the blonde. "I'm Lemon."

"Lemon?"

His grin widened. "Gimme a squeeze."

"He's really Lennon, not Lemon," said a man with bright blue eyes and shaggy brown hair. "I'm Bryce."

"I'm Milagro. You can call me Mil."

Bryce tried to take my hand, but I slapped him away. "Behave yourself," I said, which threw them into gales of laughter as they mimicked me and slapped at their buddy.

"Where do you live, Mil?" asked Lemon. "Got room for guests?"

"I'm here with my boyfriend. We live on the other side of the mountain."

"I don't see a boyfriend," Lemon said. "Anyone see any boyfriends?"

There was a chorus of no's.

"Here's the tasting room," I said. "Have fun."

Beyond the wide doorway was a gift shop and beyond that was a light-filled room with a long bar at the end. I was disheartened at the idea of rejoining the tour, but Bryce said, "How can we have any laughs without you? Share a round with us."

"Well . . ." I supposed that it would have been rude to say no to these visitors. I didn't want them returning home saying that we Californians were unfriendly, which would have a domino effect and eventually devastate the entire tourist economy in our state. "I guess I have time for a glass."

The guys bellied up to the bar, where a pair of slim, neat bartenders were pouring small amounts of red wine in glasses and attempting to describe the vintage and the characteristics of the ruby liquid. It was impossible to hear them because Lemon said something about the small portions and the bartender's anatomy.

"You stingy bastard!" Bryce bellowed. "Give the lady a proper drink!"

I guess by "lady" he meant me, because all the other customers had edged away from our group. After dealing with Willem on my own the night before, I was happy to have a lowland sun idolater advocating on my behalf. "Thanks," I said, "but I'm fine."

Lemon threw crumpled bills on the counter and his pals followed suit. "Start pouring, mates," he said with a wink to the bartenders.

The bartenders filled our glasses to the top with red wine, and the Aussies insisted on toasting to me, Aussie-American relations, Disneyland, nude beaches, beer, and the La Brea Tar Pits. They had a strapping Down Under charisma that increased considerably after my second glass of wine.

In the back of my mind, I was aware that I'd been away from the Grants for too long, but I felt no eagerness to return and struggle to make conversation with Oswald's taciturn parents.

"Any more at home like you?" Lemon asked, leaning against me. "Or any sexy girlfriends? We'll take you out tonight, you name the place. I think I'm falling in lust, I mean, love with you." His eyes strayed down the front of my blouse.

I shoved him away and laughed. "You'll have to entertain yourselves." They were doing a pretty good job of this now, since one of the guys had grabbed some open bottles of wine, which they started tossing to one another. A bottle of zinfandel (intense flavors of blackberry, cedar, and spice, according to the bartender) slipped and exploded on the floor.

It was at this point that I noticed Oswald and his parents in the doorway. Two men in dark suits nudged the Grant family aside as they approached my new amigos.

I quickly moved to a brochure display and pretended to read a pamphlet on viniculture. As the Aussies were escorted off the premises shouting their good-byes, I joined Oswald. "Sorry about that," I whispered to him. "They thought it was funny to take the mickey out of the bartenders."

"The what?" Oswald asked.

"I'm not really sure. I think it has something to do with their visit to Disneyland."

"Your blouse," Mrs. Grant said.

Looking down, I saw that red wine had splattered all over the front of my blouse, and the damp fabric was clinging to my exuberant girly parts. I looked like an extra for *The Texas Chainsaw Massacre*. For the first time, interest flashed in Mr. Grant's eyes.

Oswald had to buy a case of merlot in order to persuade the men in suits to let me stay. When we sat at the outdoor café, I tried to get one of the seats facing away from the rest of the tables, but Oswald's parents took them because they wanted to admire the view off the deck.

I was shamefully aware of other diners staring at me. I wanted to tell them, "Oh, you think I'm bad—this nice-looking older guy swills blood from a silver hip flask."

Mrs. Grant looked at me over the top of her menu and said, "I hope we're not taking away from your large friends."

She didn't say "you tacky ho," but she didn't need to.

"Not at all. I was merely showing them a little hospitality," I said, keeping my voice even. "It's so seldom that people treat each other with real courtesy."

"Is that what you were doing?" she said with a tight smile.

I glanced at Oswald, but he and his father were studying the menu as intently as if they were the Dead Sea Scrolls.

"Perhaps things got out of hand," I said. "Different cultures have different standards of behavior. Here, we're very tolerant of others, even when their ways seem, oh, strange and frightening."

Oswald looked up then and said quickly, "Let's start with

the antipasto platter. It's very good." He gave me an irritated look, and I knew I'd gone too far.

I swallowed my pride, which made me too full to enjoy the meal. I pushed my food around the plate and listened to Oswald talk about his practice, his investments, and a paper he'd published in a professional slicing-and-dicing journal.

Mrs. Grant angled her body toward Oswald, and all her conversation flowed in that direction. I had a strong suspicion that she wouldn't be referring to me as "my son's lovely girl-friend" anytime soon. Mr. Grant stared out at the view and made occasional comments to his son about all of his wise decisions. No one talked to me.

The ride back was tense, at least for me. I sat silently in the backseat with Conrad Grant, while Evelyn Grant listened in fascination as Oswald described maintenance procedures at the ranch, such as the digging of a new well. I resisted the urge to kick the back of Oswald's seat all the way home.

When we finally got back to the ranch, I quickly left Oswald and his parents outside. I found Edna in the small parlor reading an Italian cookbook. "Studying up on the foods of the lower lands?" I asked, and plopped down beside her on the velvet loveseat.

"No one dictates my menu," answered Edna. She noticed my blouse and pointedly did not ask about the stains. "How did you get along with my daughter-in-law?"

"She hates me with a deep and burning passion."

"I mean, besides that." Edna gave me a quick smile.

Edna looked and acted nothing like my *abuelita,* the grand-mother who had rescued me from my mother's clutches for a few brief happy years. But when Edna talked to me like this, I felt the same warmth and affection.

I leaned gently against the older woman. "Oh, other than that, fine, except that your grandson did not stand up for me against his mother's hostility."

"Oswald knows better than to get involved in a fight between two women. Don't put him in a position where he has to choose."

"I did not . . . ," I began defensively. "Well, maybe I did. She seems to have an innate dislike for me."

"When we met, you didn't care if I liked you."

This was true. She had been icier than a blender of margaritas. "You know, I don't mind outright antagonism. I have a problem with veiled hostility, though, and being ignored." My mother Regina had ignored me for most of my life. It was as if she thought that not recognizing my existence would negate it. "But how can I win Evelyn over?"

"I think I'm the wrong person to ask that question."

"She doesn't like you, or you don't like her?"

"We like each other just fine, Young Lady, especially when there are large bodies of water between us," she said. "You should know better than anyone that you cannot choose your relatives."

I sighed. "If I could, I would have chosen Evelyn over my mother Regina. Evelyn adores Oswald. I think it's mutual."

"And that's as it should be. She has been a good mother to him and a good wife to Conrad, and I am grateful for that."

"Too bad she's not any fun."

Edna narrowed her great green eyes. "Were you having fun when you ruined your blouse?"

I grinned. "As a matter of fact, I was. Do you want to know how?"

"No, thank you. I will hear Evelyn's version of the story soon enough."

I cringed thinking of the unpleasant slant that Evelyn could put on a completely innocent situation. "I could have behaved with more decorum, I suppose."

Edna patted my knee. "Don't hope for the impossible."

"Very funny, Edna. What's on the menu for tonight's it's-not-a-party?"

After I changed my blouse, I had to hard-boil dozens of tiny brown speckled quail eggs. The menu included vamp favorite red foods: French toast with mascarpone and berries, beet salad with oranges, very rare leg of lamb, and raspberry sorbet. Bloody Marys and the merlot that Oswald purchased today would be served.

"Eggs, Bloody Marys, French toast," I said. "It's a midnight brunch."

"Yes, you could call it that. Young Lady, do keep Daisy out from under my feet."

I had put aside the end of a baguette for Daisy and now I shooed her outside and tossed the treat.

When I was done helping Edna, I went to the Love Shack. I fully expected Oswald to scold me for baiting his mother and carousing with rambunctious foreigners. All my self-righteousness had dissipated with the residual effects of the wine. When Oswald acted as if nothing had happened, I was so relieved that I treated him to an exhilarating tumble.

I was feeling a warm zuzziness toward him, and I said, "Oswald, I'm sorry about that incident at the winery. I got caught up in the silliness, and . . ."

"It's all right. It must be boring for you here all the time. I know it's quiet and isolated compared to your old life."

My old life consisted of borderline poverty, rats in my apartment, not enough time to write, and a yearning for a fabulous relationship and a home with people who loved me and whom I loved. "No, I love being here." I did love living at the ranch, but perhaps I also missed a few of the City's charms.

"If you're tired it's okay to skip the meal tonight."

Pulling away from his embrace, I said, "Why do I get the feeling you're brushing me off? I guess it's okay to have the help from the lower lands do the cooking and cleaning and servicing the master's sexual needs, but not to have her actually socializing with the high and mighty—"

"Stop, stop." Oswald took my hand in his. "I'm not brushing you off. It's just . . . I was giving you an out if you wanted one, especially since you do such an incredible servicing job."

"I told you already, I want to be there."

Still, I couldn't help feeling excluded and resentful as I watched Oswald leave for the baby's naming ceremony.

I took a copy of Brönte's *Villette* to read while soaking in a bubble bath. I had loved Jane Eyre like a friend, but I found Lucy Snowe disturbing. I was at a scene where the spooky, sexually repressed Lucy thinks she sees the ghost of a nun when I heard an eerie thump at the bathroom door. The thump came again. I dropped my book in the water and sat up just as Daisy bashed her way into the room.

"I wish you wouldn't do that when I'm reading scary stuff." I fished the paperback out of the water and set it on the floor on a towel. Experience had taught me that slower methods of drying books worked better than sticking them under the broiler, trying to blow-dry them, or putting them in the microwave and hitting the "popcorn" button.

When my toes were thoroughly prunified, I got out, slipped on one of my new dresses, a pretty floral print with little buttons up the front. After brushing my hair and putting on eye makeup and lipstick, I selected a dark shawl, the better for concealment, and slipped my feet into flat leather shoes.

I took a flashlight and went outside into the night.

The cottage was surrounded by tall shrubs and vines, so it was easy for me to stand in them and survey the Big House and the pool compound. The house was almost dark, except for the fairy lights twinkling in the trees around the patio. Light glowed at the pool compound. They must have retracted the roof.

Daisy wanted to come with me, but she had no grasp of subterfuge, so I kept her in the fenced garden. The moon was full tonight and bright enough to let me make my way without the flashlight. I avoided taking the shortest route, the path to the pool, because the gravel would crunch with every step.

I stumbled once on the uneven ground, but caught myself. The knothole was difficult to find in the dark. I covered the flashlight with my hand to obscure its beam and flicked it on. When my fingers found the chunk of wood, I turned off the flashlight. Slowly, carefully, I pulled out the chunk of wood. Then I put my eye to the hole.

I expected to see the group looking like country-clubbers at their annual members meeting and social. Instead, I saw people wearing hooded scarlet robes that were edged with black borders. Their faces were shadowed and eerie in the flickering light of candles and torches that formed a circle around them.

I searched for Oswald, thinking that surely I would recognize him immediately, but he was as anonymous as the others. When I finally identified him as the man in the second row of chairs, he didn't look much like the man I knew and loved; it was as if someone else, someone serious and soulless, was inhabiting his body.

I had a better view of Willem Dunlop, his face looking jaundiced and waxy, as he stood on the platform. His robe was all black, and he wavered weakly as he threw a handful of leaves onto a brazier on the altar. Bitter smoke billowed toward me in the breeze. The platform itself was covered with a layer of birch branches.

Silas was by Willem's side, holding my little baby friend. Willem spoke in a language that sounded like glass breaking, like metal twisting, like something that should never come out of a human mouth.

A couple moved forward, golden hair swinging out from under one hood, and I realized that the pair was Winnie and Sam. They echoed a long, harsh phrase in monotone voices. The people behind them repeated the phrase three times, like a chant.

My gut clenched with anxiety.

A movement from behind the chairs caught my attention. Ian Ducharme stood there, dressed in an elegant light suit and cream-colored shirt. He'd cut his curly black hair short, which brought out his strong, indolent features. He had dark eyes with hooded lids, a prominent nose, and a full, sensuous mouth. He was only average in height, and his tailored clothes hid his broad chest and muscular body.

Now he watched Willem with bored amusement. Reaching into his pocket, Ian took out a gold case. He opened it and pulled out a cigarette. Then he strolled into the dark shadows at the far end of the compound.

I turned my attention back to Willem. He gestured to Silas, who held the baby over the stone basin on the table. Something glinted in the candlelight, a delicate glass goblet.

Silas spoke for the first time, saying, "The blood iss the river, the blood iss the life." He was translating for Willem. "Blood must be taken, and blood must be given, for it iss written."

Willem reached to the table and lifted an object. He held it tremulously aloft. It was a knife with a jeweled handle.

It was a knife by the baby, my baby, and I had to stop it. I opened my mouth, but a hand closed over it and I felt myself in an iron grip. I twisted and kicked back hard, and bit down on the hand, even as I smelled Ian's familiar spicy cologne and heard him whisper, "Calm down, *querida*."

four

fiesta con los vampiros

The baby was in danger, so I did not calm down. I writhed
and kicked back, and one shoe flew off. I bit Ian's palm and
jabbed my elbows into his ribs. Years of garden work had made
me a strong girl, but he didn't flinch or loosen his grip.

In fact, I got the distinct impression that he was enjoying
the physical contact.

Bending my head forward in preparation for throwing it
back so I could break his nose, I heard him whisper, "The infant will not be hurt or harmed. I promise you this."

The odd thing was that I believed him.

When I stopped trying to hurt him, Ian said, "Now, I'm
going to let you go." He nuzzled his face against my hair, and I
felt his lips briefly on my neck.

I remembered with crystal clarity our brief liaison. I thought
it must be very wrong to be aroused by another man when I

loved Oswald. I *knew* it was absolutely wrong for him to seek arousal from a young woman in a committed relationship.

Ian released me; I didn't bother looking for my shoe and immediately put my eye back to the peephole. Edna, her hood pushed back away from her face, held the happy, healthy baby. Sam and Winnie, who had also pushed back their hoods, stood beside the marble basin. Silas handed Sam the knife.

Poor Sam looked as if he was the unwilling guest at a costume party. Holding his left palm out, Sam said slowly, "This child is my blood and my life. I will love and protect this child always." He winced and cut his palm. The incision was too tentative to cut his skin. Sam gazed helplessly at Winnie, who took the knife from him.

She caught his gaze and smiled reassuringly. She then made a small incision. She immediately cut her own palm and said in her sweet, firm voice, "This child is my blood and my life. I will love and protect this child always."

I teared up at this expression of parental devotion.

Sam and Winnie held their hands over the basin and Willem picked up the crystal chalice. It held what I assumed was water, which sloshed in his shaky grip. He splashed the water over the couple's hands and spoke in that unspeakable language; like a dubbed film, the sounds did not match the movement of his mouth.

Silas said, "It iss sso proclaimed that this child shall henceforth be Elizsabeth Tabitha Grant-Harding."

Sam and Winnie grinned as Edna handed them back the wriggling baby. Elizabeth!

I turned to face Ian and stomped on his foot.

"Why, darling?" he asked quietly. He picked up my wayward shoe and handed it to me.

"Because you took pleasure in my fear," I whispered. Ian still had the disconcerting ability to make me think: sex, sex, sex.

"Ah, but I find your presence so uplifting. Now hurry and arrange yourself so that Oswald doesn't suspect you've been out here spying. We'll talk later."

Ian walked toward the swimming compound, whistling cheerfully, and I loped off across the field. When I arrived back at the shack I noticed that my neat little shoes were dusty and the top buttons on my dress had popped off, exposing most of my *tetas* in their pretty pink bra. Damn Ian Ducharme.

I kicked off the shoes and took off the dress to survey the damage. Perhaps it could be repaired. I looked through a cigar box with safety pins, stray buttons, and a few bobbins of thread. But none of the buttons came close to matching.

The front door opened, and I grabbed the first thing I touched in the closet, a ruby-red dress in a stretchy jersey. I pulled it over my head and wiggled it down over my hips. If Winnie had worn this dress, it would have looked stylish, but the cut and clinginess accentuated all my curves. This was a high-heels type of dress and I jammed my feet into black open-toe stilettos. I was smoothing my hair with my hands when Oswald came into the bedroom.

"Oh, you're still up."

"Of course I am. But I fell asleep dressed and, uh, I have to just tidy up."

"Okay," he said with a somewhat befuddled expression. "If you're sure you want to go."

"Oswald, if you don't want me to go, would you just say so?" When he didn't answer, I stomped into the bathroom. Looking into the mirror, I saw that my grappling with Ian had smeared my lipstick across my face. As for the dress, I could have worn it soliciting, and jaded hookers would have thought me trampy. No wonder Oswald was hesitant.

I could have changed, but then I thought, these people have just been wearing weird robes and performing a creepy ceremony, why the heck do I need to impress them? I repaired my makeup, and Oswald and I went outside.

He hesitated and said, "Don't you want a sweater? It's getting chilly."

"I'm fine. How was the baby event?"

"Long and dull," he said, pulling his eyes up to my face. After a moment, he added, "Ian finally showed up."

"Um, Winnie will be happy."

I had to walk on the balls of my feet across the field so that my heels wouldn't sink into the soil. The glimmering fairy lights in the trees, the glowing lanterns, and the cheerful pots of flowers on the patio made the earlier scene at the swimming compound all the more unreal. White blooms of nicotiana delicately perfumed the air.

"There's a breeze kicking up," Oswald said, glancing again at my clinging red dress. "I can run back and get a coat for you. It will only take a minute."

"Thanks, but I'm fine."

The guests milled about with Bloody Marys and small plates of food. Ian stood across the patio, talking to Sam's parents. He saw me but did not approach.

The baby was in her basinet, snoozing innocently, while Winnie adjusted a ribbon-trimmed pink blanket over her. "Hi, Win," I said. "How is little Elizabeth?"

"Oh, Oswald ruined my surprise. I wanted to tell you myself."

I smiled innocently.

midnight brunch

"We're calling her Libby."

Gabriel joined us. "Libby is so old-fashioned," he said. "I'm going to call her Za, I think."

Gabriel and I wandered over to the drinks table. "Miss Milagro, I'm not complaining, but whatever inspired you to wear this scandalous dress?"

"It was an accident, but difficult to explain."

"I'm sure the uncles appreciate it, but you can bet that the aunts will poke out their eyes if they catch them looking." He poured two glasses for us, but we didn't have a chance to talk. The aunts surrounded Gabriel. They stroked his pretty red hair and admired his complexion as if he was a chubby three-year-old instead of a sleek urban creature.

I edged away from the group and walked smack into Silas. "Misss De Loss Ssantoss," he said, fully enjoying all the *s*'s in my name.

"Misster Silass," I said softly, trying to figure out this guy. My internal Geiger counter didn't register him anywhere on the sexual scale of straight and gay. His eyes didn't stray from my face.

He sidled close to me. "I do hope you don't judge Willem based on the ideas he expressed yesterday," he said with twice as many *s*'s as needed. "I ssit beside him in order to assuage any outbursts that are so uncharacteristic of the honorable and noble man he once wass." Silas subtly reached his fingertips to his head. "You understand?"

Was Willem in the first stages of dementia? "I think so."

Silas gave a relieved smile. "Reasoning with him now is futile. But we try to treat him with the respect he earned in the decades before. We choose tolerance over censure."

"I take it he was a different man."

"He was a gentleman and a sscholar, a shining light!" said Silas. "It ssaddens my heart to witness his deterioration, but I feel honored to be of assistance in the ssunset years of his life."

I liked Silas's formal way of speaking. I imagined him as someone who had spent too much time with old papers, and not enough with people. His lack of sexuality, too, was interesting. "That's very kind of you."

"Winnie mentioned that you are a writer. How exciting that must be!"

I warmed to him. "It sounds exciting, but I just sit at a desk for hours."

"I'm sure you are too modesst. Tell me, what do you write?"

People frequently reacted negatively when I told them about my political horror stories, but Silas seemed fascinated. I told him about my short stories, my attempts at screenwriting, my novel, and the new *Uno! Dos! Terror!* novellas.

"I know someone will recognize your talent sssoon, Misss De Loss Santoss. You possesss a unique character," he said. "I'm also intrigued by your personal story of ssurvival. May I call you and set up a time to have a coffee?"

"I don't have my own phone, but you can call the house and they'll give me the message."

Suddenly, Silas's elderly charge bellowed loudly, "An abomination!"

Now, whenever I heard someone say "abomination," I naturally assumed they were talking to me.

But Willem pointed at Gabriel and said, "The homosexual is an abomination. Your duty to your family is to marry, continue our blood and traditions. Your parents were right to disown you for the shame you have brought to us all."

I waited for Gabriel's blistering reply. But my friend, usually so quick-witted, stood in shock, a blush suffusing his lovely face.

I took in the stunned expressions of the guests, the yelp of an animal in the distance, a moth battering itself against the glass shade of a lantern, Silas looking dismayed.

I didn't care if Willem had been a nice person once. I wanted to tackle him and crack his egghead open on the slate pavers until his brain leaked out like a rotten yolk. I wondered if "justifiable irkiness" was a defense against vampire-slaughter.

Ian was suddenly beside the wretched old man. He said in a cold tone, "Dunlop, you have offended all thinking people. You will leave now and go back to your dark little world." For all his bonhomie, Ian had gravitas and his words penetrated the eggman's shell.

The older man gaped, and then gazed helplessly at his aide. Silas looked around the gathering and said politely, "Thank you sso much for your generous hosspitality. You have been more than kind. We must go now, but please continue to enjoy yourselvess."

Willem tottered into the house. Silas paused to tell Gabriel, "I am very ssorry for Willem's behavior. He'd had a good sspell, but the travel has upset his routine."

Gabriel was silent and Silas glided away.

Then Ian put his arm through Gabriel's and led him to the shadows under a tall oak.

The silence was broken by Edna turning to me and saying, "And I thought *you* would be the one to make even more of a spectacle of yourself, Young Lady."

"The night is still young, Edna. Wait a little longer and I may," I said.

Everyone laughed nervously and then began to talk again. Oswald left his parents and came to me.

"Do you think Gabriel's all right?" I asked him.

He glanced at his cousin and said, "His folks can't come to grips with his being gay."

I wondered if that was part of my connection with Gabriel: we weren't what our parents wanted. My parents hadn't wanted me at all, and his parents had wanted a different kind of child. "He can't choose his sexual orientation," I said.

"It's not the orientation that bothers them as much as the family line dying out." Oswald looked nervous, as though he'd divulged too much of his cousin's confidences.

Who knows what Ian was saying to him, but a few moments later Gabriel was smiling, and everyone started having fun.

I was trying to figure out if I really wanted to eat little quail eggs and, if so, how to go about it, when I realized that the awful incident had made me momentarily forget about the eerie ceremony. Maybe it was the vodka in my drink, but the faces around me looked mysterious, not in a glamorous way but in a what's-hiding-under-that-old-log kind of way.

The problem with being raised by an abnormal family was that I had no standard for normal behavior.

I drifted at the periphery of the party, watching and listening. The conversation was perfectly ordinary, but the guests would disappear off to the barn. I wended my way there and entered the dark building. I loved the rich aroma of animals and hay. Light and laughter spilled out of an open stable door. I knew what I would see as I moved toward it and looked around the door frame.

Oswald and his parents were engrossed in conversation as they drank pink-tinged drinks. Ernie, the ranch hand, was mixing the drinks: spring water with organic, grass-fed lamb's blood. When I had been infected, the sight and smell of blood had excited me. One taste was enough to send a rush of bliss, like a drug, through me. But my immune system overcame the contamination, and those days were gone. I left the barn and went back to the patio.

Ian, the only one who had not worn the weird robes and the only one who had spoken out against Willem, sauntered over to me. "Milagro, so good to see you again." As he kissed me on the cheeks, he said sotto voce, "I like this dress even better than the one you had on earlier."

"Nice to see you, too, Ian. How've you been?" I was conscious that Oswald was not nearby.

"Oh, feeling rather sentimental of late. My sister sends her love."

The last time I'd laid eyes on his sister, Cornelia, she was spitting venomously because I'd stopped seeing Ian. "Tell her that I miss her just as much as she misses me," I said. "Are you staying in town?"

"I'm driving to the City tonight. Would you like to join me?"

"Thank you, but no. I have to head there anyway in a few days for my friend's wedding."

"You don't look happy about it."

"Oswald will be gone and I'm going to look like such a pathetic loser all by myself," I blurted. "He has an excellent reason for not joining me. He's going to the border to do pro bono work for children, and that's wonderful, but . . ."

"But?" he said.

"But I really don't fit in with my friend's friends. They completely ignore me."

"No one should ignore you, Young Lady. If you will permit, I would like to escort you."

"Really?" I quickly weighed the pros and cons of this scenario. What harm could come of attending a public event with Ian? "Okay, but I don't think we need to tell Oswald. He's got some Issues about our, um, friendship." I gave Ian the phone number of my friend Mercedes so we could coordinate when I was in the City.

Later, in the Love Shack, I lay in bed and watched Oswald checking his luggage. He was driving to the airport tomorrow after breakfast.

"Do you think Gabriel's okay?" I asked.

Oswald frowned. "He's a resilient guy. He'll come out of this fine."

"At least Ian spoke up for him."

Oswald gave me an irritated look. "Did you have a nice reunion with him?"

"Yes, I did. He told me that his sister sends her love. I told him I reciprocated her feelings." Oswald and Cornelia used to be friends, so I asked, "I always thought that Cornelia had a thing for you. I overheard her say something once about 'sharing lovers' with you."

"Not lovers, *blubber*. We took a trip to the Arctic once and had a traditional Inuit meal."

"You expect me to believe that?"

"Yes, and I'll believe that Ian didn't make a pass at you."

This seemed like a reasonable agreement. I asked Oswald, "Your supplies will be delivered, right?" He could go for days without drinking blood, but he'd languish.

"The bio firm will have a delivery for me the day after tomorrow." He pulled a folder out of his leather messenger bag and examined a few pages. "Here's a copy of my itinerary. I might not be able to call, but leave a message for anything important. Or anything at all."

"There's not going to be any emergency. Don't worry about me." I crawled out of bed and put my arms around him. "You're wonderful and amazing, and I'm sure everything will go brilliantly."

Unfortunately, predicting the future was not one of my talents.

five

bad to the bone

A gentle prodding awoke me. I reached out for Oswald and touched fur. Daisy was standing beside the bed, her head resting on my pillow, her nose an inch from my face. Her amber eyes gazed solemnly at me. When she saw that I was awake, she did a little skittering dance of happiness, her nails clicking on the hardwood floor.

I glanced at the clock and saw that it was already late. Hopping out of bed, I hurried to the kitchen and scooped kibble into a bowl for Daisy. Then I pulled on jeans and a light sweater and put my hair in a ponytail. I brushed my teeth, dashed on some mascara and gloss, and ran to the Big House.

Oswald was sitting outside, drinking coffee with his father. I threw my arms around him and gave him a kiss. "Morning."

"Morning, babe. I was letting you sleep in. There's a fresh pot of coffee."

I went inside and poured a mug. "Where's Gabriel?" I asked Edna.

"He had to take care of some business," she said.

The relatives were talking about their sightseeing plans. They were going to take Libby with them, so I extricated her from Winnie's arms and took her to the study with me for a few minutes of quality time. We settled in the desk chair and I put my feet on the desk. She grinned gummily and made a grab for my hair.

I stared into her huge brown eyes and all I saw was a little girl I loved. "You are a normal girl," I told her. "Very special, but normal."

"No, she isn't."

Oswald's mother, Evelyn, stepped into the study and closed the door behind her.

I took my feet off the desk and sat up straight.

"She's not a normal baby and she's not going to have a normal life." Mrs. Grant sat on the sofa.

I got that sinking "Miss De Los Santos, the dean would like to have a word with you" feeling. "She's got a genetic condition," I said. "Lots of people have genetic conditions."

"Not like ours," Evelyn said, and then sighed. "I believe my son thinks he loves you, Milagro, but do you really love him or are you impressed by his position and money?"

"Mrs. Grant, I fell for Oswald when I thought he was an unemployed slacker. I wasn't hunting for a rich man."

"Say you do love him, are you going to want to stay with him when you can't have children together?"

"You don't know that." Oswald and I had not even discussed marriage yet.

She repeated what I'd already heard from Winnie: centuries

before, children born from intermarriage with outsiders died at high rates. "Could you bear to see your child die?" she asked. "Could Oswald bear it? How long would it be before you blame and hate each other?"

Tears welled in my eyes and I turned my face down toward the baby.

"Let him go, Milagro. Let him have a chance at having a family of his own."

I wanted to say, "He is my family. *This* is my family." But it wasn't. They still hid things from me and left me out.

"We are happy," I said in a thick voice.

"Don't be selfish. If you love him, you'll do what's best for him. You're young and attractive enough, I suppose. You'll get married and have children and forget all about Oswald."

"We can adopt," I said. "Or get a sperm donor." Why was I even discussing this with her? "We can take a child left at the mall." The year after my grandmother died, my mother Regina left me in a shopping mall. I sat on a bench, euphoric with the hope that some kind family would take me home with them. The cleaning lady who found me was unconvinced that I was an orphan.

"You may be Mother Edna's little pet, but I don't find you very amusing," she said. "With Winnie, he had a future with a woman who knew how to behave decently in public. Before you stole him away with your trashy ways."

"Oswald never loved Winnie. He loves me. You know that or you'd be talking to him."

She stared me directly in the eye. "Of course I have, Milagro. I told him to give you enough money so you can get an apartment somewhere and pay for expenses until you find a real job. I hope he'll think about it while he's away. It would be the best thing for all concerned—even you." She stood up. "Don't doubt that I will do anything I can to make sure my son has a happy life." She left the room, shutting the door after her.

I had a difficult time controlling myself long enough to return Libby to her mother and get back to the shack without anyone else seeing me.

Oswald was in the bedroom picking up his suitcase and briefcase. "Time for me to go," he said before he saw my face. "Milagro? Is anything wrong?"

My face felt hot and tears welled in my eyes. "Is anything wrong? Yes, *everything* is wrong," I shouted. "Your mother hates me and she wants you to pay me to go away. You invited a bigot here and you keep secrets from me."

Oswald shook his head. "I don't have time for this right now."

"You'd have time if you'd told me these things before instead of telling me your mother would love me and then trying to keep me in the shack, away from your very important friends and relatives."

"Willem Dunlop is not a friend. I only had him here because it was important to Winnie and Sam's parents. As for my mother, I'm a grown man and I make my own decisions."

"What about all the secrets you keep from me? How come you never really explained how your people live?"

"Because I can't count on you to be discreet," he said angrily. "You can't even behave politely for a few hours with my parents. No, you take off and start partying in the winery with a bunch of beach bums."

"It's not as if any of you were paying attention to me. I didn't even get to ride the funicular!"

"What are you, twelve?" he said coldly. "That afternoon

63

wasn't for you, it was for my parents. But you always need people to pay attention to you. Isn't that why you wore that dress
for Ian last night? And then you tell me there's nothing between you."

"*You* bought me that dress, Oswald. You're the one who
bought all the hoochie-mama clothing—but maybe that's how
you think of me, as just your little sex toy!" I'd crossed the line
from hurt to pure blue anger.

"Stop being ridiculous. If I wanted just a sex toy, I would get
someone who wasn't as much trouble as you. My life is more
complicated than you can understand. I have to balance a lot of
competing interests, keep my business going, deal with life and
death every single day, and then come home to the demands of
my family and you. And I always, *always* have to think about
keeping my family safe."

We'd had arguments, but he'd never taken this harsh tone
with me. "I apologize if I've been so demanding, Dr. Grant.
Forgive me for presuming that I was worth your time." At least
this is what I tried to say. My words were garbled by my sobs.
"At least I never nearly killed you." As soon as the words came
out, I wished I could grab them back again.

"I knew you'd throw that in my face one day. It was an accident, and I'm sorry, Milagro. I will always be sorry." He looked
beaten, but I wasn't happy for the victory.

"Are you sorry that you met me?"

"We'll deal with this when I get back. I left some cash on the
kitchen table for groceries or whatever."

Oswald walked out of the room. I ran to the kitchen and
grabbed the money. As he was opening the front door, I threw
the cash at him and yelled, "I don't want your damn money! I
don't want anything from you."

He gave me one long furious look and walked off toward the car park. I slammed the front door and cried a million tears.

When I was dehydrated from crying, I picked myself up off the sofa and drank a bottle of water. Desperate times called for desperate measures. I needed guidance from my own spiritual rock. I'd been planning on staying with my best friend, Mercedes, for the wedding, and I was sure she'd enjoy having me a day early.

First I dropped off Petunia at the barn, so that Ernie could make sure she was safe in the coop at night. I told him I was leaving Daisy there, so he would include her in runs with the other dogs. As I returned to the Love Shack, I scoped out the car park. The relatives had already gone for the day.

I listlessly packed my clothes and remembered that I needed accessories. I crawled behind the racks in the closet to find the box where I'd hidden the gifts from Ian. There was an enameled fountain pen with gold filigree, an ornate necklace of dark red stones and matching earrings, bracelets that chimed together gently when worn, a small portrait in a locket, carved obsidian animals, and various other trinkets.

Each item was beautiful.

I packed the earrings and necklace, along with the obsidian animals, which Mercedes would like. I put drops in my eyes to clear the redness and dabbed concealer to cover the shadows under my eyes. Then I hauled my things to my truck and went in the Big House and found Edna.

"I'm leaving early to spend time with Mercedes," I said with false cheerfulness. "Thanks for telling Oswald about the clothes."

She lifted her eyebrows. "I wouldn't have done it if I'd known he was going to buy that scanty excuse for a dress you wore yesterday."

"Look who's judging me," I said more sharply than I intended. "I mean, you must have worn outrageous things, too." She knew something was wrong and didn't respond.

"Edna, please tell everyone good-bye for me and be sure to say that I hope to see them when they visit again."

"Young Lady, should I be concerned about you?"

"You know me," I said with a smile. "I can take care of myself."

"They'll be gone soon and things will get back to normal," she said. "Oh, a package came for you this morning."

I hugged her briefly, afraid that if I held on I would relapse into tears. "Bye, Edna. I'll be home soon."

I grabbed the cardboard box on my way out. The return label was from a telecommunications company, and I was so curious I opened it once I got in my truck.

Inside was a nifty little phone, packing papers, and one of those "A Gift From" cards that said, "Dear Miss De Los Santos, Thank you for being so understanding when we met. Here is a small gift to commemorate the beginning of our friendship. Sincerely, Silas Madison. P.S. I have taken care of all charges and fees for one year."

His thoughtfulness really touched me, especially since I was feeling so tender and vulnerable.

I took off toward the City, stopping at my favorite burger joint for lunch and to examine my new phone. Mercedes was the first one I called.

She hadn't yet left for My Dive, the club she owned. " 'lo," she said briskly.

"*Hola*, Señorita Ochoa-McPherson." Mercedes's mother was a Cuban immigrant and her father came from Scotland.

"Hi, Mil, can we talk tomorrow? I'm out the door."

"It's your lucky day. I'll be there in about an hour or so."

She said a few rude words in both Spanish and English. "I'll be at the club. You still have my spare key?"

"Absolutely. I visit your house when you're gone and move things around to make you feel crazy, like in that movie *Gaslight*."

"Milagro," she said, "all you have to do is show up to make me feel crazy."

"I love you, too. Will you be home late?"

"*No sé*. We're booked for a corporate party tonight so they may be gone by ten or hang on," she said. "Come by if you want to. I'll put your name on the list."

"Ha, ha, and ha. As if I ever needed to be on a list with Lennie working the door."

"I'm only comping you one drink. Don't forget to tip."

"I always tip. Later, *mi amor*."

While the rest of the world was enjoying warm weather, the City was shrouded in fog. The diffused light softened the edges of buildings, like gel on a lens. The old girl was past her heyday, but still quite a looker.

Mercedes's two-story house was the nicest one on the block, but now neighbors were beginning to restore their small Victorians and Edwardians. Bay windows had been repaired, facades repainted, and fanciful gingerbread trim reattached.

Mercedes was only a few years older than me, but she'd packed a lot of work into those years by dropping out of college and getting a high-tech job. She'd bought a seedy nightclub in foreclosure and the house when the neighborhood was downright scary. Tenants in the first-floor flat helped pay the mortgage for the house, and the club was doing well.

I drove around the neighborhood for ten minutes looking

for parking. When a space opened up across the street from her house, I took it as a good omen. I unlocked the front door and lugged my things upstairs to her cozy flat.

The place was very attractive and decorated with an eclectic selection of comfortable furniture, original prints, and warm colors. There was a place for everything and everything was in its place.

Being at Mercedes's made me feel as though I was on the edge of illumination. She had a rational, dispassionate approach to life, and she would make sense out of Oswald's blow-up, doddering bigots, albino acolytes, spooky costume dramas, and irrational women who wanted to get rid of their sons' delightful girlfriends. She would tell me that I was being too emotional, too paranoid, and too insecure. She would make the world right again.

I flicked on the sound system and music filled the room. After a few seconds of thinking really hard, I recognized Ellington's thrilling *Far East Suite*. Mercedes, the daughter of classically trained musicians who were also ethnomusicologists, had spent a lot of time giving me a musical education.

Singing "dadda-dah-dah-dah" along with Ellington as best I could, I unpacked my things, made a pot of Darjeeling tea, and then called my friends to tell them I finally had my own phone number. When they asked how things were going with my beau, I told them that everything was fabulous.

In the bedroom, Mercedes had a long desk on one wall with three computers. She was a geek who secretly indulged in hacking. She used her powers for good, not evil, though, and her skills had helped extricate me from SLIME's nefarious clutches.

I hung my dress in her closet and checked her bathroom to see if she had any interesting new products. I found a bottle of

Obsession that looked as if it had never been used. I spritzed it in the air and walked through it.

Although the home values had increased in the neighborhood, there was still a dangerous edge of gang activity. When I went out to pick up something for dinner, I saw a few cholos kicking back on a corner ahead, all elaborate black tattoos, perfectly pressed pants, and deadly attitude. I crossed the street, buttoned my jacket to cover up, and kept my gaze straight ahead.

A police car cruised up and the men vanished into the shadows.

My favorite taqueria was about six blocks away, in a mishmash of cafés, restaurants, bars, and small shops. Because my paperback hadn't dried, I needed a book. I thought about getting another Brönte novel but discovered a used hardback of Waugh's *Brideshead Revisited*.

I took my tacos and *horchata* back to Mercedes's and read while I ate. This solitary activity usually brought me joy, but my mind kept drifting from the character Sebastian Flyte to the Sebastian I knew, SLIME. Sometimes life intrudes on fiction that way. Sebastian had been so beautiful and clever that I never sensed the corruption at his core. I'd thought that love would overcome the differences of class and culture.

Reading about Sebastian Flyte's descent into depravity made me mourn SLIME's descent into amorality.

Disturbing thoughts were scurrying like beetles around my brain, bringing in crumbs of information. I brushed them away, resisting the idea that I might be similarly deluded with Oswald.

It was late when I spackled on nighttime makeup and sprayed and gooped my hair until it had doubled in volume. I went down to the street and hailed a cab, which was easier than driving downtown.

Mercedes's club was located in a bleak neighborhood of cheap residential hotels, a soup kitchen, strip clubs, and tiny marvelous Vietnamese diners. It had a plain black exterior with small red letters that said "MY DIVE." A few people in disheveled business attire were smoking on the sidewalk and I could hear the music throbbing within.

Lenny, the doorman, smiled when he saw me get out of the cab, but a deep wrinkle between his brows showed that he was tense. "Hey, girl, good to see you. Give me some sugar."

Lenny always took advantage of hugs and this was no exception. He grabbed my behind in his hands and squeezed. "Good to feel you, too, 'specially when you got something to grab on to."

I stepped back before he explored further.

He had shaved his head and I ran my hand over the glossy dark pate. "When did you do this?"

"When there was more skin than hair. What do you think?"

"Sexy, Lenny. You'll be getting all the groupies."

"Groupies, huh. Don't you tell my wife." He winked. Lenny was married to a minister.

I walked into the club's lobby, waved to the coat-check girl, and entered the main room. I stood for a few minutes, letting my eyes adjust to the darkness and my ears adjust to the noise. In addition to the usual suspects in a rock band, there was a saxophonist, two oud players, a conga player, and someone on a didgeridoo.

It shouldn't have worked. The lead singer was shrieking, and the song veered into total dissonance before suddenly falling into place. I couldn't even tell what genre of music they were playing or the lyrics of the song. But it didn't matter. The waves of sound filled me. Nothing seemed to matter but the music. I wanted to fling myself into the crowd of gyrating, glassy-eyed corporate types, but first I had to say hello to Mercedes.

On the staircase I stumbled over three people doing something that I was pretty sure was prohibited in the corporate handbook. They didn't even notice me. I found Mercedes on the balcony by the sound booth. She looked worried and gave me a quick *abrazo* before turning back to look at the room below.

"Your hair! It's so cute," I said, touching the neat little dreadlocks.

She ducked her head away. "*No me moleste,*" she said. "Do you see what's going on down there?"

"That band is on fire. I've never heard anything like it."

"They're trouble."

"What's wrong with people having a good time?"

She spoke into my ear so I could hear her. "Tribal rhythms mimicking pulse, like trance music, with the rock component. People get loco."

Glass shattered down below. A young man in a suit jumped on the bar and began stripping and howling. A high heel flew through the air and struck him on the head. He fell into the crowd.

"Oh, hell no," Mercedes said angrily. "The deposit is not going to cover this." To me she said, "You might want to get out of here."

"But I haven't even danced yet."

Two women clamored onto the stage and began pulling down the lead singer's jeans. Mercedes got on her walkie-talkie and hurried downstairs. The man who'd been stripping was hoisted aloft in the crowd. He looked unconscious. I waved to the sound guy and reluctantly made my way downstairs. A man was spraying a fire extinguisher on the crowd, and a woman leapt on his back and pummeled him.

I'd never seen this kind of mayhem in My Dive before, and it was especially shocking when the hooligans had MBAs instead of police records.

Lenny came striding into the club, a walkie-talkie in one hand. He put his mouth to my ear and said, "Better clear out. The cops are on their way." Then he shouted into the walkie-talkie, "Shut it down now!"

The electricity onstage went out, throwing the band into darkness and cutting off the amplification. People were screaming and howling with laughter as Lenny and another bouncer began shoving them toward the exit and telling them, "Move along, move along!"

The people started toward the door, but circled back to the dance floor in a daze. I pushed my way through them and outside. Paramedics and police arrived as I got into a cab.

When Mercedes came home, I ran a bath for her, dumping in a generous amount of honeysuckle foaming gel. Then I went to the Caribbean blue kitchen and opened a bottle of zinfandel that I'd brought. I poured two glasses and took one to Mercedes in the bath.

I took my book and curled up on the sofa, becoming more and more engrossed in the story, until the city sounds faded away and I forgot where I was. So when the large pale shape loomed in front of me, I screamed and threw the book at the apparition, which amazingly transformed into Mercedes wearing a soft coral quilted robe.

"What the . . . ," she said, glaring at me.

"Sorry!" I caught my breath and said, "You surprised me."

She shook her head and her dreads bounced a little. "You

and your books." She picked up the novel and tossed it to me.

Mercedes had caramel skin and a scattering of freckles across her open, honest features. She was just above average height with a sturdy build. She wasn't delicate enough to be pretty, never wore makeup, and didn't practice any feminine wiles, but there was no shortage of musicians and managers who pursued her.

She plopped on the sofa with a sigh. "Okay, I think I'll recover. The company's CFO said they'd pay for all the damage. He's smoothing things over with the cops."

"That doesn't sound so bad."

She shrugged. "I'm not booking that band again. Now I understand why they call themselves the Dervishes."

"Speaking of craziness, I wanted to talk to you about something. I'm freaking out a little bit."

"You've been living with a pack of vampires for a year, and now you're freaking out?"

"Why do you keep calling them vampires?"

"I am not the one in denial about my identity."

"Let us not quibble over semantics. I had a big fight with Oswald before he left."

"Fight and flight. Do I have to hear about this tonight?"

"Yes," I said, and refilled our glasses. "I mentioned that the vamps were having a party of sorts for the baby? Oh, and her name is Elizabeth, and we're calling her Libby."

I described how I'd very accidentally found a peephole in the fence, "just like you find a side entrance in a computer program," and told her about the scene I'd witnessed, the vile and reprehensible eggheaded creature, my close encounter of the maternal kind, and Oswald's awful behavior.

When I finished, Mercedes stared at me for a moment, then said, "And that is why I like living alone. I'm going to bed now."

"Don't you have anything to say about this horrible situation?"

"I like your friends, especially Gabriel, but like my mother says, *Hay gato encerrado.*"

"Your Cuban sayings never make any sense. What do you mean there's a cat locked up?"

"They've got big secrets. Why should they tell you everything when you could bail on Oswald when the infatuation burns out?"

"You are the most unromantic person I have ever met. Except for this argument, Oswald and I are deliriously happy together."

"Yeah, that's why you're close to tears. What the hell was his family doing and why are you going on a date with Ian?"

"He's not a date, he's Ian. I didn't tell Oswald because I didn't feel like arguing about something that's perfectly innocent. He didn't tell me about the ceremony because . . . because they're not used to outsiders."

"Don't be such a *tonta.*"

"I am not being stupid. I am being flexible and understanding. You might try it sometime."

"Believe me, I'm trying it now, *mujer,*" she said with a smile. She was quiet and I let her think. She was good at that. She finally said, "Even though you love each other, it's always good to be self-sufficient. Try to get on your feet financially and you won't feel as resentful about his money."

"I'm so not resentful about Oswald's money."

"Yeah, right. Not that there's anything to worry about, but always keep me up-to-date on what's happening . . . just in case."

The "just in case" was ominous. Just in case I learned they had skeletons in the closet . . . or bodies thumping in the dryer.

six

swells, swell friends, and swelled heads

There was something about Mercedes's matter-of-fact acceptance of my fight with Oswald that made me feel calmer. Fighting was normal when people lived together. I'd been unused to it because my parents never fought. Both were in perfect accordance that my father's life's work was to worship at my mother Regina's pedicured feet. I got blankets from the closet and made up the sofa. I would call Oswald tomorrow evening and we would apologize to each other and everything would be fine.

The next morning, while Mercedes and I were enjoying our third cup of sweet Cuban coffee and I was feeling a caffeine-induced sense of possibility, my new phone rang. The caller identification was blocked, so I answered with a tentative "Yello?"

"Hello, Misss De Loss Ssantoss, this iss Silass Madisson."

"Hello, Mr. Madison," I said. "Thank you so much for the phone."

"A ssmall token. I was calling to enssure that you had received it."

"It was a very generous gift," I said.

"I was hoping that we could get together ssoon. I have been researching our family's ssociopolitical alliances over the centuries."

At long last, I was talking to someone who wanted to help me understand the family and maybe, too, understand Oswald. "Yes, I'd like that." I told him that I was in the City for a wedding.

"Iss Dr. Grant with you?" he asked.

"No, I'm all on my own." That sounded self-pitying, so I added, "Actually, Ian Ducharme is standing in for Oswald and is accompanying me to a friend's wedding."

"He must hold you in high essteem. You are a remarkable young woman."

His praise soothed my battered ego. Silas and I agreed to meet at a café the day after the wedding.

"Misss De Loss Santos, would you mind not mentioning our meeting to Monsieur Ducharme? I only assk because others of our kind disapprove of open intellectual inquiry and discoursse, and there iss also the last dustup with Willem."

At least Silas trusted me to be discreet. "Of course, Mr. Madison. The meeting will be confidential."

The wedding was in the afternoon. Mercedes had heard a lot about Ian and wanted to meet the man for herself. She usually left for the club midday, but she stayed home and watched me prepare for my not-a-date.

Mercedes practiced her bagpipes while I got ready. Her genius was recognizing musical talent in others, not playing. Although she could plunk out a tune on a piano or guitar, her skill on the bagpipes was barely rudimentary.

I came out of the bathroom wearing the rose silk halter dress. The top was cut into a low V-neck, and I liked the way the fuller skirt swirled at my knees when I turned. I was glad I'd done some nude sunbathing in the privacy of the pool compound at the ranch and had an even tan.

I asked Mercedes, "How do your neighbors like you playing Scottish dirges?"

"It's a ballad, not a dirge. My tenants are fine with it and I'm fine with their parties. The neighbors to the north sometimes call the cops and complain."

"What happens then?"

"I tell them, 'Do I *look* like someone who plays the bagpipes?'"

"Your father thinks you do." The bagpipes were far from my favorite instrument, but Mr. McPherson could play songs that brought tears to my eyes.

"My father also thinks Americans should head-butt more in fights. That dress looks good on you, but there should probably be more of it. Is that jewelry real?"

I was wearing the red stone necklace and earrings that Ian had given me. "I have no idea. Will you help me with my hair?" I held up a hank.

She blew a long, baleful squeal on her instrument. "Sorry, but I don't know how to deal with straight hair. It's too slippery. Wait a minute."

Mercedes went to the hall closet and rooted around. She pulled out a cardboard box and handed it to me. "*Mi mami* is always giving me this stuff. She keeps hoping I'll start dressing more feminine."

"Tell her that I love you just the way you are."

Inside the box was a bevy of beauty supplies and products. I used a curling iron to make a mass of curls that I gathered atop my head. I slipped on a pair of high-heeled sandals with thin straps and said, "I feel very tall with my hair and my shoes. I feel so tall I can reach things on the top shelf. How do I look? Extremely tall?"

"Nice, but still shortish." Mercedes wasn't big on fashion.

I was adding an extra coat of mascara when Ian arrived. He was wearing one of his beautifully made suits and a snowy shirt. He doubtless had a tailor locked up in a dungeon somewhere sewing day and night. He kissed my cheeks and I smelled his subtle spicy aftershave. It made me think of a library filled with old books, a fireplace, leather furniture, and tobacco. It made me think of the times he had taken off my clothes and stroked my skin.

When I introduced him to Mercedes, I was half afraid he'd bow over her hand and say, "*Enchanté.*" He sussed her out, however, and shook her hand.

He chatted with Mercedes, inquiring about her club, asking informed questions about Croatian folk music, Cuban *son,* and Hawaiian slack guitar. When we left the house, he said, "I very much like your friend. She's like a pure note, isn't she?"

"You are an astute man, Ian Ducharme."

"I'd tell you how beautiful you look, but I don't want to be accused of flirting."

As I general rule, I loved flirting. It made me feel like Barbara Stanwyck in old black-and-white movies, snapping out clever lines that could lure a man in. But I saw a fin circling in the water, so I wasn't about to cast a line now.

A sleek racing-green Jag was parked across the street. Ian

opened the door for me. When we were on our way, I asked, "Ian, who is Willem Dunlop and why is he important to the family?"

"He's an ugly relic." Ian deftly wove through the crowded intersections. Ian always drove as if each road was familiar to him. "He officiates at meaningless vampire ceremonies, probably more for his own benefit than anyone else's." Unlike Edna's clan, Ian was unapologetic about calling himself a vampire.

"Is he a priest or a minister?"

"Vampirism is a condition, my dear, not a religion," he said with a grin. "I'd call him a historian and officiant. Sam and Winnie's families give him more respect than he is due."

"How did you know I was hiding behind the fence?"

Ian chuckled. "A bright and curious girl would be spying, wouldn't she? Open the glove compartment and take out my cigarette case. I have something for you."

Inside the glove compartment was the slim gold case. "I don't smoke and didn't know you did."

"Only on those occasions when I need an excuse to wander away. Nicotine is not addictive to me."

I was learning something already. I flicked open the clasp and saw two buttons from my dress. "Ha, ha, and ha, Ian." I slipped the buttons into my clutch and returned the gold case to the glove compartment. "Oswald thinks that there's something between us because of the way I was dressed for Edna's midnight brunch."

"He senses the inevitable. Did you have a lovers' quarrel?"

"As you know, I am truly, madly, and deeply in love with Oswald. I should probably give you back all those gifts. They are beautiful and I thank you, but . . ."

"A gift given is a gift given. That necklace looks lovely on you. I take pleasure in thinking of the blood coursing through your veins beneath your skin, the same tincture as the stones."

"My gory flesh, what a lovely image," I said. "You know, Ian, I've always found your interest in me perplexing."

"Yes, I'm aware of that."

"You could have stunning women, you could have rich women, and you could have women who are both rich and stunning."

"And I have."

"Not that I lack self-confidence, mind you," I said. "I like to think that I have a number of admirable qualities, and my youthful naïveté must be charming to a roué like you."

"You talk as if I'm longing to snatch you from convent school." Ian grinned wickedly. "I have told you already why I admire you. Do you remember?"

Of course I did. He'd said I tasted like life and death and life again, a description that I found both unsettling and intriguing. "I vaguely recall some rather morbid nonsense."

He laughed, then said quite seriously, "I am fully aware of *who* you are, Milagro, even if others only sense it."

We were approaching the church. Guests were going through the tall carved doors, and red-vested parking valets waited on the sidewalk. "That sounds a little fatalistic for me. I'm a believer in self-determination."

"Then you might ask yourself, how did you find yourself among us?"

"Pure chance."

He pulled over to the curb and got out of the car. A valet opened my door and handed me out before turning to Ian. Ian handed over his keys with a cupped hand, saying, "Thank you, my good fellow."

I knew he was palming a huge tip to the valet. He gave everyone huge tips; it was one of the reasons going out with him was rather fab.

You had to hand it to the vampires; they knew how to throw around cash.

We sat on the bride's side of the stark modern church. The bridesmaids, many of them F.U. alumnae, came up the aisle wearing pale pink dresses, their hair a uniform shade of honey blond, each with a single strand of pearls, a neat little nose, and a perfect tan. Nancy was very detail oriented when she wanted to be.

Nancy wore a serious expression as she walked down the aisle. Her hair was one shade more golden than her bridesmaids', and her dress one shade more delicate. The dress, made of a shimmery fabric with a tight bodice and a full skirt embroidered with seed pearls, made her look very fairy princessy.

Her fiancé, Todd, who'd been two years ahead of us at F.U., stood stiffly at the front of the church. He looked as if he was fulfilling a duty, like filing his taxes or having a colorectal exam. I never understood Nancy's passion for a man who didn't seem to have any.

To Nancy's credit, the ceremony was neither cloying nor snore-inducingly elaborate. I may even have teared up at some point before I remembered that she was marrying a robotoid who barely tolerated my company.

After the ceremony, Ian and I stood in the crowd to watch the newlyweds and the wedding party as they posed for photos. I tried to catch Nancy's eye, but she was out of range. "I'll introduce you at the reception," I said to Ian. I recognized some of the Bright Young Things, but they were all too busy talking to one another to notice me. They did, however, shoot glances at Ian.

The reception was being hosted at Nancy's socialite god-mother's house. Nancy had cultivated the patronage of Gigi Barton, heiress to the Barton facial tissue and toilet paper for-tune ("It's not worth sneezing at if it isn't Barton's!"), and her in-vestment of time and flattery was paying off.

I had been inside a few of the City's lavish homes, but Bar-ton House set its own standard. My general impression was: a quarry of marble floors, acres of oriental rugs, forests of paneled walls, and a few museums' worth of art.

Nancy's friends and family were almost exclusively of a light hue. I tried not to be overly sensitive about race, but it was something I always noticed. Most people, Oswald's family in-cluded, felt more comfortable among their own. I smiled at a sorority sister of Nancy's, and she knit her eyebrows as if she was trying to recollect who I was.

I was suffering a minor I-don't-belong-here attack when Ian took my arm in his and escorted me to the receiving line. Nancy's parents, her mother flushed with pleasure, were at the front of the line. We exchanged hellos and Nancy's mother said, "You next, Milagro! Is this your special friend?"

"I would like to think so," Ian said smoothly. "Ian Ducharme." When he shook her hand, I noticed that his gold cuff links were engraved with a crest. I wondered if there was a bat on it.

Nancy's mother giggled like a twelve-year-old and her father gave Ian a second look. It wasn't what Ian said, it was the way he said it, as if he'd met the world's most fascinating people and found you the most fascinating of them all.

When we got to Nancy, she screamed a ladylike scream and said, "Hi, honey, are you über-thrilled for me?"

"I'm totally über-thrilled for you," I answered. "This is

Ian Ducharme. Ian, meet Nancy-pants, now Mrs. Nancy-pants."

Nancy grinned mischievously and pulled me into a hug. She whispered, "Very interesting! So sorry about the table."

Todd greeted me with a terse and unconvincing "Hello, glad you could make it."

I looked at Ian, who seemed amused.

Ian guided me into the crowd of guests, all in tight little groups, only opening when a waiter passed by with champagne or hors d'oeuvres. I was scanning the crowd looking for a friendly face when a brassy voice said, "Why, damn my eyes if it isn't Ian Ducharme."

Gigi Barton, her beautifully angled face recognizable from photos in dozens of society columns, descended on Ian. A former model of indeterminate age, she wore her garish outfit with panache: a designer dress in a wild print of neon colors, blue eye shadow, fake eyelashes, and a mass of blond hair. Her signature look was layers of mismatched costume jewelry around her slender wrists and long neck. She was famous for saying that she'd rather invest her money in stocks, not rocks.

Gigi gushed about a ski weekend at Ian's chalet, asked about his beautiful sister, mentioned boating in the Aegean, and swore eternal love now that they were reunited. She embraced me as her new BFF and confessed that she no longer regretted all the wedding hassle, since we were there.

Suddenly the waiters circled us. Other guests were drawn into orbit by the gravitational pull of our delightfulness.

When it was time for the meal, Gigi said to us, "Where did they put you? Let's sit together."

I found out exactly why Nancy had apologized about the table. My little calligraphied place card was on the table by the door used by the waiters as they rushed back and forth to the kitchen.

"Well, this is a bitch," said Gigi, observing the table. "It's not going to do."

"Darling, please don't concern yourself," Ian said. "We are very happy to sit wherever there is a place."

"Lord Ian, you're not sitting by the kitchen in my house," Gigi said. She went to the raised dais where the wedding party was seated and grabbed her own place card. Then she spoke to Nancy and Nancy's mother. The conversation looked quite animated, judging from the raised arms and dismayed expressions.

Gigi teetered back on her high heels. "Things will be fixed in a jiffy."

She waved her arm and the head waiter was at her side. After a few words with him, waiters rushed to slide open pocket doors on a wall to reveal an intimate jewel of a room. All the guests at our table were moved to a table there. A waiter cleared Gigi's setting from the top table and moved it to ours. Nancy looked momentarily upset, then regained her cheerful expression. Todd glared in our direction.

An older man in an ill-fitting navy suit, his wife in a shiny polyester flowered dress, and their adult children and spouses tentatively entered the dining room. The woman said, "I'm the bride's aunt Tiny. I guess we're supposed to be here now," she said, as if she didn't know whether this was a reward or a punishment. Tiny was pleasingly plump, and I guessed that her nickname came from her small, birdlike voice.

Gigi patted a chair. "Make yourself comfortable and let's get acquainted."

"Hi, I'm Uncle Dill," said the man. "Glad we don't have to sit with all the fancy people."

Gigi thought this was hilarious. When she stopped laughing, she said, "Uncle Dill, you're at the fanciest table of them all, so you must be one of the fanciest people."

It was like being in the VIP room of a club that usually won't let you in the door. Gigi's cellar was raided for her favorite wines, and the service was flawless. Our conversation seemed wittier, and everyone was instantly more attractive.

Nancy's cousins, who lived in Indiana near their parents, and I shared Nancy stories.

Sharon, who was close to our age, said, "You know that her parents sent her to a speech therapist, right? They thought she had a learning disability."

"How much money did they throw away on that?" Aunt Tiny asked Dill, who shook his head. "Turns out that girl just liked talking nonsense, and she still does."

"That's what I've always loved about her," I said. "She's like an impressionist painter with language, giving you a feeling of something's essence."

Uncle Dill choked on his wine. "What the heck did they teach you girls in that snobby school of yours?"

Gigi kept batting her false eyelashes at Ian. I couldn't tell if this was how the superrich socialized or if she was disrespecting what would have been my territory if this had been an actual date. Other than that quibble, I was having a great time. I smiled at Ian. He returned my smile, his dark eyes looking into mine, and I felt an understanding between us. Unfortunately, I couldn't quite identify the nature of the understanding. I hoped it was just a friendly connection.

In the main room, toasts were made to the happyish couple. We knew because our table was chattering away when we realized the hall had gone silent. Todd's voice, amplified by a microphone, said, "And we'd like to express our gratitude to Gigi Barton, who has been so kind to host our reception. Gigi?"

"Whoops, that's me!" our hostess said with a hoot. She stood up and walked into the hall. She waved to the guests and they all clapped, and then she came back to our table and kicked off her heels. "Now, Lord Ian, tell me all about your summer plans."

He looked at me and said, "I have intentions, but no plans thus far."

I turned back to Nancy's cousins and asked, "You said she beheaded your Barbies?"

Afternoon became evening. The band played, the dance floor became crowded, and the flower girl and ring bearer fell asleep under a piano. Ian and I danced with each other and with others, who all assumed we were a couple.

Nancy insisted on having a slow dance with me. "Let me lead," she said. "I'm so OD'ing on girly stuff I'm practically peeing pink."

"You look stunning today."

"So do you," she said as she steered me haphazardly on the dance floor. "You were not supposed to show up the bride."

"I'm not showing up the bride. All eyes are on the bride and will the bride please not bash her guest into the waiters?"

"Where did you find that guy? He looks like he eats glass and ravishes virgins for breakfast. I'm all goose bumpy."

"Oh, I thought you'd like him."

"I do. He's utterly lustalicious," she said. "Are you sure he's not your lover?"

"Ouch, will you stop stomping on my feet? No, he is not my lover."

"Have you slept with him ever?" When I didn't answer, she said, "Ha, I thought so, you dirty girl."

Ignoring her snipe, I said, "I live with Oswald, who is away doing reconstructive facial surgeries on poor kids. He can fix a cleft palate in fifteen minutes and sculpt a nose when a nose is no more."

"I riddle you this, how is a nose not a nose?"

"When a dog eats it. Evelyn Waugh wrote a very amusing story about a girl who was too appealing until a dog chomped on her nose."

"So you're sticking with this story that you're shacked up with a surgeon?" She gave me a look, and, yes, it did sound implausible for someone with a history of dating unemployed arty types.

"Okay, Oz hates weddings and he's out with his buddies for the weekend fishing and drinking beer and sneaking off to a strip club."

"You could have just said so in the first place. Isn't Gigi fabulous?"

"Gigi is fabulous. How does it feel to be married?"

"I am loving it so far. I'm going to go all Miss Havisham and wear my wedding dress every day forever."

"Excellent plan, and I had no idea you'd read Dickens."

"Don't be silly. I watched a Dickens festival on TV when I had the flu. I think I'd like to be a pickpocket someday or collect bodies from rivers."

"You're full of brilliant schemes today."

"Marriage is very inspiring. Todd and I have everything worked out on a twenty-five-year plan. Actually, his financial planner came up with the schedule and now I don't even have to think about when to have children or what charitable board to join; I check the calendar and it tells me."

The idea was so hideous that I wanted to shake her until

sense came to her. But maybe Nancy was the sensible one, while I merely la-la'd about with no concrete goals. "I hope it works out for you, Nancy. Make sure the financial planner schedules me in."

"Oh, absolutely. I insisted on girl-bonding time," she said. "Now that I'm a wedding expert, I can help you when you get married."

I thought with horror about the year of planning and the enormous sums of money that had gone into this production. I imagined Evelyn Grant stopping the ceremony with a list of objections to the marriage. "I think I'll just exchange oaths under the sky and hire a guy to play the ukulele."

"Every girl wants a big wedding. Every girl wants to be a princess for a day."

"I am not every girl," I answered.

"I don't know why I am friends with such a weirdo."

At the end of our dance, Todd approached. I thought he wanted to dance with his bride, but instead he held his arms out to me. "Milagro, if I may."

Nancy smiled and skittered off with the best man.

"Of course, Todd. Congratulations." I didn't like touching him. He was stiff and moved badly.

"Are you enjoying yourself?"

"Yes, it's a lovely wedding." Todd and I had never been buddies, but things had gone downhill calamitously when he'd joined CACA.

"It must be nice to be sitting at Gigi's special table," he said coldly. "Sebastian was supposed to be my best man."

I kept my gaze over his shoulder. Gigi had her long-nailed hand on Ian's shoulder. "Nancy mentioned it."

"It wasn't enough for you to keep my friend from being at

my side, now you drag Gigi to your table to humiliate me."

I dropped my arms and looked into his face. He was one of those men you think are handsome because he was tall with sandy hair and blue eyes. But his features were blunt and his expression harsh. "I had nothing to do with that, Todd, and I had nothing to do with Sebastian dropping out of the wedding."

"I never liked you. You think that reading books makes you special. You're not special. Your father mows lawns."

"That's nothing," said a boozy voice behind me. "My family made its fortune because people have to wipe their asses."

I turned to see Gigi holding a tumbler of amber liquid. She hooked arms with me and added, "Luckily, there will never be any shortage of asses, right, Todd?"

He was speechless, which I found very rewarding.

"I need some air," Gigi said to me. "Let's go out in the garden."

It was late and the overcast sky was a dark pewter color. The formal garden was perfectly maintained, with clipped boxwood bordering quadrants of lawn around a fountain.

"Thanks for coming to my rescue," I said.

"My pleasure. That toad has always rubbed me the wrong way. Good luck to Nancy because she'll need it." Gigi sat atop a ledge decorated with mosaics. "I've been married and divorced three times. What about you?"

"Not even close."

"You aren't taking Ian Ducharme seriously, are you?"

"Ian and I are friends, that's all," I said. "He's the second or eighth cousin of a friend of mine."

She chuckled. "Honey, a man like that isn't just friends with a girl like you. But if you're not involved with him, you won't mind if I play through."

I didn't need to ask what she meant by "a girl like you." When you had more curves than angles, people always assumed that no man would be interested in a platonic relationship. "I have no claims on him. Knock yourself out." Even as I said it, I felt a twinge of jealousy, which I'm sure was merely female competitiveness and nothing more. What did I care if Gigi and Ian got involved?

"What do you do for entertainment, Milagro?"

"I write and I garden. I don't have a landscaper's license so my work is smaller projects."

Gigi tilted her chin outward toward a magnificent rhododendron. "What do you think of the landscaping here?"

"It's beautiful, but it feels more like a park than your garden."

"Really?" she said. "What would you do?"

I considered her exuberance and flamboyant style and began sketching out a dream garden. I didn't think she was listening, but I liked being out of the hot, crowded room, smelling the damp coastal breeze, and listening to the rustling of the trees.

She finished her drink, tilting the glass so that the ice cubes tumbled together. "Write all that down for me and send it to me, okay?"

"Sure. Your turn. What do you do for entertainment?"

Gigi grinned. "I take lovers, buy things, give to charity, play the stock market, and explore ways to stay young, honey." She saw me looking for telltale signs of plastic surgery, and she said, "I prefer treatments other than the knife. I don't like being cut."

"Neither do I," I said as I thought of how Oswald used the scalpel on my skin.

A chilly breeze raised goose bumps on my arms.

"It's getting cold. Let's go back in."

Gigi was immediately subsumed by Nancy's relatives and I

went to a table with petits fours, handmade chocolates, and pots of tea and coffee. I drank a cup of tea and shifted from one foot to the other.

Ian left a group of young women and came to my side. "You look as if your feet hurt."

"Nancy trod all over them. I'll never let her lead again."

"Would you like to go?"

We said our good-byes and business cards were pushed into our hands with promises of dinners, golf outings, sailing afternoons, and whatnot. People always thought Ian was one of them.

"Here," he said, picking up a party favor left on a table. He opened my clutch bag and, as he put the favor inside, noticed my phone. "Ah, so you have a phone."

"I don't know why everyone is so surprised. I am not a Luddite."

We walked out of the house and waited for the valet to bring the car around.

Ian began fiddling with my phone. "There," he said. "Now you have my number in case you should ever need an escort again.

seven

sorry, i don't prey that way

As Ian drove me back to Mercedes's, I slipped off my shoes and rubbed my feet. There were no parking spaces, so he left his car double-parked. The windows of the house were dark. I was well aware that Mercedes wouldn't get home from My Dive for hours. Ian walked me to the door.

"Ian, thank you so much for coming with me. I had a good time."

"We always have a good time, *querida*." He stepped close to me. "I've missed you."

He took my hand and turned it. He bent his lips to the veins of my wrist. His mouth was warm and his teeth very gently nipped the skin. "Come with me," he said. "We belong together."

"I can't. You know that."

"Let me have one kiss. Then I'll leave you."

He was looking at me gravely. I didn't know if I was attracted to him because he was so effortlessly sexy, or because he respected me despite my inclination toward silliness. Nancy had always said that it didn't count as cheating if you had sex with someone you'd been with before. This wasn't sex and there would be no sex. This was only a single friendly kiss between single friends.

"One kiss as a friend and then you go."

His mouth was on mine then, his lips soft, his tongue slipping into my mouth, and he pressed me close to him. The kiss was slow, lingering. I hadn't been kissed by anyone but Oswald for months. The kiss felt strange, yet familiar, reminding me of all the pleasure Ian had given me. I knew then that I was doing something very wrong.

I broke away from him, and my voice was shaky as I said, "Good night."

"Until next time," he said. He brushed his fingers along my throat. "Dream of me."

I put the key in the lock and opened the door. I turned to wave good-bye. That was when I saw the movement between two cars. A figure was squatting down. Ian was standing by his car, looking down the street. The figure, dressed in dark jeans, a black-and-white plaid shirt, and a ski mask, began moving in a crouch.

I dropped my shoes and took the steps two at a time. "Ian!" I cried as I ran across the sidewalk.

There was a flash of metal in the man's hand that I saw as I tackled him. I felt nothing for a moment, then wetness on my arm.

The man scrambled out from under me and I saw alarm in his hazel eyes. He said something that sounded like "oh-oh-oh-oh."

"Milagro!" Ian shouted.

Suddenly the man was gone and I heard footsteps running away. It wasn't until I looked at my arm and saw the blood flowing from a deep gash that I felt the pain. I was able to recover from small cuts, but this was no small cut.

Ian lifted me in his arms and carried me inside. He kicked the door shut and carried me up the stairs and into Mercedes's bedroom.

"Call an ambulance," I said.

"No time."

"This is bad, isn't it?" I felt oblivion pulling at me and I closed my eyes.

"Milagro, try to stay awake."

I opened my eyes. Blood drenched Mercedes's creamy comforter. I really thought he should be calling an ambulance instead of taking out a gold penknife. I needed a doctor, not another trinket. My skin was clammy and I heard a sound that I realized was my own rapid, shallow breathing. I was so cold.

Ian shrugged off his jacket and yanked up his sleeve. Then he flicked open the knife. "This is going to hurt, darling, but it must be done." Then he sliced his left palm with the knife and said, "Be brave." The penknife clattered to the hardwood floor.

He pressed his hand to my open wound.

I screamed, but Ian's right hand was over my mouth, muffling the sound.

It felt as if he was holding a branding iron to my flesh, pain so overwhelming that I fought against him, trying to stop it.

Ian said, "Bite down if it helps."

I bit hard, going through the skin, tasting human blood for the first time since Oswald had infected me. Through my agony, I was aware that Ian's blood was warm and viscous and delicious. Pleasure flooded over the pain, washing it away. I sucked on his hand and filled my mouth with his blood, felt it slipping down my throat.

"Milagro, please, do not die," Ian said. His dark eyes, filled with something that looked like affection, gazed into mine.

I was in a bewildering place between pain and pleasure. Sensation surged through me and I felt as if I was moving toward something that might be death or ultimate delectation. I resisted the pain, I resisted the pleasure, and I held on. I released his palm from my teeth.

Ian bent over and kissed my brow, my temple, my cheek. He tucked his head against my neck and I felt safer.

"I'm cold," I said.

Still gripping my arm with his hand, he folded the comforter over me and he lay down beside me. "Is that better?"

"Yes."

"Why did you put yourself in harm's way?" For the first time in our acquaintance, Ian sounded puzzled.

"To save you."

"Milagro, I saw him. I was waiting for him to get closer. Promise you'll never do anything like that again."

I was too sleepy to think through any promises. I felt very peaceful and I worried that it might be the treacherous type of peace you feel when you are freezing to death, like in a Jack London story. So I did a survey of my body functions. Toes and fingers wiggleable: check. Eyeballs able to focus on objects both near and far: check. Lungs and heart operating in the normal range: check.

Ian released my arm. I shifted it out from under the comforter. Under the wash of red, I could see a long line demarking the gash. Ian brought my arm toward him and, like a cat grooming her kitten, began licking away at the smears of blood.

Placing my hand atop his head, I said, "I miss your curls." Then I closed my eyes and went to sleep.

eight

i'm not sick, but i'm not well

When I awoke, I reached for Oswald. I opened my eyes and recognized Mercedes's sunny yellow ceiling with rosette molding around the vintage light fixture. I snuggled under the blankets for a second before I remembered what had happened: the mugger, the knife, the blood, Ian.

Panic squeezed me like an old tube of toothpaste. But I was safe here and now, breathing in and out, in and out. My body felt tender all over, even in places I never thought about, the insides of my elbows, the skin between my toes, the small of my back.

I glanced down and saw that the stained comforter had been replaced by blankets. I was wearing a long-sleeved, oversized My Dive T-shirt. After a moment's hesitation, I shoved up the sleeve of the shirt and saw a shiny pink line of new skin on my arm.

A carafe of water and a tumbler were on the bedside. I sat up in bed and sharp pains like needles went through me. The room spun. I clenched the blankets in my hands and waited for the pain and dizziness to subside. I was so thirsty. By concentrating very hard, I was able to reach the carafe and bring it to my mouth. I drank all the water, felt it dribbling down my face, running along my neck.

Mercedes came into the room just as I was contemplating the advisability of standing up. She put her hands on her hips and stared at me.

I couldn't bear seeing the anguish on the face that I loved so. "Morning, sunshine," I said, my voice hoarse. "Why don't you turn that frown upside down?"

"Milagro De Los Santos, don't you ever do that again!"

"Do what?"

"Scare me to death. There was blood on the stairs and all over the comforter."

"I plan to avoid any further displays of blood spillage."

"How are you feeling?"

"A little weird, but alive," I rasped. "Where is Ian?"

"He stayed until he was sure you were okay, but said he had to leave to take care of something urgent. I got the feeling he was going out looking for the guy who hurt you."

She sat on the bed beside me. I reached for her hand and suddenly saw a confusing image of red, red, red all over the creamy comforter, blood covering my arm, blood soaking Ian's ivory shirt. My body flushed with heat, and I felt a surge of nausea. I released Mercedes's hand and closed my eyes until the feelings passed. I hoped I was merely suffering from blood loss.

"A man with a knife tried to mug Ian," I said. "For his money or his car, I don't know."

"Ian said you got hurt protecting him."

"I just reacted. It was faster than saying, 'Watch out, there's a guy creeping out from between the cars.' "

"I thought we should take you to the hospital, but the wound was, well, *mira,* what the hell is that?"

I held out my arm. "My new and improved ability to heal. I don't want to go to the hospital, but I do want to call the cops. Hell, Mercedes, you never told me things have gotten this bad here."

"I called the police last night," she said grimly. "I had to tell them that it was an attempted mugging, because there was no way I could explain your arm. They said you could go down to the station today."

"What?" I said, as outraged as a vegan at the Cattlemen's Banquet.

"They were handling a couple of drive-bys last night. Two teenage boys died. They didn't have time for an attempted robbery."

"What kind of society is this where violent crime is a normal occurrence?" I said, and we shared a sad look. "I'm supposed to meet Silas later, but if you fix me a cup of coffee now, I have time to file a police report. Where's the closest station?"

I waited until Mercedes had left the room before I tried to get up. My body felt as it had during puberty, when things were mysteriously changing, when even my bones ached. I forced my legs over the side of the bed. Then I lurched up, and everything went woo-woo-woo. After I steadied myself, I walked slowly to the bathroom. I sat in the tub and let the shower wash away the remnants of dried blood.

Mercedes already had *cafecitos* and *pan dulce* on the kitchen table. "Ian called while you were in the shower," she said. "He wanted to know how you were."

I took a sip of the coffee, but something tasted off. "Did he say anything else?"

"Only that he wants you to go back to the ranch, where it's safer. He said he had something urgent he had to do and he'll be in touch later."

I took a bite of the *pan dulce*, but the bread had the consistency of papier-mâché in my mouth. I ate and drank anyway so Mercedes wouldn't think I didn't appreciate her hospitality. "Did you ask the neighbors if they saw anything?"

"I talked to my tenants. They were in their bedroom in the back and didn't hear anything. I checked with the people across the street. They said they didn't see anything, but even if they did they'd say that. People won't get involved because of payback."

The thin scar on my arm felt hot and itchy, and I rubbed at it. "Mercedes, I think you should sell this place and move. You shouldn't be living in a war zone."

My friend twisted one of her locks. "Usually the dealers just fight with each other. It's not the suburbs, Milagro."

"Maybe I've been out in the country too long. I was nervous walking down the street the other day, and I never used to feel like that."

"You were used to it," Mercedes said. "I'll go with you to the station."

When Mercedes was glancing at her newspaper, I cleared our plates and slid the bread into the trash.

"Are you going to tell Oswald what happened?"

"I don't know. The Ian factor would aggravate things. And I'm not going to have him rushing back when I'm fine."

Mercedes let out an exasperated breath. "Milagro, you know how to survive, but sometimes I wonder if you know how to live."

I ignored her ad hominem comment and asked, "What did you think of Ian?"

"*Muy suave.* He's got charisma, like a performer. He seems to be in love with you."

"He's only interested because I turned him down." I washed out the tiny cups she used for coffee and our plates. I wanted Oswald with me. He would have sewed up my cut and made jokes and put a bandage over the injury. "I hate feeling frightened. I'm no good at it."

"No one is."

At the police station, we had to stand in line to talk to the desk sergeant. I was given a form to fill out and then we had to wait for almost an hour to talk to a weary middle-aged detective, who had golden hair shot through with silver that contrasted fantastically with his ebony skin. His name was Antwon Jefferson. Despite his presidential last name, he didn't strike me as likely to be a vampire. He listened to my description of the attack and said skeptically, "So the guy ran off after you tackled him? And he had a knife?"

"Yes, he ran off. I'm very scary when I'm angry."

"Yeah, a lot of women are."

Detective Jefferson tapped his pen annoyingly on the edge of his chair and read over my form. Finally he said, "Could be anyone. Gangs usually work in teams. Less risk, higher payoff. But if your boyfriend was driving a Jaguar, it sounds like a crime of opportunity."

"He isn't my boyfriend."

"Why didn't he call us last night?"

"I called," Mercedes said. "You were too busy to send someone."

In the end, the detective took my report and said he'd get back to me if he learned anything.

I said, "Detective Jefferson, it's very disappointing that a man with such fabulous hair is showing such apathy about this attack."

He exhaled a breath that smelled of refreshing spearmint gum. "Look, I'm sorry you had a scare, but since you weren't hurt, this isn't a priority. We have a backlog of violent assaults and murders. Some teenager gets shot in broad daylight on a crowded street and not one damn person will come forward as a witness. Welcome to my world."

We walked out of the station and I said, "That was a major waste of time. Will you drop me off for my meeting with Silas?"

"Are you sure you don't want to cancel and go back to the house and rest?"

"No, I want to get my mind off things. This guy is rather intriguing in an ascetic, neuter way."

"You think all men are intriguing. I'll drop you off, then I've got to run home. I'll be at the club later. Be careful, okay?"

She drove me to a café on the busy waterfront. I felt more comfortable here, among office workers striding hither and thither, and tourists meandering and staring into store windows.

The café was all brushed stainless steel and honey-colored wood. I didn't see Silas among the casually chic people who worked intently at the small square metal tables. Someone walked by with a bright red frozen drink that looked delicious. I went to the counter and ordered a raspberry smoothie.

Then I picked up a local weekly and read it while I waited for Silas. I'd gotten through an editorial advocating the banning of all motorized vehicles in the City when my phone rang.

"Yello, talk at me," I said.

"Misss De Loss Santoss," the caller hissed.

"Hi, Mr. Madison," I said. I felt silly calling him that, but I liked feeling silly. "I'm here as arranged."

"That'ss why I'm calling. I apologize, but other businesss hass held me up. Please accept my most ssincere regretss."

"It's okay. Things happen."

"I would like to make it up to you, Misss De Loss Santoss. Could you meet me tonight for a drink at a private club? I am an investor and I think you will like it."

"That would be fine."

I heard a commotion at the other end of the line. Then Silas came back on. "Excellent. I must rush off, but I will call you later with the address and directionsss."

We said our good-byes. I stared out the window at the gray-green bay and wondered what I should do. Should I call Oswald and tell him about the attack or wait until he returned? Should I go to the Museum of Modern Art or go see a movie?

A small, sleek man dressed in jeans and a gray sweater stopped at my table. His head was shaved, which made his oversized black-frame glasses look even larger. I smiled tentatively at him, not encouraging him, but not wanting to seem hostile either.

"Hi. I don't mean to bother you, but I recognize you from college," he said. "You and Sebastian Beckett-Witherspoon used to go to the English Department parties, right?"

"Guilty," I said.

He saw me staring at him and laughed while he rubbed his head. "I used to have lots of hair then, and I wouldn't wear my glasses half the time." He pulled off his glasses and grabbed a napkin and put it on top of his head. "Look familiar now?"

I'd never been good with faces, so I said, "Yes, a little. I'm Milagro De Los Santos."

"Skip Taylor." He held out his hand and we shook. "I was in the grad film program, but I had friends in the English Department."

Skip seemed pleasant, so I said, "My friend just canceled. Would you like to join me?"

"Sure."

When he returned from the counter with some gigantic and elaborate coffee concoction, he said, "I saw a big article a while back on Beckett-Witherspoon in the alumni mag. He seems to be doing well with his novels."

"The critics loved the first one. I haven't heard much about the second."

"Do you stay in touch?"

"I saw him when he stopped in the City last year on his book tour, but we don't keep up." I didn't think it was necessary to add that SLIME had tried to kidnap me and then wanted to keep me as his concubine after he'd married his posh F.U. sweetheart. "I was here for the wedding of my frosh roomie. I got mugged last night."

"No crap! Are you serious?"

I was glad to see that someone was suitably shocked by my ordeal, and I told him the public version of the story. "Do you live here?" I asked.

"No, I had a few meetings with backers of my next project and with the idiot screenwriter." He mimicked the expression of Edward Munch's *The Scream*.

"You're still doing film, then?"

"Yeah, I'm producing, mostly actioners." He named several movies, and some sounded familiar. "It's me in the middle of all the University of Second Best dudes."

We shared a superior F.U. chuckle over the nickname for USB, a rival private university. "I wrote a few spec scripts," I said. "I couldn't get past the D-girls."

Skip flicked his fingers in a disdainful gesture. "Spec scripts are useless. You've got to know someone and set up a pitch meeting before bothering to write anything more than a treatment."

"Well, now I know you," I said.

"Yeah, now you know me." Skip gave me a long look and said, "You and Beckett-Witherspoon were kind of an odd couple, weren't you?"

"We weren't a couple. But if you mean it was all *Love Story* or *The Way We Were,* because he was WASP and rich and establishment, and I was the wacky ethnic scholarship girl, then yes, we were an odd couple."

Skip laughed. "You're funny."

We chatted about our time at F.U., and how much we liked all the movies shown on campus. We discussed Hitchcock, Fellini, French New Wave, Wertmüller, and noir. I bemoaned the lack of women directors and a female sensibility in film, and he mused about Japanese sci-fi movies of the fifties and sixties. "Gojira was a political creature, and the movie was an allegory for the destruction of World War Two," he said. "They changed the movie's name to *Godzilla,* dubbed it, and lost the powerful symbolism."

I stared at him in wonderment. "You don't know how amazing it is to hear that. My last piece, two novellas, was inspired by *Frankenstein* and the political messages in Mary Wollstonecraft and Mary Wollstonecraft Shelley's writings. One novella is about man's attempt to create life and beauty, but he creates a hideous creature that he disowns. The creature is alone in the world, yet sentient. What is the creature to make of this rejection? Who is the real monster?"

"Sounds really amazing," Skip said. "Here"—he pulled out a business card with his name and a Los Angeles address—"I'd like to look at your stuff if you want to send something to me."

"I'd love to." I took a pen from my bag and scribbled on a napkin. "This is my phone number in case you hear of anyone looking for my type of work."

Skip folded the napkin, put it in his pocket, and stood. "I gotta run. I'm having nothing but headaches because the idiot screenwriter turned in an unworkable script and refuses to do a rewrite. Great talking to you, Milagro. Let's keep in touch."

I felt exhilarated by both the conversation and having made a real connection with a producer. I was so elated that I temporarily forgot my problems. My stomach cramped oddly. I needed some food and had a yearning for a really rare, juicy burger.

And then I thought, oh no.

You didn't have to be an F.U. alumna to realize that a yen for rawish burger was bad news to anyone who'd been in recent contact with a vampire's bodily fluids. I walked to an underground metro station and took the train to a stop close to a supermarket.

I walked past the deli to the meat department. I selected a ribeye steak, glistening dark red and moist behind cellophane wrapping, and tried to be disgusted instead of excited. I wanted to tear open the package and suck every drop of blood from the meat, but even in a city that was blasé about gangland murders, this type of behavior was considered uncouth.

I hailed a cab because I felt too uneasy about walking back to Mercedes's. When we arrived, I asked the driver not to leave until I was safely behind the front door. After looking around and seeing no one, I slowly got out of the cab and ran up the steps of the house. The driver sped off, and I shakily opened the door, rushed in, and slammed it behind me. I locked it and tested the lock.

Only then did I go up to Mercedes's flat. I tore a corner of the package of meat and then lifted the package to my mouth and drank the red fluid, enjoying the delightful mineral earthiness. When I'd drained the liquid from the package, I tore the rest of the wrapping off and licked the steak and the Styrofoam tray.

I thought I'd come to terms with vampirism, but I didn't want to be one of Them. If that is what I was.

Did that mean that I hadn't truly accepted them? Could it be that I harbored ignorant prejudices? And I wondered what unspoken prejudices Oswald might have about me, other than his unfair assessment that I was a pain in the butt. I considered these ugly thoughts as I chewed on a corner of the raw steak.

I tried to read but found myself staring at the pages without comprehension. I kept thinking about monsters born and monsters created by circumstance. I wanted to believe in redemption, not only for the beautiful, dissolute Sebastian of *Brideshead Revisited,* but for people like SLIME, for Frankenstein's monster, and maybe even for my mother Regina.

I thought that there was a connection between the monster books and *Brideshead,* a lesson for me if I could find it. Before I could let these ideas marinate, the doorbell rang. I went downstairs and peered through the peephole in the front door. I saw a delivery man with large packages.

"Yes?" I shouted.

"Delivery for Ochoa-McPherson."

I opened the door and signed for the boxes. They were from an expensive store that specialized in imported linens. I thought this a little out of character because Mercedes was usually very practical in her purchases.

I called Mercedes and said, "Since when do you buy hoity-toity linens?"

"I think you must have been hit on your *cabeza* yesterday. What are you talking about?"

"You just got an express delivery of boxes. I thought you'd want to know."

"I didn't order anything. Open them and see what they are."

Mercedes stayed on the line while I used a key to slash through the packing tape. Inside the box was a beautiful soft silk and down comforter, and a set of Egyptian cotton sheets. "It's a comforter and sheet set," I said. "We can safely assume that Ian sent them."

"He didn't need to do that."

"It's their culture. They're very generous." I told her about my exciting encounter with Skip and also that I'd be going out to meet Silas later.

"Are you up to such a busy day?"

I was still feeling content from my grotesque snack. "Yes, I'm fine."

Silas phoned as promised and gave me the address of the club. "Memberss only," he said, "sso please do not release the information. You understand how there are people who sstill want to harm uss."

I didn't know if the club had a dress code, but I wore jeans, a T-shirt under a sweater, and sneakers. I felt less vulnerable out at night if I didn't draw attention and was able to run. I decided not to carry a handbag and put my phone, money, and ID in my pocket.

Before I left, I stood hidden behind the curtain of the window facing the street. I watched for five minutes to make sure that no one was lurking in the shadows or between parked cars. The cold bluish light of the sparsely spaced halogen streetlamps illuminated only small areas of sidewalk.

However, my night vision, which had been excellent since my first infection, was even better now. A *viejo* walked a scruffy terrier and each of them was outlined with a delicate phosphorescent glow. I was fascinated by the creepy wonder of my new ability. Not that it balanced out the other side effects of my recent contamination.

I pulled my phone out of my pocket and called Ian. He didn't answer so I left a polite message, the gist of which was "What the hell is happening to me?" Then I calmed myself and left the house. On the street, I threaded my keys between my fingers, the urban girl's version of brass knuckles, and walked purposefully toward a busy street. An available cab was driving by just as I reached a large intersection, and I flagged it down.

When I gave the cabbie the address, he said, "Nothing's down there, is it?"

"I'm meeting a friend," I answered. There were only a few areas in the City that were still undeveloped because they were too violent, had toxic waste, or were caught in redevelopment agency red tape. This desolate once industrial neighborhood fell into the last category.

The cabbie slowed down on a block of dark buildings with boarded windows and stopped in front of a plain-fronted structure with a large metal door. I'd been to plenty of clubs in down-and-out locations, but this place looked incurably bleak and abandoned.

The door opened partially and a sliver of light escaped. Then the door closed again, but at least I knew someone was in the building. My curiosity overcame my caution; I paid the cabbie and stepped out into the cold, gusty darkness.

nine

blood is the drug

Shards of broken glass on the sidewalk crunched beneath my shoes. Just as I raised my hand to knock, the door swung open and I had to step back to avoid being hit.

A pasty string bean of a young man wearing a black Nehru jacket and loose trousers stared at me. "Private club," he snapped, and began to close the door.

I wanted to say, "Well, aren't we special?" I kicked my foot in the door before it shut. "Silas Madison invited me."

"Oh, can you wait here?"

"No, my cab is gone and I'm not standing out here on the street." I pushed my way in and the string bean closed the metal door with a loud clang.

I expected a dingy club with exposed pipes, concrete floors, and questionable conceptual art. Instead, the long, narrow room had a black carpet with an ivory deco leaf design, Pompeii red glazed walls, sparkling crystal sconces and chandeliers, gleaming black tables, and a sleek metal bar.

On a small stage at the back, a trio played, and an exquisite chanteuse dressed in white tie and tails sang. She was as lovely as Marlene Dietrich, but had a much better voice. Her song, which was in German, could have been about daisies and bunnies or decay and termite damage. It didn't matter to me because I thought she was fabulous.

The pale customers wore chic but subdued clothes, the type a successful designer might wear: fabric and cut were more important than color and pattern. They drank clear pomegranate-colored drinks in martini glasses; brownish red drinks garnished with celery; and frothy fuchsia beverages in flutes.

A few nonvamps, done up in black PVC, leather, and velvet and black eyeliner, sat beside the vamps. These were the thralls, a term which really annoyed me since it went against my egalitarian beliefs.

There was an intricate game of role-playing between some vamps and people in the vamp Goth world. Vampires pretended to believe that they were the mythical undead creatures who slept in coffins, could only be killed with a stake through the heart or a silver bullet, and drank blood. Their thralls either went along with this game or believed it themselves.

The thralls got their ya-yas serving the vamps, and the vamps got their ya-yas from having willing, if deluded, sources of human blood.

Silas sat at a table set off to one side. He wore a black shirt buttoned to the neck and black slacks. Although he was alone in a social setting, he looked composed. I got the impression that all the other people in the club were aware of him. In front of Silas was a tall bottle of mineral water, a small carafe of red liquid nestled in a bucket of ice, and two wineglasses.

When I walked over, Silas looked up and said, "Misss De Loss Santoss." His smile lit up his pale face. He looked as pleased as a mouse that has figured out how to push the lever for food pellets.

"Mr. Madison," I said. He rose smoothly and pulled out a chair for me. In the busyness at the ranch, I hadn't noticed his physical grace before.

"I'm sso glad you could come. I realize a club issn't the best place for a sserious talk, but I thought you might like thiss."

"It's wonderful," I said, and I meant it. "The singer is very talented, too."

"Do you share our taste? Would you like a drink?" Silas indicated the carafe. "Organic rabbit, very mild and relaxing."

Rabbit blood was the chamomile tea of the vamp world. I intended to say no, but when I opened my mouth "That would be fantastic" came out.

Silas poured about a teaspoon of blood into each glass and filled them with mineral water. He handed me a glass and raised his own. "To our friendship, Misss De Loss Santoss."

We clinked glasses and sipped. The rabbit juice was delicate and herbaceous, nothing like Ian's blood. "I didn't know your people had clubs."

He smiled. "Only a few in the United States. We have more in Europe, South America, and Asia. My favorite is one on a beautiful beach in Thailand. It's a relief to have a place to socialize where we can be ourselvess."

"So you don't subscribe to Willem's beliefs about the lower lands?"

Silas gave a weary smile. "Poor Willem. He's been expounding ideas that he sstudied and dismissed earlier in his career. I totally reject any system of beliefss that holdss one group of humans in less regard than another."

"I am relieved to hear you say that. I agree with you completely." The drink was sending a delightful zing through me. I felt beyond urbane as I listened to the music, drank a decadent cocktail, and chatted with Silas. "Silas, I hope this isn't too sensitive a question, but what do you call those of your kind?"

He said a few words in the car-crash language and added, "That is the old term, which means children of the blood, because blood unites us." He smiled. "But because no one can pronounce it and as it is a dead language, perhapss I misspronouce ass well. We call ourselves vampire."

"You don't find the word offensive?"

"Sometimes the victim embraces the epithet and attemptss to transform it. You are familiar with this tactic?"

"Like bitch or the N-word?"

"Yess, although I am not convinced that this doess more good than harm." Silas frowned, then shook off his mood. "Enough talk of me. Tell me, has your visit to the City been pleasant? Did you enjoy the wedding?"

"I did," I said. "But I got mugged last night when I came home. Not me, exactly. I stepped in to stop a mugging."

"How astonishing!" Silas looked appropriately shocked. "Were you hurt? Wass anything stolen?"

"I'm fine," I said. If I admitted to the injury, I'd also have to admit to other physical changes. "I surprised the mugger and he ran off. It was probably more of an attempted carjacking than a mugging, because Ian had dropped me off and he was driving an expensive car."

"Was he hurt?"

"Not a scratch. The whole incident has put a sour taste in

my mouth, though, about living in the City." I tipped my glass back to get the last few drops of my tasty cocktail.

"You are an extraordinary young woman, so brave."

He made me feel brave and strong, instead of foolish and scared. But his praise embarrassed me, so I changed the subject. "Where did you meet Willem?"

"I wass an army brat," he said, and began refilling our glasses. "Although because of our condition, my father served in the military as a consultant. I sspent most of my youth on army basess, here and around the world. For that reasson, my speech ssounds a little different than mosst Americanss, doess it not?"

"It does, but I like the way you speak."

"My mother made sure we contacted other family members, no matter where we went, sso we wouldn't feel sso adrift. Willem was living near Sstuttgart when we first met."

"Where is he now?"

"He went back to Prague after visiting the Grants. Such an unfortunate end to a festive occasion!" He tut-tutted, which charmed me to no end.

"Oswald's parents were in Prague, too, last year," I said. Odd that they hadn't mentioned whether they'd seen or spent time with Willem there.

"It is one of the great cities of the world," he said. "Also, the real estate is fantastic."

Vampires were crazy about investing in real estate. From the recesses of my mind, I recalled Oswald's father droning on about an apartment building that was undergoing a conversion. "Yes, that's what I've heard. Mr. Madison, I'd love to learn more about your people's history. My friends are rather reserved on the topic."

"That iss quite normal," he said. "We have been persecuted for sso long that we've learned that ssilence is our best companion." He refilled our glasses.

"I understand, but I've been living with the Grants for a year now, and it's very frustrating to have information withheld as if they don't trust me."

"Misss De Loss Santoss, do not judge your friends too harshly. We are all bewildered by you." He said it with a kind smile. "When you and Dr. Grant marry and have children, things will transform."

"We're not at that stage in our relationship," I said, wondering if we would ever be there. "Besides, having children . . . isn't that a big risk?"

"For the average person, but you are not the average person. There is some historical evidence that survivors of the infection had undiminished fertility."

"Really? But Winnie told me the opposite—that children born from intermarriages had a high mortality rate."

"That iss what we have always believed. However, I've discovered evidence that this sstory wass invented to discourage a vampire from even attempting intermarriage. Mosst sspousess would not survive beyond the honeymoon, sso it was important to stop all intermarriage—for the ssake of the partnerss."

I felt my heart lift. "That's wonderful."

"In fact," Silas said, leaning toward me, "there iss even a possibility that the children of vampire and nonvampire would have all the benefits of our condition without our photosensitivity."

"I can't tell you how glad I am to learn this."

The singer was taking a break, so there was lots of conversation to cover ours. Some of the thralls hurried to her side and they all went to the far end of the club, where a bulky man sat by a door. He rose and opened the door for them. When they went through it, he pulled it shut again.

"What's in the back?" I asked.

"Hmm?" Silas followed my gaze. "The singer'ss dressing room. It iss only a storage room with a dressing table and mirror, but the thrallss will remodel it. It iss on their to-do list. They've just completed a meditation room, too."

"Really? You contract out your remodeling to the thralls?"

He laughed. "Oh, no. They are honored to provide for uss for free. We give them many assignmentss, from housecleaning to tax preparation. Sso useful."

"That sounds a little, well, exploitive."

"Iss it exploitive to allow people to do that which pleasess and fulfillss them?"

I considered this for a moment, and then said, "Yes, if you know better than they that they are victimizing themselves."

"I admire your analytical mind, Misss De Loss Ssantoss, and I would agree if we were taking advantage of them. Our relationship is ssymbiotic. They do things for uss, and we do thingss for them. For example, our credit union offerss low-interest loanss for students and home buyers."

Well, this vampire world was much more organized than I'd suspected. "Tell me about your people."

I'd already heard most of the story that he told, but I liked listening to him talk. The vampires originated in villages on the coast of the Black Sea. Willem's research had discovered a link with the trade caravans along the Silk Route from China, Tibet, and India. "Willem's theory iss that some of the traderss had a recessive genetic condition. When these men took wives from the villages, the children had a unique genetic combination that resulted in our people." These people then migrated west and north, most settling in Eastern Europe, but some traveling all the way to the Baltic Sea.

SLIME's family connection with the vampires could be traced back to the conflicts between Slavic pre-Christian beliefs and Roman Christianity in the ninth century. Secret alliances and organizations were formed then, and they still exist today, albeit for very different purposes. All the men in SLIME's family were members of a clandestine order called Chalice of Blood, who knew of the existence of the clans and perpetuated horrifying myths.

"How many of you are there in all?" I asked.

"Not enough," he said.

Trying to get a straight answer out of a vampire was harder than cross-examining a schizophrenic. "A ballpark figure is fine," I said. "A, zero to five hundred. B, five hundred to one thousand. C, one thousand to—"

"We don't know the numbers ourselves," Silas said with a patient smile. "Some of our kind 'pass' as normal and vanish." He sipped on his drink, gave a small "mmm" of pleasure. "Perhaps they have set up lives elsewhere. I try to take the more optimistic view."

The pessimistic view was that anti-vampire nuts had tracked them down and killed them.

"But I have taken sso much of your time, Misss De Loss Santoss, especially after your traumatic experience."

I *was* a little tired. "Thank you for telling me so much. You said you had documents?"

"Yess." He leaned closer. "I feel that we are kindred sspirits, that you, too, have the ssoul of an academic and value the life of the mind. I would like to share my studies with you, but thiss is a sserious undertaking. There are family members who would be very displeased for someone outside to have ssuch a confidence." He wrinkled his brow. "Perhaps I am alone in thinking that study can lead to advances in civilization."

"I don't want to get you in any trouble."

Silas winked. "If you can keep a ssecret, Miss De Loss Santoss, sso can I."

He told me that if I wanted to read his research, historical documents, and Willem's works we could meet here tomorrow during the day when the club was closed. "If you find the material fasscinating, as I think you will, you may want to stay and sstudy longer. We have an apartment upstairss that iss kept for guestss of the club."

I might never have this opportunity again. Maybe understanding the vampires' history would help me understand Oswald's character and his mother's objections to me. "That would be wonderful."

"I am not so brave as you, however, so you cannot tell anyone, even your friends."

"You have my word."

He said, "Thank you. We have excellent ssecurity, but one cannot be too cautious when one possesses preciouss and unique antiquities."

Silas had to stay at the club for another meeting, but offered me a ride home with one of the club's staff. He went to a back room and returned in a few minutes with a tall young man with longish dark brown hair. "This is Xavier. He will see you home safely."

Xavier was in his early twenties and wore an inexpensive navy blue suit and scuffed shoes. He was lean and sinewy, with high cheekbones and thick eyebrows. I could see the black edge of a tattoo on his neck covered by the collar of his white shirt, and dark pinpoints on his ears from multiple piercings. A scar ran through his right eyebrow, and he wore several silver rings on his fingers, and a black leather studded wristband. In short, he didn't look like your typical suit-wearer.

He gazed at me and nodded his head. "Hey, how's it going?"

"Hey," I responded, and we walked outside. "I'm Milagro."

"Nice name. Does it mean anything?"

"It means *miracle*. It's kind of silly."

"I like it," he said. "Not as bad as Xavier. Vampires always give their kids sucky names."

I thought it impolite to point out the appropriateness of this.

"Call me Zave," he said. "I'm parked over here." He stopped at a dark midsize car. I saw a rat scuttling near a Dumpster, and I wondered if my extra-sharp vision was necessarily a good thing.

We got in the car, and I told Zave the address. "Do you need directions?"

"Nah, I know that street." He looked at me and said, "You want some music?"

"Sure."

He turned on the stereo and Metallica came blasting out.

"You like the classics," I said loudly.

"Yeah." He kept taking peeks at me as he drove.

"Does something about me bother you, Zave?"

He startled. "Huh? No, it's just weird, you know, meeting you. I didn't know your kind was real."

"What kind, Latinas or someone immune to infection?"

He thought this was pretty funny, and that scored points with me. "I mean that you're someone who drank our blood, like in the movies."

"It was accidental. I didn't know your kind was real either. What's your tattoo?"

"It's a coffin and a wooden stake. I was like wanting to be empowered for who I am." He bashed on his horn and hit the gas to roar around a car that was going the speed limit.

"Whatever turns your engine, Zave."

The light up ahead was yellow, turning red, and he sped through the intersection.

I studied his hands. One of the rings was a skull, but the others were bulky plain bands. His fingernails were short and broken, and his fingers were stained.

"What kind of work do you do, Zave?"

"Stuff for Silas."

"I mean with your hands. You look like a man who knows how to use your hands." I didn't mean the comment to sound so suggestive.

"I totally restored my '73 Camaro Z28. It's got a Turbo 400 trans, a torque converter, new cam and lifters, and a new paint job, silver with black stripes. It runs like a bat outta hell."

"Sounds like a sweet ride."

"She is," he said. "It's still early. You wanna go for a drink? I know a place." He named a warehouse that was known for punk bands and brawling.

Before Oswald, this was exactly the sort of thing I would have done for fun, and Zave definitely had a loose-cannon appeal. "Thanks, but I've had a long day."

"Yeah, okay, I know I don't have money like Ducharme, but I've got ideas and plans," he said defensively. "And I'm not some geezer." Zave evidently defined geezer as anyone over thirty.

"I don't know who told you that I was going out with Ian Ducharme, but we're just friends."

"You mean you're not . . ."

"No, Oswald Grant is my boyfriend. Do you know the Grant family?"

"The ones with all the attitude? Like they're too good for anyone?"

"They're really very nice," I said.

We arrived at Mercedes's house. Zave parked across the driveway and got out of the car. I looked around before stepping out. Mercedes was still at the club, and the windows were dark.

Zave walked up to the front door, triggering the motion-detector porch light. He stood at the door and waited while I unlocked it.

"Thanks for the ride, Zave."

He watched me with a worried look and said, "You know, maybe it's time for me to move on. Maybe you want to move on, too, get away from these tired old vamps."

"I'm just getting used to them."

"Why bother? It's a big world out there. My car's gassed up, ready to hit the highway." His dark brown eyes stared into mine with promises of exhilarating and possibly illicit adventures.

"Zave, we just met, and I'm in a relationship."

"Things change." He took a piece of paper out of his pocket and handed it to me. "Here's my number anyway. You got a fire in you and I can tell . . . we could have some good times."

"Thanks for the ride, Zave. *Buenas noches.*"

He stood there until I was inside. Peering though the peephole, I saw him jam his hands into his pockets. The idea of a road trip with an aimless and energetic young man seemed romantic and impossible, and I felt a pang that my life had become so routine; I was not that wild girl.

Then Zave turned and went back to his car.

It was late and I thought Oswald would be asleep now. I

called his phone and his recorded message played. "Hi, Oz, I hope your trip is going well," I said in a cheerful voice. "I'm sorry about the argument and we'll work it out." I told him I now had a phone, and he could call me if he had a chance. "See you soon."

I called Ian again and left a message that I really, really needed to talk to him. Then I made up my bed on the sofa and lay in the dark, listening to the clatter, buzzing, and roar of the City, thinking of my last few days. I felt as if I'd turned a corner and that big things were happening in my life, things that would radically change my state-of-the-*chica* analysis. Like Silas, I tried to take an optimistic view.

The next morning, I packed my bags before Mercedes was up. I folded my blankets and tried unsuccessfully to make Cuban coffee. The result was not foamy and rich but flat and bitter. I tossed it in the sink and made a pot of very strong tea.

When I heard Mercedes moving around, I fixed toast with marmalade for her and toast with strawberry jam for myself. I was having a strong red craving.

"Morning," Mercedes said, coming into the kitchen in her robe. "You're up early. Going back to the ranch?"

"Yes," I said. Of course I lied occasionally, especially when answering questions like, "Do you like my new haircut?" However, lying to Mercedes felt very, very wrong, and I promised myself that I'd make it up to her somehow. "If that detective gets back to you, which I doubt he will, give him my phone number."

"Sure." She poured some milk in her tea. "I smell coffee."

"I ruined it. But I had a great day yesterday." I told her about meeting Skip and said that I'd had a drink with Silas. She didn't ask me the name of the bar, so I didn't have to prevaricate.

As I said good-bye, I gave Mercedes a hug. The visions of red pulsing through veins and flesh exploded in my head. I held tight to her sturdy frame, waiting for them to dissipate. But they continued, worse than yesterday morning when . . . when Mercedes had touched me.

"Milagro?"

I let go of Mercedes and fought the urge to let my knees buckle. The images quickly faded.

It couldn't be. It couldn't be that touching someone would do this to me.

"I'm fine," I said with a broad smile. "I just hate to say good-bye."

"It's just *hasta la vista*, not *adios, mujer*."

She walked me out to my truck. I got in and rolled down the window. "*Muchas gracias por todo*."

Looking more serious than usual, she replied, "If you need anything, just call, okay?"

"You know I will."

I drove until I was out of her view. Then I pulled into the first parking space I saw and dropped my head onto the steering wheel.

What had Ian done to me? I tried to think rationally. I'd been very sick after my initial accidental infection with Oswald's blood. I'd suffered a relapse early on and a second ingestion of his blood had helped me to recover. The quantities I'd taken in were mere drops, nothing compared to the amount that I'd received from Ian. And Ian was different from the other vamps. He was physically stronger, and he never seemed affected by alcohol or exhaustion. But those traits could be unrelated to his vampire condition.

I needed to know more. I needed to see Silas.

ten

played for a (blood) sucker

The block of empty warehouses looked even more dismal in the daylight. Layers of soot covered the buildings, and even the graffiti was uninspired obscenities. I parked in a lot behind the club, where Silas had told me the truck would be safe.

I knocked on the front door of the club, and the string bean, looking as colorless and nasty as a jar of marshmallow cream, opened it.

"Hi, Silas is meeting me here," I said.

Without a word, he swung open the door, and I entered the cool darkness of the club. I followed him to the back door. He pushed a button and a few seconds later Silas opened the door. He looked younger, his small, thin body clad in jeans and a white T-shirt, his pale hair wet and spiky.

"Misss De Losss Santoss, I'm sso happy that you came."

"So am I, Silas."

He ushered me into a nondescript hallway with gray industrial carpeting and said, "Let'ss go upstairs to the apartment, so we can talk and I can show you our hisstorical manuscripts."

We walked to the far end of the building. The windows here had been painted black, and pendant lamps illuminated the narrow stairs to the second floor.

The apartment was enormous by city standards and starkly furnished. The large room had only a sofa, a few armchairs, a coffee table, and a dining set. To one side was an open kitchen and I guessed the bedrooms were behind the closed doors.

"You've got a lot of space here," I said.

"No need to be polite. Xavier was supposed to put this place together for me, but he got into some sort of confrontation with one of the IKEA salespeople over bookshelves."

Laughing, I said, "Xavier in IKEA? He doesn't seem like a guy who's interested in household furnishings."

"No, he's happier in an auto parts store, but I have hopess for him. May I offer you ssomething to drink?"

"Yes, that would be nice," I said. I was happy when he went to the refrigerator and took out a plastic pouch of blood. "Animal, right?"

"Calf." He filled two glasses with ice, added some blood to each, and then topped them off with Italian mineral water. Eyeing the glasses, he said, "Maybe a garnish? I'm not very good at these domestic embellishmentss."

"No, it's fine, thanks."

"Drink up and I'll sshow you the sstudy."

I preferred to sip, but I was craving blood anyway, so I guzzled.

We went by the living room area to a locked door. Silas reached under his collar and pulled a silver chain with a key over his head. He opened the door, saying, "These papersss are irreplaceable."

The windowless room was dark until Silas turned on a lamp by the door. Three long oak tables were set end to end. One was bare except for green-shaded banker's lamps, and the other two were covered with papers and stacks of books. Cardboard boxes of books sat on the floor, and maps and diagrams covered the walls. The only seats were wooden straight-back chairs. The air was cool and I could feel a draft from the humming ventilation system.

"If you please," said Silas, and handed me a pair of thin white gloves from a box. "The oils from our fingerss can damage the ancient paperss. Sso can direct and fluorescent light and materials with acidity."

Silas unlocked a cabinet and took out a large cardboard box. He set this on the empty table and turned on a lamp. After removing the top of the box, he gently lifted out a book. The leather cover was worn through in places and the frayed edges looked as if mice had munched on them.

"What is this?" I asked, running my gloved finger over the strange gilt letters on the cover.

"*The Book of Blood,*" he said. "Our earliest hisstory."

I carefully lifted the cover. Thin transparent sheets separated and protected the pages. "What alphabet is this?"

"It iss related to the glagolitic alphabet. The accepted theory is that St. Csyril and his brother, St. Methodiuss, created thiss alphabet, but Willem's research showss that this version may well have derived from the Slavic runes used in pre-Christian ssacred textss."

As I stared at the strange letters, a chill ran down my spine. I'm sure it was only because they were so unfamiliar, the dark black marks on thick yellow sheets, the exquisite, brilliantly colored geometric illustrations that decorated the work.

Silas was watching me and he said excitedly, "You feel the effect? The texts are not mere books. They are totemss, they have power."

I was never going to disagree with someone who said a book had power, unless he was talking about books made from movies. "But the power of books is in the words, the meaning," I said.

"Yess, but a rare few bookss have power in their very exisstence."

We sat down at a table and Silas talked about the book and gave a general translation of the contents, which correlated to his description of the vampire history. It was fascinating to be examining such an old tome and to think of the scholars who had painstakingly made these letters and intricate illuminations.

"But I must be boring you, Misss De Loss Santoss," Silas said, and he returned the book to its box, and the box to the cabinet. "You must have questionss."

I leaned back in the wooden chair. "I do. I'd like to know what role religion plays in your lives."

"Ah, do you mean if we have our own religion? No, Misss De Loss Santoss, we don't have an 'official' faith, and mosst of us follow one of the major religionss. We do have ritess that celebrate our heritage and culture. We do not believe in the old ssuperstitionss, but I think it iss important to presserve these ancient customs sso they are not losst in the fog of time. Willem wass instrumental in reviving ssome of these practicess."

His explanation demystified the strange ceremony at the

ranch. "You know, there's a group of Cuban anthropologists who sing folk songs as a way of preserving them."

"Yess, this has an anthropological basiss."

"Do all of you have exactly the same abilities? I mean, fast healing and immunity from disease? Or do some of you have other abilities?"

"The majority of uss have these characteristicss at about the same level. Ssome have less, ssome have more."

"Like Ian Ducharme?"

"Yess, hiss line hass more pronounced abilities, as you put it."

"Why is that?"

"Geneticss are not my forte, Misss De Loss Santoss, but I believe that thiss can be traced to the original intermarriages of the traders with the villagerss. A variation within an anomaly, but I am not privy to the details of his family line."

"I suppose his sister, Cornelia, shares those traits."

"Sssister?" Silas looked at me quizzically. "Cornelia is not hiss ssister. They are, ass they ssay, kissing coussins. Hiss family took her in when her own parentss died in a boating accident. It wass assumed that they would marry."

Gee, and I'd thought I couldn't feel any creepier about Cornelia. "What about the Grant family?"

"Very distinguished," said Silas. "There wass the incident with Edna Grant's book . . ."

"*Chalice of Blood,*" I volunteered.

"Yess, but she wass young. The young can be sso impetuouss," he said sympathetically. "Ssadly, it caused the demise of her marriage."

"Oswald's told me that your lifespan is a little longer."

"Yess, many of us live healthily to one hundred—which can sseem like an eternity, I ssuppose."

"I imagine so. Also, do you have any, um, sensory differences from nonvampires? For example, if you touch someone, can you sense their, ah, inner organs?"

"What an extraordinary question, Misss De Loss Santoss! Unlike comic book superheroes, we do not have X-ray vision. When I touch someone, I ssee only what you would ssee. No more, no lesss."

"Oh," I said. I was the only one. "When was the last time someone survived infection?"

"More than three hundred yearss ago, or sso the story goess." He smiled. "Sso you ssee, you are a rara avis."

I didn't want to be a rare bird. I wanted to be just one of the flock. Silas must have interpreted the expression on my face as hunger, because he said, "I have another meeting to attend, but pleasse have lunch here. If you can sstay, I have a report that may interest you, and we can continue our converssation thiss evening."

I wanted to learn as much as I could. "Yes, I can stay. My things are down in my truck."

"Give me your keyss and I will have one of the sstaff bring them up."

I handed over my keys.

He opened a file cabinet and took out a bound report. "You will find this very informative."

The report was called "Development, Migratory Patterns, and Evolution of Vampire Folklore." Just glancing at the heavily annotated and footnoted pages made me long for a margarita and a gardening magazine. "I can't wait to really get into it," I said, "after lunch, of course."

"When you have finished it, I will share a most important document, Willem's Project for a New Vampire Century."

"A one-hundred-year plan? I can hardly figure out what to do next week."

Silas laughed politely. "All good thingss take time, and with our extended lifespan, we have more time than most. The project is Willem's most brilliant work, his theoriess on how we can influence policiess to create a better world for everyone." Silas's pale eyes shone with a passion I hadn't seen before.

"That sounds ambitious," I said, trying to sound as neutral as Switzerland, except that I had no intention of shielding the bank accounts of evildoers. "What are your goals?"

"I cannot explain them all now, but in brief, we promote national fisscal ressponssibility, an elected parliamentary ssystem, and ssupport for familiess and children. With economic equality and ssocial justice, there comes peace."

Thinking about Gabriel, I asked, "What about gay families?"

"The private ssexual practicess of individualss are unimportant to us," he said with a patient smile. "We are concerned about sstable, ssafe homes for children and responsible parenting. Is the child fed healthy foodss, clothed, educated, and loved? Is the child ssafe and are there ruless, but not abuse?"

He should have a chat with my mother Regina about his standards for good child care. "It sounds wonderful, but how do you deal with corporate power and greed that circumvents the greater good of nations and peoples?"

"Ah, Misss De Losss Santosss, that is a problem for economists, and a few good minds are working on that now. There can be change for the better, I musst believe that, and the will of the people should not be underesstimated."

His idealism was a warm breeze in a cold world.

We removed our gloves and left the research room. Silas locked the door behind us.

He showed me the bedroom I would be using. It was a small, austere room, done all in white like the quarters in a rest home in a chilly mountain village where one would go hoping to be cured of consumption: white coverlet, white walls, white flat-weave rug, white melamine furniture. Through a door I could see an all-white bathroom.

"My own needs are minimal, Misss De Loss Santosss, and I hope this will not be too uncomfortable for you."

"It's very nice. Where is it that you stay, Mr. Madison?"

"Some thrallss allow me to use their guest cottage when I am in the City. Otherwise I will work all night and exhaust myself."

I imagined Silas toiling away, unaware of the hour, working on his important annotations and footnotes.

"Cuthbertson, our doorman, will be here if you need anything. You may call downstairs on this intercom. I will have lunch ssent up shortly."

So he left and I found myself holding the hefty report. I read the introduction, which was a mind-numbing explanation of research techniques and methodology.

I had just finished this section, by which I mean that I had let my eyes move in total apathy over the pages, when Cutherbertson, the string bean, came upstairs with a white paper deli sack and my overnight bag.

"Your lunch," he said, dropping the bag on the table. He tossed my bag onto the sofa.

"Thank you."

He gave me a long look, then turned and left. I opened the white bag and took out a clear plastic container of fruit salad, a chicken sandwich, a bottle of water, and an oatmeal raisin cookie. I tried not to think of the blood in the refrigerator as I ate my meal.

When I was finished eating, I made myself cozy on the sofa and returned to the report. Silas was a very diligent researcher, but his intriguing personality could not be found in his writing. I would have had fun reading through the history of vampire myths if he'd thrown in a handful of active verbs and a sprinkling of adjectives. I liked learning trivia, such as the old-timey belief that if you put seeds on a vampire's grave, he would get so preoccupied counting them that he wouldn't run amok, eating villagers in the dark hours.

The report lulled me to sleep, and I awoke to footsteps on the stairs. I sat up, ran my fingers through my hair, and tried to look as if I was fully alert. When Silas entered the apartment, I said, "I've been so engrossed in your report that I lost all track of time."

"You are too kind, Misss De Loss Santoss. When I checked on you earlier, my stolid work had made you doze off."

I shrugged. "It wasn't your writing. I was very tired. What time is it?"

"Just past ten. I hope you don't mind me letting you ssleep sso long, but you sseemed to need the rest. It's almost time for an exhilarating event."

"Really?" I was glad we weren't going to spend the entire evening discussing his report.

"Yess. Perhaps I am being precipitouss in asking, but you've shown such interest . . . would you like to participate in one of our most important ceremonies? It requiress a survivor, and when I heard about you, I knew you were the one. I've wanted to revive this rite ever ssince I first learned of its existence in a Latvian text on the mythology of the Latvju Dainas."

This sounded as if it would fit Oswald's description of his peoples' ceremonies as long and boring. "Do I have to recite anything? Because if I do, I'd need time to memorize."

"No, we will do all the sspeaking. Your role is ssymbolic."

"Do I get to wear a folk costume?" I wistfully envisioned something with wooden clogs and an embroidered red felt hat.

Silas beamed. "Yess, you will look very beautiful in the traditional white ssilk gown."

I liked dressing up, so I said, "Well, okay, then."

Neither of us was very hungry, so we had fruit and cheese and blood spritzers. "What is the purpose of the ceremony?" I asked.

He opened his mouth and the strange noises came out. "It meanss ssolicitation to the ssun. You can imagine how anguished our forebears were without ssunscreen. They longed to walk in the ssunlight without harm. They believed that a ssurvivor would lead them to a new sstage and they would not fear the ssun's rayss, but flourish in them."

"That's so poignant," I said. "The sun always symbolizes life and growth, of course." At least the latest infection hadn't rendered me susceptible to UVA rays.

"We will begin ssoon. The gown is in the meditation room, and you can change there. The ceremony will be held on the stage of the club."

We started downstairs, and I said, "Wait, let me get something." I ran back up and grabbed my overnight bag and my purse, then returned to Silas. "I've got a few lipsticks, so I'll see what goes best with the gown," I said, holding up my purse. Then I indicated my overnight bag and added, "Luckily I brought all my things for the wedding so I can fix my hair, too. I want to look my best if I'm going to be onstage."

"I appreciate your zeal."

As Silas opened the door to the meditation room, Cuthbertson, in a red Nehru jacket and black pants, came through the door at the end of the hall that led to the club. In a moment, I saw a crowd of pale faces, thralls and vampires, all dressed in ruby robes, and I heard the eerie keening of the chanteuse, singing in the awful language. A chill ran down my spine.

Cuthbertson closed the door and came to Silas. "We are ready, sir." The string bean's jacket bulged at his side. I knew he had a weapon hidden. I knew without a doubt that it was the jeweled knife. His eyes homed in on me like a shark homes in on a seal.

"Thank you, Cuthbertson, we shall be ready momentarily." Silas waited for me to go into the meditation room. The room had soft gray walls, large sitting cushions on the gray rug, and a low table. An aromatherapy candle was burning. The only window was painted black. It really was a meditation room.

On the table was a decanter of greenish liquid, a small carved wooden cup, and a neatly folded white item of clothing. Silas lifted the fabric and shook out the gossamer silk. The long gown was indeed beautiful, with a low, gathered neckline and an empire waist. The bodice was richly embroidered with a sun motif in gold thread.

"I will give you a few minutes to prepare," Silas said. "Please have a cup of our traditional beverage." He poured the greenish liquid into the cup and handed it to me.

I sniffed. It smelled herby. "What is this?"

"A fermented grain beverage, distilled with herbs. The alcohol content is minimal, but I thought you would enjoy experiencing all asspectss of our anthropological research. For the ssake of authenticity."

"Thanks." I put the cup to my lips and took a sip. It tasted like rubbing alcohol, dirt, and grass. I suspected that it would serve as nail polish remover in an emergency. "Mmm, nice green notes," I said. "I'll save it until I'm doing my makeup."

"The tradition is to drink it quickly. Bottomss up," Silas said.

I had to drink it if I wanted him to think I was complacent. I tipped the cup back and swallowed the vile beverage. I hoped the alcohol wouldn't hit me too soon and too fast.

"Fabulous," I said as calmly as I could. "Um, no one is going to walk in while I change?"

"Cuthbertson will guard the door. I must get ready, too." He smiled broadly. "We will relive history tonight, Misss De Loss Santoss. We will pay homage to the sspirits of our ancestorss."

I was pretty sure my ancestors would have lopped off his ancestors' heads and rolled them down a pyramid, but now wasn't the time to discuss cultural differences.

The moment Silas left the room and shut the door behind him, I went to the one window in the room. I opened it slowly and quietly, then saw to my dismay that security bars blocked my escape to the parking lot below. A small lock held the bars in place.

I got my phone out of my bag. The police wouldn't come on my suspicion alone. Ian was nowhere around. I needed someone who could find this place fast and get me out. Zave's scrap of paper was in my pocket. I took it out and called him. He answered right away.

"Zave," I whispered. "It's Milagro. I'm at the club and I have a feeling Silas is planning something bad."

"Mil! I tried to warn you last night. They're gonna bleed you."

"Warn me? You asked me out for a drink last night. I'm in the meditation room and Cuthbertson is guarding the door. A pack of vampires and thralls are in the club. How do I get out?"

He paused so long that I said, "Zave, are you still there?"

"Yeah. You gotta get the key from Cuthbertson. He keeps a ring of keys in his pocket and he's got keys for the window bars. I'm coming round back to get you."

"How do I get the key from him?"

"Punch him out. He's going to be using the knife on you."

I'd seen the meanness in Cuthbertson's face. I knew he'd enjoy hurting me. "Punch him out with what? The only thing in this room is pillows." There was a tap at the door and I quickly put the phone away.

"Miss De Los Santos," said Cuthbertson. "Are you almost ready?"

I went to the door and opened it a few inches. "Actually, I'm really nervous about being onstage. I always choked in my acting classes. Do you think I could have some champagne? Bring a bottle."

His pupils were dilated and I could smell the herby alcohol on his breath. He stared at me hungrily and nodded. I didn't want to know what he was thinking.

I put my bag and purse by the window and waited for his return. When he tapped on the door again, I opened it and ushered him in. He held a bottle of champagne in one hand and a flute in the other.

I took the bottle and said, "I think I'm going to have a little trouble with this dress. It's not going to fit over my chest. Can you help?"

When he walked unsteadily toward the low table, I kicked the door shut and said, "Has everyone been imbibing this amazing grog?"

"Yes, we are all very, very excited." He leaned toward me. "Is it true what they say?"

"What?"

135

"Is it true your blood is an aphrodisiac? That it arouses and strengthens? That it grants fertility?"

It took me a second to take in what he'd said, and then I answered in a husky voice, "All that and more, Cuthbertson. Will you be doing the cutting?"

His mouth was slack. He nodded. "Yes, I want to feel the knife going through your flesh."

Any ambivalence I'd had about what I was going to do vanished. "Get the gown for me, would you? You can help me get into it."

When he bent over to pick up the gown, I swung the bottle at his noggin. It connected with a sickening thud and Cuthbertson collapsed forward. "Better you than me," I said.

He was breathing, but unconscious. I dragged the table to the door and jammed it underneath the knob to block entry. Then I fished in his pockets while thinking, "Ew, ew, ew," and found the keys. I poured the rest of the grog over his face and shirt.

I ran to the window and examined the key ring. There were three smaller keys that might fit the lock. The first one worked. I swung out the security bars and hoisted myself on the windowsill. The ground was about fifteen feet below and I didn't see my truck in the parking lot. I tossed out my bag and my purse. I hoped I wouldn't break my legs in the fall.

I took a breath and counted, "One, two—" and then I heard the roar of a powerful engine. A silver and black Camaro swerved into the parking lot. Zave left the engine running as he jumped out and came to the window. He wore a beat-up black leather jacket, a faded black T-shirt, and old jeans.

"Jump," he said, looking like a rock-and-roll Romeo.

"Three." I jumped. I was not a frail and delicate creature,

but he was able to catch me, even though the impact knocked us to the ground. He smelled of motor oil, sweat, and beer, and I thought it was the most fantastic aroma on earth.

We scrambled up and he grabbed my bags. "Let's roll," he said, and I had already thrown myself into the leather bucket seat and slammed the car door. He tore out of the parking lot and he was right; the car raced like a bat out of hell.

eleven

children of the gravely mistaken

"Where's my truck?" I asked Zave.

"Silas told me to get rid of it. It's at a long-term lot at the airport." He looked at me and grinned. "Did you knock Cuthbertson out?"

"I did. I had a little help, since he was bombed on that weird vampire booze."

"Lucky you didn't drink that. I had a cupful once and woke up naked by the tracks two days later."

Zave had probably had a bottle, not a cup, because I felt clearheaded. "Where are we going?"

"I can take you to your truck, or maybe you want to come with me." He tore around a bus that was trying to merge into traffic. "We can drive north, south, whatever you want, wherever the wind takes us, Milagro."

"You don't know how good that sounds, Zave. But you don't have to do that for me."

"I owe you," he said quietly. "The other night in front of your friend's house, when you were with Ducharme . . ."

It took a moment for the realization to hit. "That was you?"

"Silas wanted to send a message to Ducharme. He was mad about something Ducharme said to Willem Dunlop."

"So he sent you to kill Ian?"

Zave laughed. "A knife's not going to kill him. But it would hurt and maybe he'd back down from opposing the Project for a New Vampire Century."

"Why would Ian oppose it if it's so nice and good? Silas told me he believed that everyone was equal."

"Yeah, sure, all *humans* are equal," he said. "He thinks it's our destiny as superior beings to lead and direct humans. 'Peace and harmony through control and direction.' "

"Do you believe that?"

"I don't really care about that stuff."

"What does Silas want with me?"

"He says you're the omen of the new era of nonvampires who are in alignment with us and maybe even can have hybrid offspring. Your blood is supposed to be, what was the word he used? Transformative."

"I'm not a symbol. I'm a normal girl."

"You healed up, though, from a real bad slice," he said. "That's *not* normal, even for us. The only ones who heal like that . . . the only one I know . . ."

"I'm a normal girl with a few quirks. Did you tell Silas what happened?"

He frowned. "I told him you got in the way. I didn't tell him you got cut bad 'cause he would have slit my throat."

"That's merely a figure of speech, right?" When he didn't answer, I asked, "Are my friends, the Grants, involved in this movement at all?"

"Silas didn't say anything, but you're like his special project," Zave said. "I'm real sorry about the other night. You came at me and the knife slipped. I'd never hurt a girl."

"I am all atwitter that chivalry is not dead."

Zave laughed, then said, "I like you."

I felt a strange exhilaration, feeling a rush from escaping the neovamps and racing along the streets with Zave, the world open before us. If I went with him, I wouldn't have to be careful about what I said or what I did or how I dressed or if I had a career. If I went with him, I wouldn't have to worry that Evelyn was right and that eventually Oswald and I would hate each other. "Would you take me to my truck, Zave?"

He sighed. "What are you going to do?"

"I don't know yet. What are you going to do?"

"Get out of here. I'm bored with it all. Not enough hot girls."

"What about the thralls?"

"I don't like submissive chicks. I like them with fight in them, like you."

I asked Zave how'd he'd gotten involved with Silas and he said, "He recruits guys dropping out of school, or maybe with some substance abuse problems. You join the movement and you get an apartment, a salary, a job. He gets you on track. It's okay for a while."

"What about the ideology?"

"He paid off my college loans, so I was like, yeah, new vampire century, whatever."

When we got to my truck in the airport parking lot, he leaned over to kiss me. His lips landed on my cheek, and gory images burst in my head. I wanted to jerk back from the contact, but I kept control until he pulled away. "Maybe next time," he said.

"Maybe," I answered.

He waited as I lugged my bag out of the car and tossed it in the back of the truck. "Bye, Zave. And thank you."

"*Hasta la vista*, baby."

He took off and I stood there for a minute, paralyzed by the reality that both human and vampire contact gave me these waking nightmares. I could have broken down then, collapsed on the cold asphalt, and cried in anguish. But that was not who I was. That was not how I had lived through the loss of my *abuelita* and the years of loneliness in my mother Regina's house.

As always, my instincts took over. I got in my truck and drove to the pay booth.

The attendant said, "The guy in the Camaro paid for you."

Zave's small kindness was enough to make me hope. I drove out of the lot and back toward my comfort zone, the City. Silas knew I'd stayed at Mercedes's, so I couldn't go there, and he knew I'd possibly head for the ranch. And then it occurred to me: Nancy was gone on her honeymoon and she'd kept her old apartment for days of shopping and shows in the City.

I parked a few blocks from Nancy's apartment building in an upscale, very trendy neighborhood of overpriced boutiques, day spas, cafés, and restaurants. After checking to see that no one was around, I used an eyeliner crayon to alter my license plates, changing a *C* to an *O*, and a 3 to an 8.

Unbeknownst to Todd, Nancy had never asked me to return the key that she had given me. Her place was in a smaller building, only eight units total, and she was on the third floor. It wasn't until I opened the door that I remembered that Nancy was redecorating it as what she called "a lady's bedsit."

Todd and Nancy's cavernous monster of a home was done in a minimalist design, but she'd brought balance to her life by cramming every ruffled, flowered, fluffy thing into this apartment. I put the bolt on the door, threw my bag in the bedroom, and poured myself a vodka tonic.

Then I fished Detective Jefferson's card out of my wallet. I rehearsed what I would tell him: the mugger had been a member of a neovampire movement, and they'd tried to drug me with an ancient grain alcohol and feed on my blood in order to initiate the beginning of a new vampire era.

Despite our brief acquaintance, Detective Jefferson did not seem like a man who would find my story credible. I put his card back in my wallet.

I needed an escape from reality, so I turned on the television to my favorite channel, the classic movie station. I'd seen *Now, Voyager* before and found it particularly fascinating because the story features not one but two horrible, heartless mothers.

Although Oswald's mother treated me badly, I couldn't hate her. At least she loved and admired her child, the way mothers were supposed to.

I called Oswald, who didn't answer. I was relieved, because it would be easier to tell him in person that I'd met with Silas. I didn't know how to explain my reinfection without mentioning Ian, though.

Then I called Gabriel. As the security dude, he would need to know about Silas, and I hoped he would have some suggestions on how to punish him sufficiently for his bad behavior. Gabriel's message said, "I am taking personal time off, and I will not be checking messages."

Ian was next, and I struck out again. "Ian, new issues of serious concern for both of us. Call me."

I was feeling oddly ambivalent about my friends at the ranch. Did I really want to tell them all the gory details of my awful incidents, when they had been the ones who had invited Willem and Silas to the baby's event? I wondered how much they knew about the Project for a New Vampire Century, and how much they supported the movement.

When I called the Big House, Winnie answered. Before I could say anything, she put the baby on the phone. "Hi, Libby, hi, my little baby friend. How are you? Do you miss me? Is my dog behaving?" The conversation was necessarily one-sided.

After I'd babbled for a few minutes, Winnie got back on and asked, "How was the wedding?"

"Very beautiful, although the bridegroom is still a jerk. How is everything there?"

Winnie told me that the last of the relatives had left, that Edna was annoyed I wasn't around to help, and that no, Oswald hadn't called, but he usually didn't when he went on these trips. The baby started crying, and Winnie said, "She's exhausted from all the activity, and off her schedule. I've got to take care of her. Call me back, okay, Young Lady?"

"Absolutely, Winsome."

I hung up the phone and let my mind go blank. I hadn't a clue what to do. I had already imposed all this crazy vampire stuff on Mercedes, and I didn't want to bother her again—especially since I had falsely blamed her neighborhood for the assault.

My phone rang. I checked the incoming number. It had a Los Angeles area code. "Hello?" I said cautiously.

"Milagro, Skip Taylor here. You know how I said I was having problems with my screenwriter?"

"Yes, of course."

"Yeah, so I was thinking, you know, screw him."

"Hmm," I said. Was he trying to impress me so he could ask me out?

"Okay, so you want to do my rewrite for me?"

I gripped the phone tight, afraid it would fly away with his words. "Could you repeat that?"

"You're a writer, and I feel like we're on the same frequency. So if you want the job, it's a flat-fee rewrite, no screen credit, but you do get WGA membership and stuff."

"Skip, I am officially in love with you," I said. "When do you need it? When can you send it?"

"The thing is I need it now, but I'll be shuttling between the location and my offices for the next month. I was wondering if you wouldn't mind staying at the location, writing there, so we can meet and go over stuff. I'm on a tight schedule here."

"Where would I stay?"

"Don't worry about that. I'll put you up in a casita at the Paragon Spa and Resort. You ever been there? Nice place, a lot of industry types frequent it, desert air and stuff. You'll have your own little place, catered meals, and a private patio and pool."

"The Paragon? Where is that?" I asked.

"In the desert outside a town called La Basura. It's a nice quiet place to work on 'Teeth of Sharpness.' "

For a moment, I was still with fear that Skip knew everything about the vampires.

"Milagro," he said. "Are you still there?"

"Yes."

"So do you want to work on the screenplay, 'Teeth of Sharpness'? That's just the working title. We might change it to something about flying death or shadow of the beast."

It was only a title and I'd been overreacting. "That will suit me fine, Skip," I said. "I'll drive down tomorrow."

Given my situation, it seemed entirely fitting that I should escape to a town called The Garbage.

twelve

welcome to the hotel california

I went to bed early but didn't sleep well. My night was full of vivid dreams of knives and blood and Ian and sex, and I didn't even want to think about them when I awoke early. I wanted them out of my brain.

I jogged to a twenty-four-hour market, bought two steaks, and went back to Nancy's. After consuming my breakfast, I went to Nancy's closet. I'd only brought clothes for a few days and I needed spa wear. Nancy had once advised me that high-quality accessories are more important than clothes. This was probably a truism for her social class, so I grabbed handbags, scarves, belts, and sunglasses. She was a petite chick, and most of her things didn't fit me, but I found three pair of sandals that were roomy enough for my *patas*.

I stuffed these things in a carryall that still had its price tag. Even though I knew that Nancy squandered money, I was still shocked to see what she would pay for a bag that she might never use.

I took all my loot and went to the block where my truck was parked. I surveyed the area for ten minutes before deciding that Silas's underlings weren't around. Then I hurried to the truck and was on the road heading south. Even at this early hour, commuters crowded the freeway, but most of them were heading into the City, not away. Once I got beyond the region's perimeters, I could speed up, and I did so without even thinking about it. I was dashing around slower cars, seeing all the action ahead as clearly as the plot of a familiar book.

And I thought, Ian drives like this.

It was just then that my phone buzzed. I glanced at the screen and saw that Ian was calling.

"Ian," I said, "where have you been?"

"You sound well, darling."

"That is a matter for debate, Ian. I'm drinking animal blood and have really fast reactions. Also, Silas wanted to use me in a bloodletting ritual welcoming a new vampire era." I didn't tell him about the visions. What if he was as horrified as I was? What if they were a sign of insanity?

"You sound as if you are full of vitality, my dear."

I was upset that he sounded calm. "Do you know that Silas sent one of his followers to stab you?"

"I suspected as much. Madison has a petty, vindictive nature. How did you learn this?"

"Because I made the mistake of meeting with him. He promised to tell me about vampire history. He told me about something called the Project for a New Vampire Century. Do you know about it?"

"Willem wrote that manifesto years ago, but none of us took it seriously. He couldn't organize a poker game, let alone a political movement. Silas resurrected the project," Ian said. "But I'm curious why he told you all this. Did he try to take the buttons from your dress?"

"No, he has a loftier view of my role in vampire society. In fact, he thinks I can produce an army of hybrid bloodsucking babies to promote the Project for a New Vampire Century."

Ian had the nerve to laugh.

"It is *so* not funny, Ian," I said, all fuming.

"Milagro, please believe that I take Silas Madison's attacks on you very seriously . . . deadly seriously. I'm only laughing out of relief that you obviously escaped and are well. I will always bet on you in a fight."

"I'd rather avoid fighting altogether," I said. "He's operating out of a vampire bar. He suggested that I participate in an old folk custom and made it sound like an academic exercise. Then I found out that he planned to serve me as the main course."

"Silas is not superstitious, Young Lady, but he does believe in continuing the old practices for the sake of tradition."

"Oh, that makes me feel much better. Why didn't anyone ever tell me there are vampire bars?" I told him the address.

"I know the club. The singer's quite good."

"She's terrific except when she's singing in that hideous language. But back to the topic, I'd like to know what's happening to me physically."

"Would that I could tell you, but it's all rather speculative at this point. My hope is that when you are fully recovered, you will enjoy beneficial changes. I make no promises, however. You aren't like anyone else in the world."

"Yes, and every snowflake is unique," I said. "What does it mean that you're the Dark Lord?"

He chuckled. "An ancestor bought property in cold and boggy province. Worthless as farmland, but he got a title." Ian paused and said more seriously, "Milagro, I've got to go now. I couldn't call you before because I was trying to deal with Madison through official channels. The result was unsatisfactory, so I'll have to take another approach."

"I haven't quite figured out what your 'official channels' are, Ian."

"We have a council that decides on judicial matters. They have been ignoring Madison's activities because some of the older members support the movement," he said. "Milagro, Silas won't dare touch you on family property, so please stay at the ranch. Do you understand?"

"Believe me, I understand the danger." I thought of Cuthbertson's zombielike movements and the chilling desire in his voice when he said he wanted to feel the knife cut me. "Silas wants my blood, Ian. He thinks it has unique properties."

"He may be correct, darling. Save it all for me, though," he said seriously. "Go home and be careful. I will be in touch."

"Bye, Ian."

I'd told Ian that I understood, not that I agreed. Until I worked out my friends' relationship to Silas's group, I'd rather hide away out in the middle of nowhere. Maybe, too, as time passed, so would the visions and the craving for blood.

I glanced at the phone and realized that Silas could use it to track me. I pulled over at the next town, a mess of fast food restaurants, gas stations, and mini-malls. I deleted all the information and my message from the phone, and then found a post office and mailed the phone to Santa Claus, Nome, Alaska. "That's not a valid address," the clerk told me.

"I promised my niece that I would mail her present to Santa," I said with a smile.

I got a strawberry soda and an extra-rare roast beef sandwich at a deli, and I was back on the road.

I didn't doubt that Ian was telling the truth: I was an anomaly and the vampires could not predict what I would become.

I wondered if my vampire friends saw the flesh and blood as I had. If so, why hadn't they told me? Because I was an outsider and would always be an outsider. Maybe every time Oswald held me, touched me, and made love to me, he was delighting in seeing a red and raw carcass in his arms. I couldn't bear the thought that I would never be able to show him affection again, to make love to him, without seeing those images.

I yearned to hear his voice and I had an awful feeling that he was calling me now, on the phone that I'd just mailed away.

I made one more stop on the road, at a midsize town dominated by new oversized tract houses. First, I found an off-brand store staffed by sly young men who didn't think it was necessary to run a national security check on me before I bought a prepaid phone. I did, however, agree to have a beer with them when I came back through town.

Then I went to a large thrift store and sorted quickly through the racks for clothes that said serious writer slash spa guest. The only desert clothing I could think of was from the fabulous old movie *Lawrence of Arabia*. I found myself paying a pittance for white cotton shirts, khaki shorts, khaki trousers, and an absurd pale olive jacket with epaulets and gold buttons.

When I left with my bundle, I could smell rich aromas coming from a cozy Mexican restaurant. I had one of the dinner *platas* and lingered over my book, trying to puzzle out the author's intentions about the romance. When I looked up from the page, it was late and evening had fallen. I got back on the lonely road.

In a case of life imitating art, I felt like the main character of *Uno, Dos, Terror!* I'd been in control when I had written about a Latina heroine escaping fascists and the monster she had created. The bitter irony was that I was my own monster and I could never outrun myself.

The highway through the desert was lonely. My headlights picked out the flat, dry terrain. I could see the creatures moving in the darkness: small rodents and insects. Something dashed swiftly in the dark and I nearly slammed on my breaks. It was a lithe gray fox with a black-tipped tail, the first real fox I had ever seen. The brown shrubs shivered in a slight wind, and Joshua trees stood like sentinels. Mountain ranges, riven from the earth and thrust up by major fault lines, were solid black masses on the horizon.

A huge white moth splattered on my windshield and I turned on my windshield wipers to scrape it away. To my right I saw a turn onto a paved road with a discreet sign saying PARAGON WAY.

The lane was bordered by Canary Island palms dramatically up-lit with spotlights. At the end of the road was a sprawling, low pale yellow modern building with a circular drive around a fountain made from massive sandstone blocks.

Carved into a wall behind spiky agaves were the words PARAGON SPRING—SANCTUARY, SPA, & RESORT. It took me a moment to recognize a pop-pop-pop sound as a tennis ball being hit, and I thought I could spy courts beyond the building. I drove into the guest parking lot and sat for a few minutes.

This was as good a place as any to wait and see if my skin

grew scales, my hair fell out in clumps, and I began running with packs of wild dogs at night, feasting on the flesh of jackrabbits and rattlesnakes.

I heard a crunch-crunch-crunch on the gravel outside, so I got out of my truck.

A valet was walking toward the truck with the smile of someone who is well paid to be pleasant.

"Evening, miss. Welcome to the Paragon. May I be of assistance?"

"Yes, I've got a reservation here."

He blew a whistle and a bellhop trotted over to haul my luggage. A raked gravel and boulder courtyard led to a vast lobby with walls frescoed in soothing ocher hues. To one side was a long slate reception desk. The staff, dressed in dark burgundy tunics, were as lean and immaculate as Tibetan monks.

A bar was on the other side of the lobby. Next to the bar were tall, copper-paneled doors to a restaurant. The place smelled like expensive places do, absolutely clean with the faintest scent of woody aromatics, like sandalwood, and delicate florals, like orange blossoms.

The spa's patrons seemed to be a homogenous bunch of tanned and rested nonethnic rich people who enjoyed colorful cocktails. I was definitely out of my comfort zone. At least the staff was a mixed bunch.

I gave my name at the desk, and the receptionist signaled to the concierge, who came over with a smile.

"Ms. De Los Santos, welcome to the Paragon," he said. "My name is Charles Arthur and I'm here to ensure that your stay is serene and rejuvenating." He was a big, meaty man with a thick, neatly trimmed brown beard and kind blue eyes. His suit was well tailored, but he reminded me of those guys in the City who wore flannel shirts, built stuff with power tools, and had brunch every Sunday with their boyfriends. I liked him instantly.

"Thanks. I'd just like to go to my room. Also, is there a café here?"

"Yes, but if you would like to unwind in the privacy of your casita, our restaurant will prepare anything on the menu. Mr. Taylor has taken care of everything for you." He dropped his voice and said, "He also included service, so there is no need to tip the staff."

Charles then escorted me out a side entrance to a small yard with golf carts. We got in one and he drove down a path that led beyond the back of the main building to cottages that were hidden behind fences, shrubbery, and dark red bougainvillea. He parked in front of the last casita.

We went through a small garden and into the casita. "Most of our guests enjoy the open layout," he said, waving like a game show hostess to display a wide room that served as a living room and dining area. The back wall had floor-to-ceiling windows that opened onto a private courtyard with a small pool that glowed blue. There was a sort of minimalist/desert theme, as if an ambivalent hermit had decorated and his taste ran to animal skins, adobe, and stainless steel.

"That door leads to a kitchenette, which is stocked with some Paragon favorites. There's a guest bath here." His soft leather shoes made no noise as he crossed the stone pavers to a hallway. "The bedroom suite is through here." A huge platform bed was covered in elegant mushroom-colored linens, and a large TV screen was set above the fireplace. The Saltillo-tiled bathroom had a step-up bathtub that was large enough for a party.

On the other side of the casita was a roomy office that had all the necessities for a modern scriptwriter. On the desk were a black granite plaque engraved with my name and a gift basket.

The bellhop arrived with my bags. I handed him a tip before I remembered not to make physical contact.

Charles noticed my shocked expression, and when the bellhop left he said, "Oh, you forgot that tips were included—but don't worry, they are always appreciated."

When he handed me the card key, I took it carefully by the edge. After he said good night, I locked the door and gave a sigh of relief; in this vampire-free zone, I could reflect and recover.

I called Skip and gave him my new number. We arranged to meet the next morning. Then I tried Oswald, but he didn't answer. "Oswald, it's me. Here's my new number. I know you're busy, and it's not an emergency, but I miss you." I hated sounding so needy and pathetic.

I phoned the ranch and Sam picked up. "Hi, Sam, I've decided to stay a few extra days with Mercedes." I told him I had a new phone and gave him the number. "Please don't give it out, because, you know, the psychos."

"I am not in the habit of releasing personal information," Sam said, all lawyer-y. "Libby said 'da-da' today!"

"Really? Isn't she a little young to be talking?"

"Grandmama says that I imagined it, but I think Libby is an especially advanced child. You can tell, can't you?"

I agreed that she was exceptional. I felt a sharp pang at the thought that I couldn't hold her until I was well. I missed her warm babyness. "I'm going to try to teach her to say 'Milagro' when I come back," I said lightly, as if my life was nothing but parties and buying ribbons for my hair. "Sam, you know what? I ran into this old schoolmate, and he's a producer and wants me to do a rewrite of a screenplay."

"That's great news, Young Lady. Send me a copy of your contract and I'll look it over," Sam said. "If there are any red flags, I can check with an acquaintance in entertainment law."

"No contract, yet, Sam, but it's a flat fee, and it can't be that complicated."

"People without attorneys always say that," he said. "Get something in writing and don't sign it until I review it, okay?"

I said that I would and asked about the family. I edged the conversation to Gabriel. "I tried to call Gabriel and got an odd message. Is he there by any chance?"

"No," he said much too quickly. "Why do you want to talk to him?"

"I just want to gossip with him about my new clothes and things. If he calls, tell him I'm absolutely frantic to dish." I hung up thinking that all was not right in the wide, wacky world of vampires.

I opened the gift basket, which contained Paragon lotions and soaps. I ate some fruit from an arrangement on the sideboard, took a quick shower, and examined my body for any outward evidence of my disturbing internal changes.

I slipped between the cool, high-thread-count sheets of the bed and listened to the night. I missed Oswald beside me and my dog sleeping on the bedside rug. At some point the muted sounds of the spa guests faded and only the insects could be heard.

I wanted desperately to be with Oswald, ask him a hundred questions, and make him answer each one in exhausting detail. I hadn't asked before because I didn't want to be a nagging girlfriend. I'd wanted him to open up on his own. If the family had only been honest with me, I wouldn't be here now with a strange condition, once again pursued by lunatics.

I couldn't pretend the family was anything other than what they were: vampires.

What was I?

thirteen

lights, camera, tension

Skip Taylor was late for our meeting the next morning. I waited for him in the office, familiarizing myself with the screenplay program and making a backup of the "Teeth of Sharpness" file.

As the minutes passed, I called Mercedes in a panic.

"Mercedes, I was so wrong. The mugger wasn't someone from the hood. He was one of Silas's people waiting to attack Ian."

"What are you talking about?"

I gave her a brief rundown of the last two days. "I feel awful calling you about my troubles, it's just . . . it's just . . ."

"It's okay, Mil. That's what friends are for."

"But you never share your troubles with me."

"I vent to you *all* the time. You don't mind because you like hearing about the club," she said. "What have your friends said about all this?"

"I'm not at the ranch. I am mutating into some grotesque, bloodthirsty creature. That guy I told you about, Skip Taylor, offered me a job rewriting a screenplay, so I'm at the Paragon Springs Sanctuary, Spa, and Resort, which is just outside La Basura."

"You would find yourself in *la basura*."

"Ha, ha, and ha. My friends think I'm with you, but I feel safer here."

"Are you making this up?"

"No, I really am having strobe-light visions of bloody flesh every time I touch someone."

"No, I meant about the screenwriting job," she said with exasperation. "That's a very expensive hotel."

"It's also a sanctuary. Me and the Hunchback of Notre Dame both need one," I said, then cried, "Sanctuary! Sanctuary!" I glanced at the clock. "The producer is really late for our meeting."

"It's a Hollywood power thing, making someone wait. What did Gabriel say?"

I told her that I couldn't get in touch with him and elaborated on the freak show going on in my head: "Have you ever seen a David Cronenberg film? It's like that, but without any artistic content."

"I'm having a hard time believing your condition is serious when you talk like this."

"Mercedes, if I stop kidding, I'll start screaming and I'll never stop."

She was quiet for a moment, and then she said, "I'd worry about you more, but I know you're strong, *mujer*."

"I wish *strong* was synonymous with *sane*."

She was telling me that she'd try to track Gabriel down

online through a hacker connection when the doorbell rang.

"I have to go," I said.

Skip came in, saying, "Glad you're on my team." He reached his hand toward me.

I braced myself for the contact. As he gripped my hand, I saw an image that glistened with carmine rivulets; I saw white teeth scraping against white bone as they ripped away flesh.

He'd already walked past me into the large room. "Settled in? Good, good. Nice place. Hope you're ready to rock and roll."

He was already sitting at the dining table, unpacking papers from his leather satchel and jittering a knee, before I closed the door.

When we'd first met, I hadn't noticed how smooth and pink Skip's complexion was. I found it mesmerizing. "Millie, here's the current version of 'Teeth of Sharpness.'" He dropped a huge manuscript on the table.

I flipped open the front page and was shocked to see the writer's name. He had been a wunderkind, paid enormous figures for action-packed, violent movies. I said the first thing that came into my head. "You didn't tell me I'm rewriting *his* screenplay."

"Everyone's got to start somewhere." He pointed at the screenplay as if accusing it of heinous war crimes. "You see the problem here?"

The screenplay was 324 pages long. Each page would be roughly one minute of screen time. I did a quick calculation and said, "As it is, the script is over five hours long."

"He thinks he's an artist, but it's a mess, completely unproduceable. You're a good fit for this material because it's about a *chupacabra* attacking a small town."

"The goat-killing flying demon of Latin American lore?"

"Yes, I hoped it would work as both a horror film and an allegory, but he's too heavy-handed. He's got scenes that work as horror, and scenes that work as allegory, but nothing that works as both. There's no synergy."

"What is the allegory?"

"The *chupacabra* symbolizes our fear of the anonymous consumer culture and how it sucks away our souls. We're left as mere husks of real people."

"That's an amazing theme," I said, feeling a rush of excitement. "Do you have any specific instructions?"

When he rummaged in his satchel and pulled out a few pages that were clipped together, a pen rolled out. I grabbed it before it hit the floor.

"Good reactions," he said. "Here are my notes. Cut it down to a fast one hundred minutes. Show, don't tell. Nuke the whole business in the middle—you'll see what I mean." He snapped his fingers. "Oh, yeah, keep one or two of *his* poetic ramblings to make him happy. Otherwise, use your own creative talent."

I realized that I'd stopped writing and was staring dreamily at Skip, imagining all the fragile capillaries that brought a bloom to his cheeks.

"What?" he asked.

"Uh, I was just noticing your fantastic complexion. It's so healthy and richly colored."

"Huh? Thanks, I guess," he said, confused. "So you ready to go?"

"Time frame?" I asked.

"We're scheduled to start shooting in four weeks. If you can get it to me sooner, there's a bonus of an additional ten percent."

My father, Jerry D ("Let Jerry D-light you with a wonderful lawn!"), had not imparted much wisdom to his only child, but he did stress the importance of settling money issues up front. I tried to sound calm and confident as I said, "Do you have a contract for me? Just so we're clear on the terms."

Skip shrugged. "I do a lot of my business on a handshake. If there's no trust, why bother?"

He put out his hand. I took his hand and breathed slowly as a horror show played in my head.

"Good to have you on board, Millie."

"My name is Milagro."

"Hey, don't rip my head off," Skip said, and threw up his hands.

Laughing, I replied, "I'm really trying not to." The thought of Skip's exposed throat spewing blood like a hydrant made me ache with desire.

Skip glanced at his wristwatch. "Gotta go meet Thomas Cook. He just agreed to do 'Teeth,' but we gotta get him into shape for the role."

"Thomas Cook is here?" I asked, my voice breaking on a high note. Thomas Cook, named by his Central American mother after the travel agency, had vanished from the A-list as quickly as he'd appeared. I'd adored him, and I still watched his movies whenever they were shown on late-night television.

Skip shook his head and said, "Hiring him is a risk, but my director thinks he's still got It."

I didn't have to ask what It was, because memories of It were making me feel all squiggly inside. "I always liked his acting."

"You haven't seen him lately, have you?" Skip said. "Forget I said that. I'll touch base later in the week." His phone rang and he walked away with a wave.

I thought, holy cow, Thomas Cook is at the Paragon! I should have been thinking, holy cow, my boyfriend, who won't call me, neglected to tell me about a group of crazy neovamps, or, holy cow, I yearn to drain people of their bodily fluids, but sometimes you're not as sincere and serious as you'd like to be.

I went out to the private pool and sat at the edge. An iridescent blue dragonfly darted over the surface of the water. I was grateful that I could be in the sun without my skin frying, as it had done during my first infection.

At least my career had taken a marked turn for the better. Being a blood-swilling beast was probably not a hindrance to a screenwriting career. The thought of blood made my stomach cramp with hunger. I needed to find a source of the stuff.

I padded inside the house, leaving a trail of wet footprints, and found the menu for the spa. The Paragon offered various raw fish dishes, but no raw beef. I ordered a very, very rare burger and fresh tomato and red pepper juice in the hope that I could wean myself off the hard stuff.

A plump waiter brought my meal. When I tipped the waiter and his moist, chubby fingers touched mine, I had a mad urge to throw him on the tile floor and bite him all over like a rabid ferret. Obviously, I was going to have to work on self-discipline.

The food held me over as I began going through the manuscript. It didn't take me long to figure out that it was inspired by Joseph Conrad's *Heart of Darkness*. The narrator's voice-over told of a midlevel manager who is sent to a desert town to find out what's happened to a legendary land developer, Kiltz. The land developer has "gone native"—shacking up with a barmaid, hiring a shaman, ingesting hallucinogens, and forgetting his responsibilities to the home office.

"Teeth of Sharpness" was a disaster of major proportions. Sections of dialogue were written in iambic pentameter for no reason. The chupacabra spoke in riddles. Characters occasionally burst into songs that were more Lerner and Lowe than Brecht. I couldn't stop reading until I had turned the final page. There was a beauty to its insanity.

I read it through twice, marking dialogue and scenes that seemed extraneous. Evening came and my craving resurged, stronger than before. La Basura would surely have a grocery store, where I could buy meat. I slipped on my tennis shoes and trod off to my truck in the guest parking lot. The temperature had dropped and a breeze carried interesting, unfamiliar scents.

I hopped in my truck, but when I turned the key, the usually reliable engine made a strangled gargle that devolved into a whine. After a few attempts to start the vehicle, acrid smoke began pouring out of the hood.

A man with a cancerous tan who was parking his sparkling Mercedes looked at me as if my malfunctioning truck was a sign of my own unworthiness as a Paragon guest.

I got out of the truck and leaned my head against the window. My mechanical skills were limited to turning something on and then turning it off. Someone was approaching and I said, "Yes?"

"Ms. De Los Santos, could I be of service?"

I turned to see Charles, the concierge, wearing a dapper suit.

"My truck seems to be having problems. Do you know of a garage with a tow-truck service?"

"I do," he answered. "There's an excellent mechanic under contract with the Paragon. He maintains all our vehicles. Why don't you give me your keys, and I'll arrange everything for you?"

His eyes shone with helpfulness and I wanted to grab him in *un gran abrazo*. I dropped the keys into his open hand and said, "Thank you, Charles. I really appreciate this."

"My pleasure, Ms. De Los Santos."

"Call me Milagro, won't you? Could you please tell me how far it is into town?"

"Several miles. If you'd like to exercise, we recommend that you stay on our trails, which are inspected hourly for rattlesnakes, scorpions, tarantulas, and other venomous creatures."

"Oh, I just needed to pick up a few things."

"Write out a list and we'll get them for you," he said. "We also offer many quality items in our guest shops."

"Right, okay, thanks."

"If you need to go tonight, I'd be happy to offer you a ride. I drive through La Basura on my way to visit my girlfriend."

It took me a second to register that he really meant, girlfriend. That was odd. My gaydar had definitely swung to the gay side of the gauge with him. "Thanks, but really, I'm fine."

Charles said he'd have the truck towed and repaired in the morning. When I asked to talk to the mechanic first about the charges, he held up his hand and said, "Mr. Taylor has instructed that all your expenses be charged to his business account." He must have seen my surprised expression, because he added wryly, "Movie people."

"I don't know what I'll do without my truck," I said.

"As the Dalai Lama says, when one door closes, another one opens."

I appreciated his effort to cheer me up. "Thank you, Charles. Have a good evening."

After walking around the resort grounds, I veered into the dusk of the desert. When I was well clear of the Paragon, I broke into a run. There were no humans anywhere and I felt safe.

I noticed all sorts of critters, mostly skittery little lizards and beetles, going about their business. I could see the outlines of rocks, mounds, and pits well enough to easily traverse the soft soil. The stars above were coming out, and I thought I detected the pungent scent of native salvias in the dry air.

The miles passed, and soon I saw the lights from a small town. I slowed to a walk and realized that I was breathing easily, which would probably be useful when I was trying to outrun the cops if I degenerated further and committed a vicious assault.

The two-lane highway went through the center of town, which consisted of small shops, including Lefty's Happy Looky-Dat! Club, a chiropractor, a gas station, a doctor's office, and a midsize grocery store. Vampires, who had a fondness for luxury and sophistication, wouldn't be caught undead in La Basura.

The chilled air of the grocery store felt marvelous on my hot skin. I grabbed a basket and tried to look as if I was shopping for a meal. This market held products that would have caused general hysteria among the food elite. I picked up fluffy white sliced bread, iceberg lettuce, tinned spaghetti sauce, a cardboard container of parmesan cheese, and spaghetti noodles. Then I went to the meat section, as if it was an afterthought.

The pickings were slim. There were packages of hot dogs, grayish chicken parts, and hamburger. I checked out the frozen food section, thinking that frozen burger patties might be more appealing, when I noticed strange dark sausages half hidden behind giant bags of microwaveable buffalo wings.

A label identified the frosty sausages as *boudin noir*. I didn't know what they were, but some part of me went, "Whoa, baby, that's what I'm talking about." By the luncheon meats I found in plastic containers chicken livers sloshing enticingly in dark scarlet liquid. I put all of the packets of sausages and the liver containers in my basket.

The middle-aged woman who rang up my purchases looked at me when she saw the sausages. "You like these?" she asked.

"Sure," I said, picking up a pack of wintergreen gum.

"We only stock them 'cause of Lefty. Those Frenchies will eat anything."

Perhaps she expected me to join in a rousing condemnation of our brothers and sisters in *liberté, egalité, fraternité*. I was unable to read anything but *pommes frites* on a French menu, but I said, "Their food is fabulous."

"If you think sausages made of blood is fab-u-lous," she said. "La-di-da. You like liver, too?"

"One of my friends gave me a Julia Child cookbook," I said. "I'm working my way through all the recipes. Um, do you have shallots and Spanish oloroso here?"

"If shallots are onions, I got green and yellow ones by the potatoes. What's that Spanish thing you said?"

I had to buy a moldy yellow onion and a bottle of cooking sherry as cover for my story. I left the store and slipped into the parking area out back. I hid behind a Dumpster and tore open a packet of sausages with my teeth. Saying the *boudin noir* tasted like a chewy, salty blood popsicle cannot express the amazing scrumptiousness of this frozen confection. After gobbling the sausages, I chomped a piece of gum to freshen my breath.

The snack had made me thirsty, so I decided to drop in at the local watering hole. Lefty's Happy Looky-Dat! Club looked like the result of a fatal collision between a Western bar and a Victorian whorehouse. Which is to say: red velvet flocked wallpaper, brass chandeliers, mounted animal heads, ornate gilded mirrors, rusty horse shoes, stolen highway signs, and spittoons.

I checked out the crowd, and they checked out me. It was a surprisingly mixed group of people, mostly white, but with Latinos, African-Americans, and a few Asians, too. The majority wore jeans, but a few people wore business clothes, rumpled after a long day.

One fellow caught my attention because he was sitting by himself, a pile of newspapers and notebooks on the table in front of him. He was a paunchy man in his forties with a receding hairline in a plaid short-sleeved shirt. I sat at the empty table next to his and looked around.

"There's no waitress," the man said, glancing my way. "Let me get you the house special."

He was gone before I could say "No thanks." He conferred with the annoyed bartender and returned with an unlabeled wine bottle and two glasses.

"Lefty makes his own wine. It won't win any prizes, but it hasn't killed anyone yet."

The pale gold wine glugged out of the bottle as he poured. "I'm Bernie Vines."

"Milagro De Los Santos."

He grinned. "Finally in La Basura there is a *milagro de los santos*. We've been waiting long enough."

"I've wondered how this town got this name," I said.

"One of my favorite stories." He took a sip of his wine and made a face. "Once there was a Spanish don who had a beautiful but troublesome mistress named Carmelita. He owned this land and built a hacienda for her, saying that he would join her soon. But he never came—he'd just thrown her out like the trash, *la basura,* and she went mad with waiting. Some say that

Carmelita still waits for him. If you listen to the wind you can hear her calling him."

"I hope she's calling him bad names," I said. "Is that story true?"

Bernie shrugged. "Could be, or it could be that radioactive waste was dumped here once."

"Which do you believe?"

"Night like this, I'm inclined to hear Carmelita's lonesome cry as I wend my way home."

"You're a poetic soul, Bernard. What is it you do?"

"By day, I'm a high school English teacher. I'm also a stringer for the *Weekly Exposition*."

"The tabloid? The one that runs stories about alien babies and two-headed goats?"

"I see you're familiar with our illustrious publication," he said with a smirk. "Your turn. What do you do?"

I tried not to sound as if I was bragging when I told him about my rewriting job. I didn't tell him the name of the screenwriter, but I did say, "The script's got a lunatic beauty."

"Now you're the one with the poetic soul." He asked about the plot and when I mentioned chupacabras, he started laughing.

"What?" I said.

"I've written a couple of stories about chupa sightings for the *Weekly Exposition* is all," he said.

"You expect me to believe that you've seen a chupacabra?" I asked, laughing.

"Milagro, in the desert, you see all sorts of things. Chupas, werewolves, aliens, vampires, Elvis . . ." He was watching me as he said this, and then I caught him glance across the room.

A woman sitting with a few girlfriends was staring at us. She was in her late thirties, I guessed, and very attractive if you went for thin, extremely tan, extremely angry dames.

"A woman over there is staring daggers at you," I said. "I get the distinct feeling she'd rather be throwing them."

"That's my ex-wife. She dumped me for a golf pro at the Paragon."

"Why is she mad at you?"

"She never realized how much time golf pros spend playing golf. She thinks I should have told her before she kicked my ass to the curb." He shook his head, then snorted, "The Paragon!"

"What do you have against the Paragon?"

"Something bothers me about that place. There are things that happen in La Basura, and I wonder if there's a connection."

"What things?"

"Chupacabra attacks." He grinned, just daring me to question him. "Or something. People disappear and show up confused and burnt out a couple of days later."

"I live in the country, Bernie. It's an ugly secret that lots of bored people do lots of hard drugs," I said. "Has anyone actually seen a chupacabra? Anyone sober and sane?"

"I saw something once. Wouldn't bet that it was a chupa— but I wouldn't bet that it wasn't one."

I finished my drink. The wine had a very low alcohol content, because I'd had a few glasses and felt almost nothing. "I've got to take off," I said, picking up my bag of groceries. I didn't want the meat to go too long without refrigeration. "I'm expecting a call from my boyfriend."

"It's time for me to get home, too," he said.

He stood up and we walked out of the bar and directly into an argument. Technically, it wasn't an argument because one belligerent, hairy, large man was shouting and cursing at some poor old skinny drunk, who wavered on his feet. It was an extended rant with phrases repeated over and over with a Mamet-like rhythm and intensity. This La Basura Sasquatch made me yearn to curse, too, except that every time I did, I pictured my *abuelita* shaking her head in shame.

Then the large, angry man looked at Bernie and stopped shouting. "Uh, evening, Mr. Vines," he said politely.

"Get outta here, Joe," Bernie said. The man went into the bar, and the drunk crumpled to the ground. "Joe was one of my students," Bernie explained as we watched the drunk crawl on the sidewalk. "I didn't mind his bad temper, but he couldn't punctuate worth a damn. Since his abduction, all he does is rant."

"Abduction?"

"Joe went missing for three days. Came back dumber than ever. Give me a hand with this guy, will you?" Bernie went to the drunk and took one arm.

I steadied myself for the shock of gory visions, but when I took the drunk's arm . . . nothing. Nothing. Maybe I had overcome the nasty, cannibalistic condition. My joy was so great that I laughed out loud.

But before I had time to linger on this feeling, the drunk turned toward me. I was stunned. This shriveled old man was Thomas Cook. His copper skin, stretched tightly on high cheekbones, had a gray hue. There were dark hollows under his eyes, his clothes hung from his large, gaunt frame, and his straight black hair was greasy.

"Well, if it isn't Thomas Cook," Bernie said.

"Hey, baby," Thomas mumbled with an attempt at a leer.

It was a magical moment, the man of a million fantasies flirting with me. Of course, the fact that he was blind drunk and began retching immediately afterward somewhat tarnished the effect.

When Cook had emptied his guts and I'd nearly lost my dinner, Bernie handed him a crumpled tissue from his pocket.

"Wipe your mouth, Cook. Where're you staying?"

"Spa," Thomas said.

Bernie looked at me. "Can you give him a ride back?"

"Actually, one of the drivers dropped me off in town so I could pick up some groceries."

If Bernie thought this was strange, and he did, he didn't say. "You can drive his car." Bernie shook Thomas's shoulder. "Cook, where's your car?"

The actor muttered something about PCH and a party and the police and "I was set up."

Bernie frowned and said, "I'll take him back. You coming?"

"Sure. I call shotgun."

We hauled Thomas into the backseat of a beat-up brown car, rolling down the window so he could hang his head out like a dog.

"You aren't going to write about this for the *Weekly Exposition,* are you?"

Bernie glanced my way. "A has-been is not news. No one cares about this guy anymore."

Thomas was snoring loudly. I looked back at him and thought that people should care about him, people *would* care about him again.

Once we got to the Paragon, we tried unsuccessfully to find out his room number. He kept muttering, "Nine-oh-two-one-oh."

"Isn't that too long to be a room number?" I asked.

"It's the zip code for Beverly Hills. Look, it's better if you keep him tonight to make sure he doesn't choke on his vomit."

"Why me?"

"I've got to teach tomorrow. All you're doing is writing."

"No one thinks writing is work," I complained.

"That's because it isn't."

We threw Thomas in the back of a golf cart and took him to my casita.

Bernie picked up Thomas under the arms, and I took his feet. Bernie was walking backward, looking over his shoulder as we walked through the gate and the small courtyard, and into my casita. "Swanky," he said.

"Tell me about it."

The actor was too long for the sofa, so we deposited him on the bed. I put mineral water and aspirin on the nightstand, and then I went back to the main room.

Bernie was surveying the view out the windows to the lighted pool. "How'd you score this?"

"The production company is paying for it." I stared at the surface of the pool. "He used to be so wonderful. What happened?"

"He wasn't immune to the hype." Bernie shook his head. "Live fast, die young, leave a good-looking corpse."

"That's a harsh judgment."

"Milagro, after J-school, I covered celebrities for five years. The stories were all the same. I just switched out the names as the actors came and went."

I must have looked disappointed, because he added, "Okay, Cook was something special. He seemed like a decent guy. He had some greedy management, got ripped off, made some bad decisions about his roles. His ex-wife took him to the cleaners.

If he gives you any trouble tonight, thwack him over the head with something solid."

"I'll be fine," I said.

As he left, Bernie said, "Milagro, you seem like a nice girl. Don't get sucked into this business."

When Bernie was safely gone, I took my groceries to the kitchenette. I shoved the sausages in the freezer behind the ice cube bin. Then I removed the livers from the containers and put them down the disposal. I moved as quickly and quietly as I could, hoping that Thomas was a sound sleeper. I poured out a bottle of Paragon's High Antioxidant Refreshing Berry Smoothie, rinsed the bottle, and poured in the blood from the livers. I put the bottle behind the other juices and mineral waters.

I washed up and changed into one of the pretty nightgowns that Oswald gave me, but when I went to my makeshift bed on the sofa, the fabric kept twisting uncomfortably around me in a tragic case of style over function. I stared at the ceiling, listening to the water lapping in the pool. Nothing seemed real anymore.

Every time I closed my eyes, I kept thinking of the vampire nightclub, remembering the madness on the faces that had gathered in the club for the bloodletting ceremony, the unnerving black script of the ancient book, and the language that predated reason.

My dreams were dark and incoherent, but frightening. I remembered knives, blood, and running from something. I kept waking up in terror, unable to separate the danger of my nightmares from the dangers of my real life. At least I'd overcome the worst symptom of my condition. I could return to the ranch when I was done here. I could hold Libby again, and I could deal with Oswald and his family face-to-face.

fourteen

the man who came for nachos

Horrible noises woke me. I was on my feet and ready to fight before I was even fully awake. I slipped on a silk wrap and stood still. Then it came again, a loud, unearthly "Agggh, Agggh!" cry, and it was getting closer.

Thomas Cook, his emaciated body clad only in boxers, walked into the room. He squinted against the sunlight streaming through the windows and scratched his hairy underarm. Upright, he was taller than I thought, over six feet. When he caught sight of me, he looked surprised, but then gave me a cool once-over. "Hey, baby," he said in his famous gravelly voice, "have a good time last night?"

"Sure, if you define a good time as hauling an unconscious *pendejo* from a bar into my bed."

"You wanted me that bad," he said with a grin.

Damn, if I didn't still see the appeal of this man. Sexiness radiated from him, like heat from hot asphalt.

"Do we know each other?" he asked.

"I know who you are. I'm Milagro De Los Santos and I'm working on the 'Teeth of Sharpness' rewrite for Skip Taylor. I found you in town last night and brought you back here."

"That's quite a name. Is it real?" His eyes dropped lower. "Are those?" He didn't wait for an answer but sat on the sofa, picked up the phone, and dialed room service. He ordered an enormous breakfast and as an afterthought said, "Do you want anything?"

I ordered fresh raspberry crepes and cranberry juice.

Thomas hung up the phone and said, "Think I'll have a shower."

"Yes, do make yourself at home." I said it sarcastically, but he didn't seem to notice. "And wash your hair!" I shouted after him.

The food arrived just as Thomas came out of the shower wrapped in a thick terry Paragon robe. He had a towel twisted around his hair the way women wear them, and the overall effect was vaguely regal. It was one of those actor things.

"How do you feel?" I asked as he examined his roasted vegetable omelet. The skin around his eyes looked like crumpled tissue paper, and he looked at least a decade older than I knew he might be.

"Like death warmed over," he said. "Okay for a vampire."

I almost spit out my juice. "What did you say?"

He said, "See if there's any hot sauce in the kitchen."

"I'm not your servant."

Thomas looked hurt. "Latinas are usually such good hostesses."

"Fine, whatever." I got up and went to the kitchen. In the cupboards with a supply of upscale condiments was a bottle of salsa picante. I put it on the table in front of him. "So you think you're a vampire?" I asked in a flat voice.

"That's what my therapist says. Emotional vampire. Sucks the life right out of a relationship."

I relaxed. "Really?"

He drank an entire glass of orange juice before saying, "I'll show you." He went into the bedroom and came back carrying his trousers. After rooting around in the pockets, he gave me a folded sheet of paper with the caption "DSM-IV Diagnostic Criteria for Narcissistic Personality Disorder."

I read aloud, "'The Narcissistic Vampire Checklist.' It's a true-or-false quiz. Do you think you're more successful than others your age?"

"Obviously."

"Are you convinced you're better-looking, brighter, et cetera, than others?"

"Sure."

"Are you a name dropper?" I asked.

"Does it count when everyone I know is famous?"

"Do you think it's critical for you to live in the right place and socialize with the right people?"

"That's what my manager tells me."

We went through the rest of the list and he answered yes to nearly all of the questions. It occurred to me that most F.U. alumni would also score high.

Handing him back the page, I said, "I think this quiz is for people who really aren't handsome and successful."

"And special and smart," he added thoughtfully.

"How could I forget?" I said. "I wouldn't take the diagnosis that seriously."

"Man, I knew that vampire thing was bogus. What do you know about psychology?"

I told him that I had taken Psych 101 at F.U. He seemed

to think that made me qualified to debunk his therapist.

"Are you here to dry out?" I asked.

"No, I've got to bulk up for 'Teeth.' I just played a POW in an Italian production so I had to go all anorexic. A couple of drinks in town and I was wrecked."

"How did you get to La Basura, anyway?"

"Good question. If you find out, let me know."

He finished his meal and went to the front door. "Have housekeeping clean and press my clothes and send them to my room."

I walked him to the gate and said, "Say please and thank you."

He opened the gate. "*Por favor* and *muchas gracias.*"

Thomas suddenly kissed me full on the mouth, but he did it in a professional, impersonal way.

"There's your thrill for today. If I get bored, I'll look you up," he said, walking toward the main building. I glanced around and saw Bernie Vines standing by a golf cart, closing a camera case.

"Bernie!" I shouted.

"Morning, Milagro. Gotta run!" Bernie said, hopping into the golf cart. "Hey, Tom, you want a ride?"

Thomas, distinguished as a sheik in his robe and turban, stepped into the cart and asked, "Do I know you?"

"Sure, we met last night. Bernie Vines, at your service."

I wanted to throw rocks at both of them, but just then my phone began to ring.

I picked up and said, "Hello."

There was a sound like wind or hollowness, and then I heard Oswald say, "Hey, babe."

My heart rose at the sound of his voice. "Oswald! Why haven't you called? I thought . . ."

"It was only an argument, Milagro," he said, and sounded very stressed. "We've got patients lined up for a block outside of the clinic, and the surgeries are scheduled from morning until late at night, and at the end of my shift I can hardly stand. It's the best thing I've ever done."

It was now official: he was a saint and I was a terrible girlfriend. "That's wonderful, Oswald."

"Sam said that you are at Mercedes's. Say hi to her for me."

I didn't want to upset the important work he was doing, so I said, "I was, but, um, I decided to stay at Nancy's for a while. She's on her honeymoon, and I can write peacefully here." The line began crackling with static. "I got a rewrite job."

"What did you say?" he asked.

"I said . . ." And the static now sounded like a roomful of obsessive-compulsives popping bubble wrap.

"Bad connection. It's hard to get reception here and I've only got a few fast breaks in the day."

I heard about every fourth word as he talked excitedly about the work he was doing and described the kids coming to the clinic and a young surgeon he was training.

Oswald said he'd try to call again in a few days. Then there was nothing but crackling on the line. I said, "Hello? Hello? Oswald, are you still there?" but no one answered.

I would feel better after a shower. But when I went to the bathroom, wet towels were crumpled in a corner, and the carefully handmade, soy-ink packaging of complimentary Paragon products was strewn on the floor. Small bottles of lotion spilled their contents on the counter.

I showered and had to wash my hair with the teaspoon of shampoo left in the bottle. After dressing in a spa-appropriate outfit of white blouse and khaki pants, I straightened the room as best I could so that the cleaning staff wouldn't think I was a complete *cochina*.

I drank a glass of mineral water mixed with a tablespoon of blood, then began working on "Teeth of Sharpness." Housekeeping came and I hovered around the kitchen nervously, and told the maid in Spanish that I didn't need the refrigerator restocked while I was here.

In the afternoon, I went to the lobby of the main building. The vampire family was on my mind, which is probably why I imagined that I saw Gabriel's back. The man I spotted was with an older couple, though, and he was arm in arm with a young woman. I almost followed them into the restaurant, but I realized that the stiff-legged man couldn't be my graceful friend.

Charles's head popped up at the concierge station and he smiled my way. I went to his desk and said, "Hi, Charles. I thought I saw a friend of mine here, Gabriel Grant. Can you see what room he's in?"

Charles bent to his computer and hit a few keys. "Sorry, no one here by that name."

"Redheaded fellow with parents and a young woman?"

"Oh," he said with a smile, "I know who you mean. That's not his name. The whole family has been coming here for years."

"My mistake. I didn't see his face. Have you heard about my truck?"

"I just talked to the mechanic. He didn't have a chance to look at it yet, but he promised to get back to me later today. I would be happy to arrange a driver for you if you need one."

"No, that's okay. I'll be working today."

I was turning to leave when he asked me if I planned to take advantage of the spa services. "We offer twenty-seven kinds of massage, including our Paragon Mineral Water Therapy. If you are seeking a more spiritual experience, may I suggest the Walk-about Dream Therapy, which simulates all the stages of an abo-riginal walkabout in one ninety-minute session. Many of our guests enjoy the Agave Massage, which helps drain toxins from your lymphatic system and restores balance."

This would be a good opportunity to test my endurance to human touch. "So many to choose from. What is the Mineral Water Therapy?"

"That's very special," Charles said. "Your massage therapist submerges you in an aged oak tub of hot spring water and works on those places of dense tissue. A nose plug is provided."

"That sounds, um, interesting, but I don't suppose you have regular deep-tissue massages?"

He looked disappointed. "Yes, of course. Shiatsu, Thai, Ko-rean, sports deep muscle . . . we have the traditional treatments. Here is a brochure with all the descriptions." He handed me a pamphlet printed on handmade paper.

I opened it and glanced through a list of oddball therapies. I thought of how nice it would be to feel another person's hands taking care of me. I'd been deprived of physical contact when I lived at my parents' home and now I sought out touch like a cat seeks a petting. "The deep-muscle massage will be fine. If you could set something up for tomorrow, I'd appreciate it."

There was a bistro in an interior courtyard and I had a very healthy and tasty salad of organic greens dressed in a citrus vinaigrette. As I was enjoying a leisurely meal by myself in this chic resort, I pretended that things were improving in my little world. My state-of-the-*chica* assessment was: fab career develop-ment correlating with financial improvement. Relationship is-sues could be worked out.

A man in a wheelchair, his face obscured by a hat, bandages, and dark glasses, sat at a far table. Even his hands were covered in bandages. An attendant cut his food and carefully fed it to him, making me realize that my own health was not so bad. Perhaps I had been staring at the mummy man, because he seemed to be looking right at me. I couldn't tell through his sunglasses. I quickly looked away.

Ian would take care of Silas and then I could go home as a successful screenwriter. Mrs. Grant couldn't say I didn't have a career then.

The invalid kept his face turned in my direction, and he made me uneasy, even if he wasn't actually looking at me. I finished my lunch and put a big tip on the table.

When I got close to my casita, I saw the front door open. I knew I had locked it, and housekeeping had already cleaned. I approached cautiously. Two large leather suitcases blocked the threshold. I shoved them aside and heard splashing. Through the open French doors, I saw the dark head and brown body of someone in the pool. The naked person had the general size and shape of a man, and the specific size and shape of Thomas Cook.

I looked down at the suitcases and saw a TC monogram.

"Hey," I said as I walked outside. "Hey!"

Thomas swam to the edge of the pool. "What's up?" he said as a greeting, not an inquiry.

"Why are you here and how did you get in?"

"A housekeeper let me in."

"Isn't that against Paragon policy? Why would she do that?"

"Because I'm Thomas Cook." He hauled himself out of the water with the lack of inhibition common to children, models, and the insane, creatures comfortable with nudity. Yes, I could have averted my gaze, but I told myself that I really needed direct eye contact to convey the depth of my annoyance. If my gaze happened to drift south, it was purely accidental.

"These jerks gave my room away. Get me a towel, would you?"

I was already fetching the towel when I realized he was ordering me around. "Get it yourself."

"Okay, I didn't want to get the floor wet."

"Oh, all right," I said. When I returned with a towel, I said, "Why were you kicked out?"

He shrugged his bony shoulders. "I couldn't get that straight. Maybe I checked out when I was ripped?" he said, as if he was asking me for an answer.

"They must have another room for you. I'll call the front desk and see."

"Actually, they were kind of hostile. They said something about damages." Thomas left the towel on the cement and walked inside.

I put the towel across a chair to dry and followed him inside. Picking up the hotel phone, I said, "I'm sure we can straighten this out." I pressed the "front desk" button and someone answered, "Front desk, would you please hold?"

"Yes," I said. I listened to soothing pan pipe music and glanced around for Thomas. I hoped he'd gone to put on some clothes.

The music stopped and a voice said, "Thank you for your patience. How may I help you, Ms. De Los Santos?"

"Hi, I was wondering if you had a—"

I heard a banging sound coming from the kitchenette.

"Ms. De Los Santos?"

"I'll have to get back to you later," I said, and hung up the phone.

181

When I got to the kitchenette, Thomas was just lifting the bottle of blood to his mouth.

"Don't do that!" I said.

But it was too late. He yelled, "Yahhg!" and spit out the blood, slamming the plastic bottle on the counter; a few precious drops of thick red liquid spurted out onto the floor. As he stepped away from the mess, he slid and fell.

"What the hell is that?" he said.

"What is what?" I said. "It's a Paragon protein drink."

He started laughing. "Leave the acting for the pros." He dipped his finger into a drop of the red liquid and smelled it. "It's blood. I went out with this girl and she was into the vampire Goth scene. Do you drink it or smear it on for sex?"

"My personal life is—"

"You can get sick that way. Yeah, I thought there was something freaky about you."

As he got up, he grimaced. "I think I sprained my ankle. Not that it was your fault, exactly, but my manager might think so. You know how they are, always wanting to call in the lawyers and sue."

He dispassionately surveyed his naked body. "Do you know there's a moral turpitude clause in film contracts, and Skip could have cause to fire you if he knew you were so kinky?"

"Why do I get the feeling that you're quoting your own agent? I don't have a contract."

"Then you really don't want this to come out. I feel like some Mexican food."

And that was how I was blackmailed into becoming the personal assistant and general dogsbody of a spoiled, egocentric Hollywood has-been.

fifteen

indentured sillitude

Thomas spent the afternoon naked by the pool, which was very distracting. I called Mercedes and updated her on recent developments.

You would think that Mercedes would be fascinated by a naked movie star in full frontal view, but she was accustomed to the exhibitionist behavior of musicians. "Did you tell him to put on some clothes?"

"Yes, and he told me to grow up," I answered. "I thought I saw Gabriel here today. But it was some dweeb in pants with a pouchy butt and a girlfriend." I told her about Gabriel's mysterious sabbatical and my friends' secrecy on the subject.

"Maybe he just doesn't want to deal with any hassles right now."

"But that's not like Gabriel. He likes jumping into the fray and fixing everything." I looked out toward the pool and sighed deeply.

"What was that sigh for?"

"Thomas just turned over. He looks ancient and awful, yet I still associate him with my teenage crush. I thought that being in love would mean that I wouldn't lust for other men, but I still do. Is something wrong with me?"

"Yes, you should grow up."

"Back on point, I'm worried about Gabriel and not just because I'm concerned about the neovamps."

"Precúpate de tú misma."

"Okay, but I don't see any purpose in worrying about myself. It just makes me all angsty and Latinos don't do angst well."

"When was the last time you listened to Astor Piazzolla or *any* tango? When was the last time you read Cortázar?"

Thomas started calling, "Milagro! Milagro!" and so I said good-bye to my friend and went outside.

"Yes?"

"What about that Mexican food? I want an enchilada platter. Whole beans, not refried."

"Where am I going to find that?"

"There's a Mexicatessen in La Basura."

"My truck is being repaired."

"Have one of the drivers take you." He closed his eyes.

I called Charles, who told me that all the drivers were booked for the afternoon. He then said, "Our chefs are happy to accommodate your dietary preferences. But if you would like food from town, I will have it delivered to you immediately."

I asked him to order the food, and then told Thomas that it would arrive soon. I decided to go for a run. The Paragon sunscreen was pleasantly sage-scented and I put some on before I trotted off. I kept to a leisurely pace. When I was far out of view of the spa grounds, I picked up speed, enjoying the sensation of the hot, dry sun on my face.

I saw a lovely yellow and black bird flitting in a Joshua tree and even spotted a few waxy pink blooms atop the spiny arms of cacti. As I ran, I began to appreciate the subtle brown and tan palate of the soil.

When I returned to the casita, Skip and Thomas were lounging on the sofa, drinking Paragon's mineral-and-vitamin-enriched water.

"Why aren't you writing?" Skip asked.

Thomas gave me a disappointed look, as if he had just learned that one of my hobbies was drowning puppies. "I thought she should be working," he said quietly.

I wanted to slug the snitch right on his enchilada-scarfing mouth. "I needed to stretch my legs. I was going to get back to work right now."

"Show me what you've got so far," Skip said.

I followed him into the study and he closed the door behind me. "Milagro, I really appreciate that you're taking a personal interest in Thomas."

"About that . . ."

"And, naturally, if you can assist him, I'll be very grateful."

"What do you mean, assist?"

Skip had a nervous heh-heh-heh laugh. "Nothing sexual, unless, you know. But keep him working out, eating right, preparing for his role." He looked me in the eyes and said, "Can I count on you?"

As if I had a choice. "Sure, Skip. I'll do what I can."

"Good!" he said, and put his hand on my shoulder.

Red, wet, slick, twisting color came into my head, a kaleidoscope of gore. Skip was already turning to the papers on my desk. Knowing that I was still a monster depressed me so much that I could barely listen to anything he said.

I would have to enter some monastery, wear drab, rough clothes woven from weeds and bark, and seek spiritual fulfillment outside of society.

Skip reached into his pocket and pulled out a small white paper bag. "These might help him," he said as he handed the bag to me. "He didn't want them, but if there's no significant improvement in his appearance, maybe you could talk to him."

Inside the bag were bubble packs with white pills. "What is this, Skip?"

"Nutritional supplements. Vitamins," he said smoothly.

I examined the packs, but there were no manufacturers' marks on the pills or the foil backing of the bubble packs.

Skip took them from me and slipped them in a desk drawer. "You'd be doing Thomas a favor."

A treadmill arrived just as Skip was leaving. We watched as two delivery guys finessed it through the doorway and into the middle of the main room.

"I'm sure the Paragon has a workout room," I said with dismay.

Skip dropped his voice and said to me, "The Paragon isn't really happy having Thomas around, so keep him on the down low."

The rest of Thomas's exercise gear came shortly thereafter. The stark furniture was pushed against the walls to accommodate bulky metal contraptions.

I threw myself into writing with desperate zeal. So long as I was concentrating on the various plotlines and characters, I didn't have to think about my own situation.

"Milagro! Milagro!" Thomas shouted through the door.

I didn't bother getting up from my desk. "What is it?"

"I can't find my shoes. Did you put them somewhere?"

His shoes were under the bed, where he had kicked them. Although he didn't seem to be doing anything but pumping iron, lolling in the pool, and consuming protein shakes, Thomas still liked to interrupt me for menial tasks. He had me kill a wasp that was buzzing against a window. He made me hold a mirror at different angles so he could examine his haircut. He asked for and then corrected my opinions on A-list movie stars. He needed to have his shirts organized from light to dark, solids to patterns.

"Milagro!" he bellowed from the pool.

I stuck a dark patterned shirt between a white one and a beige one and went outside. *"Sí, Señor Tomás."*

"Suntan lotion on my back."

"I'm not rubbing this on your butt."

"Do you know how much people would pay to do that? Just put it on my shoulders."

I picked up the bottle of Paragon Organic Sun Elixir with Beneficial Emollients, squeezed the liquid into my palm, braced myself for contact, and then tentatively touched his shoulders.

"What is your problem?" Thomas asked. "Put a little muscle into it."

I touched his shoulders again, but there were no horrific results from the contact. My fingers massaged and caressed his copper-hued skin. I was touching Thomas Cook, and I felt a buzz run through me as I remembered his film roles—and love scenes.

"That's more like it," Thomas said with a satisfied sigh. "I can tell you're into me."

I was glad he couldn't see my face. "I am absolutely not into you, Thomas."

He laughed. "Sure. Keep rubbing."

"I already told you I live with my boyfriend. His name is Oswald."

"Nobody's named Oswald. You're the worst liar I've ever met. Look, Milagro, you're here, I'm here, and if you want to, you know, whatever, I'm cool with that. Don't expect anything long term, though, because you've got it going on, but you're not my type."

I stopped massaging his shoulders and calmed myself. I stepped in front of him, thinking, don't look down, don't look down, whatever happens, don't look down. "Thomas, while your offer is more than generous, I'm afraid I'll have to decline because, one, I love Oswald, and two, you are a monumental jackass."

He stared at me and shook his head. "You know, you're kind of judgmental for someone into blood games. Can you move? You're blocking my rays."

Something occurred to me and I asked, "Do you have a health condition?"

He looked puzzled. "I told you, I'm not here to dry out."

"No, I meant something else, something that makes you different. An illness maybe?"

He shrugged slightly and said, "I've got mild anemia."

"Do you need to take medication?"

"No, but I probably shouldn't have starved down for that last role."

"Skip gave me some pills and was trying to tell me they're nutritional supplements. He wanted me to get you to take them."

"Yeah, he was trying to push those 'roids on me earlier. I'm not gonna have my *huevos* shrivel up like olives."

Later, when Thomas was in the shower, I had a blood spritzer. I washed and washed the glass and then I pushed it to the back of the cabinet.

Thomas got bored and decided that we needed to go to La Basura for drinks.

"No. We don't even have a way of getting there."

"Call your friend Bernie for a ride."

"I barely know him," I said. "I don't have his number."

"He gave me his card."

A few minutes later I was feeling really foolish as I called Bernie and asked for a ride into town. He was more than happy to pick us up, but said he couldn't make it for at least an hour. That gave me time to shower and put on a dress and makeup. I didn't know if it was the Paragon shampoo and conditioner, but my hair fell smooth and glossy over my shoulders.

Because Thomas was the celebrity, he rode in the front seat of Bernie's junker. Thomas had pulled a few designer clothes out of his suitcases and had put together a fashionably disheveled outfit.

I'd worn a casual deep lavender dress for the occasion, and I hoped I wasn't sitting on something gross in the backseat. Yellowed copies of the *Weekly Exposition* and other newspapers were piled on the floor and seat.

"Flying Bloodsucking Monster!" screamed a huge headline. The byline said, "Bernard Vines, Field Correspondent." The adjective-laden article was a thrilling account of a missing young female teacher from La Basura who'd gone for a walk in the desert, never to be seen again. Two witnesses who'd been out drinking beer and shooting bottles nearby had heard screams and seen a terrible creature coming from the sky and carrying her off.

"Nice story about the chupacabra, Bernard," I said. "You have a compelling style, except for the hyperbole."

"A tabloid without exaggeration is like a cat without fur: curious, but not appealing," Bernie said. "You have good eyesight to be reading in the dark."

"Abnormal pupils," I said, hoping I'd named the correct body part. Should I have said retinas or corneas? I felt pretty stupid now for making fun of my F.U. friends who struggled with human bio courses while I was going to loony poetry seminars. "Is any part of this story true?"

"It's all true. Maybe the woman just ran off with her best friend's husband, but maybe not. Some strange stuff happens here, especially near the Paragon."

Lefty's Happy Looky-Dat! Club was jumping by the time we got there. Bernie carried a brown paper bag and led us to two tables in the corner. A young couple was already sitting at one and Bernie said, "Get lost. I've got stuff to do."

"Yes, Mr. Vines. Is this your girlfriend?"

"Out!" Bernie barked. Once they were gone he said, "Former students." Then he pulled a stack of papers out of the bag and put them on the table in front of me, along with two red ballpoint pens. "Here, grade these."

I flipped through the papers and saw they were two-page essays on race relations in *To Kill a Mockingbird*. "Bernie, I know *nada* about grading high school papers."

"I mark down for useless filler and repetition. Otherwise grade however you want."

Thomas was recognized by a few customers, and pretty soon

he was holding forth, telling stories about his career. He was an amusing raconteur, making significant eye contact with the prettier women present, pausing for effect, dishing some intriguing dirt on celebrities.

If you listened under the surface of his anecdotes, you heard what I thought was the real story. His mother was an indigenous Indian from Central America who only spoke her tribal language when she found herself in Los Angeles and one of her employers took advantage of her. Thomas had no idea what his father's real name was or where he was.

I went through the essays, correcting typos and spelling errors, and writing comments in the margins. I tried to keep an annoyed expression on my face, but I really enjoyed reading the students' opinions, especially the eccentric ones.

Bernie came to check on me on his way back from buying another round. "How's it going?"

"I worked all day on a screenplay, you know."

"Writing is not work. We already established that."

"Right, how could I forget?" I held up a few essays that I liked. "These are rather perceptive. Why is La Basura so diverse for such an isolated community?"

"There was a train station here once. It brought in different groups. When it closed, they stayed."

I looked around at the mix of people in the bar. "It's nice. I like it."

"Hurry and finish up. The show's about to start."

As we listened to an Edith Piaf impersonator performing on a tiny stage, I thought that I was having altogether too much fun, as if I really didn't believe there was anything wrong with me. Mercedes was right: how could anyone take my condition seriously when I myself didn't? I sunk so deeply into self-recrimination that I could barely join in the sing-along for the encore of "Non, Je Ne Regrette Rien."

Bernie sat back and listened. Occasionally he would direct a comment about literature to me. He liked books set in the desert, from Westerns to ghost stories.

"Why?" I asked.

"The landscape is so alien, it's like we're on another planet," he said. "What's going on between you and Thomas?"

"Nothing. I have a boyfriend."

"Right, I forgot . . . maybe because you're hooked up with this knucklehead." He tilted his head toward Thomas, who was drinking a shot of Pernod out of a woman's cleavage.

"Why did you take pictures of Thomas leaving my place?"

"Old habits die hard," he muttered. "You never know when you'll get something good."

"I am not hooked up with Thomas. In fact, even if I was interested in him, which is laughable, I am not his type."

Bernie gave me a long up-and-down look. "Hon, you're everybody's type."

Socializing over a few drinks made me think of the ranch, and I found myself missing Edna's snipes and the *espíritu de los cocteles,* that relaxed camaraderie that came over us as we watched the sunset. Although I'd had several glasses of Lefty's high-octane *vin de table,* I felt only the faintest buzz. I recalled that Ian never showed the effects of alcohol no matter how much he drank.

"I'm tired," I said. "I'd like to go back."

We dragged Thomas out of Lefty's and headed back toward the Paragon. I was in the backseat feeling melancholy when Bernie slowed down and said, "Did you hear that?"

He pulled the car over to the side of the road and rolled down his window. I did the same. Somewhere in the distance came an eerie animal screech. Bernie must have fantastic hearing to have noticed it before I, with all my enhancements, did.

"What is that?" I asked.

"Coyote," Thomas muttered. "Let's go."

The animal cried farther in the distance, as if it was traveling away from us.

Bernie said, "That isn't any kind of desert animal."

"No," I said, "you're not going to tell us that was a chupacabra."

"I'm only saying what it *isn't*," Bernie replied.

I pondered the identity of things, not only for what they are but for what they aren't. For much of my life, I'd defined myself by what I wasn't: the blond, tall, slim girl who always said the right thing, always wore the right clothes, and knew the rules for every social situation.

Those girls didn't find themselves out in the desert with tabloid writers and emotional vampires, scanning the skies for mythical critters.

"Aren't you curious?" Bernie asked.

We got out of the car and Thomas said, "Gotta go," as he ran off toward a clump of bushes.

"You think we know everything already?" Bernie asked as he took a camera out of the trunk. He was fiddling with flashes and other equipment.

"If there were chupacabras, legitimate scientists would have discovered them by now."

"Scientists are always discovering new species."

"Not flying monkey–goat killer species."

"So much is unknown in this life, and yet you are so skeptical," Bernie lamented.

"What the hell!" Thomas shouted. He came running back, zipping up his slacks.

I heard it then, the angry craw, the whooshing of large wings. Looking up, I saw shadows against the darker night. Large shadows. "Did you see that?" I asked.

"What is that thing?" Thomas replied.

Bernie began snapping photos and the flash of the camera blinded me when he shot toward my face. I blinked and then searched the sky. I saw only stars and the solid black shape of mountains in the distance.

The animal's cry was fainter now, followed by a yet fainter one. The creature had flown away.

"I've got a flashlight somewhere." Bernie went to his trunk again and rooted around. He came back with a massive aluminum flashlight and clicked it on. We followed behind him as he scanned the ground.

"What are you looking for?" I asked.

"Like pornography, I'll know it when I see it."

I pretended to keep my eyes on the beam of light, but my night vision allowed me to see far beyond the one bright circle to the beetles scampering away, spiders, a translucent old snakeskin. With my super-vision, I should have been able to catch a better look at the flying animal.

A breeze blew and I shivered at a familiar scent.

Bernie stopped walking and said, "I see it."

Blood had clotted the sandy soil around the fresh carcass. When I forced my stare away from the purple, shining entrails that spilled out of the gaping wound, I saw that the animal was a sheep. Thomas and I crouched down for a closer look and Bernie took more pictures.

"Stop that," I said. "It's a dead sheep. What's it doing out here anyway?"

"Something brought it here," Bernie said.

"Maybe it got away and wandered here," I said. "Coyotes got it. That's happened at the ranch."

"Can coyotes do that?" Thomas pointed to the jagged rip on the sheep's belly.

The blood was so thick and rich. It glistened alluringly. The air was perfumed with the sweet scent of blood and the rancid lanolin of the wool. I jumped up and rushed off.

"Are you okay?" Bernie called.

"I'll be fine," I said.

I overheard Thomas tell Bernie, "I think she's going to be sick."

I wasn't going to be sick, but I needed to get away before I dipped my hand into the wet flesh and put it to my mouth. They were looking in the wrong direction for a monster; I was right in front of them. I walked in circles and tried to collect myself.

Thomas wondered if they should bury the sheep, but Bernie said he'd like to come back after school and take it so it could be examined.

"Good idea," I said as we returned to the car. "That way you'll find out that it was killed by a feral dog or some other predator. I bet there are mountain lions nearby."

When we were in the casita and I was gathering a pillow and my nightclothes, Thomas said, "You got excited, didn't you, by that blood. You don't need to explain to me. I'm open about things."

"A chupacabra didn't kill that sheep."

"Bernie's crazy," he said, and was done with the subject. He flicked on the television, then patted the bed and said, "There's enough room here for both of us. Come sleep with me."

"I have a boyfriend."

He gave me an annoyed look and said, "What about 'not my type' don't you understand? If I wanted you, I could have you."

"You are beyond delusional," I said. The sofa had been very uncomfortable and the luxurious bed was about the size of a football field. "Okay, but you have to at least wear boxers, and if you try anything I will pummel you to within an inch of your life."

"I am not going to 'try anything.' You are so conceited, you think every man wants you," he said. "See a therapist."

I went to the bathroom, washed up, and changed into my nightgown. Then I turned off the lights in the bedroom before I slipped into bed. Thomas was flipping rapidly through the stations when I saw a familiar black-and-white image. "Turn that back. It's *The Third Man*."

Thomas wanted to watch celebrity news, but I kept arguing until I got my way and we both settled into watching the classic film. Mercedes had introduced me to the movie. She'd been excited by the weird and wacky score by Anton Karas, with one lone zither playing. Mercedes only liked movies when she liked the music.

Joseph Cotten plays an American pulp novelist who goes to post–World War II Vienna to meet a friend. But he learns that his friend is dead. Or maybe not. Nothing is what it seems and the writer is misperceived, deceived, and manipulated. He eventually realizes that he's been a mere dupe in a game played by people far more corrupt and complicated than he ever would have imagined.

Before the movie was over, Thomas turned the sound down low. "Do you know that you were crying in your sleep last night?" he asked.

Embarrassed, I said, "I had nightmares."

"When I was little, my mom would take me with her when she went to clean offices." His gravelly voice was as comfortable as an old friend's. "One of the other cleaning ladies had a little girl. I don't remember her name, but she had the prettiest brown eyes with long lashes, and long black braids.

"We'd have a nighttime snack of instant hot chocolate. Then our mothers would fold blankets under a big desk for us and we'd lie there. The noise from the vacuum cleaners scared the little girl, so we'd face each other like this," he said, scooting down and turning toward me. "Face me," he said.

I was curious so I turned toward him.

"And I'd hold her hand like this," he said, taking my hand, and I felt comforted and safe. "So whenever she woke up, she'd see me and she wasn't afraid anymore. *Buenas noches,* Milagro."

"*Buenas noches, Tomás."* It was strange, facing him like that, but I was suddenly so sleepy I couldn't keep my eyes open. I felt his warm breath on my face and heard the water lapping against the sides of the pool. I slipped into deep, marvelous, dreamless sleep.

sixteen

retreating from sanity

When I opened my eyes, I saw that I was still facing Thomas, still holding his hand. Our foreheads were practically touching. The morning light was kind to him, and he looked much better than he had yesterday.

He opened his eyes and smiled his gorgeous Hollywood smile. "Did you sleep well?"

I couldn't remember ever sleeping so soundly, and I was relieved that I hadn't had any disturbing dreams involving Ian. "Amazingly well. How about you?"

"Terrific." He stared at me and said, "How'd you get mixed up in that freaky blood-drinking scene? Did your boyfriend drag you into it?"

"Yes and no," I answered. "It was an accident in a way and now I'm part of it."

"Where are your real clothes? All the black stuff you guys like to wear?"

"I left them at home because I wanted Skip to think I was professional."

He got out of bed and stretched.

"Thomas, I'm curious. What *is* your type?"

He did an up-and-down gesture in my direction. "Less like a girl."

"You mean you prefer guys?"

"Do I look like I'm into guys?" He snorted. "I'm into women."

"I *am* a woman."

"Not the way I like them."

That was as much of an explanation as he was prepared to give. He turned to more important matters, such as his breakfast and whether he should grow his sideburns longer.

Before I started working on "Teeth of Sharpness," I called the ranch.

Edna answered and snootily said, "I vaguely recall someone named Milagro who left here very abruptly."

I'd planned to confront them, demanding to know what they knew about Silas and the neovamps, but I found myself saying, "So you *do* miss me, Edna."

"Don't begin wallowing in cheap sentimentality, Young Lady."

"But that's my favorite kind," I said. "Oswald's called, but the connection was awful. Have you heard from him?"

"No, but he said phoning would be difficult. I know you must miss him."

It was such a polite response that it threw me off. "I miss him like crazy, Edna, but I'm very proud of him, too."

"Young Lady, Sam said something about you writing a screenplay."

"I did get a rewriting job. That's what I'm working on."

"Hmm."

"On another topic, I wanted to talk to Gabriel and he's got a strange message on his phone."

"Gabriel is occupied with other responsibilities at the moment. He doesn't have time for your fripperies."

"Is everything all right, Edna?"

"I wanted to ask the same of you." She paused and there we were, at a Mexican standoff. Or possibly a vampire standoff. "The baby is crying, so I have to go. If Oswald calls, I'll tell him you miss him."

"Edna, why do you and the family keep hiding things from me?" My voice quavered and I was close to tears. "Haven't I proved myself to you?"

"Young Lady, this is not a discussion to have over the phone. Libby's crying. We'll talk when you come back."

I hung up feeling lost and alone.

The phone rang immediately after. It was the spa reminding me of the massage Charles had scheduled for me. I worked on my screenplay until the appointment, and my mood of isolation and anxiety crept into my writing.

When I went into the main building, I followed the signs for the treatment center. A long hallway led to a wing of the building that was done in pale washes of peach and buff, or blish. Hidden speakers played water sounds, wind chimes, and birdsong.

After I checked in, I was guided to a warm room with dim lighting and scented candles. The receptionist told me to remove my clothes and put on a natural linen wrap.

I sat on the massage table and admired the photographs of desert plants on the walls until my therapist arrived. Small bells chimed on her anklets, and she said "Hello, I am Triveni" in a soft voice at odds with her large frame.

She was six feet with broad shoulders and muscled arms covered in henna tattoos. Her hair was hennaed red, in tiny braids with ribbons. Her hazel eyes were ringed dramatically with kohl, and I wondered if I could get away with that much eyeliner.

After I introduced myself, I asked, "What does your name mean?"

"It is the place where three sacred rivers meet," she said. She saw my expression and said, "But my parents named me Eugenia, after an aunt."

"No wonder you changed it."

She smiled quickly. Then she held her hands together and closed her eyes. "I will begin by asking you to breathe slowly with me."

We did this for a few minutes. I was glad Skip was picking up the tab for this treatment, because I could breathe for free on my own.

Triveni then lit a sage smudge stick and waved it around the room. "This is our circle of safety. In this place you will not be harmed. Do you feel safe here?"

Since there wasn't a group of neovamps intent on harvesting my blood, I said, "Sure. Totally."

"I will evaluate your energy field and see if there is an imbalance."

She asked me to stand and then held her hands palms forward toward me. She hummed off-key while moving her hands a few inches from all areas of my body. I thought this was loony, but I went along with it because she seemed so sincere. "You have a powerful life force," she said, "and are a conduit of regenerative energies."

"My friend Nancy says I have strong and confusing pheromones."

"Oh." Her hands hovered above my belly button. "I am sensing something unusual here, the Manipura chakra."

"What's that supposed to do?"

"It controls appetite, energy, currents of the life force. Lie down on your stomach, please."

I was glad I could hide my face for this procedure. Her hands slipped the robe down my back. When she touched me, I felt like I'd been prodded by an electric current. My body jolted as I hallucinated juicy, bloody, gory flesh, rivulets of blood, a purple heart pumping.

I was off the table and I'd flipped Triveni like a turtle onto the floor. I pinned her down, holding her hands above her head, and I could hear blood throbbing in my ears. She was as surprised as I was, especially since my *chichis* were swaying near her face.

Triveni uttered a word that you didn't expect to hear from someone at peace with herself.

I got off her as quickly as I could and pulled up my robe. I was dismayed at what I had just done and by the vision. "I'm so sorry. Are you okay?" I wanted to offer her a hand up, but was afraid I'd throw her over my shoulder.

"Holy frikken crap, what the hell was that?" Her soft spa voice was gone and I heard a Boston accent. Triveni sat up and rubbed her head. "How'd you do that?"

I remembered the spa brochure and said, "Very dense muscles. I'm really sorry. I can go now."

There was a knock at the door and someone said, "Is everything all right in there?"

Triveni didn't try getting up but called out, "All is at peace and harmony." We both stayed still until we heard footsteps receding.

Then Triveni hauled herself up. "What gives?"

"I'm kind of freaking out when anybody touches me. I think I have to work through this. Do you think you can help?"

"Have you been abused or raped?" she asked flat out. "Because then you really need a psychiatrist."

"No, but I've been ignored, and, um, stalked."

"Two extremes, hmm?" She thought for a moment. "No promises, but I can try if you pay me double for each session. And if you ever try that flip again, I'm gonna slap the taste right out of your mouth."

"Do you think you can actually help me?"

"Yeah, on the count of I'm a natural healer."

I had nothing to lose, especially since it was Skip's money.

By gripping the sides of the massage table, I was able to stop myself from repeating my earlier performance. Triveni worked on areas of my back, and I was so busy concentrating on not reacting to my bloodlust that I managed to blank out on most of her New Age yammering.

Enduring the massage was like taking the same roller-coaster ride over and over: if no less graphic, the images became less shocking.

When the session was over, Triveni scheduled me for another and recommended that I take a soak in one of the hot mineral baths to increase the benefits of the treatment. "The easiest way to get there is to go down to the end of the hall, bang a left, hook a right at the next big door, and go out of the building and around to the mineral pools."

"Thanks."

By the time I got dressed, I'd forgotten whether I was supposed to bang a right or hook a left, and I found myself in some strange back corridor of the Paragon. The passage was not bright and airy like the rest of the spa. A few dim bulbs were insufficient to illuminate the dark carpet and gray walls. While the front of the building had discreet signage, the doors I passed were unmarked. I heard voices and thought I could ask directions, so I followed the sounds.

A handsome couple was standing in a doorway, holding the door open. As I approached, I could see past them into a luxurious dark lounge, all red leather sofas and heavy black velvet hangings. When they saw me, they stopped talking. The man took the woman's hand and drew her back into the lounge.

"Hi," I said. "I'm a little lost here. I was on my way to the mineral baths and . . ." Then I glanced past the woman's shoulder and I saw the redheaded man and his mall princess girlfriend sitting on a loveseat. In the low light of the room, with his face averted, I couldn't be sure, but he looked so much like my Gabriel.

I took a step forward and the door shut in my face.

I turned the handle just as someone on the other side opened the door. A stubby, ruddy-faced man in a Paragon uniform squeezed out and quickly shut the door behind him. I guessed he was a manager because his jacket had thin gold braiding on the cuffs and collar, but unlike other employees, he did not wear a name tag.

"May I help you?" he asked officiously.

"I thought I saw my friend in there. I just want to say hello."

"I'm sorry, miss, but this is an exclusive room for our Paragon Diamond Club members only. Their privacy is paramount."

I was going to ask him to pass a message to the redheaded man, but what if he wasn't Gabriel? After all, what would

Gabriel be doing with Miss Sunshine Cream Cheese? "Of course. Would you please tell me how to get to the mineral baths? I lost my way."

I cooked in the mineral bath for an hour, but I spent the whole time worrying about my condition, my relationship, the neovamps, and the screenplay.

I hoped to talk to Charles about my truck, but the concierge desk was empty. Then I heard a familiar brassy voice saying, "Send a strapping virile masseur to my room," followed by merry laughter.

Gigi Barton was walking into the lobby, leading bellhops struggling with hillocks of suitcases. Another concierge, one I thought of as Charles-lite, was escorting her. Gigi had tied a Pucci scarf around her blond hair and was wearing wide trousers, a bat-winged blouse, and a vest in an unholy combination of fuchsia, chartreuse, orange, and magenta. So much for my theory that a khaki and white color scheme was appropriate spa apparel.

"Hi, Gigi. Remember me?"

She saw me and grinned widely before dropping her bag and tossing her arms around me. Colors even wilder than Gigi's outfit burst in my head. "Milagro, just the person I wanted to see."

I really doubted this, but gently released myself and said, "Really? Well, it's good to see you, too."

"You must be here for the new treatments. Where's Ian?"

"Oh, you know Ian. He goes wherever he goes. What new treatments?"

Before she could answer, Charles-lite oozed, "Ms. Barton, if you could just sign in, we'll take you up to your suite."

"Yes, yes, Milagro, sign in for me, would you, dear, and meet me for drinks in the bar. Sixish. Much to talk about." She flitted away to the elevators, Charles-lite following in her wake.

I went to the front desk and told the clerk, "Gigi Barton wants me to sign in for her."

She smiled and said, "Thanks, we'll take care of it."

When I got back to the casita, the red message light was aglow on the hotel phone. I thought Skip might have called, but the seven messages were all related to Thomas: asking me to set up appointments, arrange an interview, renew a gym membership.

My roommate was on the bed watching a talk show wearing silk boxers, as modest as a nun.

"Thomas, there are several messages from people who have the delusion that I am your assistant."

His eyes stayed on the television and he said, "A man in my position needs staff. It doesn't look good for me to deal with this stuff personally."

I walked in front of the television screen. "A man in your position? Your position being recumbent and half naked in bed, watching TV in the middle of the day?"

"Exactly. I'm not some jerk stuck in an office. I am Thomas Cook." He sat up a little straighter. "Milagro, I thought we agreed that we'd help each other. I help you keep Skip happy and you help me with my stuff."

He gave the distinct impression of being earnest, but he was a good actor, so I couldn't tell. "Okay, whatever, but don't expect me to keep up this farce after I finish with the screenplay."

I spent the afternoon trying to fix the second-act arc for "Teeth of Sharpness" and handling Thomas's business.

In the late afternoon Thomas interrupted me once to recite his touching monologue, "Thomas Cook: The Underwear Model Years," which shouldn't have interested me as much as it did.

Then he said, "Let's go to Lefty's for drinks."

"I can't. One, my truck isn't fixed, and two, I'm meeting someone here."

My phone rang and I automatically replied, "Good evening, Thomas Cook's suite," as I walked back to the office.

"Milagro?" There was so much static on the line that what I heard was "mmm-a-ooo."

"Oswald! Oswald, is that you?"

There was static and then a clear and angry "Tho-moo [crackle] ook," followed by more static.

"It was a joke, Oswald. How are you?"

But the line was dead.

Thomas was standing in the doorway, leaning back against the frame.

"Who are we meeting for drinks?" he asked.

"*We* are not meeting anyone. *I* am meeting Gigi Barton in the spa bar, and you may recall that they asked you never to darken their door again."

"Why do you have to be that way?" he asked, a hurt expression on his face. "Gigi and I go way back. They'll have to let me in the resort if she says so. Call Gigi and tell her I'll be joining you."

Thomas was subverting all my efforts to be a serious and accomplished screenwriter and treating me like a gofer. Since my career had become inexorably enmeshed in his happiness, however, I made the phone call. Gigi was thrilled and promised to send word to the front desk that he should not be thrown out.

He took over the bathroom while he got ready. I picked up his clothes and shoes. "Thomas, will you please hurry up so I can have a chance to fix myself?"

"You can't put a time limit on perfection," he said.

When he came out, he looked fabulous. Everything about

him gleamed, from his smooth copper skin to his espresso eyes to his sleek black hair. He was wearing one of those casual T-shirts that cost a fortune and fell just so from his shoulders. His slacks caressed his famous butt.

I was wearing my lavender dress because it was the nicest thing I had. I did a quick check in the mirror, brushed my hair, smoothed on some lip gloss, and went back out.

"You're wearing that again?" Thomas asked.

"Who's going to be looking at me when you're around?" I said sarcastically.

"That's true, but I can't be seen with just anybody. What else do you have?"

"What do you know about clothes?"

"When you model, you learn how to put together a look."

"Fine," I said, and showed him my meager stock of clothes.

He looked dissatisfied and said, "This is all hopeless. How do you expect to get a boyfriend dressing like a slag?"

"I already have a boyfriend."

"Oh, right, Eugene, the blood sports dude."

"Oswald, and he's very normal."

"Whatever." He went to his closet and pulled out a white linen shirt. "Wear this."

"With what? Slacks or a skirt?"

"Just heels."

"I am not wearing a shirt by itself and showing all my girly bits to the world."

Thomas called me a prude, a priss, repressed, and uptight. He finally compromised and loaned me a pair of white silk boxers that I wore over my own panties. I asked, "Are you sure people will think these are shorts?"

"All you ever think about is yourself." He buckled one of

Nancy's fancy belts around the shirt and adjusted it. Then he pulled the elastic band off my neat ponytail and said, "Bend over and hang your head upside down."

Thomas used half a bottle of Paragon's nonaerosol Shine and Hold spray to turn my hair into a tousled mane. He touched up my makeup, smudging eyeliner, dusting bronzer, highlighting, and shadowing the contours of my face. By the time he was done I looked like the sort of hot, pouty, edgy girl who would date an actor.

"I guess you'll have to do," he said. He took my arm and we walked to the Paragon. "What kind of massage did you get today?"

"Deep tissue. Have you heard about something called the Paragon Diamond Club? They have private lounges here. I wonder how much people have to pay for that."

"I never worry about those things. I'm Thomas Cook—everybody wants me in their private room," he said, forgetting that until recently he'd been banned from the Paragon.

Gigi had taken over the bistro courtyard for her cocktail party. Dozens of glass lamps glowed in jewel colors of turquoise, amethyst, ruby, and topaz. The bistro tables were gone and long, rough-hewn wooden tables held ceramic platters of food and earthenware pitchers of red wine. Rugs had been scattered over the courtyard and there were piles of bright pillows on them and low benches with cushions. In a corner, a man played a zither and sang a haunting, droning song in a language I couldn't identify.

Gigi left a circle of guests and came to us. She was wearing a gauzy emerald-green paisley-print caftan over skintight pants. She wore gold sandals and jangling gold necklaces, bracelets, and earrings. "Thomas, you gorgeous animal!" she said, and wrapped him in her arms.

They looked into each other's eyes and he said, "Gigi, why aren't you in the movies?"

"I am, Thomas, and if you're good, I'll let you see them someday." She laughed smuttily, then looked at me. "Milagro, sweetie, thank you for bringing Thomas. Ian would just eat you up in that outfit."

"Um, thanks. And thank you for inviting us. This is amazing," I said as I looked around. "I can't believe there's someone playing a zither. I just heard zither music on the score of *The Third Man*."

"It was a surprise to me, too," Gigi said. "I'd mentioned something to the manager before I came, so he put this together." Leaning toward me, she confided, "I don't know half the guests, but they're members of the Diamond Club, so I'm sure they're wonderful."

If the high rollers were here, there was a chance that the Gabriel clone would show up. I let Gigi and Thomas flirt with each other because I wanted to keep watch for the mystery man, and I also wanted to sample the sangria and food.

At one of the tables, a waiter was carving a leg of lamb so rare that the blood pooled on the cutting board beneath it. "Some of the lamb and wine, please," I said to him.

Perhaps at the ranch they were having a drink now and maybe missing me. I missed them.

As the waiter cut thin slices of meat and placed them on flatbread for me, I noticed how the rest of the food would have made my vampire friends happy. There were bowls of red berries, beet and goat cheese salad, a shredded red cabbage dish, gingered carrots, potatoes sprinkled with paprika, and smoked red peppers. I hovered near the table, grabbing small bites and listening to the conversations around me.

I felt uneasy all of a sudden, as if someone was behind me. When I turned, there was no one nearby. But at the far edge of the party, away from everyone else, was the bandaged man in the wheelchair. Even though he wore dark glasses, I had the feeling he was watching me. Maybe Thomas was right and I did think everything was about myself.

I tried to make conversation with an older man standing near me, and I thought he was really interested in my opinion about free trade agreements. Then his hand went to my thigh and he lurched forward, saying, "You have nice skin and so much of it."

I jumped away, stopping the flood of grisly images and said, "If you want to keep yours, you won't touch me again." Flustered, I quickly returned to the actor and the socialite.

Thomas was holding hands with Gigi, saying, "You'll come to the premiere, promise me?" and smiling full-wattage.

"Only if you promise to think about doing a commercial for Barton tissue," she said. "Milagro, dear, are you two . . ." She looked at Thomas and raised her eyebrows.

"We're not," I said quickly. "We are business associates."

"Milagro's my assistant," Thomas said blithely. "Milagro, get me a glass of wine and a plate of vegetables." He began leading Gigi to a cluster of people who were laughing.

I was assembling His Majesty's refreshments when someone behind me cleared his throat loudly. I turned to see Bernie carrying a beat-up brown paper shopping bag, a six-pack of beer, and a jar of dry-roasted peanuts. "Thought I'd surprise you with our own happy hour, but I see you've found something better." He put the beer and the peanuts on a table.

"How'd you find us?"

"I'm a reporter." He poured a glass of wine, then followed

me as I walked to Thomas and Gigi. Bernie smiled engagingly at the blond heiress and said, "Hi, I'm Bernard Vines."

"Bernie, this is Gigi Barton," I said. "Bernie writes for the *Weekly Exposition*."

"I do," he said proudly. "Barton as in Barton tissue paper? You're nothing to sneeze at." Gigi actually thought this was funny.

I handed Thomas the food and wine and told Gigi, "Thomas treats me like his assistant, but I am really here to work on a screenplay."

"I thought you were a gardener," Gigi said. "That's what I want to talk about. Later."

"You garden, Milagro?" Bernie asked.

"Yes, among other things," I said. "How's your chupacabra hunt going?"

"When I went there after school, the sheep was gone."

I gave him an I-told-you-so look. "The coyotes that killed it dragged it off."

"The dingo took my baybee!" Thomas shrieked in falsetto with an Australian accent.

"What's a chupa whatever?" Gigi asked.

"It's a creature out of Latin American folklore that kills goats," Bernie said. "We heard some strange animal in the desert the other night, and we found a sheep's carcass all torn up. I looked around and didn't see any drag marks or footprints other than ours."

I shook my head and said, "Whatever, Deerslayer."

"Go ahead and mock me with your freshman English references," Bernie said with a grin. "You did a good job on those essays."

We were an unlikely quartet, but somehow the conversation

flowed and before I knew it an hour had gone by. "Gigi, how long will you be here?" I asked.

"As long as it's interesting," she said with a flirty smile toward Thomas and Bernie. "I come a few times a year for the rejuvenating treatments. The Paragon's so innovative, and I'll try anything once."

I thought she was exhibiting ho-ish activity, but who was I to judge? Thomas got whisked away by admirers, and Gigi eased up to Bernie. She was at least three inches taller than him, and with her heels, she towered over him. "Tell me more about celebrity scandals," she said.

The groups of guests shifted and for a second I was staring right at the man in the wheelchair. "I think I'll turn in," I said. "Thanks for everything, Gigi. See you later."

I took a last look around the party, hoping to see the red-headed man, but he wasn't here. As I walked back to the casita, I looked up at the stars and thought about Oswald. Perhaps he was sleeping in a hot, humid shack, too exhausted and dusty to think about the petty problems of his girlfriend and family.

The phone was ringing as I walked in the door. I ran inside and answered on the fourth ring. "Hello?"

"Hello, Milagro?" Static broke up the line and made Oswald's voice sound different.

"Oswald, I was just thinking about you."

I heard: "[crackle] called [cackle crackle] last [crackle crackle] answered [crackle]. Where [crackle crackle] at?"

"When you called last time I answered faster? I was just outside. I was looking at the stars and wondering if you could see them, too, Oz."

I definitely heard "ook," which I took to mean that he would *look* at them and think of me. "Oz, I love you. *Te amo* like crazy."

The line died before he could answer.

Every time I began drifting off to sleep, my thoughts jumbled tonight's zither music with the vampire's chewing-metal language. I kept seeing the laden tables at Gigi's party and Silas's altar merging together, until I was on the table surrounded by pitchers of blood and the velvet drapes of the Diamond Club room were closing in.

I was grateful when Thomas finally stumbled into the room. He threw off his clothes and bumped into furniture on his way to the bathroom. "Thomas, are you okay?"

"Fine!"

I got up and fetched him a bottle of water from the kitchen. I put it on his bed table and called out, "Do you want some aspirin?"

"Just sleep."

Okay, I thought, have a massive hangover in the morning. When he came to bed, he mumbled, "This way," and I obligingly turned toward him, hoping he wasn't going to get frisky. He took my hand and twined our fingers.

"Tell me the story," I said.

He mumbled the story about sleeping under the desk, and I could have sworn that his breath smelled like hot chocolate.

I was out so soundly that I didn't hear the phone ring. I only woke when Thomas pulled his hand from mine and reached over me to answer my phone.

"Yeah," he mumbled. "Hello?" He dropped the phone on my chest and said, "No one there."

I took it anyway and said, "Hello."

Whoever was on the other end hung up. I told myself that it was probably the wrong number and fell back asleep.

seventeen

flash, cash, and stash

I sipped a blood and tomato juice cocktail as I talked on the phone with Skip about the screenplay. Through the window, I could see Thomas doing laps in the pool. I had an attack of adolescent celebrity worship at the sight of his brown naked body moving through the water.

I mentioned Thomas's progress to Skip, and he said, "Actors are like that. They're used to abusing themselves and bouncing back quickly."

I thought I would take advantage of my massage to nose around the Paragon. Perhaps my time with Edna's family had made me as suspicious as they, but I had the troubling feeling that I was just missing something important.

First, though, I checked in with the concierge. "Hi," I said to Charles. "I was hoping to hear something about my truck."

"I apologize for not contacting you earlier," he said obsequiously. "The mechanic called, saying that the damage to your vehicle is major."

The truck was used, but I had recently taken it in for its annual inspection. "I just had a full maintenance done on it," I said.

He blinked. "Oh, it wasn't a maintenance problem." He seemed to be trying to remember something. "He said that maybe you ran over a large rock or road debris and that damaged the undercarriage."

"The undercarriage?" I had no idea what an undercarriage was, but I liked the word.

"Yes, the undercarriage."

"Okay, can you find out when the work will be completed, please?"

He told me that parts had to be ordered from the East Coast. "If you approve, I'll tell the mechanic to proceed."

"Yes, go ahead. And, Charles, thanks for all your help."

He smiled broadly. "Glad to assist."

Then I poked around for a glimpse of my dear Gabriel or his clone. I visited the seven shops, including the gift shop for children, where I bought a cute tiny onesie for Libby. I peeked in the restaurant and the café, checked out the bar, walked through the bistro, and made my way to the steaming mineral pools outdoors.

I went down the corridor to the Diamond Club, but the entrance was closed. Maybe Triveni would know something.

As I walked to my treatment room in the massage center, I glanced through a doorway and saw a room with interesting stacks of laundry, including the dark maroon of maids' uniforms.

Triveni spent more time on our breathing sessions and put me through some visualizations. I imagined the bloody images transforming into scarlet blooms of amaryllis. As soon as I thought of the flowers, I felt a sense of joy.

Triveni massaged me with hands warm and slick with oil that smelled of damp earth and moss. I gripped the table and continued my visualizations.

When she was done, I swung my legs over the table and sat up. "Thank you, Triveni. I think that's helping. You know, I was thinking of joining the Diamond Club."

She tilted her head and looked at me. "You've got that kind of money, honey?"

I shrugged a shoulder and said, "A friend offered to pay for me."

"But how are you going to get past the ten-year customer requirement?"

"I thought it was only a year."

"No, it's ten years to ensure, I dunno, loyalty to the Paragon. Employees who've been here for less than two years don't even get to work in that part of the building."

"What about you? Do you work there?"

"No way. I'm into natural healing. That extreme stuff skeeves me."

"How extreme is it?"

She paused, and I could tell she was debating how much she should say. "Experimental things, I think. Things that might not be approved. When I told them I wasn't interested in working over there, I thought they were going to fire me."

"I'm glad they didn't."

When Triveni left, I dressed slowly, then opened the door a smidge until I saw her go into another treatment room. I walked out and checked that no one was around before stepping into the room with the laundry.

It took less than thirty seconds to find a uniform hanging from a rack. I put it in my Paragon gift bag under Libby's onesie, and then I walked out of the treatment area.

I hurried through the halls as if I had an appointment. When I saw a ladies' room, I went inside. A woman was touching up her lipstick in the outer room. I didn't make eye contact as I passed through and went into a stall. When I heard the door close behind her, I struggled into the uniform, which was so snug across the chest that I had to leave the top buttons undone. I pulled my hair back into a ponytail and hid my clothes in the vanity under the sink.

As I smoothed the fabric of the uniform, I felt a hard bump in the tunic. An inside pocket held an employee pass card. Figuring that I should look as if I was doing something, I picked up an arrangement of white and yellow lilies on the side table and walked into the hall with it.

I made an efficient path to the door of the Diamond Club, and then I realized how crazy it was to crash a private lounge. I continued down the hall, which ended in a metal double door. Just for the heck of it, I flashed the pass card across the magnetic reader. I heard the click of the lock releasing. Head down toward the flowers, I turned the handle and opened the door.

This area had thick carpets that muffled footsteps and nubby grass-cloth walls. It was silent except for the sound of a water fountain on one wall. A straightlaced young man sat reading a sports magazine at a reception desk. He looked up and said, "What?"

"Flowers." I lifted the arrangement but kept my eyes down in the way that the shy maids had.

He gestured toward a passage on the left, so I went that way. Suddenly the mummy man and his attendant were in front of me. I raised the arrangement in front of my face and kept walking. His attendant rolled the wheelchair by me without even looking in my direction.

Then I saw a sign on a door that said BATH ROOMS.

I opened the door and stepped into an area that resembled a medical office waiting room, all stainless steel, black-and-white tiles, and pale green walls. I placed the flowers alongside an arrangement on the coffee table.

After waiting and listening for a few moments, I crept to one of the closed doors and turned the doorknob. The room inside had a luxurious porcelain tub in the center. It was, indeed, a bath room. I quickly checked the other two rooms, and they were identical. What was the big secret about taking baths at a spa, I wondered.

I was feeling ridiculous and a bit thirsty when I noticed a stainless steel industrial refrigerator in the back of the third room. I thought I could filch a bottle of mineral water. I swung open the door and there on the shelves was row after row of plastic bags filled with dark crimson liquid.

You didn't have to have (a) lived with a vampire, or (b) lived with a doctor, or (c) lived with a vampire doctor, or (d) been infected with vampires to recognize blood when you saw it.

Desire rushed through me. I wanted to grab the bags, tear them open, and pour the blood over my face, fill my mouth with it. I wanted to take off my clothes and cover my body with the viscous, rich liquid. I wanted Oswald here, so we could make love, slipping and sliding in a puddle of blood.

My hand reached out and then I saw the labels on the bags. I realized with horror that I was about to take a pouch of human blood.

Now, I had studied the Paragon treatment brochure closely

and there was no mention of any treatments involving blood or its by-products.

I picked up the floral arrangement, left the bath rooms, and said good-bye to the guy at the reception desk.

"Yeah," he responded apathetically.

After making it back through the locked doors without encountering anyone, I thought I was home free. But as I neared the ladies' room where my bag was hidden, a voice called, "You there!"

The stubby manager who'd guarded the Diamond Club lounge was approaching me. "Where do you think you're going with those flowers?" he demanded. "I asked for clean towels in the herbal sauna ten minutes ago."

"Uh," I began. I was afraid he'd recognize me, but his eyes were firmly fixed on my cleavage.

"Don't you speak English?" he snapped. "*¿Hablo inglés?*"

"*Sí, señor,*" I said with a blank smile.

He looked at the flowers and sneered, "Leave the flowers to the florists and get the towels to the sauna." He used a key to open a closet filled with fluffy yellow towels. He grabbed an armful of the towels and shoved them on top of the flower arrangement.

Then his hand slid down. He grabbed my breast and squeezed hard, an ugly look in his nasty eyes. My thoughts went crimson and he said, "Well, *ándale, muchacha.*"

He slapped my behind as he walked off and muttered, "Dumb maid."

I dropped the flowers and the towels, and then tackled him. He hit the floor with a solid thud. I sat on his back and a sensation started in my legs and thighs and rose upward, an eruption of bloody images.

The man was too stunned to react, and I leaned close to his ear and whispered, "Don't you ever, ever treat one of the staff like that again."

He was struggling and I jerked his arm upward, fighting my desire to break it and to hear the bone snap and burst through flesh and skin.

"Who the hell . . . " he said shakily. "Let me go. You have no right!"

"I do. I'm from the Department of Fair Employment and Housing."

"Fair Employment doesn't—"

"We're a new division and we've been watching you. Some say we're rogues, out of control. Some say we leave too many broken bodies. But I think you can't take things too far in the pursuit of justice." I wanted to pull off his ears and drink from the torn flesh.

"But it was—"

"No, not a word or you're up on charges. You are never, ever to touch one of the girls here again, do you understand?"

I yanked his arm up and he groaned, "Yes!"

"I'm feeling nice today, so I'm going to let you go with this mild rebuke." I banged his head against the rug to emphasize my nice mood. "You're going to walk away from me and not look back because if I see your disgusting face again, I'm going to tear it off and make a Halloween mask out of it for my dog, Daisy."

I got off him and he stood up, rubbing his arm. My heart was racing as he hurried off. I knew I shouldn't have had so much pleasure in hurting someone. I knew I shouldn't have wanted to hurt him more.

I was a monster, I thought as I changed back into my

clothes. I hid the uniform under the sink. I thought alarms would go off and security guards would come running when I walked out of the main building, but I made it back to my place without any problems.

My emotional vampire roommate had assembled some demands in my absence: order protein powder for his shakes, tell him if a mole on his back looked cancerous, and call his agent about a beer commercial in Japan. I ordered a case of the protein powder, told him it was a pimple, not a mole, and had a chat with his agent, who said that no decision had been made yet on the commercial.

I went into the office and locked the door. I called Mercedes and when she answered I told her what I had seen. "I can't even begin to piece together what is going on here. Why is Gabriel here, if he is Gabriel, and why is there a blood supply in the 'bath rooms'? Bernie told us that strange things happened at the Paragon, and I wonder if this is what he meant."

"Occam's razor," she said.

"What?"

"Occam's razor is a maxim that the simplest explanation that encompasses all the facts is the most likely to be true. Gabriel said he's taking a break, and he's at a spa. The private wing has blood and you see someone with bandages, so the spa offers medical treatments. A large animal carried off a dead sheep. La Basura locals occasionally go on the lam for a few days. I don't see any big mysteries here."

"Mercedes, Mercedes, Mercedes, you see how facts can limit you? Something else is happening here, and it's got to be connected with vampires. Don't you think it's strangely coincidental that Gabriel and I are here at the same time?"

"Maybe it's not Gabriel. Is it odd that Gigi Barton's there

and knows Thomas? You hang around certain circles and everyone knows everyone. A mathematician named John Allen Paulos says that an absence of coincidence would be the most incredible coincidence."

"Yes, and as the Dalai Lama says, 'When one door closes, another opens.'"

Mercedes began laughing and laughing. When she finally was able to speak, she said, "That wasn't the Dalai Lama. It was Alexander Graham Bell."

"Who knew old Alex was so philosophical?" I suddenly remembered something. "Mercedes, what countries use zithers in their folk music?"

"Zithers are used all over, since always. Legend says the zither could cast a spell of enchantment. Austrian Tyrol and Bavarian music often feature it. The drone zither was a Slovenian instrument, but it's been replaced by the concert zither. Armenians use a board zither called a *kanuna*. There's the *kokle*, a Latvian zither, and a Moroccan—"

Something fell into place. "Latvians use zithers?"

"Sure, the *kokle* goes back at least two thousand years."

"Silas Madison told me the bloodletting ceremony was based on one he had first learned about in a Latvian manuscript."

"So?"

"So whither zither? The Paragon manager arranged zither music and invited Diamond Club guests to Gigi's party, and the Diamond Club has blood baths."

There was silence on the other end of the line.

"Mercedes, are you there?"

"Milagro, you know the problem with English majors? They always see associations where there are none," she said. "I will see what I can find out about the Paragon's Diamond Club, but don't let your imagination get the best of you."

As much as I wanted to ponder all these puzzling coincidences, I didn't have time. I had a deadline for the screenplay. As I tried to distill the essential truths of the screenplay, disturbing thoughts about my own identity arose. I squashed them like bugs.

The exercise equipment clanged and banged as Thomas worked out. The casita was a hive of industry for the rest of the day.

When I needed a break from writing, I changed into a clean outfit and told Thomas that I'd see him later.

"Where are you going?" Thomas asked. "Gigi's coming here with her friends and then we're going to Lefty's. Bernie says it's karaoke night."

"Sounds great, but there's something I have to take care of."

I liked the sky at early evening, and the way the color deepened through delphinium shades of clear blue to purple-blue. I bent over and sifted the earth in my hands. It was sandy and loose, but not unpleasant. I missed my soil at the ranch, with its high volcanic content and reddish hue. Dusting my hands off on my slacks, I continued to the main building.

Where would I go if I were a gay man who had inexplicably abandoned his fabulous wardrobe? I asked the concierge on duty, "Is there a sports bar here?"

"No, the Paragon is a place to escape competition."

He must have seen my disappointment, because he added, "We have a juice bar on the second-floor balcony with a small television. Sometimes the busboys watch sports at night when things are slow."

I found the juice bar and there was Gabriel sitting despondently at a table. It was him and not some clone. Beside him was Miss Daisy Fluffy-kitten. The only other customer was the bandaged man in the wheelchair, who sipped on a drink through a straw.

Gabriel stared at the screen, which flashed garish graphics of game scores and statistics. I was horrified when I got a good look at him: his hair had been hacked off into a hideous mall cut and he wore a polo shirt with a football team logo. His companion was dressed in a revolting bubble-gum-pink flouncy blouse and skirt. Her streaked hair was curled and sprayed stiff. She chewed the wedge of lemon from her drink.

"Hello, Gabriel," I said. "I thought I saw you here and I was right."

"Young Lady!" he said, unpleasantly startled. "What are you doing here? I thought you were in the City."

"I was." I pulled a chair up to his table. "Long story short, I'm working on a screenplay here. Why don't you introduce me to your friend," I said, smiling at his terminally sissified companion. Her overly sweet perfume was so strong I could practically taste it.

She smiled with huge white Chiclet teeth and said, "I'm Brittany Monroe. Gabriel and I are engaged. When we're married I'll be Mrs. Gabriel Grant, or Brittany Monroe-Grant, I haven't decided."

It was good to really laugh, and I did laugh for several seconds until I saw Gabriel's pale face. "It's a joke, right? I mean, Gabriel, you can't be engaged to a *girl*."

"I *am* engaged to Brittany, Milagro," he said quietly.

"That's the most ridiculous thing I've ever heard." My voice rose above the volume of the television. "You like men, big, strong, hairy men. We are in accord in our adoration of men."

"I was confused, but I'm not any longer. I made the wrong lifestyle choice and it was causing a lot of misery for me and my family." He stared at me as if daring me to argue with him.

"Gabriel, why are you doing this?"

"I'm doing it so I can finally be happy."

He spoke seriously, but I couldn't believe it, even though I knew he'd been going through a rough time. "Gabriel, you just have to meet the right guy. Before I met Oswald, I'd wondered if I'd ever find anybody."

Brittany gave me a curdled-milk look and said, "Gabey, who *is* this woman and why is she bothering us?"

"Milagro is my cousin's girlfriend," he said flatly. "She knows the Grant family."

"I thought I was your friend, too, Gabriel."

He looked straight at me. "Milagro, I know it's fun for you to have homosexual friends. For you, it was all about dishing and flirting harmlessly. But did you ever think of how it was for me? Did you ever think that maybe I get tired of being the gay sidekick?"

"Gabriel, you were never just the gay guy to me," I said. But was he right? Had I fit him into a neat little box? "You're brave and funny and resourceful . . ."

"And alone," he said.

"Not anymore," said Brittany, placing a possessive hand on his arm.

"You can't change your sexuality just because you decide to, Gabriel. Do you think you're going to be any less lonely living in a closet?"

"Young Lady, you may be comfortable being an outsider all your life, but I'm not," he said.

"Well, I'm going to sit right here and talk to you until you come to your senses," I said. "I have all the time in the world. If it was just Willem, he's gone and he's senile. You can't let what he said get to you."

Miss Penny Loafers practically hissed at me.

"Milagro," he said in a voice so low that I had to listen carefully to hear him. "Tell me how happy you are ten years from now, when you are still treated as an unwanted freak among our family members."

The words hurt worse than a blow. Tears came to my eyes and my voice quavered as I said, "So that's how you really see me?" I rose so quickly, the chair tottered. "Please don't let me interrupt this romantic evening. I'm sure you have a night of thrilling lovemaking ahead of you."

Brittany fluttered her mascara-clumped lashes and said, "I'm saving myself for marriage."

"I have a feeling Gabriel's not going to put up much of a fight about that," I said, and left, not caring that I'd made a scene.

Mr. Mummy watched me, his damp eyes glimmering from the recesses of the bandages.

I could hear voices and music well before I arrived at the casita. A crowd of attractive, well-groomed people filled the casita, leaning against exercise equipment, noshing from an extravagant buffet, and dancing around the pool. Thomas was sitting on the diving board with Gigi, who wore a tropical print sarong.

I went outside to ask Thomas what was going on. Someone handed me a strawberry daiquiri, and Gigi scooted off the diving board and came over to me.

"Hello, Milagro."

"Hi, Gigi," I said, trying to look pleasant even though I was in no mood for a party. "I thought you were going out."

"Change of plans. Have you been crying?"

I wiped at my eyes. "I'm allergic to tumbleweed."

She was already on another topic. "You can't imagine how thrilled I was to see you here. The treatments are fantastic, but sometimes it's deathly dull, all saunas and meditation. Won't Ian be jealous that you're here with Thomas?"

"Thomas and I aren't—"

"Milagro, please, you don't need to keep these secrets! We are women of the world," she said with a sly smile. "I admire your taste in men, and if you don't have an exclusive relationship with Thomas . . ."

"No, not at all," I said.

"He's absolutely scrumptious," she said. "Oh, and I called Ian and left a message inviting him to the Paragon, but I didn't tell him you were here. I thought it would be a surprise, and we can all have fun together and then maybe go to my place in the Hamptons. I need to have you look at my garden there."

"I really appreciate that, Gigi. Actually I wanted your advice on the procedures you get here. You know, the really special ones."

She peered at my face closely. "You're young. You don't need anything yet."

"You think I'm young. But I need to stay this way if I want to associate with men of a certain caliber, men who have high standards . . . You understand." Great, now Gigi would think I was an ambitious call girl.

She smiled conspiratorially and leaned close to whisper in my ear. "I'm just dying for the new treatment. An injection of a new blood product. Insanely expensive, but I'm told the result will be increased skin cell regeneration and immunity to disease."

"Where does it come from?" I said.

"Someone with a rare genetic condition. I've been waiting to hear when it will be available."

A man in white pants and a shirt unbuttoned to expose his hairy chest pulled Gigi away to dance to a song that had been a pop hit ten years before.

I didn't know when Bernie arrived, but I spotted him as things were winding down and people were returning to the hotel in order to prepare for evening socializing. He came up from behind me and threw his arm over my shoulders. The jolt of images made me jump, but he didn't notice. I practiced my breathing.

"Milagro, about the chupacabra . . ."

"Kindly speak to me no further of your ridiculous chupacabra theory. Don't you have to teach tomorrow?"

"We've got the day off. I really like you and I want us to be friends."

"We are friends," I said, and I supposed that we were.

"Friends forgive each other, friends remember birthdays, friends help each other out. That's what I'm talking about."

"Bernie, you sound as if you're going off to war. Yes, I understand the general definition of friendship."

I thought he was drunkenly blathering, so as he was leaving I snatched away his keys and said, "You're not driving. You're toasted."

"I'm not."

"Walk a straight line on the tiles."

Bernie did this, saying, "I'm not drunk. Will you return my keys?"

"Recite a poem."

Bernie stood straight and said,

This is my dream,
It is my own dream,
I dreamt it.
I dreamt that my hair was kempt.
Then I dreamt that my true love unkempt it.

"That totally rocks," I said. "Is it a real poem?"

"Yes, it's called 'My Dream' by Ogden Nash."

"Okay, catch." I tossed Bernie his keys.

After the staff cleaned up the place, Thomas came out of the bedroom dressed in a white shirt and black jeans. He was so beautiful that I was transfixed. He smiled and came to me. "How do I look?"

"Fabulous," I managed to say. "You look fabulous."

Smoothing his hands over his chest, he said, "I know, but it's good to hear it. I'm off with Gigi. Don't wait up."

I put on a pair of tennis shoes and left the casita. When I could no longer hear any human voices or see outdoor lights, I began to run.

Bits of broken glass shone like gems in the moonlight. I hadn't thought about where I was going, but soon I'd arrived at the place where the dead sheep had been. I don't know how I found the place, but I knew it was right.

I added a sense of geography to my list of new abilities: able to see glowing outlines on living creatures, able to heal rapidly from injuries, fantastic night vision, physical endurance, and high tolerance for wine and mood enhancers. These amazing powers might be useful in a life of fighting crime, but they did not help me figure out what was happening to all of my friends or to me.

I crouched down to examine the place where the carcass had been. A sheep is not a petite critter. It is large and cumbersome. Carrying it away would not be possible for even the most wily of coyotes. Even a cougar would have had to drag a sheep away, but I didn't see any drag marks.

I armed myself with a pile of rocks and sat on a boulder. As I waited and listened for the strange flying creature, I tried to think through recent events, looking for the simplest explanation that included all the facts. I'd seen a show about a math genius who helped FBI agents. The math genius had talked about information flowing from a source, and going back to the source. I followed the flow back to the appearance of Willem Dunlop and Silas Madison.

Their visit exposed the family's secrets and exacerbated my situation with Oswald's parents. Willem denounced Gabriel. Silas tried to hurt Ian because he'd humiliated Willem, and I'd been reinfected as a result. Silas thought I was a portent of a great new vampire era. If Silas hadn't canceled our coffee date, I wouldn't have met Skip.

If I hadn't accidentally met Skip, I wouldn't be here . . . here in a place with an altered Gabriel, a place where people went missing in the desert and appeared days later, a place where I was distracted by a movie star and given a project that fit my unusual interests, a place where socialites came for radical treatments and blood was stored in a locked wing, a place where my truck suddenly had engine problems, a place with zither music.

And I thought I was so smart because I'd gone to F.U. Silas wanted me here and not only had I come, but I hadn't told any of the people who might have helped me. If Thomas was in league with Silas, I was sleeping with the enemy. But Silas was far too clever to trust an emotional vampire, rather than a real one.

I ran back to my casita. I ate a wedge of *boudin noir,* and picked up my phone. Mercedes would either be at the club or on her computers at home. "Mercedes, hi."

I heard a lot of noise, and she said, *"Momentito,"* which could mean anything from five seconds to five hours. In a few minutes, she said from a quieter place, "What's up?"

"I applied Occam's razor, and the simplest explanation I came up with is that Silas used Skip to maneuver me here to the Paragon, and that he's behind the private wing and also connected to Gabriel being here. By the way, I talked to Gabriel tonight and I met his new fiancée, who is a girl."

"I didn't think Gabriel went for queens."

"Not a queen, an actual genetically certifiable female, one of the more odious of our gender, a major sissy."

"Why would Silas want you at the Paragon?"

"That, *mi hermana,* is where I will need the assistance of your giant brain. I can play dumb until you get here."

"I know you can," Mercedes replied.

eighteen

flunkies and flying monkeys

In the morning, the phone began ringing before seven o'clock: I answered on the first ring, hoping it was Oswald. "Hello?"

"Maria Dos Passos?"

"It's not Maria, it's—"

The woman on the other end identified herself as a reporter with a daily paper. "I want to talk to you about your relationship with Thomas Cook and your recent experiences."

She had an insinuating tone that put me on guard. "I don't have a relationship with Thomas Cook and why are you calling me here?"

"I'm following up on the report in the *Weekly Exposition*. Now, about this alleged chupacabra sighting . . ."

"No comment," I said, and hung up.

I was going to kill Bernie. I would use a dull knife to very slowly and messily dismember him and then I would leave his body parts strewn about the desert to be eaten by his beloved chupacabras.

"Thomas, Thomas, come here!" I shouted as the phone began ringing again. "Hello," I answered.

"Is this Maria Dos Passos? My name is Louie Richardson and I'm a reporter for the—"

"*No hablo inglés*. You bye-bye now." I ended the call and went looking for Thomas even as the phone began to trill again. I picked up the receiver and put it down. Then I dialed the reception desk.

"Good morning."

"Hello, this is Milagro De Los Santos in Casita Twelve. I've been receiving calls for a Maria Dos Passos. There is no one by that name here."

The receptionist asked me to hold for a moment and then came back on the line. "We do apologize, Ms. De Los Santos. We have a new staff member who thought there had been a mix-up with the names. It will not happen again."

"Thank you. I do not wish to be disturbed by reporters of any ilk." I hung up and tried to remember to look up the word "ilk."

My roommate was examining the skin under his eyes in the bathroom mirror. "Why aren't you answering the phone? It could be my agent."

"It's not your agent. Reporters are calling because there's a story about us and a chupacabra in the *Weekly Exposition*."

"Really? Do you have a copy?"

"No, I don't . . . ," I began saying as the doorbell buzzed. I went to the front door and opened it a tiny crack. "A package for Milagro De Los Santos," said the delivery guy.

"Thanks," I said, signing for an oversized manila envelope.

I closed and locked the door and programmed the phone to forward all calls to the message service. Then I made myself a drink of blood and coffee. It was an awful combination, and I only choked down half a cup before pouring the rest down the drain.

Inside the envelope was a copy of the *Weekly Exposition*. A note was attached to it with a paper clip. "Friends forgive friends. Your friend, Bernie."

I unfolded the tabloid and a shock went through me. There was a large photo of Thomas kissing me outside the casita the morning after Bernie and I had rescued him from the sidewalk.

"He could have gotten my good side," Thomas said.

"Did you know about this?"

"No," he said, but he grinned.

I picked up a small barbell and held it aloft. "The truth or you won't have a 'good side.' "

"I swear I didn't know, but I, uh, didn't *not* know." When I waved the barbell menacingly, he stepped back and added, "He's a tabloid writer. What did you expect—that he liked us for our conversation?"

"Actually, yes," I answered, feeling monumentally stupid. I looked at the tabloid. If it had featured some *chica* other than me, I would have thought it was hysterical.

The major headline was "Latin Lovebirds Tormented by Chupacabra," and a subhead read, "Love Cursed by Deadly Winged Monkey-Monster." A photo of Thomas hugging me was captioned, "Thomas Cooks Up Passion with Spicy Hot Tamale." Another of us examining the sheep's carcass said, "Latin Lovers' Beloved Pet Goat Pancho Slaughtered."

At least my face was blurred and I was identified as "Maria Dos Passos."

"Do you think that anyone can tell it's me?" I asked anxiously.

"Are you kidding? You look like every other Mexican girl, and your features aren't in focus." He didn't mean this as an insult and I didn't take it as one. Thomas pointed to a shot of us looking into the night sky at an ominous winged creature. "This is the best one. We look good together."

"I like this one," I said, indicating a photo of us at Lefty's. "I hardly ever get my hair to do that flip."

We were silent as we read the preposterous story. According to Bernie, Thomas had spotted "Maria Dos Passos" in a Fanta commercial and fallen instantly in lust. We had incurred the wrath of the chupacabra by accidentally killing one of its spawn on a drug-and-tequila-fueled road trip to Ensenada.

This fictitious Maria had been a popular extra in Mexican soap operas and regularly prayed to St. Magnus of Füssen, the patron saint of protection against vermin, to keep the chupacabra from harming her. "How could Bernie do this after I corrected papers for him?" I said, and flopped down onto the sofa.

"It's a good story," Thomas said. He went to the phone and dialed. I listened to him talk to his manager. Evidently both were overjoyed with the positive coverage. When Thomas was finished, he sat by me and grinned. "The story's getting picked up internationally. People are asking for interviews."

"You can't possibly think this is good!" I told him how my F.U. acquaintances would fall over laughing at this piece.

Thomas straightened up. "Milagro," he said in a husky voice that sent shivers through me, "let me explain something to you. They might laugh in public, but at night when they're with their boring stockbroker boyfriends, they'll be fantasizing that they're you, in my bed."

Even though I knew he could turn on his sexual energy like a spigot, I was as mesmerized as a Boy Scout in a sorority house on naked pillow fight night. "I . . . um . . ."

He placed his finger over my lips. "You ought to thank Bernie. He said you were hot."

"Thomas, I seem like an idiot in that article."

"You must have been treated very badly to have such low self-esteem. Can you get my agent on the line and also order breakfast?"

I was happy to call his agent, because I had some questions to ask her about my deal with Skip. She was ecstatic about the tabloid story.

So was Skip, who showed up in the afternoon with a too-hip-for-words publicist dressed in a severe black suit. The publicist looked me up and down and pushed her huge black-rimmed glasses up her designer nose. "You should have consulted with me before casting. I would have gone a different direction. Not so obvious."

"I was not cast," I said, spitting out every word as if it was a sharp thing. "I am a real person."

"Mmm," she said critically. "A little more class and a little less sass would be good for interviews. Don't worry—we'll get you a coach." She turned to Skip. "You know that civilians are always hard to work with."

"I know," he said. "But we didn't plant the story. We just lucked out."

"Skip, I do not consider this luck," I said, wanting to smack the little creep. "I am in a real relationship, you know. I also feel that being associated with a chupacabra sighting in a tabloid will damage my credibility as a serious author."

"Milagro, lighten up," Skip said. He turned to the publicist.

"We can replace her with an up-and-comer. Any suggestions?" They quickly became engrossed in discussing a love interest for Thomas.

Silas couldn't have scripted all of this, could he? Skip seemed genuinely excited about the publicity for the movie, and I had to believe it was a real project.

I needed to rant so I called Bernie. I left a blistering message about his mendacious nature, his ethical chasm, his questionable use of the semicolon, and his penchant for excessive alliteration.

I locked myself in the office and pretended that I was working. I picked up *Brideshead Revisited* and read the last pages. As I closed the book, I felt better. Charles, Sebastian, and Julia had survived foolishness, self-destructiveness, and broken hearts, and had matured. They had lost their innocence, but not their hope.

It was time for me to take control of those things that I could control, and one of those things was my truck. I was so eager for confrontation that when the doorman swung open the door to the Paragon, I dashed directly into the man in the wheelchair.

"Sorry, sorry," I said as I recovered my balance. "I didn't look where I was going. Are you hurt?"

"Fine," he said, his voice muffled through the gauze around his mouth. "It'sss okay."

I was across the lobby before I felt a chill go through me. It was only the bandages that had caused the sibilant *s,* I told myself as I kept walking.

Charles was at the concierge station. He was taking a long time with a guest who wanted to know all the particulars about winter vacation packages. I occupied myself by watching all the smooth and tan people who glided across the stone floor.

I stood patiently for ten minutes before I began tapping my toe, glancing at my wrist (before remembering that I didn't even own a watch), and sighing impatiently.

The concierge occasionally glanced at me sympathetically but otherwise seemed in no rush to conclude his tedious conversation. I determined to wait as long as necessary and began singing "Las Mañanitas" softly. Mercedes had told me that singing the chirpy song three times through was guaranteed to cause madness in listeners.

The guest succumbed by the second chorus, and I stepped forward with an innocent smile. "Charles, how are you?!"

"Hello. I hope you have been enjoying your stay at the Paragon and all our amenities."

"It's been beyond fab. I would like to get my truck back, though."

"It's not ready yet."

"I'd like to talk to the mechanic. Why don't you give me the name and number of the garage and I'll handle this myself."

I saw the panic flash in his blue eyes and knew he was thinking of a lie.

"He works exclusively for the spa and private clientele," he said, stroking his beard. "He hates being disturbed and our agreement with him requires that we, um, not disclose his information."

Leaning close, I looked up at him and said, "I'm holding you personally responsible for taking my truck. Get it back to me by tomorrow. Or I will be really upset with you, Charles. Do you understand?"

"Yes, I'll tell the mechanic to expedite the repairs."

"Good. Now I'm off to my massage." Although the massages were not pleasant, I felt as if I was doing something to gain control over the bloody visions. As I walked to the treatment room, I checked the door with the uniforms and laundry, but it was locked.

In the massage room, I quickly changed into a robe.

Triveni tapped on the door and came in, her ankle bracelet jangling. "How's it shaking, girlfriend?" she asked in her normal voice.

"I'm fine. Sorry I'm late."

"No sweat," she said as she put a match to the smudge stick.

"How's work going?"

She rolled her kohl-rimmed eyes. "I don't think I'm cut out for this big-resort scene. There are some perks, though. In our staff meeting they announced that we're getting two days off, full pay, in a week."

"Really? That's very generous."

"Yeah, the whole place is going to be shut down for a private party for some members of the Diamond Club."

"Why would the resort need to shut down for special guests?"

"The hell if I know. Maybe they're having a nudists retreat. Maybe they're having a greasy old orgy. Now shut your trap and meditate."

When I returned to the casita, I was thankful that Skip, Thomas, and the publicist had left. I mixed a few drops of blood with water in a wineglass; most observers would've assumed I was drinking rosé. I wrote and sipped, sipped and wrote.

Thomas came in late, waved good night, and went to bed. I stared at my phone, wishing Oswald would call, even if it was only so I could listen to crackling noises and shout that I loved him.

When everything at the spa was quiet, I slipped outside and went for a long run. The daytime hues of taupes, browns, and grays turned into grays and blacks at night. As Bernie had said, there was something alien, harsh but beautiful, about the desert. It felt as if I was the only one on the planet.

On my return route I circled the area where we had found the sheep. After a few minutes of searching, I located speakers hidden behind rocks and shrubs and also some kind of light projector. That explained why the shadow of the flying creature hadn't had a radiant outline. That desert rat, Bernie, had rigged the whole show.

Everything I'd done recently was off balance. I'd allowed Bernie and Charles to deceive me because I thought them amiable. I hadn't really objected to Thomas blackmailing me. I couldn't accept Gabriel's wishes and wanted to hold an intervention for him.

My only comfort was deep, dreamless sleep.

I was in a marvelous, cozy place, delighting in the smoothness of the luxury sheets and the squooshiness of the down pillow, and just drowsy enough to be blissfully unaware of how screwed up my life was, when I heard a nasty buzzing sound. I opened my eyes as Thomas shoved me and said, "Door."

I shoved him back, and then he pushed me so hard that I almost fell out of bed. I whacked him with my pillow, saying, "Treat me better, you jerk, or I will kick your exfoliated and waxed ass!" I grabbed a Paragon robe and looked at the clock. Who would show up at seven in the morning?

A bellhop stood at the door, shuffling from foot to foot. "Miss De Los Santos, there's a person at the front desk to see you."

"This early? I told them I wasn't to be disturbed by the media."

"Yes, we know, but this lady kept insisting and she is . . . um . . . kind of scaring people."

I sighed. "I'll be there in a few minutes. Let me shower and—"

But a golf cart came rolling down the path and stopped at my casita.

The bellhop driving it looked humiliated. I couldn't help smiling when I saw the petite woman with the oversized sun hat and the designer shades step out of the cart. She said to him, "Make sure my room is ready when I return. I want still water, not carbonated, and for goodness sake, don't have any potpourri around."

"Yes, ma'am."

The Paragon employees drove away so fast, gravel spun up.

nineteen

bleed me alone

Edna looked the picture of Paragon chic. She wore a pale aqua blouse over flowing slacks that were a shade deeper. She removed her sunglasses, and the hat cast a shadow over her face, making her amazing eyes look more mysterious.

Affection filled me and I wanted to grab her and hold her close. "Hello, Edna, won't you come in? How did you find me?"

"Young Lady, you were right."

"Really," I said, brightening up. "About what?"

"That if I waited long enough you would make a spectacle of yourself." She pulled out a copy of the *Weekly Exposition* and handed it to me as she came into the casita. "What are you doing here? You said you were in the City."

"I have a job rewriting a screenplay, but it's a lot more complicated than that."

Someone yawned loudly behind me and I remembered too late that I had an unauthorized roommate.

Edna took a long, lingering look at Thomas and said, "Young man, put on some clothes and order breakfast for us."

Thomas grinned cheerfully. "I am at your service . . ."

"Edna Grant," I said. "Edna, meet Thomas Cook, the actor."

"Edna," he repeated before hurrying off to get dressed.

Edna walked outside to inspect the patio. "Oswald called me and was beside himself about you. How are you going to explain your addled paramour to him?"

"Thomas may be addled, but he isn't my paramour. He's my ward," I said. "You have some explaining to do yourself."

"How so?"

I pulled up my sleeve. "Look, Edna." I put my finger to the edge of the shiny pink scar. "This is where Silas Madison's underling slashed me."

And, for the first time since I'd met her, Edna was speechless. She sat down in a chair and gazed at me, her eyes wide and full of sympathy.

"It happened the night of Nancy's wedding. I went with Ian, just as a friend. Silas sent this guy after him, but I was the one who got cut."

"Was it serious?"

"Serious enough that Ian gave me some of his blood to help me heal." I saw her shocked expression and said, "There have been some side effects."

"Tell me . . ." she began, and then Thomas returned. He was dressed in a blue button-down shirt, a tie, and slacks. His sleek black hair was brushed neatly back and he was wearing cologne.

"Breakfast will be here soon," he said so cheerfully that I wondered if he'd been replaced by an alien replicant.

"Thank you, Thomas," Edna said, pulling herself together. "I believe I recognize you."

"You look very familiar to me, too," he said dreamily. I waited for him to launch into his filmography, but he was busy gazing at Edna.

Breakfast was delivered, and she directed that it be set up in a shady spot on the patio. Thomas held out a chair for Edna, and she said, "Run along now. Milagro and I have some personal business to discuss."

He chewed disconsolately on a lemon-oatmeal scone as he walked away from us.

When he was inside, she said, "Tell me everything."

Until now I had been trying to hold myself together. But now Edna was here and when I looked at her, I trusted that she loved me. I trusted that she would help me.

I didn't bother to wipe away my tears as I told her everything that had happened. I felt an enormous relief as I confessed about the visions. "Edna, it's horrible. Every time someone touches me I see these things, blood and internal organs, and they seem so real. It's awful and I'm awful because under my revulsion is some sick desire."

"Oh, Young Lady," she said gently.

She reached for my hand, and then pulled back. "Except for Thomas," I said. "He's anemic so I don't have that reaction to him. What is it like for you? What do you see?"

She shook her head. "I don't experience anything like that."

"So it is just me. I'm the only one like this. How can I be with Oswald when I'm like this?"

"Oswald loves you deeply, Young Lady."

"He loved a girl who was affectionate. He won't love a girl who can never touch him or be touched by him."

"We will figure things out," she said. "You will survive, Milagro."

245

I thought about Mercedes's words. "I know how to survive, Edna, but maybe I don't know how to live." I closed my eyes and did a breathing exercise. "What do you know about the neovamps?"

"There's no such thing as—"

"Yes, Edna, yes, there *are* vampires and they tried to capture me and drink my blood in a primitive rite. They could have killed me, so please, please don't tell me there's no such thing!"

"You're right." She gave a nod. "Gabriel discouraged Winnie and Sam from inviting Willem and Silas, but the baby's grandparents insisted on having the traditional ceremony. There's a big division regarding the group. I didn't know Silas would go so far as to try to unseat Ian on the council."

"Silas mentioned the council. Tell me more about it."

"It's an international council of family representatives. Ian is a member. The jurisprudence branch officiates on matters that we prefer not go to other courts."

"Matters like assault with a deadly weapon?"

"Yes, criminal matters," she said. "Silas has been gathering followers, but I'm astonished they could do this."

"Yours is a blood-based culture."

"As is yours, Young Lady, but I don't expect you to capture enemies and cut out their beating hearts."

"It would be nice to have that option," I mused.

The edge of her mouth tilted up, but she looked tired.

I said, "You must have been driving all night. Why not get some rest and we'll figure out what to do later. I wish we could ask Gabriel for help."

"We will. I'd heard he was considering a conversion attempt, and I've been very saddened that he felt the need to go ahead with it."

"He said he wants to be normal," I said glumly.

"Young Lady, the longer I live, the more I am aware that there is no such thing as 'normal.'" She tapped her foot on the patio. "Is he here with his parents?"

"I think so, and some dreadful girl who looks as if she was raised on milk and broccoli and has had a subscription to *Brides* magazine since she was twelve."

"You paint a damning picture," she said. "Is Silas here?"

"I haven't seen him, and I've been in and out of the spa and snooping around," I said. "I don't know how much Skip Taylor knows, and I have a feeling that Thomas doesn't have a clue."

She glanced in through the windows. Thomas was wearing shorts and a tight T-shirt and making a great show of exercising. "An extremely good-looking man."

"Yes, but incredibly self-centered. I'm surprised he hasn't asked me to walk backward in front of him holding a mirror."

"I'm sure you're exaggerating," she said. "In the evening, we'll talk about how to bring Gabriel back to his senses."

Edna said good-bye and walked back to the Paragon. Thomas watched her go and said, "Now, *that's* a woman."

So that's what he meant by "less like a girl."

I completed the first draft of "Teeth of Sharpness" while waiting for Edna to call me. I printed it out and put it on the corner of my desk. I stared at the clean type on the pages and felt a squiggle of pride because I thought the result was very good. I would let it stew in my brain before looking at it again.

Edna summoned me to her room at cocktail hour, and I walked into the main building feeling anxious yet optimistic, as unpleasant a mixture as coffee and blood. I ran into Charles on the landing of the wide staircase and said, "Charles, come meet a friend who's just arrived."

"I'm just signing out for the evening and—"

"No excuses. I've been very understanding about the slow repairs to my truck, so you can take a minute to say hello and make sure my friend is comfortable."

"Yes, of course. Is this your friend's first stay here?"

"I think so. She's more of a city person."

"A college friend?" Charles asked politely.

I led him to a corner suite and he looked nervously at his watch. "I really . . . ," he began as I knocked on the door.

Edna opened the door and took a look at me and my companion.

"Hi, Edna. I wanted you to meet Charles, who works here as a concierge. Charles, this is my friend, Mrs. Grant."

"Come in," she said. "Close the door behind you. Young Lady, there's a bottle of wine chilling. Please open it and serve us."

Charles stood at the doorway and smiled. "Thank you, but I can't stay. Welcome to the Paragon and please call our desk should you require—"

Edna turned and glared at the man. "I said, come in and close the door behind you."

Her brusqueness confused both Charles and me. I wondered if she was going to lambaste him for some hotel crime like having a torn "sanitized for your safety" band on a water glass.

"Edna," I began as I walked in, "Charles only has a minute." The room had marvelous windows looking out toward the dark mountains. A sleeping area was visible behind woven reed screens and there was a sitting area with a fireplace and a bar. I went to the bar and took the wine out of the ice bucket.

She pointed to the sofa and said to him, "You sit there."

He did so as docilely as a trained seal. "Yes, Mrs. Grant. I hope you find your room comfortable."

She took the glass of wine that I offered her. "I find my room very comfortable. What I find uncomfortable is that you are working here."

He looked befuddled. "I am well qualified for my job and trained at some of the finest establishments in the world."

"That's not what I'm talking about." She sat across from him and said, "Look me in the eye, Charlie Arthur, and tell me what you're doing here."

"Edna, really, what has Charles done to offend you?"

"Young Lady, don't you see? He's one of us. Isn't it obvious?"

I read his name tag again. Charles Arthur, Concierge. "He can't be. There was no President Arthur."

"Chester Arthur," Charles said miserably. "Eighteen eighty-one to eighteen eighty-five. Everyone forgets about him."

My F.U. education had failed me. I dropped to sit on the sofa beside him.

"The last time I saw you, Charlie, you were three years old at a family picnic shoving cupcakes in your face," Edna said. "You look exactly the same."

"*Et tu*, Chuck?" I asked sadly.

twenty

biting the hand that bleeds you

Charles broke like a piñata. Instead of delicious candy treats spilling out of him, he gave us jaw-breaking, foul-tasting facts.

Silas had recruited Charles for the neovamp group when he had been flunking out of an MFA program. "He told me we would use our difference to make a difference," Charles said. "We'd replace the old guard, install our own members on the council, and leverage our power. Some of the ideas he had, like reviving the ancient ways, sounded pretty cool. I didn't really know what the old ways were, but I'd done a history minor and was interested in that stuff."

" 'That stuff' like genetic supremacy?" I asked.

"I thought he meant the language and, you know, wood carving and boat making," Charles said. "I wasn't paying that much attention because I was partying a lot then. That's how he usually recruits: he finds guys at loose ends."

Zave had told me the same thing.

"Where is Silas?" Even as I asked the question, I already knew the answer.

"Here, the man in the wheelchair," he said. "He's still recovering from, um . . . I don't know the details, but I heard that Ian Ducharme almost killed him. The council's detained Ducharme and is holding a hearing about his attack against one of our own."

"Is Silas involved in Skip's movie?" I asked.

Charles sunk deeper in the sofa. "No and yes. It's a real movie and Silas is one of the financial backers. They needed a rewrite and he thought he'd kill two birds with one stone, so he asked Skip Taylor to hire you. Skip doesn't know what we are, but he knows that Silas is up to something." He gave me an "I'm sorry" look and added, "When Silas was investigating you, he found a short story that he liked, so he thought you'd do a decent job as a screenwriter. A story about a yak."

"A llama," I corrected. Actually the story had been about *La Llorona*, the mythical wailing woman of Latin folklore, but a terrible mistake with my computer's spell-check had replaced all the "*Llorona*"s with "llama"s.

"Silas is fascinated with you," Charles said.

"Yes, I know. He wants to use me to create vampire hybrid babies." Some things are impossible to say without sounding ridiculous. "He tried to drug me with some vile alcohol and then he was going to have a bloodletting ceremony. I managed to get away, though."

He looked shocked. "That isn't what he told me. He told me that you've been threatening to expose our people and that you were allied with Sebastian Beckett-Witherspoon and CACA and that's why we had to keep you occupied here."

"Edna, please enlighten Charlie."

"Milagro helped save us from CACA," she said. "She's on our side."

I asked, "Charlie, what's happening in that locked wing with the blood bathing rooms? Is Silas involved with the shutdown of the Paragon for the Diamond Club event?"

Charles bit a fingernail. "He bought a share of ownership in the Paragon, and he's been planning a big celebration for our movement. The word is that your blood is, uh, stimulating like an aphrodisiac. According to legend, the blood of a survivor increases our fertility."

"Charles, Chas, Chuckles, Charlie," I said, "I can't express the depth of my dismay that you would want to do this to me. I thought we had a connection, we were simpatico."

He gulped his wine. "I'm sorry."

"What will happen at the ceremony?" Edna asked.

"The usual drinks, dancing, and food for most guests. Milagro will be given the ancient drink to make her more relaxed, then there's that gibberish ritual and blood will be taken, but only enough for our people to have a few drops each. Milagro will be kept sedated in a suite next to the Diamond Club lounge and one of our staff, a registered phlebotomist, will begin regularly harvesting her blood for our new treatments."

I said, "Do people in the Diamond Club know they're dealing with vampires?"

Charles shook his head. "They think the ceremony is just entertainment. They don't ask a lot of questions as long as they get access to cutting-edge treatments. Some of them might know, but those kinds of people keep secrets for each other."

"Now, what about my grandson Gabriel?" asked Edna. "How did you lure him here?"

"That was a coincidence," Charles said. "Silas offers guidance to people who are confused and helps get them on the path. It works. I was like Gabriel, and now I have a girlfriend and everything."

"So you're straight and you're not the least bit interested that gorgeous, smoking-hot Thomas Cook is here at the hotel?"

"I am only interested in Mr. Cook in my capacity as a concierge," he said.

I was really tired of people denying who they were. A big gesture was needed. I turned to Charles and, pulling him to me, shoved my body hard against his. Gruesome images detonated in my head, but I endured them as I put my lips over his mouth and kissed him deeply and passionately. My hands ran up his meaty back. I wish I could have enjoyed the fact that he was a big, hunky grab.

When I released him, his face was as pink as a peony and his eyes were wide. I looked at Edna and said, "As I suspected, one hundred percent gay."

Edna's eyebrow went up. "Young Lady, I could have told you that without the graphic display."

"Sure, but it wouldn't have had the dramatic impact."

Charles composed himself and said, "I am absolutely *not* gay. I am in a healthy romantic relationship with a woman."

"Then you won't care if I tell you that if you come to my casita, you can see Thomas Cook swimming naked."

"Really!" he said excitedly. Then he hid his head in his hands and said, "How did I get in this mess?"

"Wanton carelessness," Edna said. "But if you help us, we will try to get you out of it."

Our first order of business was reclaiming Gabriel.

"I always thought he was okay with who he was," I said.

"His parents are entirely behind this. They have baby fever," Edna announced. She turned to Charles and asked, "Are they staying here?"

"No, those are Brittany Monroe's parents. They come every year."

"The Monroes," Edna sneered. "Social climbers. I'll take care of this."

I hopped up and started to follow her.

"You stay here and keep Charlie company," she said, and left the room.

I watched the door close and then hunted through the honor bar. There were a few bags of organic whole wheat pretzels. I tossed one to Charles. He held the cellophane bag in his hands and stared at it.

"So, Charlie, how did a nice boy like you get mixed up with a group like this?"

He turned the bag over and over in his hands. "I just wanted to fit in somewhere. It sounded like a good group."

"Tell me," I said.

He told me that Silas preached an idealistic philosophy of a world led by wise, benevolent vamps. The reality was tawdrier: that the newly indoctrinated vamps were placed in positions where they could collect information in order to blackmail, extort, and influence the wealthy and powerful.

I asked Charlie, "What's up with Silas's weird vibe? He doesn't register on any sexual scale."

"He says that our leaders shouldn't be distracted by sexual drive. He takes progestin as a form of chemical castration. It's a female hormone that inhibits testosterone production."

We were talking about what it was like being on the outside of mainstream society when Edna returned with Gabriel in tow.

He turned to me and said coldly, "Milagro, I can't believe you brought Grandmama here when it was clear that I wanted you to leave me alone."

Edna gave him a look that would reduce most people to mere piles of ash. "Milagro did not ask me to come. Someone in town brought to my attention that she was in a tabloid article with an actor."

"Thomas Cook," I said. "He swims in my pool naked almost every day." When Edna glared at me, I added, "I'm sorry, but it's really an impressive sight. Thomas Cook. Naked. In my pool. Although Gabriel wouldn't have any interest in that since he's now a raging heterosexual."

"Gabriel," Edna said, "please sit down."

He took a chair at a distance from us and sat straight. "I only have a few minutes. Brittany is waiting for me."

Edna turned to him and said, "Do you know that Silas sent someone to stab Ian, but it was Milagro who was badly injured?"

Something flickered in Gabriel's pond-green eyes. "I didn't know she'd been hurt." He looked at me and asked, "What were you doing with Ian?"

"Why, are you jealous? Oh, I forgot, you're not interested in hot, sexy men anymore."

"You're so obsessed with men that you think everyone else is, too," he said bitchily.

Edna glared at us. "Ian went to her friend's wedding with her. Silas also had her down at that nightclub in the City and he was about to perform the"—and here Edna spoke a few words in the ugly old language—"and you know what that means, Gabriel."

Lifting his eyes to mine, Gabriel said, "I'm very sorry to hear that you had to go through that. If you had asked me . . ."

"I *did* ask you about Silas," I said angrily. "You never said that he was assembling a force of neovamps in order to seek global domination."

"There's no such thing as vampires," he said without conviction.

"Will you children stop bickering so we can discuss this?" Edna snapped. "Silas also tricked Milagro into coming here and plans to use her blood for his followers and sell it to members of the Paragon's Diamond Club as rejuvenative therapy. Did you know about this?"

Gabriel blanched like an almond. Then he stood up. "I'm sorry, but I can't disclose any of Silas's confidences," he said with a tremor in his voice. "I appreciate your concern, but I'm taking a new direction with my life, one that embraces my legacy and identity. Please support me in this, because I'm going to sever all toxic relations. I think the best thing for you is to leave here now."

Edna stared at her grandson. "You know that I have always loved you and accepted you as you are. I could not have asked for a better grandson. I can talk to your parents. You don't have to pretend to be something you're not for me."

"Yes, Grandmama, I know," Gabriel said softly. "But that isn't enough anymore."

"Gabriel, don't tell Silas that Milagro is aware of his machinations and don't tell him I'm here. Will you do that for me?"

He nodded his head. "Yes, Grandmama, but please don't ask anything else of me. Good night."

He walked out the door and we sat there stunned.

"We're to blame," Edna said sadly. "We tolerated Willem Dunlop and his followers when we should have denounced them."

"Why didn't you tell me what was happening?" I asked.

"Knowledge is a burden, Young Lady. You already had enough to absorb about our lives. Perhaps, too, we took the easy route." She gave a hard look at Charles and said, "You have a choice: you can go to Silas now, or you can help us to put an end to his plans."

Edna won over people by both intimidating and impressing them. Charlie was no exception.

Our discussion lasted for hours. Charlie told us that the private section of the spa hoped to lure more vampire customers by offering special services, including "free-range blood" and blood and mineral water soaks.

"Well, that gives a new definition to 'blood bath,'" I said. "What's free-range blood?"

Charles hung his head and mumbled so incoherently that Edna snapped, "Sit up straight and speak clearly."

He did as she ordered. "Some of the guys put on these alien suits and take young adults from La Basura. They're kept in a room that looks like a spaceship exam room. When they get really scared, their blood is harvested. Just a pint or so every day, nothing harmful. The adrenaline in it is a real rush. He charges extra for that. Then he drugs them and returns them."

"Charlie Arthur, I can't believe that you participated in such reprehensible and criminal activity," Edna scolded. "Your good mother would weep with shame if she had any idea—"

'Please don't tell my mother!' Charlie said in a panic.

While Edna threatened and guilt-tripped Charlie, I found myself oddly amused that at least one of Bernie's stories had a basis in reality.

Charlie said that Silas's launch party for the neovamp movement would take place in the Paragon's ballroom. Thralls would serve as waitstaff, since they could be counted on for loyalty and they worked for free. The party would start early, and the ceremony would take place at midnight.

"Silas really wants to make this an ongoing venture," Charlie said. "If Milagro's blood really does help our fertility, our numbers will grow and he'll be in on the ground floor of vampire spas."

"Does the council approve of Silas's activities?" I asked Edna.

"So far they've turned a blind eye to all this," Edna said.

"Silas says they get off on it," said Charlie. "They're proud of the old ways and most of them believe we really are superior to the normals."

Edna thought a moment. "If we go to them now, Silas can deny everything. We have to have evidence and take it to the entire council, not just the reactionary members." She looked at me. "But it's up to you, Young Lady. If you like, we can pack your things and leave here now. How far do you want to go?"

"All the way, Edna. I say, bring it on."

It was very late when I returned to the casita. Thomas was awake, sitting on the sofa in striped pajamas, wearing glasses, and reading my screenplay. He put down the pages as I came in.

"Where have you been? Bernie and I waited around for you."

"I was with Edna, catching up on things." I sat beside him on the sofa and pulled off his glasses. I looked through them and saw that the lenses were plain glass. I handed them back to him. "Why would Bernie think I'd want to have anything to do with him after that fallacious article?"

"You mean . . ." Thomas made an obscene gesture with his mouth and hand.

"No, fallacious means false."

"Oh," Thomas said, looking disappointed. "Bernie wanted to get together because we're all friends."

"How about tomorrow?" I suggested, and he brightened. He was a man who lived in the moment. "What do you think about my first draft?"

"Not bad," he said. "But I've got some suggestions."

I'd thought that Thomas would want changes that expanded his role, but his ideas were really good in terms of improving the plot and characters. Clearly, wearing fake glasses had made him smarter.

I thought they were a nifty prop and I tucked them in my handbag when I went to the main building the next day. Charlie was at the front desk, as nervous as a virgin in a whorehouse.

"Good morning, Charles," I said. "I wanted to pick up some brochures for my mother Regina. She loves spas."

"Of course, Miss De Los Santos." Charlie handed me two brochures, making sure that I felt the keys hidden beneath them. "The top one describes our accommodations and the bottom one has directions about transportation."

I flipped up the top brochure and saw a note with his car's license plate, make, and color, as well as a diagram of its location in the day visitors' parking area.

"Thank you. I'll put these to good use."

I found his car exactly where he'd told me it would be. In the backseat was a bag with two maid's uniforms, a staff parking permit, a housekeeping pass key, and a few maps sketched out on binder paper. I liked Charlie and hoped I wasn't making a mistake trusting him again.

Mercedes was waiting in a room at the budget motel on the

259

edge of La Basura. We caught up on things and she said, "You look healthier than I've ever seen you."

"Weird, huh? I'm feeling strong and have good endurance and reactions. How was your drive down?"

"No traffic. I got here fast, but after this, I'm going to crash."

"I really appreciate your help, Mercedes." I wished that I could hug her.

"Hey, it's not just for you; it's for the good of humanity."

"Who knew there were so many cults and extremists around?" I mused.

"How's Oswald feel about what happened?" she asked.

"He doesn't know yet."

Mercedes frowned and said, "You've gotta tell him, Milagro."

"He's coming back soon. I'll tell him then."

"What's going on with Gabriel?"

"It's so sad it makes me want to cry. He's like a dry husk of his former self. I could understand him trying to be straight with some amazing androgynous chick, but it's as if he decided to punish himself with this festering mass of pink and blond girlitude."

We changed into the maid's uniforms, and I twisted my hair into a bun and put on Thomas's clear eyeglasses. Mercedes took one glance at me and said, "You look smarter." She wore a kerchief over her dreads.

I told her I was probably the only Paragon maid with an F.U. degree.

We got in Mercedes's car and she propped the parking permit in her windshield. We didn't speak much on the tense trip to the spa. We stopped on the highway just before Paragon Way and waited for Charlie's phone call. It came in a few minutes.

We drove into the employee parking lot and walked through the service entrance of the main building. Mercedes carried a canvas shopping bag.

Charlie was waiting for us in a storage room, sweat on his brow. After I introduced him to Mercedes, he said, "Silas just went for a sauna, but he never stays long, so hurry."

He pushed a cleaning cart to us and said, "Good luck."

Mercedes hid her canvas bag behind the dusting rags on the cart and said, "We'll be careful."

My friend and I took the service elevator to the top floor.

I knocked on Silas's door and said in a heavily accented voice, "Cleaning es-staff." I listened carefully and heard nothing, so I opened the door. The enormous suite was designed to accommodate someone needing medical care. I could see a hospital bed through a doorway and railings on the walls.

We put a "Housekeeping in Progress" sign on the doorknob and closed the door behind us. "Cleaning es-staff!" I called again. *"El hauskipin."*

"There's no one here," Mercedes said. "Let's find his papers and computer."

The desk only contained the usual hotel notepaper, Paragon brochures, and local tour guides. We opened drawers and cabinets and Mercedes said, "Bingo."

She pulled a laptop computer from a case in the closet. "Find the hormones."

That was an easy task. They were on the bedside table with an array of Paragon skin products. I flushed the progestin down the toilet and refilled the bottle with the steroids that Skip had wanted Thomas to take. "Check," I said to Mercedes.

"You keep watch and I'll get the files." From her canvas bag she took a few small electronic components.

I picked up a rag and swiped at surfaces while listening for anyone coming. Mercedes was chuckling, and I said, "What?"

"This guy wants to take over the world and he doesn't protect his computer as much as a teenager who's hiding porn from his parents." Her fingers were flying over the keyboard, and she grinned and said, "*Ahorita.*"

Ahorita was like *momentito,* and it made me crazy because "a little now" could mean one minute or one hour or one day. I paced in front of the door.

I heard footsteps and the low buzz of a wheelchair coming down the corridor. "Dive, dive, dive!" I whispered sharply, because some piece of my brain thought that submarine lingo would emphasize my urgency.

Mercedes was sliding the laptop back in its case when a voice in the hallway said, "Houssekeeping? They were already here thisss morning."

I tossed a bottle of glass cleaner and a towel in Mercedes's general direction and then I held a feather duster in front of my face. The lock clicked open and Silas, still protected by bandages, zipped his wheelchair into the room.

I glanced toward Mercedes, who was industriously rubbing a towel on the window. "*Está bien,*" she said. "Ees good now."

Silas's companion stepped into the suite. It was the manager I'd tackled. "What are you doing in here? This room was supposed to be cleaned this morning."

"Yes, meester," said Mercedes, "but, *pero,* the girl this morning say there is something on the window. I clean for you berry good." She smiled proudly. "Ees good now."

"Fine, please leave," the manager said.

Mercedes had hidden her computer equipment under the towel and I hoped the men wouldn't notice the bulky shape.

The manager walked us to the door and said quietly, "I will have a talk with your supervisor about this. Where are your badges?" Silas's back was to us as the manager yanked away the feather duster and saw my face.

I smiled at the manager and whispered, *"¡Hola!"* and put the feather duster up again.

He turned red and choked out, "Thank you very much for your help."

Mercedes and I wheeled the cleaning cart out the door and raced down the hall with it. Once we got around a corner, we grabbed her canvas bag and ditched the cart. We ran down a stairwell, out of the building, and were back in her car in a few minutes. It wasn't until she was speeding down the highway that I rolled down my window, stuck my head out, and hollered, "We don't need no stinkin' badges!"

"Who was that guy?" Mercedes asked.

"Some *cabrón*. Don't worry about him." I turned on the stereo and an insane cacophony blasted out. "Hey, is this the Dervishes?"

"Yes, guaranteed to blow your mind."

"I like them."

"They totally rock. Do you know what I found out after that disaster at the club? They'd bribed one of the bartenders to replace the house vodka with some high-octane vodka from the Balkans."

"Well, that explains some of the mayhem," I said and turned up the volume.

I left Mercedes at the motel to nap and later search through Silas's information. I drove Charlie's car back to the Paragon, leaving it where I'd found it.

Thomas was running on the treadmill when I came in. "What are our plans? Bernie's called three times."

"Doesn't Bernie know I'm furious with him?"

"Grow up, Milagro."

I called Bernie and yelled at him for several minutes while he laughed and apologized.

"Your beloved pet goat Pancho," he said. "Tell me that's not funny!"

"It wasn't a goat. It was a sheep. Where did you get that, anyway? That was awful."

"A butcher in town was a student of mine. Milagro, it was all meant in love."

I wanted to spend time with Edna away from the Paragon, so I asked, "Do you know how to cook?"

"I can grill burgers," he said. "Why?"

"You're cooking dinner for me and my friends tonight."

My truck had finally been returned, so I was going to drive to Bernie's with Thomas. Edna said she would meet us there a little later.

Thomas was walking around in his boxer shorts while I put on some makeup in the bathroom. When the doorbell rang, I called out, "Get that, please."

"Sure, honey buns," he joked.

I heard footsteps come through the bedroom, and I said, "Who was it, sugar cakes?"

"Milagro."

I looked in the doorway and there was Oswald.

twenty-one

every breath you take

Oswald was dirty and sweaty and rumpled in a T-shirt and jeans. His hair stuck out in odd ways and he hadn't shaved. He was the most beautiful thing I'd ever seen and I stared at him speechless. Perhaps I desired him so much that he'd manifested as a vision. Except that visions were rarely olfactory and he had a definite aroma.

"Do you want to tell me what's going on?" he said with a hard edge to his voice.

"Oswald!" I moved to him, but then I stopped short, terrified of poisoning my passion for him with ugly images. "Oswald, you're really here." My breathing was shallow and I felt dizzy with happiness and confusion. "You're back."

"You didn't wait long, did you, to find someone else?"

"There's only you, Oswald. There's only ever been you."

Thomas, rubbing his firm abs, walked up behind Oswald.

"So you're the boyfriend," he said. "I thought she was making you up."

I wanted to drown Thomas in the step-up Jacuzzi tub, but that would have taken me away from staring at Oswald.

"You're Thomas Cook," Oswald said angrily. He stepped toward Thomas.

"Yes, I'm here getting in shape for my next role. Milagro's done a nice little job as my assistant."

"I am not your damn assistant. I'm a screenwriter." I pulled Oswald into the bathroom, taking care to only hold on to the fabric of his shirt, and slammed the door shut in Thomas's face. Then I carefully placed my arms around Oswald's waist, averting my face so that my skin wouldn't have contact with his. "Oswald, I've missed you so much."

"If you've missed me that much, why don't I rate a kiss?" he said, and I heard the hurt in his voice.

I stepped away from him. "I want to, more than anything. Didn't your grandmother tell you what happened to me?"

"No, she said I should hear everything from you," he said. "You know how I found out you were here? An anesthesiologist brought a copy of the *Weekly Exposition* when he flew in yesterday. I've been traveling here since then."

I sat on the edge of the tub, thinking of the last time I'd had a conversation with Oswald in the bathroom. "Let me talk and don't say anything until I've finished. It started when Silas Madison said he wanted to meet with me and talk to me about your people's history."

I related the story, feeling more and more embarrassed at my gullibility and rash behavior. When I finished I said, "I'm an idiot. If I hadn't been so insecure, I wouldn't have tried to get information from Silas and I wouldn't have needed to go to the wedding with someone who I thought would impress Nancy's friends."

Oswald sighed. "Oh, babe, it's my fault," he said, and sat beside me. His gray eyes were as clear and shining as a child's. "I'm sorry about things I said to you. I've been sorry ever since I left. I'm sorry I didn't tell you more. It's my fault you got hurt."

"No, it's Silas's fault," I said.

He touched my knee and I could feel the warmth of his hand through the denim of my jeans. "Are you sure I can't touch you?"

I did my visualizations and controlled my breathing. Then I put my forefinger on his hand. Blood, a pulsating heart, deep purple organs blasted through my thoughts of flowers. I jerked my hand back.

I closed my eyes so that he wouldn't see the tears.

"Milagro, we'll find a way to get over this. Winnie and I can work on it, and there are research doctors in the family."

"Sure, of course," I said. "I got over the earlier contamination. I'll get over this one." I forced myself to smile and said, "Why don't you take a shower? We're having dinner at Bernie's."

"Take a shower with me." He brushed his lips on the shoulder of my blouse.

"Next time," I said, even as I wondered if there would ever be a next time.

I left the bathroom, because it would hurt too much to watch him undress and not be able to touch him.

When he had showered and dressed, he came into the bedroom, where I was trying to pay attention to the evening news. He looked around and said, "Where does Thomas sleep?"

"You're going to hate the answer. We share the bed."

"You just told me that you weren't having sex with him!"

"I'm not! It's entirely platonic." Thinking of Gabriel's accusation, I said, "You're so obsessed with me, you think everyone wants to have sex with me, but they don't. I'm not even Thomas's type."

"You want me to actually believe that you share the same bed and don't do anything?"

I looked him in the eye. "Yes, because it's true. In fact, it's all very innocent and sweet." I recited Thomas's story about holding hands with the little girl and told him how we slept facing each other. "He's so good at telling his story, I always imagine that I can smell the hot chocolate on his breath."

Oswald's expression changed from irate to calculating. I'd seen that look when he was trying to puzzle out a health problem with one of the animals at the ranch. "You said he looked terrible when you first met him?"

"Yes, but every day he looks better and better. It's amazing, really, what sleep, protein drinks, and exercise can do. He's the only one who doesn't set off the gory visions. He's got a mild form of anemia."

"Amazing," Oswald said coldly. He strode out of the bedroom to the living area, where Thomas was sprawling in a chair reading *Variety*.

"You sleep with her, facing her, and you don't do anything sexually?" Oswald demanded.

"Whatever she says," Thomas said, flipping a page.

Oswald grabbed the paper away from Thomas and smacked it down on the sofa. "What kind of anemia do you have?"

"A mild kind, not that it's any of your business. Are we ready to go yet, Milagro?"

"Gestational anemia?"

"Yes, that's it."

"Only pregnant women get that."

Thomas shrugged eloquently. "It's got some other name, then."

"You're sleeping close enough to Milagro to be breathing in each other's faces?"

"There's nothing wrong with that."

"Oswald," I said, "can you stop hectoring Thomas? He hasn't tried to seduce me. He hasn't done anything wrong."

"You're an incubus!" Oswald barked in Thomas's face.

It was an insane thing to say, and I wondered if Oswald had forgotten to drink bottled water on his trip.

Thomas maintained his cool, though. "You're one to be calling me names, you freaky vampire perv."

Oswald's fist swung out, but Thomas jumped up and out of range. "You're the one who got Milagro into your sick fetish."

Oswald let his arms hang down. He looked guilty and I said quickly, "Thomas knows we're into the vampire Goth scene, hon. He knows we like to play-act that way." I was still trying to process what Oswald had said. I remembered a class I'd taken in mythology at F.U. and said, "What do you mean Thomas is an incubus? There's no such thing. The myth was generated as an explanation for night terrors and night paralysis."

Looking defeated, Oswald said, "There's no such thing as the *mythical* creature. There are, however, people with a rare genetic anomaly of their hypothalami that results in their condition as subacute hyperventilators. Do you know what hyperventilation is?"

"Yes, breathing in too much oxygen," I answered.

"Common misconception," Oswald said. "It's *exhaling* too much carbon dioxide. The CO_2 in our systems is the main determinant of the body's acid-base balance. If your CO_2 is off, it negatively affects all of your body functions. He was restoring the balance of his CO_2 by breathing in your exhalations."

"Boring," Thomas said. "Bernie is waiting."

So now there were incubi, too, but they weren't *really* incubi? Next I'd learn that there were zombies, who weren't zombies but people with a biological disorder that made them eat human flesh. "You're telling me that Thomas was using me for my carbon dioxide?"

"Yes, that's why he always needed to face you." Looking at Thomas, he said, "Admit to Milagro that you used her."

Thomas exhaled a long, possibly carbon dioxide–deficient breath and said, "It's not my fault. My father was one. There's nothing wrong with what I did, and it helped her. She was miserable and having crying nightmares."

Oswald glanced at me.

I nodded. "I've never slept so well in my life. I didn't have any nightmares—or any dreams at all."

"There's a symbiotic aspect of the relationship," Oswald said, in full medical doctor mode now. "The process helped to regulate your own breathing, provide you with additional oxygen, calm you down, and assist in your sleep."

"See, no problem," Thomas said.

I should have been angry with him, but I was grateful for those dreamless nights. "Thomas," I said, "does Skip know about your condition? Is that why he wanted you here with me?"

He shook his head. "No, I told him I needed an assistant, that's all."

"Listen to me, Cook," Oswald said. "That was then; this is now. She's my girl, and you're not sleeping with her again, do you understand?" Oswald sounded belligerent now. "You can just breathe in a paper bag and self-regulate your CO_2."

"It's not like I need her," Thomas said. "I could make a phone call and have a dozen just like her here in two hours."

This time Thomas didn't see the punch coming until it was too late. I drew my fist back and rubbed my knuckles. "Ouch," I said. "I hope that hurt you more than it hurt me."

Oswald couldn't stop laughing as the actor massaged his jaw. Thomas gave me a look as if I'd been a terrible disappointment to him and said, "You know I won't be able to give you a good reference after this."

Before we left, Thomas called Gigi and she said she would get him a room near her suite. While he talked, I motioned Oswald into the bedroom and whispered, "Why doesn't he set off the bloody visions?"

"I can only theorize, baby. Maybe the visions are in reaction to the respiratory gases carried by red blood cells."

We went back to the living room as Thomas hung up the phone. "Gigi wants me to stay for some big private party next week, so I guess I'll do that."

The ride to Bernie's was difficult, not only because Oswald and Thomas were annoyed with each other, but because Oswald was close to me, yet I couldn't touch him.

Bernie was good-natured about barbecuing for us in his backyard, a barren square of dirt with a cement slab and a rickety trellis. I introduced him to Oswald and he said, "So you're the lucky guy. Milagro always talks about you."

"And you're the guy who made her famous."

"I made Maria Dos Passos famous," Bernie said. "But I've got faith that Milagro will make her own name as a writer."

I felt a general zuzziness at the compliment.

Bernie poured beer in a glass for me and said, "I'm glad we're still pals."

"I am questioning my own sanity for even talking to you again."

"Stop insulting our host, Young Lady," Edna said as she came up behind me.

"Now you're . . ." Bernie looked at Edna, then at me, trying to figure out our relationship.

"Edna is my friend and Oswald's grandmother," I said.

Bernie stared at Edna and grinned. "There was a devastating novelist some time back named Dena Franklin—I was crazy about an old black-and-white photo of her that I found in some newspaper archives—anyway, you resemble her. You're much too young to be her, of course."

"Of course." Edna smiled and said, "Milagro told me that you have expertise with hidden cameras and recording equipment."

"Oh, you mean that chupa story . . . Well, it was all in good fun."

"I thought it was most diverting," Edna said. "How would you like a job recording some antics at the Paragon party? It's a private job. I just want copies for myself and my friends."

"I'll be at that party," Thomas said. He angled his head. "This is my good side."

"Are we talking about blackmail?" Bernie asked.

"We're talking about persuasion," Edna said with a smile. "Thomas, we don't need any photos of you or of Gigi, so let's keep this our secret."

He grinned foolishly. "Whatever you want."

My friend turned her charm back to Bernie. "Are you interested?"

"Interested? Hell, I'm captivated. How do you like your burger?"

"I like it rare. Very rare."

"She wants it very rare," Thomas repeated.

The evening had an odd poignancy; I felt as if I was playing the role of someone I wanted to be: an up-and-coming screenwriter with only good things in my future, fabulous friends, a fabulous boyfriend, youth, and health.

After dinner, Edna pulled Oswald to one side of the patio to fill him in on the situation with the neovamps. I stood nearby, adding the occasional fact, but letting her relay the events. When she began to describe the situation with Gabriel, I saw the sadness and concern on Oswald's face. I felt as if I was intruding, and I left them so they could have some privacy.

Bernie offered to show me his "library." He said the word as if he was joking, but when we went inside his ramshackle house, I saw that every wall was lined with bookcases. I held my head sideways as I read all the titles. There was a dizzying assortment of both familiar and unfamiliar names, great works and obscure collections of poetry.

"You can borrow anything you like, except first editions of American writers. What do you think?"

"I could live the rest of my life in this room," I said. "You have so many hardbacks, too."

"Some men gamble or take mistresses. I buy hardbacks."

Mercedes called as we were starting in on bowls of vanilla ice cream. I went out front to talk to her in privacy. "Speak to me," I said.

"I've got all the financial records and my pals are doing a little digging." She meant her hacker buddies. "It's the stuff we expected, a copy of the manifesto, records of payoffs to the neo-vamps, blackmail, and extortion, but there's something more interesting."

"Really? Tell me."

"Silas Madison was once in a rock band. Sort of metal, very heavy. Drugs, booze, groupies. He was lead singer and wrote songs, too, not half bad."

"The artistic instinct, when thwarted, often goes awry," I mused. "Hitler, Charles Manson, Silas Madison."

"You know," Mercedes said, "in my experience, you can never really take the rock out of someone."

"Nope," I said. "Never can. Silas is still drawn to music. That's why he has the chanteuse at the nightclub and that's why he had the zither player. What do you have in mind?"

"Do you remember how I told you that centuries ago people thought that a zither could cast a spell? Same with the lute. The oud is a form of the lute."

She let me make the association. I felt like the teacher's pet when I said, "And the Dervishes have an oud in their band. But the spell casting is just a myth."

"Sure, but the havoc those guys can cause is a proven fact, *chiquita*," she said, and told me her idea.

Oswald was exhausted from all his traveling and worrying. We left the others talking in Bernie's backyard and went back to the casita. Oswald wrapped me in a bedsheet and put his arm over me, careful not to touch my skin with his own. I wanted desperately to kiss him, to hold him.

"Oswald, do you think I'll get better?"

"Of course you will, babe," he said gently. But he sounded as if he was trying to convince himself.

"What about Gabriel?"

"I'll talk to him . . ." he began, but sleep overwhelmed him and his eyes closed.

It was best this way. I knew that people had cybersex and alternative ways to pleasure themselves. But I needed to touch the man I loved and to be touched by him. It was better to be able to watch him sleep all night than to try to make love without our skin touching.

I still loved him madly. I loved him so much that his happiness was more important than my own. There was a moment when the sky outside was still dark but a few birds began calling out. It was then that I suddenly understood what Evelyn Grant had been asking of me.

twenty-two

let's get the bloody party started

Oswald had just left to find Gabriel and talk to him when Skip showed up to collect the screenplay. Even though he didn't know the details of Silas's evil plans for me, I really, really wanted to drag him to the pool and drown him.

"Skip, first we have to take care of some business. Our contract." I handed him a few pages. "I talked to Thomas's agent and she drew this up for me. You'll see that it's all standard."

"I can't believe you don't trust me." Skip let out an annoyed huff and flicked through the pages.

"It's not about trust. It's about business."

"It looks fine," he said. "You know, now you're gonna have to give your agent a fifteen percent cut. Your loss." He pulled a slick silver pen out of his pocket and signed the copies, then handed the pen to me.

I signed the papers and then fetched "Teeth of Sharpness."

"I think it's good. I hope you like it."

"Gotta be better than anything a USB guy would do, right?" he asked with a grin.

"Right," I answered.

Later, Oswald returned with upsetting news. Gabriel was determined to remain part of the Project for a New Vampire Century.

"We can abduct him," I said. "We'll tie him to a chair, play techno and old-school disco music, and force him to look at *International Male* catalogs. Did you meet Brittany? She's Putrid in Pink."

Oswald smiled wearily. "I met her, but she's a symptom of the disease, not the disease itself. We have to go to the source."

When Gabriel refused to set up a meeting with Silas, Oswald went through Charlie. In the evening, we were summoned to meet with Silas at his suite.

I had nothing that would pass as a cocktail dress, so I followed Thomas's fashion tips and put on one of the gorgeous shirts he had left behind. I belted it with a long scarf and wore khaki shorts. I smoothed Paragon's Nourishing Agave Emollient Lotion on my legs and put on espadrilles and jewelry.

Oswald took one look at me and said, "What happened to all the clothes I gave you?"

"There're at the ranch. Are you staring at my legs?"

"Yes."

"Then this outfit is fine. Let's go."

When Charles met us in the lobby, I noticed many guests were checking out. He led us to Silas's suite.

One of the neovamp flunkies opened the door to Silas's suite. The bar was set up with a small carafe of blood, bottles of still water, and those delicious fish-shaped cheese crackers. I tried not to stare at the blood, but I'd been rationing my last few teaspoons of chicken liver blood, which was beginning to taste a bit funky.

Silas's bandages had been removed and he was out of the wheelchair, standing by the window. When he turned to us, I saw that all the hair on his face was gone and his skin was glossy pink, like my scar. His pale blue eyes stood out eerily against his new skin. "Dr. Grant, Misss De Loss Santoss," he said. "Do come in." He nodded to his flunkie, who went to the bar and began mixing blood cocktails.

"Good to see you again," said Oswald, stepping forward to shake Silas's hand. "Do call me Oswald."

Silas stared at me and said, "The lasst time we met, you left quite precipitoussly."

I smiled and let him wait for my reply. "I was as disappointed as you. I regret to tell you that Cuthbertson . . ." I stopped for a moment as if I was considering how much to reveal. "He was very stoned and very crude, but that doesn't excuse what he tried to do to me. I acted in self-defense, although that liquor may have caused me to overreact a little."

Silas was taken aback. "I had thought that Xavier might have . . . He is not the most reliable young man, and in fact has gone missing."

"Zave always treated me with the utmost respect." Glancing at Oswald, I said, "I wasn't going to let the doorman at Silas's club abuse me."

The chemically castrated Silas might not have believed me, but the steroids seemed to be having an effect, because Silas now gazed up and down at me and said, "Misss De Loss Santoss, I am very ssorry. Cuthbertson indulged too carelessly, but he told uss a different story."

"He would, wouldn't he?"

Oswald said sternly, "Silas, I don't hold you responsible for your employee's assault on *my* girlfriend, but I insist that you hold him responsible."

Silas nodded. "I shall ssee to it today. You have my word on it."

"Good." Oswald sat on the sofa and I sat beside him. The flunkie brought the drinks to us. The fresh mineral tang of the blood tasted wonderful.

Oswald gazed at Silas and said, "Do you mind my asking what happened to you?"

Silas's bitter smile, which he directed at me, looked especially bizarre on his taut, pink-skinned face. "Ian Ducharme told me that you had been cut."

I said, "Do you mean the knife incident? Zave apologized for the accident, and I understood that it was just between you and Ian."

"Ducharme considers you his personal property. He gave me one hundred cutss for the one 'nick' you ssuffered, Misss De Loss Santoss. Every time one began healing, he cut me again. We do recover, but we are not invulnerable to pain."

It wasn't difficult to believe that Ian had done this, and I felt emotions too dark to analyze now.

"I'm well aware of Ducharme's attitude toward Milagro," Oswald said. "He's no friend of mine and he was invited to my ranch only as a courtesy due to his position."

"I thought ass much," Silas said.

"Can we please drop the subject of Ian?" I asked. "I admit that I made a mistake with him, and I'd like to move on to other things. More exciting things, like the Project for a New Vampire Century."

"Sure, babe," Oswald said. "Silas, Milagro and my cousin Gabriel have been telling me more about your project."

Silas was skeptical. "You don't strike me ass an idealisst, Oswald. No offensse."

My boyfriend gave a lopsided smile that made me ache. "I'm not. I am more interested in my professional development and new ventures. I've outgrown my small practice and I'm looking for something I can invest in that will give me a bigger return."

"You're sspeaking about our new treatment center?" Silas asked.

"Yes, and I think you could use a plastic surgeon with my skills who knows how to treat both vampires and normals."

"What about the goalss of the project?"

"Do they really matter if we're bringing in the money?" Oswald said. "Let me buy into this place and you won't regret it."

The thing about corrupt people is that they always believe that everyone else is just as corrupt. Silas understood greed.

I gave him a seductive look and said, "Now isn't this much more interesting than conducting academic research? You get to use my blood, but this isn't a charity project. I want a cut of the take."

Silas returned my look. "I thought there wass more to you than an earnest bookworm. I say, let'ss cselebrate our new partnership."

The flunkie brought out a bottle of partridge blood and a bottle of champagne. Silas sketched out the overall goals of the Project for a New Vampire Century. They sounded great if you didn't listen too closely. Willem had envisioned a utopia where stability, both communal and financial, was paramount.

His first step was working to eradicate all things that threatened the family. "We've started with campaignss againsst gay marriage, on the grassrootss level," Silas said. "Sso easy to get support for that. Then we will move on to restrict divorce. Our ultimate goal iss mandatory arranged marriagess, and no divorce. We have an eight- to ten-year plan for that."

"What about people who have children harum-scarum?" I asked.

"Our kind are already overwhelmed. Various sscares can be created to encourage a limit of two children. Eventually, we will reduce that to one human child per couple, until our numberss reach parity. Reducing family size for humanss will also encourage financial ssolvency. We have plans to increase interest ratess to an onerous level, discouraging borrowing and unnecessary purchasess."

"You know, I had student loans for school, and most people can't buy a house without a mortgage," I said.

"In many countriess there are no home mortgagess or sstudent loanss. People must learn to do without those thingss they cannot afford."

"How does the elimination of all personal debt advance the vampire agenda?" I asked.

"Lesss dependence on corporate structure and more dependence on our moral authority. Individuality has been elevated in thiss country over the national good. Life is not only the purssuit of pleassure," he said.

Oswald chuckled. "You don't have to give her long explanations. All she really cares about is partying, flirting, and spending my money."

I laughed and said, "Oswald knows me too well."

"How is living with Thomas Cook?" Silas asked.

"Ah, Silas, very clever of you to keep me occupied while I was here. And thank you. I loved having that hunk of eye candy around. Oswald was so jealous that he's promised me a convertible!"

Oswald rolled his eyes.

Seeing that this was a sore subject, Silas said to Oswald, "It is ssuch a benefit to uss to have Gabriel'ss ssecurity resources and skills. Perhapss, too, you can help me recruit Ssam and Winnie."

"I was thinking the same thing," Oswald replied.

Silas told us about the launch party for the new treatment center. "It will take place, two nightss from now," Silas said. "Milagro, you will be a prominent participant in thiss event. We would like to offer tastess of your fresh blood to our important dignitariess at the gala. I'd also like to have a pint for our spa saless."

"Are you sure you can afford a whole pint?" I said. "I am a rara avis."

"Let me negotiate that with Silas, honey," Oswald said. "I can also draw the blood, no charge."

"I knew you would be of sservice," Silas said.

We chatted a bit more about the new treatment center and Silas said he'd give Oswald a tour the next day. Then we exchanged good nights and went back to the casita. Oswald automatically reached for my hand and I jumped away. He said, "It's killing me not to touch you."

"I'm getting better, but slowly."

"We'll be done with Silas in a few days, and then we can deal with your condition."

I nodded. "Okay." Our shoes crunched the gravel below our feet. "Silas thinks you're unethical and greedy and he thinks I'm slutty and greedy."

"Then we were successful."

"Yes, you were very convincing when you said that all I cared about was partying, flirting, and spending your money."

He laughed. "What about you calling Thomas a 'hunk of eye candy'?"

"If I sounded like I was telling the truth, it was because I do think Thomas is a hunk of eye candy!" I skipped out of his range.

"Why do you torment me, Maria Dos Passos?"

"Because I am crushed by the loss of my beloved pet goat, Pancho," I intoned. I started laughing every time I thought of that line.

When we went into the casita, Oswald said gently, "Milagro, we can still find ways to be with each other now. I love you. Come on."

I followed him to the bedroom. He opened his medical bag and took out a narrow box of surgical gloves. "See," he said. "We just need to be creative. You have a degree in creative writing, so it will be easy."

He placed a pair of the gloves on the bed and quickly put a pair on his own hands. He smiled and came toward me.

"You have got to be kidding, Oswald Grant," I said. "I am not going to start having safe sex with you now. You can just wait until I'm better."

"It's been a long time. I don't want to wait."

"Oswald," I said more seriously. "It will be better when we can touch each other and I can kiss you again. Do you mind?"

He groaned. "Yes, but it doesn't seem like I have much of a choice."

I took off my sandals and my shorts and washed up. I slipped into bed and Oswald wrapped the sheet over me and then embraced me through the sheet. Occasionally his hands would wander, rubbing here and rubbing there.

"Cut it out, Oswald. Go to sleep."

"You are torturing me."

"Good. Maybe next time you won't keep secrets from me."

Before I'd met Oswald, I'd thought that being in love with a man and having him love me in return would solve all of my problems. Now, even though my problems weren't solved, I knew that I wasn't alone. I had to believe that I would get better. The alternative was too dismal to contemplate.

twenty-three

when it's time to party,
we will party hard

On the day of the party, I felt sick with anxiety. Charles had arranged for Mercedes to act as the gala's head bartender. A biker friend, Ernest "Pepper" Culpepper, and his crew were on their way to replace the original security team. The Dervishes were already at the motel in La Basura and they'd been a big hit at Lefty's on open-mike night.

Bernie and Charlie had visited an electronics superstore and bought cameras that they hid throughout the Paragon ballroom, which was on the back of the top floor of the main building. Mercedes had made up a nice dossier on Silas's criminal activities. Sam had provided contact information for the council members, and they would receive the dossier after the event, along with a video that we had tentatively titled "Vamps Gone Wild."

I hadn't seen Gabriel again, but he'd had a heated discussion with Oswald and tried to get us to leave the Paragon.

I went for a long run to work off my energy. I was cooling off, circling around the back of the Paragon, when I saw several men unloading a long, heavy wooden crate from a truck. Silas, wearing a Panama hat, long-sleeved T-shirt, and jeans, was directing them, saying, "Be careful. That'ss pricelesss."

As I watched, he came over to me, so close that his hip touched mine. "Milagro, thiss iss the altar." He smiled suggestively, and now my internal gauge registered a strong heterosexual reading. "Are you excited?"

"I'll be more excited when you deposit that money in my bank account."

He laughed. "We'll give them a good show, won't we? I know you don't take the ritualss sseriously, but they have a power. They can be a real turn-on."

"I'm looking forward to it," I said.

His hand drifted to my thigh and I didn't brush it away. "I'm sso curiouss about you, Milagro. What iss it that you do that makess ssomeone like Ducharme sseek revenge for you?"

I looked at him from under my lashes. "Play your cards right and you might find out."

Then I walked away swinging my hips. Inside, I was thinking, "Ew, ew, ew, ew!" I wished there was a way to bleach away the memory of flirting with Silas from my brain.

At least I didn't have to worry about what to wear this evening. One of the neovamps had delivered a white gown for the ceremony and the most exquisite white silk slippers embroidered with flowers and glittering with red jewels like drops of blood.

When I tried them on, I said, "Oswald, do you think I'll be able to keep these shoes?"

"I don't see why not. They look as if they were made for you."

I sat and put my legs straight out, the better to admire the slippers. There was a tapping at our door and when Oswald answered, Silas came in.

"Hello," he said. He saw me and looked pleased. "I'm glad at leasst one thing arrived on time."

"Why?" asked Oswald. "Is there a problem?"

"That'ss why I'm here. Our family knife wass ssupossed to be delivered yesterday, flown in from Prague, but Willem made an error in shipping. It arrived jusst now, but it iss too precious for me to trust one of the thrallss to pick it up. My own men are sso busy." Silas said that the knife was at a shipping store near the airport. "Could I assk you to pick it up? I know that it'ss a long drive."

Oswald looked at his watch. "I can go now and I'll be back by ten thirty at the latest, in plenty of time for the ceremony. That is, if Milagro doesn't mind if I miss the cocktail reception?"

"As long as you're back for the main event, darling," I said.

"Thank you," Silas said. He handed a yellow sheet of paper to Oswald. "Here iss the receipt and my authorization for you to ssign for the delivery."

When Silas left, Oswald said, "You sure you don't mind?"

"It's fine. There's no traffic here and you'll have lots of time. What's a ritual bloodletting without the ritual knife?"

He took off and I was glad to have solitude to prepare for the night. I took a long bath and read the copy of *Vile Bodies* that Bernie had loaned me. I thought about my own once reliable but now vile body.

I put on the pristine gown carefully. It was beautiful, the silk flowing down to a few inches above my ankles. The neckline was perfect. It revealed just enough to entice without seeming slutty. Since I would be on camera tonight, I took my time with my makeup, and even let the first layer of mascara dry before adding the second. Inspired by Trevini's hairstyle, I made a few slender braids and let the rest of my hair hang loose around my shoulders.

I had checked in with my accomplices and told them that Oswald had gone to pick up the knife but would be back long before the actual ceremony. I was worrying that my slippers would get dusty on the walk to the hotel when the doorbell rang.

Silas stood there, looking sleek and stylish in a black suit and white shirt. "I thought you might want a ride." He gestured to the golf cart behind him.

"Thanks, Silas. You must have read my mind. I didn't want to muss these pretty slippers." I picked up a shawl to keep me warm against the breeze.

"A fitting adornment for ssuch a beautiful woman."

"Did you deposit the money?"

He pulled a slip of paper from his pocket. "Here'ss the deposit sslip."

I took it and looked at the sum. It was like holding a winning lottery ticket: incredible that the numbers were real. I said, "Excuse me," and then I went to the bedroom and put the deposit slip in the small hotel safe.

I returned to Silas. When I saw that he was going to take my arm, I shifted the shawl so that it blocked his touch on my bare skin. He led me to the golf cart, then got behind the wheel.

"Is anyone there yet?"

"A few memberss of the Diamond Club. Mosst will come fashionably late."

"Oh, good. Then Oswald won't miss much."

We arrived at the Paragon and I got out of the cart before Silas tried to hand me out. He walked around to me, looking like the evil twin of the gentle academic I'd first met. His pale blue eyes boldly ran over me. "The question iss, will you miss Oswald much?"

I returned his stare. "Let me take a good look at your customer base, and then we'll talk of romance."

"You are teasing me, Milagro."

I laughed girlishly, as I imagined Brittany would, all hair flipping and teeth. "I assure you, Silas, that if I like what I see, I won't tease much longer." I hated using feminine wiles on someone I hated.

The lobby was decorated with towering urns filled with long-stemmed red roses, velvety burgundy gladioli, and creamy tuberoses that perfumed the air with their heady fragrance. A red carpet led the way to the elevators. One of the neovamps held it for us and said, "Good evening, Mr. Madison, Miss De Los Santos."

Silas punched the button for the top floor. When the doors opened again, I saw two guards in front of the ballroom entrance. I hardly recognized our biker pal, Pepper, dressed as he was in a suit with his beard trimmed.

Pepper opened the door to the ballroom, and when Silas wasn't looking, he gave me a wink.

The ballroom's magnificent windows had been cloaked in lavish inky-black velvet drapes. Urns with flowers were placed between the windows and by the doorways. On the stage, the Dervishes, dressed neatly in black shirts and black slacks, played gentle folk music. I recognized a tune from the sixties about love and daisies. Mercedes said that they always started out quite innocently.

Refined vampires and wealthy degenerates attired in designer clothes milled about the dance floor and sat at tables covered in white linens. Each table had an arrangement of red roses and numerous candles in gleaming silver candlesticks. Goth waiters in black and white circulated with trays of drinks and tasty-looking chow.

As we went by the main bar, I made eye contact with Mercedes. She looked ridiculous in heavy eyeliner, a conservative church-lady wig, and a black suit. "Let's have a drink, Silas," I said. I turned to Mercedes and said, "Champagne, please."

Silas asked for a vodka martini. When we got our drinks, I said, "Bottoms up," and I tossed mine back, hoping that I was still as resistant to chemical enhancements as Ian. Silas looked amused and said, "Here'ss blood in your eye." His glass was filled to the brim, and he drank the martini in one long gulp.

"Another round, miss," I told Mercedes. As she poured the drinks, I said to Silas, "You must be a little tense about tonight."

"Not too much." Leaning close, he said, "Sso are you impressed with the clientele?"

I looked around as if calculating the wealth of the guests. Diamonds sparkled on ears and necks; rubies and emeralds hung from ears. Most of the men wore tailored suits and had the well-groomed, self-satisfied look of the very affluent. One guy in a bad haircut, grubby polo shirt, and ill-fitting khakis was at the center of a group. His glasses were held together with tape.

"Who is that?" I asked.

Silas mentioned a high-tech company. "He's sso rich, he

doesn't give a damn about appearancess. But his wife wantss our new treatment."

I raised my second glass of champagne. "To you and the success of your new venture." I drank the whole glass.

"Thankss." He took one sip and said, "This vodka is a little rough," and put down the drink. What I knew and he didn't was that his martini was made with the insanely potent Balkan vodka. Other drinks were being spiked with 190 proof grain alcohol, brought over the state border by our biker buddies.

Silas was already wavering on his feet as we went across the room to the front table. Gigi sat there, one long golden leg crossed over the other, wearing a tight red strapless dress. Silas was pulled away by a guest, and Gigi waved me to her side. "Milagro, darling," she purred. "I adore your fashion sense. White looks fabulous on you."

"Thank you. You look amazing."

"You can take the girl off the runway, but you can't take the haute couture off the girl. Or, you can't take it off until the end of the evening." She gave me a sly look and asked, "Did one of your special friends pay for your membership to the Diamond Club?"

"Silas Madison asked me to come. Do you know him?"

"Of course, I know Silas. I met him in Krakow. Krakow is the new Prague, you know. He spoke at a small dinner we had in my friend Jadwiga's castle. He was so passionate about world peace that we all wrote checks to him immediately. Then Jadwiga showed us her new boobs, which are fantastic, and Silas told us about the innovative beauty treatments here."

"So this is the nexus of politics and vanity."

Gigi laughed merrily. "You're just like Nancy—you always

intellectualize everything!" She stood up and called out "Darling!" to someone across the room, and she was gone.

Silas came to me and handed me another drink. "You see, they only care about themselvesss. They need guidance."

"And you are good enough to guide them."

"You jesst, Milagro, but if not me, who?" he said. "I can do both, you ssee, advance our agenda, help them, and make enough sso that I am comfortable."

"You're a visionary, Silas. A visionary who knows the importance of having a good time, I hope."

He smiled at me and a red light went off in my head. I looked around the room and spotted a badly cut thatch of red hair. "Oh, there's Gabriel. I must clear up an awful misunderstanding we had earlier. Please excuse me."

"Don't disappear," he said.

I made my way through the tables to Gabriel. I thought he had never looked more miserable, but I was wrong. When he saw me coming, his anguish increased visibly.

"Are you still here?" he said.

Miss Misty Roseybottom was by his side, encased like a sausage in something made of shiny pink material. She had applied excessive amounts of shiny makeup products, like goopy pink lip gloss and sparkly blue eye shadow.

"Hello, Brittany. Aren't you a vision today? You look as wonderfully fluffy and sweet as cotton candy, doesn't she, Gabriel?"

Brittany didn't know whether I was complimenting her or insulting her, but Gabriel knew exactly what I meant. "Milagro, I already asked you to leave the Paragon."

"Yes, you did, but since you're not the boss of me, I decided to stay. Besides, I promised Silas I'd hang around." I turned to Brittany. "When's the big day? What's your color scheme? One of my friends just did a blush-and-white scheme. It was fabulous."

She brightened. "I think I'm going to do deep rose and spring green, but maybe pink and lilac—"

Gabriel cut her off and said to me, "You've got to go now, Young Lady. You don't know what's coming."

His use of my nickname threw me off. "Actually, I do. Because I'm getting paid to participate. See, I'm on your team now, Gabriel."

Before he could answer, Thomas Cook was grabbing my hand and dragging me away. "What is it, Thomas?"

"I need you to send photos of this party to my publicist so they can get me in the columns. Take one with me and Gigi and her friends. Find someone hot and get a shot of that, too."

"Thomas, I am not working for you."

"You're telling *me*! That's why I had to let you go. Remember to get my good side."

It was no use arguing with him. "Fine. I'm on it. Don't worry about a thing. They'll be candids."

The party progressed as large parties do: exchanges of compliments, truncated conversations, and introductions that I would never remember. The music got louder as the Dervishes played covers to classic rock songs. The room grew warmer and voices rose to be heard. Several couples ventured onto the dance floor.

When the main bar cleared for a moment, I took the opportunity to say to Mercedes, "Nice hair. You look like a hellacious black Betty Crocker. How are things going?"

"Bitch," she replied. "Everyone loves the drinks."

"Keep pouring. This will all be over soon."

I found Edna, but Thomas was monopolizing her, providing

her with good camouflage as someone here to celebrate and socialize.

Even though Oswald was expected back soon, I kept looking at the entrance to the ballroom, waiting for him to come through it. In a very short time, the band had finished playing retro covers and began playing their originals. The noise was deafening and the walls throbbed with the music. The lead singer threw himself around the stage, shrieking. I thought he looked like a scrawny hairless monkey, yet I had a difficult time tearing my eyes from him.

People bumped into me as they talked and danced. Their faces were red with excitement, their eyes glassy. Many had broad smiles, but a few were wailing and tearful in conversation.

Ladies' shoulder straps had fallen down, exposing creamy flesh, and men had pulled off their ties and unbuttoned their shirts. The hot room smelled of perfume and chemical sweat and spilled booze and danger and sex.

On one of my circles around the room I bumped right into Silas.

"What are you thinking?" he asked.

I told him the truth. "I was thinking of my old life, before I even knew there were vampires. What astonishes me is not only your existence, but your openness in a place like this."

"We're hiding in plain sssight," he said. "We are ssafe sso long ass we know more about them than they do about uss."

"Knowledge is power." I said. "Do you ever resent them?"

"Iss a party the time to assk these things?" Then in a firmer voice, he said, "I grew up resenting and hating them for what they have done to us through the centuries, treating us like monsters. Eradicating us with no more thought than if we were vermin. Willem opened my eyes to a bright new future, a new dawn." Although he was smiling, I heard the rage in his voice. He had lost his sibilant *s* and stood up straighter. "They tortured us, they hanged us, they burned us, and they drowned us. They had moral certitude that they were in the right as they confiscated all that was ours and deprived us of any legal recourse."

"Deny your enemy's humanity and eliminate the need to treat them humanely," I said. "And now?"

"And now it is our turn to rule." He grabbed my hand and an electric crimson shock went through me. The room became red, red, red, blood pouring down the walls. The music pounded out a heartbeat, and I could smell it, the rich, copper scent of all the blood in the room. "The time to begin is now."

"Oswald hasn't returned yet with the knife," I said. I barely heard my own voice through the blood beating in my head. I pulled away, but Silas kept gripping my hand.

"Do you miss him?" Silas asked for the second time that evening, as he dragged me past the dance floor to a door that led behind the stage.

"Silas, stop messing up my costume!"

We were backstage. He let go of me. A few dim lights marked a short set of stairs and the exits.

I said, "What's the rush?" I followed his gaze to the rear of the stage, which had been blocked off from the ballroom by red curtains. In the middle was the stone altar. On it were silver candelabras, an earthenware pitcher and cups, and a large silver bell. To one side of the altar was an ornately carved black and silver armchair.

Silas poured the nasty herbal essence into the cups and said, "Let's drink to us, Milagro."

"That would be fab, Silas." A few cups of this stuff on top of the megavodka should make Silas fall apart.

I took the cup from him and drank it quickly so I wouldn't have to taste it. Silas watched me and took only a few sips. If Zave was right about the potency of this stuff, Silas should turn into a slobbering mess in a matter of minutes.

What I didn't count on was that he would first go through an ugly transition.

He looked at his watch and said, "Now is the time."

"Time for what? The night is young, Silas, and Oswald—"

"Oswald is on a fool's errand," he said. "We have the real knife here and his car will have an unfortunate problem on his return."

I tried to act like the avaricious tramp that he thought I was. "And your reasoning for this is?"

"Tonight is our wedding night, Milagro. You are a radiant bride."

My previous aversion to complicated weddings seemed inconsequential when compared to my shuddering revulsion at the prospect of marrying a freaky vampire cult leader at a debauched society soiree.

The beautiful white gown, the lovely slippers—if I had been a girl like Brittany, I would have realized before that this looked like a wedding dress. "Oswald will not be happy."

Silas stepped close. His pupils were so dilated that his eyes were black with a pale aquamarine rim. His sweat smelled acrid. "You're wasted on Grant. I want to have you in all the ways Ducharme had you, the ways that made him willing to kill for you."

Silas made my skin crawl. I smiled and said, "I amused him momentarily. But let's take a big-picture view. If you humiliate

Oswald now, you lose a valuable ally. If you wait, I can stage it so he breaks up with me. It'll be easy. His parents already want him to pay me off. I'll make them double their offer, and then I can come to you. It will be a win-win situation."

"That's what I admire about you, Milagro. We think alike. But I've waited a long time and I can't wait any longer." He picked up the silver bell and clanged it loudly. Suddenly the band stopped playing, the curtains to the ballroom rose, and a spotlight glared down at me. I looked out into the ballroom and saw Willem coming forward, escorted by neovamps, who were bumping one another drunkenly as they walked. Willem was dressed in the black robe he had worn when officiating the baby's naming ceremony.

The chanteuse from the vampire nightclub followed Willem. She started singing a song from hell. The Dervishes, who had been standing to one side, moved to their instruments and began playing along. The chanteuse looked surprised but pleased at the accompaniment.

The neovamps helped Willem up to the stage and to the ornate chair. The hood slid off his bald noggin. His skull looked as translucent and fragile as porcelain. I saw then that he held the jeweled knife. Willem glared at me and said, "You are not worthy of being among us."

Silas stared down Willem and hissed in a low voice, "Shut up, you old fool, and do as you're told or I'll lock you back up in that home until you rot to death."

The elderly man cringed and looked down at the floor.

"Silas?" I said.

"Don't worry, Milagro. Willem knows that if he behaves, I'll treat him well."

Silas took my hand and pulled me forward to face the guests.

I saw a flood of red rising until it covered everything. I could smell blood. I licked my lips as I imagined the taste of it.

Silas said, "Welcome, friends! Thank you for sharing this joyous occasion with us. We are here to celebrate the opening of our new treatment center at the Paragon, where you will receive the most innovative, most remarkable therapies for retaining your youth and beauty."

Looking out onto the guests, I saw the skin stripped from their faces and bloody eye sockets. They were glistening meat. Silas released my hand for a moment, and in that moment they transformed into the intoxicated, self-indulgent hedonists that they really were and I wondered how I ever could have been intimidated by people I despised so much.

"Funds from this new center will go toward cosmetic research, as well as to my project to bring morality, order, and harmony to our country. I call it Benevolent Guidance."

His listeners clapped and hooted enthusiastically. I could see that a few chairs had been knocked over and tablecloths were soggy with spilled drinks. Someone had taken the roses out of an urn and scattered them on the floor.

"This night is also very special because you are all guests at my wedding to the only woman in the world for me, a unique creature, or as I call her, my rara avis, Milagro De Los Santos."

He took my hand again. The crowd was cheering wildly and I tried to practice my breathing exercises, but then I thought, no, no, no. I jerked away from Silas's grip, and I ripped the knife from Willem's hand and shouted, "No, no, no!" I pushed Silas against the altar.

The Dervishes started playing loudly, wildly, and their music was the soundtrack of insanity. Everyone was laughing at the show, howling, and I held the knife against Silas's throat. Just as

Cuthbertson wanted to feel the knife in my flesh, I savored the moment before I would slice into Silas's pale, pale skin.

I heard someone shouting, "Milagro, no!" But I was not Milagro anymore. I was something that needed, craved, yearned for, and deserved to drink the blood of others.

"You're magnificent," Silas choked out. He put his hand over mine, caressing it, and that surprised me so much that I was caught unaware when he tried to push it away.

Crimson images swam in front of me. He was strong, but I was strong, too. People were shouting, but their words were only part of the deafening noise of a party whirling out of control.

I bit Silas's arm, wanting to rip and tear his flesh like an animal, and he groaned, "Oh, baby, yeah, to the bone," but all I got was a disappointing mouthful of suit.

We struggled and fell to the floor. I was on top of him, holding the knife above him, trying to decide if a stab to his throat would be more satisfying then a stab to his heart.

His flunkies jumped onstage, but a few were so drunk that they fell off immediately. "Stay back or he dies," I shouted. "Dies sooner."

My anticipation was like foreplay. I let it build and build.

"Milagro," came the annoying voice again. Gabriel was standing nearby. "Milagro, put down the knife," he said.

Anger cut through the bloodlust momentarily. "Go away!"

"Milagro, let him go. You're screwing everything up!" Gabriel began to approach me, but I pressed the knife against Silas's skin. Undaunted, Gabriel announced, "Silas Madison, I hereby take you into custody on the authority of the High Council for treason, felony assault on a normal, attempted assault on a council member, misuse of council property, elder abuse, and illicit theft of blood."

The ancient grog was having its effect now, because Silas began laughing uncontrollably. I watched in exquisite expectation as his throat moved with the sound. His throat, I would cut his throat.

But just as I was basking in my blood passion, I saw Oswald standing before me. "We'll drink together, Oswald," I yelled over the music. I heard glass breaking, screaming, and china shattering.

"Milagro, put the knife down," he said calmly. "Put the knife down."

Maybe a knife wasn't the way to go. Perhaps I could bash Silas's skull on the stone altar and see blood pour from his ears and nose. I wanted to rip his arms from their sockets, hear the crunch of his bones, and bathe in his hot, rich, sticky blood.

Silas saw my expression and groaned, "Blood is the river and blood is the life. Blood shall be taken and blood shall be given."

"Milagro!" Oswald reached out for me.

I jerked away, dragging Silas a few inches with me. I'd never felt so strong. "It's his fault I can't touch you anymore, Oswald. He steals blood from locals. He's cruel and horrible and wants to enslave people!"

Silas grunted out, "Kill me, then. Take my blood. You are the one foretold." He leaned his head back, exposing his neck.

Willem began speaking the old language, and in my blood passion, it sounded like music. "As it is foretold," he said in English, "the one who survives slaughters her mates and drinks of their blood in her rise to power."

I clutched at Silas, my thoughts becoming confused, remembering fields of scarlet flowers, growth, life. I flung the knife across the floor and rolled off Silas. I was on my back, staring at the bright stage lights. The party raged on. I closed my eyes and heard Silas screaming, "Let go of me!"

In retrospect, we shouldn't have told the bikers that the booze was spiked. They might have been more efficient and less violent as security guards if they hadn't been pilfering drinks all night.

I heard thudding on the stage, like a body in the dryer, and Silas's voice receded.

Oswald was kneeling by me and he said, "It's all right now. I'm here now." I wanted his arms around me, I wanted to feel the comfort of his flesh, but I could not.

I'd never felt so alone and angry in my life. I screamed. I screamed and I screamed.

I was aware of Oswald running off. He returned pulling Thomas. Oswald said, "Help her!"

Thomas came beside me. He took my hand and forced me to look at him. His breath was like spring air. He said, "You're safe. Go to sleep, Milagro."

I slept.

twenty-four

love bites back

I awoke the next morning to see Oswald dozing in a chair by the side of my bed. For a moment I was puzzled, but then the events of the night before hit me like a shovel.

"Oswald," I said, and his eyes opened immediately.

He smiled, but it was an even, controlled smile, not one of his carefree, lopsided grins. "Hey, baby," he said softly. "How are you feeling?"

"What happened?"

Oswald reached out and brushed the hair away from my face. He was wearing surgical gloves and I felt as if I was contaminated, some hateful, untouchable thing.

"We all had our own agendas," he said. "Gabriel had infiltrated the group on behalf of the council. He was still gathering evidence when you came along and changed Silas's timetable."

This was one happy stitch in the miserable tapestry of my

life. "I knew it couldn't be true that he would marry that nasty ruffled pink creature."

Oswald smiled. "Gabriel's already gone to the airport with Silas. He'll present the case against him to the council. The video from last night will help."

"Where does the council meet?"

"Even I don't know that," Oswald said. "I don't have the level of clearance that Gabriel has."

"I should have trusted him," I said. My guilt about treating Gabriel badly was like the chopped cilantro in the salsa of my bad feelings: not the main component, but an essential ingredient.

"He needed us *not* to trust him."

"We should have trusted him anyway," I said. "What brought you back from the errand? Silas told me they'd rigged your car."

"Yep, and when my phone also went out, it was too coincidental. I thought no one would pick me up on the road at night, but some friendly hippie chick stopped and gave me a lift."

"Was her name Trevini?"

"How did you know?" he said.

"She works at the spa. She's wonderful."

I sat up in bed. I was wearing the long nightgown that Oswald had bought me. "Oswald, this nightgown always twists around me, and I can't help but think it's a metaphor for something—maybe that things that seem appealing are often impractical in real life."

"You've been through a lot, Milagro. We'll have breakfast and then we'll go back home."

"I can't go back with you, Oz."

He smiled, but now it was a nervous smile. "You're tired.

303

You need time to rest and recuperate. We can take care of you best at the ranch. Grandmama will help you pack."

I plucked the glove on his hand. "Is this how you want to live? Do you think that we could have a meaningful relationship while I'm like this?"

"You won't always be like this."

I looked into his clear, gray, honest eyes. "We don't know that."

"I love you, Milagro De Los Santos. I want to be with you always."

"I want to be with you, too, Oswald." I shook my head. "But not now."

"I thought you loved me."

"I do, Oswald, more than anything."

"Then give me one good reason you can't come back—and don't say it's because we can't have sex now, because I can wait."

I knew what I had felt, but now I was ashamed to tell Oswald. "Because I'm afraid I'll kill someone. I'm afraid I'll hurt the baby."

"That doesn't even make sense. Okay, you got out of control with Silas and he deserved . . . Who wouldn't want to hurt him, but . . ."

"Oswald, it wasn't just that I wanted to hurt him. I was so excited by the idea of killing him." I watched his face then, to make sure he really understood what I was saying. "It wasn't anger that I was feeling. It was pleasure. It was erotic. It felt amazing."

"That's not you."

"It's not who I was. It's who I am now. You let Silas and Willem on the ranch out of deference to others. Are you willing to risk having me there? Because I'm not willing to take the chance of hurting the ones I love."

Oswald stood and looked down angrily at me. "You're going to stay with Thomas, aren't you? Or is it Ian?"

"I'm going to stay with myself. I'm either going to overcome this or I'll have to learn to live with it somehow on my own."

When Oswald couldn't make me change my mind, Edna came into the room and made him leave. "Young Lady, my grandson tells me you have gotten a ridiculous notion in your silly little head that you are a menace to society and, as such, should not return to the ranch with us."

"Your grandson related the essential points, Edna."

She sighed dramatically and raised her eyes to the ceiling. "Young Lady, you are not fit to set loose upon the world, particularly with your unnatural propensity to attract the attention of extremists and incite mayhem. I will not even speak of your unfortunate wardrobe choices."

Oh, la, for those not-so-long-ago days when I could gaily exchange insults with Edna. But that time was gone, and now I looked seriously at my friend and said sincerely, "I now know one of the side effects of my contamination with Ian's blood, Edna. I get a thrill out of hurting someone when I have physical contact with them."

She thought for a moment and said, "You don't want to hurt any of us."

"No, I don't want to hurt anybody. Especially the baby."

"Young Lady, are you sure of your decision?"

When I nodded, she said, "Where will you live? What will you do?"

"I have some money from my screenwriting job and the deposit Silas made to my account. I'll be fine."

"When you're well, you'll come home."

Mercedes was the only one who thought it was a good idea

for me to be by myself. "Don't think of it as being alone. Think of it as having time to yourself."

"I know what it is to live alone, Mercedes."

"No, you don't. You know what it is to live by yourself while you hope you meet someone who will live with you. Living alone is different. Living alone can be very peaceful."

"You mean, it's peaceful as long as your friends don't come crashing in with problems and craziness."

She fiddled with one of her locks. "If I have peace the rest of the time, I can deal with a *loca* on my doorstep every now and then."

My friends kept finding reasons to delay their departure and made a dozen phone calls. Gabriel called Oswald and told him that Ian had been released from detention and that Silas was being delivered to them.

Oswald handed the phone to me and said, "Gabriel wants to talk to you."

"Hello, Miss Thing," he said cheerfully.

"Gabriel! I'm so glad you're you again."

He laughed. "You don't know what a burden it is to be straight. I'm sorry about that huge mess, but I kept trying to get you to leave. How are you doing?"

"Well . . ."

I heard announcements and chatter in the background. "Gotta go, Young Lady," Gabriel said. "That's our plane. See you back at home!"

I handed the phone to Oswald. "He doesn't know I'm not going home?" I asked.

"He knows. He's just hoping you'll change your mind. We're all hoping."

In the end, I made them all leave. It broke my heart to

watch Oswald walk away. I crawled into bed and cried and cried. I went through boxes of Barton tissues.

Oswald, Mercedes, and my other friends called. It was painful for me to talk to them so I stopped answering the phone. Then the new concierge at the Paragon informed me that Skip's production company had only paid for one more night.

I was slumping around the casita, packing my belongings, when I found the white vampire dress in the back of the closet. I was going to throw it away, but I wondered what the maids would think of a girl so spoiled that she threw away beautiful clothes. I folded it and left it on a chair.

The doorbell rang, then someone knocked. When I didn't answer, Bernie yelled, "Milagro, I know you're in there!"

I opened the door and he shambled inside. "You look like hell," he said.

"Thank you for your frank assessment. I'm leaving here tomorrow. I've reached the end of the line."

"You going back home? Or to L.A.?"

"I don't know where I'm going. It doesn't matter."

"Faulkner said, 'Between grief and nothing, I will take grief.'"

"Everyone keeps quoting things to me," I said listlessly. "'When one door closes, another opens.' Do you know who said that?"

"Bob Marley?"

"Good guess. Alexander Graham Bell."

"Your friend Mercedes got hold of all the video of the other night, but I had an extra camera there for myself."

"Oh." I remembered Thomas's request. "Thomas wants you to send any good pictures to him for the columns."

"Milagro, I won't release the other pictures. I covered Hollywood for half a decade, and I've seen worse things."

"Thanks," I said listlessly.

Bernie sighed. "You want my place? I'm moving into Gigi's suite for a while, and then she wants me to hang out with her this summer. I've got the lease through the end of the year."

La Basura was as good a place as any for me now. I said yes.

I had just checked out of the Paragon when I ran into Thomas in the lobby.

"I'll come visit when you go back to Edna's," he said.

"I don't know that I'm going back."

"Sure you'll go back. I've seen sad endings and I've seen happy endings, and you're a happy ending type."

"You're talking about movies, not real life."

"Same difference," he said. He gave me a big hug, and I said good-bye to the only person I could touch without pain.

I moved into Bernie's place, and the enormity of my situation and the possible end of my relationship with Oswald made me feel incapable of doing anything. I called the ranch when I knew Oswald would not be there and told Edna where I was staying. I hung up quickly before she could ask any questions, but the next day a special-delivery package came. Inside were two pouches of calf's blood.

There was one thing, however, that kept crashing at the door of my pity party: every time I looked out the kitchen window, I saw the barren yard. Finally, I decided to add a few grim and gray-leaved plants that would not distract me from my gloomy mood. Well, that was the plan, and the best-laid plants of girls and vampires do sometimes get replaced.

I put a palo verde in the back corner and filled a small plot with succulents. I covered a planter in blue mosaic tiles for a sago palm. I hung a basket of burro's-tail sedum by the door and placed an apricot angel's trumpet so that it was the first thing I spied out the window. I couldn't decide between red or purple bougainvillea, so I planted one of each so that they would intertwine, deep and rich as blood.

Oswald called daily. Even though I didn't answer, I listened to his messages over and over. "I miss you, Milagro. Maybe you don't miss me anymore, but I miss you. Daisy misses you. We all miss you. Libby misses you. I'm teaching her to say 'Young Lady.' Petunia is pining. Her feathers have lost their sheen."

Gabriel left a message saying that Silas had been banned from this continent and had joined the Dervishes on a tour of Asia. Sam submitted a petition to the council demanding that I have full rights as a family member. Ian had sponsored the petition. The baby was happy, and Winnie was in contact with the family research scientists and wanted a sample of my blood so they could investigate treatment possibilities.

I didn't want to find out that there was no treatment, though.

Bernie came by one day with a bag of papers to grade. As we worked together, he said, "We've got a teacher out on disability, and I need you to substitute."

"I don't know anything about teaching teenagers."

"If you can subdue a man with a knife, you can handle teenagers."

My face went hot with shame. "I might hurt someone."

"No, you won't," he said calmly. "Do this for a few days or the tape of your friends goes out."

"You're blackmailing me?"

"I'm persuading you."

My fear of reacting to physical contact overcame my fear of the students. They were reading *Huck Finn* and complained annoy-

ingly about the dialect and story. From the back of the class-
room, one boy slumped in his chair and said, "You're one hella
boring bitch."

I froze and the class went silent with anticipation. But when
I didn't feel the desire to plunge my hands into the boy's stomach and pull out his steaming, dripping guts, I knew that I
might actually be able to teach. "Shut up," I said happily, staring him down until he looked away and slumped further.

I made them close their books and told them why I loved
Twain. Twain had lost his beloved brother, his daughter, eventually his wife, but he had always retained his tender and fierce
understanding of the human condition. We spoke then about
loss and hope and freedom and humanity.

It wasn't one of those after-school-special moments with
dust motes floating on beams of sunlight through the window
and students' faces open with wonder and the worst student
having an epiphany and going on to Harvard. But they did stop
hitting one another and making body-function sounds for
about five minutes.

On the way home, I went into the grocery store and
picked up cartons of yogurt and cereal, things I could eat
without effort.

"How's that cooking coming along?" the woman at check-
out asked, looking disdainfully at my groceries.

"Cooking?"

"You said you were doing all the Julia Child recipes."

"Oh, that. It's too much trouble to cook just for one."

A voice behind me said, "You could invite me to dinner."

I turned to see my former masseuse in a long hippie skirt,
her hair loose and wavy. "Trevini, how are you?"

"Good, now that I'm not at the Paragon anymore."

"What happened?"

She raised her arms with a minor crashing of colored glass bracelets. "They had a big shake-up and anyone who wanted to leave got a deal. I set up a massage room at my place."

"So it worked out."

"Absolutely. What's doing with you?"

Instead of answering, I said, "You're welcome to come to dinner. I have strawberry yogurt."

"Puhleeze."

We made pasta with fresh tomatoes and herbs. I found a bottle of Lefty's wine in the back of the refrigerator and we sat in the backyard.

"It's wicked serene here," she said. "I feel the spirit of the garden. Maybe it will help your heart chakra."

"To be honest, Trevini, I don't really buy into all this New Age stuff."

"New Age? This stuff's been around forever," she said. "I used to want to be a cop, you know. But I always had a sense of the mind-body connection, and besides, I didn't like the idea of ever having to bust my friends."

"That would be a bummer," I agreed.

"Totally," she said. "You should talk to your grandmother more."

"My grandmother is dead."

"You are the most limited person ever."

I thought she was nuts, but then I realized that I hadn't visited my *abuelita*'s grave since her funeral. I drove hundreds of miles to the cemetery where she was buried. When I found her grave, I was surprised to see a bouquet of bright, clean plastic flowers by the headstone. I wondered who had left them.

I placed my own flowers beside them and sat there for a long time, remembering her love and kindness.

One sweltering evening I went to Trevini's with a bag of ice for frozen lemonades. I said, "It's too hot for anything but ice. I'm so sweaty I'm going to slide off the chair with a big sucking sound."

She started laughing and put her hand on my bare arm— I felt a delightful frisson. It was a rosy, warm, joyous sensation.

Because I'd mistakenly believed that I was cured before, I was afraid that my visions would return. They didn't. On the last day of school, I was able to hug my students good-bye. I felt prouder than I had when I'd received my F.U. diploma and practically skipped down the sidewalk on the way home.

A gray Porsche was parked in front of my house and a man was leaning against the front door.

Coming up the sidewalk, I said, "Hello, Ian."

"My dear girl," he answered. He kissed me on the cheeks and I felt a flare of delight. "You're looking very well."

"And you, as always. Won't you come in?"

"I've brought a picnic for us." He picked up a basket beside him and we went inside.

I turned on the small air conditioner and he opened a bottle of wine. We looked at each other.

"I was unavoidably detained," he finally said.

"I heard the council kept you in custody."

"So they did, but there've been changes recently, which I have long wanted. No more reminiscing about our glorious vampire heritage. Sam waged a gallant fight on your behalf, arguing for your rights. I believe they will be granted soon."

"Sam is a good egg," I said. "I hear you also lobbied for me."

"I had my own selfish reasons. I like to talk to you." He said gently, "Edna told me you've had a hard time, my love."

"There were times when I thought you should have let me die, Ian. But I got over it."

Ian said wryly, "Dying is for other people, not for you."

"I almost killed Silas, you know, and I was really enjoying it. That scared me."

"Power can be frightening."

"Silas told me you cut him one hundred times."

"Did he?" Ian said, neither confirming nor denying the story.

"I'm better now and when I touch people . . ." I walked to him, put my hand on his neck, and enjoyed the sensation. "Now when I touch people, it's as if I can feel the life inside them and it's fantastic."

Ian looked genuinely happy. "I'm so relieved. That's what I feel, too. But Edna's family, the majority of vampires, don't have it. It's just a rare few."

"Why are you different?"

"A genetic mutation passed down directly in the original line, but not in the branches. I'm a little more resilient than others."

"What am I, Ian?" I asked. "Am I vampire or am I human? Am I like the Grants, or am I like you?"

"You are yourself, Milagro De Los Santos, unique and indefinable. Decide what it is you want to be, although I do hope you won't continue being so serious."

"I have big things on my mind, Ian," I said. "Do you think I'll ever be able to have children?"

"I don't see why not. Would you like to try now?" he asked, taking my wrist and tugging me close. "I've studied the technique at great length."

I laughed. "I'm being serious, Ian. Evelyn Grant says I have no future with Oswald because we can't have babies together. But Silas seemed to think that I may be a baby factory."

Ian looked deep into my eyes and suddenly I wasn't laughing anymore. "Milagro, you are enough for any man just as you are."

Nervously I pulled away and said, "Let's have that picnic now."

Afterward I took him to Lefty's, and even Lefty was friendly to him. When we walked back to the house, he said, "I was hoping to get you intoxicated and take advantage of you."

"No luck, my dark lordish amigo. I am now impervious to chemical enhancements. I'm as sober as a nun."

"Pity you absorbed that ability." We'd arrived at the house and he came close. "May I stay the night? I've been living on the memories of making love to you." He drew me in his arms and a marvelous sensation pulsed through me.

"No, Ian. I still love Oswald. I will always love Oswald."

"Oswald need never know." His lips were on my cheek, then near my ear.

I'd been so lonely, so hungry for affection. I had to make Ian leave before I gave in. "I'll know, though. You'll know." I drew away from him.

Ian let me go and smiled one of those world-weary, been-there-done-that smiles.

"You'll make me jealous."

"I can call and get a room for you at the Paragon. They have twenty-seven kinds of massage."

"No, I'll drive on. I have something for you." He went to the car and returned with a file folder. "Here."

I opened it and looked at the pages, half of them in a language that looked Eastern European. "What is this?"

"The Grant family's petitions to the council requesting your rights. The earlier statements, here," he said, and pulled pages from the folder, "are Oswald's refusal of council orders to give you up to custody in return for a sizable financial reward."

The amount was staggering. "If I'd let you stay, would you have showed this to me?"

"Perhaps, but perhaps not," Ian said with a wicked grin. "I can wait until this infatuation of yours is over."

"You don't give up," I said with a laugh.

"Nor do you, my love."

I put my hands on the sides of his head, bent it down, and kissed his wide brow. "Thank you, Ian. Thank you for saving me. Thank you for giving me this gift."

"I'll say good-bye for now," he said. "You have my number. Do call if you get bored, or need an escort or want to practice making a baby."

After he left, I went to the bedroom and found a box wrapped in glossy paper on the dresser. I hadn't seen him bring it in. I untied the pale blue ribbon and lifted the cover off the box. Nestled in tissue paper was a red dress almost identical to the one that had been ruined the night I'd been cut. The design and the color were the same, but even I could tell that the dress was better made, the fabric finer.

Beneath the dress was a small box. I opened it. A beautiful ring glinted against black velvet. The dark, clear, red oval gem was set in a heavy gold band inscribed with symbols. I knew it would fit perfectly on my wedding ring finger, and it did. I felt a strange, guilty satisfaction at his attentions. I placed the ring back in the box.

twenty-five

home is where the heartthrob is

When Bernie came by the next day, I returned the keys to his house and he loaned me a sackful of books. He patted me on the shoulder and said, "I'm glad to see that you've made a full recovery from the tragic demise of your beloved pet goat Pancho."

When I stopped laughing, I said, "Thanks for everything, Bernie. You're a prince among tabloid writers."

"You were my muse," he said. "*Vaya con Dios.*"

The drive seemed to take forever because I was so impatient. I arrived at twilight. The automatic gate opened for me and I drove under the protective branches of the huge walnut trees. The fields had turned golden in the hot weather and the wildflowers finished their season.

The family was on the front porch, just as they should be at this time. When they saw my truck coming down the drive, they stood motionless, in a tableau that could have been titled "Happy Hour *Con Los Vampiros*." The dogs, being dogs, had no respect for stunned silence and they raced to meet my truck, barking wildly, just as they had the very first time I'd come to the ranch.

I parked on the drive and got out of the truck. Daisy leapt up and I caught her in my arms, which almost knocked me backward. Stumbling a step, I let her down and scrubbed her back with my fingers, getting nothing but the pleasure one gets from petting one's faithful companion.

My friends stared at me as I walked to the porch. Libby was in Sam's arms, yanking at his earlobe. Winnie was leaning against the railing, the picture of casual elegance. Edna sat beside Gabriel. He had his arm thrown back over her shoulders and his hair had grown longer. But Oswald was not here.

"Where is Oswald?" I said, panicking, wondering if I had been gone too long, and if he had manufactured a girlfriend out of spare parts from his patients.

"Young Lady," Edna said, "that is hardly an appropriate greeting from someone who has been so late in returning."

I came forward and threw my arms around her, jostling her drink. "I've missed you, too. Now where's Oswald?"

"He's in the shack," Gabriel said. He pulled me away from Edna and hugged me tightly. "Tell me you're better."

When he finally released me, I said to everyone, "I'm better. No more homicidal rages."

Winnie kissed my cheek and said, "I knew you could do it." She looked at Sam, her eyes communicating something. He handed the baby to me and said, "Libby refused to say 'Young Lady.' We'll have to come up with another nickname."

Even though I believed I was well, this was my biggest test. I hesitated and then held out my arms. Libby smiled at me and clutched a handful of my hair. She felt like life and joy. I tucked my head down on her soft silver-gold locks, and felt happy and peaceful until she yanked down on my earring.

"And that's why I'm not wearing any jewelry," said Winnie as she disengaged her daughter's tiny fingers from my earring.

"She's got a thing about ears," her father said with concern. "I hope it's not a fixation. Winnie, did you check the book? Does it say anything about infantile obsessive-compulsive disorder?"

Edna rolled her eyes, and even Sam laughed. It was grand to be here at last, but I was getting as shy as a schoolgirl at the thought of seeing Oswald again. Gabriel poured a margarita and handed it to me. "We were just thinking about you, Milagro."

I lifted the glass to him. "How's your fiancée?"

He grinned. "I regret to say that she was not heartbroken over my departure from her life. She got back together with an old boyfriend of hers, Xavier Pierce."

"Zave?" I said in shock. "He went for that My Little Pony confection of sissitude?"

"Tell us how you really feel," Gabriel said. He looked at his family. "When Milagro met Brittany, it was like watching a mongoose and a mouse, fascinating and horrible." Lowering his voice, he said to me, "I'm sorry for all the hateful things I said. They had to have an element of truth so you would believe them, but they aren't the truth, Young Lady."

I kissed his cheek. "All is forgiven."

I finished my drink and looked across the field to the Love Shack.

"Go on," Edna said. "We can catch up later."

I smiled at my friends and said, "Wish me luck."

I tried to walk sedately toward the shack but found myself moving faster and faster, until I was running, Daisy at my side. I fumbled with the gate's latch, and then I was at the front door. Daisy scratched at the door, while I was deciding if I should knock or go in.

The door swung open and Oswald said, "Daisy, stop that . . ."

"Hi, Oswald. I'm back if you'll have me."

A smile came to his mouth, the crazy crooked one of real happiness, and my shyness evaporated like fog in sunshine. I slipped my arms under his T-shirt and around his back, holding him tightly, feeling an incredible zinging go through me.

He didn't reciprocate.

"Are you all right now?" Oswald asked.

"Better than all right. New and improved."

"Can I touch you now?"

"Oh, yes, Oswald, you can and you better and soon, or I will die of yearning." I put my hands on the sides of his wonderful face and kissed him. I pushed him backward into the shack and kicked the door shut behind me.

We kissed and grabbed at each other, pulling off our clothes, and crashing into the wall in our haste and eagerness. Even as we were pressing against each other, I kept looking around the room, assuring myself that all was the same and that I was really back.

Oswald's marvelous hands were on my body and I closed my eyes, enjoying the sensation of skin on skin and his smell, his taste, his essential Oswaldness.

"Milagro, you don't know how much I've missed you," he said as he tumbled onto the sofa with me.

"Let me show you how much I've missed you." And I did.

I had thought that making love to Oswald was something that could not be improved upon. I was wrong. My new ability added a dimension of pleasure that I didn't know existed. It was a pleasure that was as much emotional as it was physical.

There was a point when he brought out the scalpel and asked, "May I?"

I took his wrist and moved his hand away. "No. No one is ever going to cut me again, Oswald. Do you mind?"

He put down the scalpel. His hands caressed my thighs and I sighed with pleasure. "No," he said, "I don't mind."

A few hours later, when we were resting on the pile of blankets and pillows we'd dragged down from the bed to the floor, I told Oswald about the remarkable new sensations I felt when I touched people.

He said, "This is where I usually say, damn Ian Ducharme. But he did save your life."

"There is that, but next time I hope he'll just dial 911."

"He told Edna he visited you in La Basura."

"Yes, he did. I talked to him about my condition." I entwined my fingers in Oswald's. "We need to talk about children."

"Can't that wait? We're not even—"

"Actually, it can't. There is some uncertainty that we'll ever be able to have children."

"Do you want children, Milagro?"

"I think so. I think I'd like a few. What about you?"

"I wouldn't mind them," he said. "I'm in no hurry, though."

I squeezed his hand. "So what happens if you decide you really want them, but we can't have them?"

"I've been thinking about that," he said. "When I was taking care of those kids at the clinic, I was thinking that I'd like to give a child a home." He gave me a tentative look, as if he expected me to argue with him.

"I like that idea," I said. "If my mother Regina has taught me anything, it's that biology is irrelevant to family. Besides, I always wanted someone to rescue me."

"Like from a shopping mall?" Oswald said with a grin.

"Did your mother tell you that?"

When Oswald stopped laughing long enough to talk, he said, "Winnie never got into it like you did with my mother."

I hit him with a pillow. "That's because Winnie is the perfect vampire professional and spouse and your mother loved her."

Oswald looked at me with astonishment. "Where did you get that idea? My mother thought Winnie would have spent too much time on her career and not enough on me. No one is good enough for Evelyn's perfect son."

"How are we going to manage a relationship if your mother hates me?"

My beautiful man grinned beautifully. "We let Grandmama run interference for us."

I sighed. "Can we forget about possible problems for a minute?" I kissed Oswald's neck and moved downward over his smooth belly.

"I'm forgetting, I'm forgetting!" shouted Oswald.

Epilogue

I now knew that I was a good teacher. I applied to a graduate program so I could start working on my credentials through extension courses. It seemed like a long, arduous process, but Mercedes said, "A little hard work won't hurt you."

I wanted to tell her that writing was work, but I remembered Bernie's opinion that it was not.

I was disappointed to learn that my rewrite of "Teeth of Sharpness" was merely used to manipulate Mr. Famous Screenwriter to make changes, which he did. I added "Script Doctor" to my résumé and it looked swell there. I continue to send my short stories to publications, and I'm confident that someday soon an agent or publisher will recognize their worth.

Whenever anybody asks me about my writing, I tell them, "I rewrote a screenplay, and Thomas Cook would swim naked in my pool every day." They are always very impressed and ask me lots of questions, mostly about Thomas.

Thomas does not swim naked in the pool at the ranch, or at least he has worn swim trunks on those occasions when I've seen him. He has taken to visiting us, or rather, he has taken to courting Edna. They are the oddest pair, but he adores her and she seems amused by him. I badger Edna constantly about the nature of their relationship.

"Young Lady, you think everyone should be in love."

"Not everyone. Not the Pope." I thought about it. "Yes, even the Pope. It wouldn't be hard to find a date for him. He's got the fabulous villas, the clothes, the bling, the cool Popemobile."

"Being in love is highly overrated."

I looked at her and skeptically raised one eyebrow.

"Now she usurps my expressions," Edna said to the ceiling.

"Edna, does Thomas ever ask why the pool is covered and why you wear sunscreen and hats all the time?"

"No," she said, trying to hide a smile. "He has a talent for being incurious about anything that doesn't directly affect Thomas Cook."

As to my condition: Winnie sent a sample of my blood to the family's top medical research lab in Minnesota. The researchers found no trace of any infection. "I don't understand," I said. "I have these changes in my system."

"Many things are still mysteries," Winnie answered. "You're definitely one of them."

Gigi called and asked for my advice on a landscape contractor to install my garden design. She invited me to stay at her house while the crew worked, and I went for two consecutive weekends. Bernie was ensconced in her mansion, and he was contemplating the idea of becoming the next Mr. Gigi Barton. "Don't know if I'm ready to be on this side of the tabloids," he said. "But she's a great broad once you drag her away from the stores and salons."

The heiress looked affectionately at the paunchy man beside her and said, "He'd be a cheap husband. All he ever wants is books."

When I left she presented me with a generous check.

"I didn't expect to be paid," I said.

"Take the check, honey. It's like prostitution—if you don't get paid you're just an enthusiastic amateur." Gigi referred me to her friends. I've done a few modest designs, and I always take the check.

A job here and a job there, and I've been cobbling together a living even if I still can't devote myself to one career. I haven't used the credit card Oswald gave me, but I'm more open-minded about sharing the wealth.

Winnie, Sam, and Libby moved to their house, which was a huge adjustment for the rest of us. I worried that Edna would feel lonely, but she announced that she wanted to move into the Love Shack. Once Oswald and I traded places with her, Gabriel began visiting more often, and he frequently brought Charlie Arthur along. They're just friends now, but I have hopes.

When Nancy returned from her honeymoon, she called and I told her about my writing job at the Paragon. "Thomas Cook swam naked in my pool almost every day."

"Naked is the new black," she said. "After my private beach on my honeymoon, I can hardly bear to wear clothes, they're so passé. Trust me, in New York next season, no one will be wearing clothes. When will I see you?"

"You may not want to get together with me. Todd must really hate me after the wedding."

She gave a giddy laugh. "You're so silly, Milly. Why should that stop our friendship? Todd's always hated you."

Trevini moved north and works just over the mountain from us at the hippie nudie spa. The place is a little run-down, but they're on the cutting edge of mind-body therapies. She's been trying to invent her own massage techniques and so far the frontrunner is something she calls the Piñata, where she uses small wooden bats to "activize" pressure points.

Summer ended and the first rains came. The fields were muddy, but the air smelled crisp and promising. I took a stroll by the creek, which showed a trickle of water. Oswald found me there. I was thinking of the winter to come, of the seeds that would lie dormant, waiting, and of the growth to come.

"Milagro," he said.

I reached out my hand and took his. We stood together and he said, "I'd like to take you out tonight, somewhere special."

My boots were once again covered in mud and there was hay in my hair from helping unload bales in the barn. "I will require several hours of intense work to get ready to go out. Can't we open a bottle of champagne and sit in front of the fireplace and smooch fiercely? I might even let you get to third base."

"You don't want to go out?"

"Not when it's so much fun staying in." I looked at Oswald's eyes, the color of the rain clouds above, the stones in the creek, the weathered fence posts. "I like how you're color-coordinated with the landscape."

"I knew there was a reason you liked me. I thought it was because of my vast intellect."

"That's the second reason. Why do you like me?"

"Because of your vast intellect."

"That's a very good reason," I said. "I was worried it was because you'd heard that writers make a fortune."

"That, too," he said.

His rich chestnut hair was brushed back neatly, the way he wore it to the office.

"Do you want to hear a poem?" I asked.

> *This is my dream,*
> *It is my own dream,*

I dreamt it.
I dreamt that my hair was kempt.
Then I dreamt that my true love unkempt it.

I put my hand in his hair, mussing it up.

"Am I your true love, Milagro?"

"There is no other."

"Milagro," he said, "you know how we never really talk about the future?"

"Talking about the future is too complicated," I said nervously. I was always worried that one day Oswald would decide that I wasn't serious or sincere enough for him. "Let's just go on the way we do now."

"My mother," he began. "You remember my mother?"

"Yes," I said, wondering what awful news was coming.

"My mother called and told me they're coming to visit. She told me that Brittany Monroe would be joining them."

"Miss Fruity Petticoats?" I said.

"The very same. The Monroes are concerned because Brittany has been dating your friend Zave. My mother thinks Brittany is a delightful young lady. She admires her femininity, her excellent family background, and, um, fashion sense."

Oswald let me stew in a nasty broth of suspicion and insecurity. "Well, it's your ranch, Oswald. If you want to invite that ripe carbuncle of polyester lace and strawberry-flavored lip gloss, it's your own decision."

"Thank you for your support," he said. "I told Mom that I thought Miss Assembled Trousseau might have her hopes dashed when she found out I was engaged."

"Oh," I said, confused.

He faced me and took my hands in his. "Milagro De Los

Santos, will you please save me from this threat and all threats to come? Will you protect me and love me and humor me and marry me?"

I felt a catch in my throat. "Oswald, stop joking."

"I'm not joking. Okay, I was a little bit, but I'm not joking about marrying you." He looked in my eyes. "I know I'm not what you expected. Maybe I should have let you go so you would have a chance with someone without my condition . . ."

"*Our* condition, Oswald."

"No, Milagro, so far as we know, you're fine. You could meet some great guy and have a great life without worrying about neovampires, political extremists, and crazy relatives. If that's what you want, I'll let you go, babe, but I want you to know that I love you. I'll always love you."

"Oswald K. Grant, if you think I'll leave you vulnerable to the predatory plottings of Miss Ruffles LaBoink, you are sadly mistaken."

"You won't have a normal life with me," he warned.

"There's no such thing as normal. I'm abandoning the entire concept of normality, normalness, whatever."

"I was going to wait and get a ring, but I thought you'd want to choose it, and—"

"Oswald, a ring is only a ring." I'd hidden Ian's ring with the other gifts he'd sent me. It didn't mean anything. "Yes, I will marry you. You're the only one I want." I nestled against him, still astonished that such a wonderful man loved me back. "Are you happy?" I asked him.

"I'm beyond happy," he murmured. "I'm ecstatic."

"Me, too," I said.

A breeze carried the scent of renewal and life and the seasons to come.

Acknowledgments

This book wouldn't have been possible without the help of very special people. My wonderful editor, Maggie Crawford, encouraged me to write a second novel about the Casa Dracula crowd. Julie Castiglia, my agent, is always supportive and available to answer my many questions. Thanks, too, to Jean Anne Rose, Melissa Gramstad, and Jessica Sylvester, in the Pocket Books publicity department for helping spread the word.

My dear friends Peggy and Michael Gough invited me to their beautiful ranch to write and relax and were always happy to give advice. I'm lucky that my brother and sister-in-law, Marlo and Margie Manqueros, read my manuscripts and offer honest evaluations.

Tracy McBride brought her talents to the design of my website, and Dan Sonnier, M.D., once again, answered my nutty medical questions.

Of course, I'm eternally grateful to my fabulous husband, Miguel, who has always been there for me.